D0209531

Racing the Dark

Racing the Dark

Alaya Dawn Johnson

A Bolden Book

AGATE

CHICAGO

Printed in Canada.

Library of Congress Cataloging-in-Publication Data

Johnson, Alaya Dawn, 1982–
    Racing the dark / by Alaya Dawn Johnson.
        p.   cm.
    "A Bolden book."
    Summary: "Fantasy fiction. A young woman's coming-of-age
story set in a world where wielding the power of magic requires
understanding the true meaning of sacrifice"—Provided by
publisher.
    ISBN-13: 978-1-932841-28-2
    ISBN-10: 1-932841-28-8
    I. Title.
    PS3610.O315R33 2007
    813'.6—dc22
                                   2007016675

9 8 7 6 5 4 3 2 1

Bolden Books is an imprint of Agate Publishing.
Agate books are available in bulk at discount prices.
Single copies are available prepaid direct from the publisher.

Agatepublishing.com

To Lauren,
my partner in crime and novel agony aunt.
You don't get to pick your sister,
but you do get to pick your best friend.

To Scott,
who opened up my world
so I could write this one.

〰

Prologue

O N THE SECOND NIGHT, the girl who was not yet an angel fell asleep and dreamed. She dreamed of water, thick and viscous as blood, home to what seemed like a thousand terrifyingly alien creatures. They caressed her adult wings as they pulled her deeper into the water and she cried out in pain. She could hardly see them through the murk—but what she glimpsed seemed inverted, impossible, sickening. A disembodied heart with grasping hands. A monstrous fish whose tail had melted into its head. She shrieked and struggled to swim away, but her wings weighed her down, and she sank deeper. When she opened her mouth, the water came flowing in and now it really was blood—metallic, salty (and slightly sweet?). Was it her own? It seemed to be streaming from her back.

She used to love water. Even through all the pain and fear, she remembered that. But the old love had been replaced by terror, and she knew her longing for the past was futile. No, she could not turn back now—she could only plummet. As she descended, the pressure drove at her ears relentlessly. First the left, then the right—she felt them pop and rupture. Her screams tore at her vocal chords, but she could not hear a sound.

And still she sank.

The strange creatures around her grew more substantial, and subtly less menacing. A silent crowd of them accompanied her on her descent, and in their gazes she saw a wary acceptance and—

could that be fear? No one had ever told her it was possible for a spirit to fear a human. But then again, she was more than half spirit herself, this far down—a creature of wind and water and earth and death. Yes, perhaps death most of all.

As they neared the bottom of this ocean of blood and water, she felt a growing anticipation. Something was waiting for her down there. She felt herself sinking into its consciousness as though it were a physical force, at once repelling her and reeling her in. Her limbs jerked and spasmed, while the pain in her back grew more intense. Her wings were the first to touch the mud-soft clay of the sea floor: a sudden, searing pain. When she opened her mouth to scream, she felt the unbearable force emanating from the creature that had been waiting for her. It rushed down her throat, then gripped her heart and her bowels. She would die, she thought. A relief.

Who are you? she thought, since she couldn't very well speak, or hear herself even if she could.

To her surprise, the creature eased its bodiless grip and its outline slowly emerged from the sea's red-tinged fog.

This was entirely different from your average dream phantom. It *existed,* in far more concrete terms than any of the spirits that had accompanied her here. And yet, sure as she was of its existence, she had a much harder time comprehending its appearance. Massive, with oddly malleable edges that seemed to shrink and expand at whim. Were those wings she saw, or fins? Or hands? But feathers—of those she was certain—coated its body in slick cerulean and a black dark as octopus ink. Two eyes that seemed almost normal until you actually looked into them and noticed how they reflected your face like shards of a broken mirror, shattering the watcher into infinity. She shrank back at the sight—somehow, in those horrifying eyes, infinity felt like nonexistence.

Is that death, then, or something beyond it?

"Both," the creature said, its surprisingly gentle voice somehow penetrating her thoughts. She shuddered.

Who are you? What are you? Panic, desperation, infinitely reflected in those impossible eyes.

The voice smiled. "You don't realize, even now?"

A possibility occurred to her. *The waterbird? But why?*

"A glimpse of your future. Do you understand yet, Lana?"

No. No, no, no.

"You will."

And when she awoke, alone except for the death among the long-deserted ruins, the dream seeped from her mind, wrung free by blood and pain and fear like water from a rag.

PART I

. . .

Bloody Sunrise

THE WET SAND BETWEEN HER LEGS was stained dark red. The insides of her thighs were sticky with it, but she resisted the urge to rub the blood away. It was her first, and it must remain there until cleansed by the ocean itself. Lana curled her toes in the sand and shivered as the wind lashed the early-morning drizzle against her naked body. It was a sun shower—half the sky was dark and cloudy while dawn brightened the rest. A good omen, Lana supposed, although to be certain she would have to ask Okilani later.

It seemed as though everyone on the whole island had turned out for her trial of womanhood, although common sense told her it was only half as many. The elders were there, of course, dressed in sea-green robes and leibo, the traditional diving pants that Lana too would earn this day if she could harvest her own mandagah jewel. At their head stood Okilani. She was more than sixty years old, but her beauty had always dazzled Lana. Her long, bone-white hair blew around her shoulders, brushing against her necklace of the finest mandagah jewels. At their center was a jewel of bright orange—the color of the sunset, and the rarest of all because it could only be taken from a dying fish. Its harvest years ago, at Okilani's own first blood, had marked her for life.

Lana bit her lip as a particularly harsh gust splashed the cold water against her body. Her stomach was churning so badly that she was afraid she might vomit if they didn't let her into the water soon. The elders looked as though they were waiting for something, but she couldn't imagine what. Lana squinted in the rain and looked out at the horizon. The wisps of clouds that surrounded the dawn sun looked as though they had been streaked with blood. The color surprised Lana—it was unusual for a sunrise on her island to be so unrelentingly red. And stranger still that she would have her first blood during such a dawn. She had awakened two hours earlier with a terrible stomachache and a strange wet sensation between her legs. For all she had been expecting it, she had taken nearly ten minutes to realize what had happened. She had rolled off of her pallet and onto the cold wooden floor and stared at the worn ceiling beams. It crossed her mind to keep her first blood secret until the next month—she didn't feel at all ready for her first solo dive. She could barely hold her breath for a minute and a half, let alone the four and even five minutes her mother and Okilani could accomplish. How could she possibly complete her dive? And coming up without a mandagah jewel would be a terrible shame for both her and her family. Now that she was thirteen, Lana was too old for her age to be an excuse. She had lain on the floor in a state of terrible indecision until her mother entered the room and solved the problem for her. She knew her mother would not consider even the idea of spurning tradition and hiding her daughter's first blood until the next month. So Lana had stood up and tried to pretend that she was ready for her rite of passage.

As she waited on the sand, she was still attempting to convince herself.

"Iolana bei'Leilani."

The sound of Okilani's powerful voice booming above the surf made Lana's head snap up as though it had been tied to a puppet string. Okilani was using her formal name. The trial was starting. Lana hadn't thought it possible, but her heart started beating faster, and her stomach gave another lurch.

"Today it will be decided whether you will attain womanhood

or remain a child. You have your first blood—what remains to be seen is whether you can pass the test that all who wish to harvest the sacred mandagah jewels must face. Are you ready, Iolana?"

Lana swallowed. She wanted to shake her head and run straight back home, but she felt her mother's eyes on her back and knew that was not an option. She took a deep breath, raised her head, and stared straight into Okilani's wide brown eyes.

"I'm ready," she said.

The elders stood behind her as she walked alone towards the surf. Lana wished that she could have been initiated at sunset instead—the tide always made diving at dawn more difficult than in the evening. She bit her lip. No time for regrets now. She had never entered the water for a dive alone before—her mother or one of the other experienced divers had always accompanied her, to show her how to breathe properly on the surface and how to maintain her air supply under the waves, how to find the mandagah fish and then carefully harvest the jewels hidden in the tiny pouches inside their mouths. It was a delicate process, and one that could only be accomplished in early morning and late evening, which is when the mandagah schools would move from one shoal to another. Lana stared at the blood-red sunrise and balled her hands into fists. She couldn't fail. Despite the steady rain, she was startled to see the silhouette of one of the sacred outer islands—the death shrine. She shivered. It was rarely visible from the shore, even on clear days.

Feeling the anticipation of the crowd waiting behind her, she stepped far enough into the surf that the waves came up to her waist. With a holler that was as much a cry for strength as it was the traditional diver's prayer to the water spirit, she bent her knees and sucked in air until it hurt. Before fear could force it from her lungs, she dove.

She pushed herself against the undercurrent with powerful strokes, plunging as deep as she could. The water around all of these small islands was fresh, not salty. This allowed the mandagah fish to flourish, which in turn made it possible for Lana's people to harvest the jewels and trade them on the main islands. The mandagah, and the fish trade in general, sustained the islanders in these remote regions. Lana felt her ears beginning to hurt and used a small amount of her air to ease their pressure. She opened her eyes.

She had reached perhaps thirty feet below the surface. All around her was the beautiful living coral that she had become so familiar with, growing up here and diving with her mother. She began to relax—this wouldn't be so difficult. At first, she simply swam around the reef, hoping to find something that caught her eye. The mandagah could be tricky to see because their colors blended so well with the ocean floor. She paused. Had something moved below her? As slowly as she dared, she swam closer to the sandy bottom and peered underneath a sharply jutting piece of coral.

She almost exhaled in relief, but caught herself. She had found one. But why was it alone? She hadn't seen any others near it moving together to another shoal. The large fish stared at her with its oddly human-like face, while she contemplated how to harvest its jewel. Usually she had to grasp and hold them to prevent them from getting away, but something was strange about this fish—its sunken eyes made her think it didn't have the energy to move at all. Unsure of what else to do, she gently moved her fingers towards its thick lips. She had barely touched it, let alone started the process of prying out the jewel, when its mouth sprang open of its own accord. Her mind went numb. Mandagah fish never willingly surrendered their jewels. Before she could even recover from that surprise, the fish moved its head slightly, and not one but two jewels fell from its mouth into her palm. Her heart pounded, and the churning in her stomach changed into some strange mixture of excitement and dread.

She had found a dying mandagah fish. Only the dying mandagah produced two jewels—and only on the rarest occasions were they of two different colors. This mandagah, still staring at her passively, had first produced a striking jewel of common blue. The other, however, was orange-red, like the color of the dawn above the surface of the water. The only other person Lana had ever heard of who'd recovered a jewel liked this was Okilani; it had been her discovery of that orange jewel that had marked Okilani for training as an elder. Lana's mind whirled. Even though she knew how proud her mother would be if Lana was marked with the distinction of becoming an elder, Lana herself didn't want that responsibility—she wanted the freedom to travel to other islands when she got older, and to marry, and make love to a man. For an instant Lana wanted nothing more than to toss the strange red jewel into the sand and pretend that she had never found it. But she had received a willing gift from a dying mandagah and she could not throw it away. She couldn't even leave it here and come back for it later, because by then the sea would have claimed it. Mandagah jewels, once yielded by the fish that had formed them, had to be cured right away—otherwise they dissolved within a day.

Lana felt herself growing light-headed, and she realized she would run out of air if she didn't surface soon. How long had she been under? Two minutes? Three? Certainly longer than she'd ever managed before. The red jewel felt like it was burning her hand. She made a decision. Whatever happened, she could not let anyone else know she had found it. She would keep it and cure it herself, but it would be her secret. No one—especially not Okilani—could know that she had been marked.

Lana looked at the mandagah. Its eyes were fluttering, and she realized it was dying even as she watched. Impulsively, she brushed its mouth with her finger and then touched it to her forehead. She had to leave. Taking one last look at the dying fish, she kicked off and swam with powerful strokes back to the surface.

Leilani had endured the first two minutes in silence, radiating an outward appearance of calm. Inwardly, she wondered if her daughter was at all prepared for this task. Lana could barely hold her breath for a minute, and only luck would allow her to harvest a mandagah jewel in such a short time. After two minutes had passed, she turned to her husband Kapa, panic in her eyes. He looked worried as well, but pressed her hand in a way that made her keep silent. She kept staring at the choppy water, hoping that any second her daughter would surface triumphantly, holding a mandagah jewel. Another minute passed. Was it possible that her daughter had actually chosen to drown rather than face the shame of surfacing without a jewel? Hot and cold chased each other across her skin. She should have let Lana hide her first blood and wait until she was ready. Had she killed her only child with her stubborn desire to follow tradition? Kapa looked at her again, this time with a similar sort of terror in his eyes. She stared at the waves breaking on the shore. Nothing. It had been nearly four minutes since Lana dove. Damning propriety, Leilani left her husband and strode forward to the line of elders. Okilani broke their ranks and turned to meet her.

"Could she have drowned herself?" Okilani asked.

Leilani felt as though she had been punched in the stomach. "I don't know. I can't imagine … please, let me dive and save her. It's been too long."

Okilani's face was grim. "Not yet, Leilani. The rite cannot be considered failed yet. She has only been under four minutes. Your normal dive is at least that long and we've both done as long as six. We cannot break the rite until there is no possibility she has succeeded."

"But she's young! She's never managed for longer than two minutes. Do you want her to die?"

Leilani's shout echoed across the beach. Everyone was staring at the two of them, but Leilani didn't care how much they talked later.

"Lei," Okilani said softly. She had opened her mouth to say something else when they both heard Kapa yell. He was pointing to the water.

Leilani sank to her knees in the sand.

Lana had surfaced, and in her upraised hand she held a blue mandagah jewel, glinting in the sunlight.

Her father rushed toward her as she climbed out of the ocean. Lana was exhausted—far more exhausted than she had felt moments before, under the water. He handed her a robe, which she wrapped around herself gratefully. He made as though to carry her, but she pushed him away. She was a woman now, after all. Her left hand was balled in a tight fist, which she made an effort to distract from by holding out the normal jewel in her right hand.

"How … long was I under?" Lana asked her father as they walked toward Okilani. Her mother was standing next to the elder, with wet sand stains visible on the knees of her leibo.

He looked down at her, with a small smile, and she saw the relief in his tense face. "Nearly six minutes," he said.

Six minutes? She pushed the shock from her mind; she had reached Okilani. She allowed her father to step away from her, and then she bowed slightly to the elder.

"I have passed the test, honorable elders. I return with this jewel, taken from the mouth of a sacred mandagah." She thought of the ancient creature and the way it had stared at her, how it had given her its jewels as a gift. It was probably dead by now, she realized.

Okilani took the jewel and stared hard at Lana. She cringed inwardly under Okilani's gaze but managed to keep her face calm. The elder glanced at Lana's tightly closed left fist and then at her eyes. Blood was rushing in Lana's ears, but she met Okilani's stare. She could not let Okilani discover the red jewel. The elder could suspect all she wanted, but Lana would not betray that secret. To Lana's relief, Okilani looked away from her and toward the other six elders.

"She has passed the test. Do any object?"

There was silence.

"Very well. Iolana bei'Leilani, you have passed the rite of womanhood. You are now, and for the rest of your life, a diver for the sacred fish and a disciple of the water spirit."

There was a cheering on the beach, but it seemed like an insignificant buzz in her ears. She had passed the test. She had become a diver—like every woman in her family had been for generations. She should be happy, or at least relieved. But all she could think about was finding some excuse to get away and hide the red jewel in her left hand before it was discovered.

Her mother came up to her and hugged her tightly. Lana was shocked to feel the sudden wetness of a tear on her forehead. Was her mother crying?

"I'm … I'm so proud of you, Lana," she said.

Lana realized suddenly how long those almost six minutes must have been for her mother. She hugged her back just as tightly.

"Don't worry, Mama. I'm fine."

Her mother broke away and smiled, wiping her eyes.

"This is an incredible specimen," Lana heard, and she turned to see Aya, one of the other elders, reaching out to hand her blue jewel back to her. "Larger than normal, and such beautiful swirls of color. I imagine it will be even more breathtaking once it's cured. Such a good omen—don't you agree, Okilani?"

Okilani looked speculatively at Lana and at her jewel. "Perhaps."

"Honorable elders," Lana said, and bowed again, "I'm afraid I am a little strained from my dive. If it would be permissible …"

Okilani smiled slightly. "Of course, Lana. You may go rest." She raised her voice so it could be heard further away. "Tonight we celebrate Iolana's passage to womanhood with a feast."

Back home with her parents, Lana ran to her room as soon as they'd climbed the stairs and quickly placed the red jewel under her straw pillow. She would have to cure both jewels soon. She paused, her hand hovering in the air above the hidden jewel. For the first time, she was struck by the implications of her deception. The sacred fish had marked her as one for the spirits. Her mother would be horrified to learn that she would subvert her destiny like this. Leilani would turn it into a privilege, an honor, but Lana already knew the honor cost too much. Maybe she was irresponsible, maybe she was selfish, but even now the thought of going back to Okilani and admitting what she had found was untenable. She wanted her life to be her own, not the spirits'. She wanted to make her own decisions. She wanted … for a moment, the face of Kohaku, her teacher from the outer islands, flashed across her mind. She wanted love. She had enough defiance to hide this—even though she couldn't bring herself to destroy the mandagah's unwanted gift entirely. She heard her mother's soft footsteps outside her room.

"Lana? Can I come in?"

She made certain the red jewel was completely hidden, and then pulled back the curtains. Her mother was holding some rags that Lana was afraid she recognized.

"Why don't we sit down?" her mother said, gesturing toward Lana's sleeping mat.

Lana shook her head. "I'll just bleed all over it again."

Her mother smiled. "All right. I just wanted to show you how to use these. And don't grimace like that. It's part of becoming a woman."

Lana suppressed the urge to roll her eyes.

"You have to face it sometime," Leilani said. Her reproving expression was ruined by the slight smile turning up the corners of her mouth.

Lana laughed a little herself. "All right, Mama."

She went outside to the pump to clean herself off after her mother had explained how to swaddle herself in the women's rags. Lana felt uncomfortable, but she supposed she would get used to it eventually. The sky had cleared since she had returned home, and even this early in the morning it felt like it would be one of the hotter days of the season. As she pumped water into a large bucket, she wondered if she should heat it, but the air was already too hot to take the trouble. She poured some of the water over her body, shivered with the icy shock of it, and then grabbed the half-used bar of soap set beside the bucket on the wooden platform. She scrubbed her entire body, making sure to clean the last of the dried blood from her thighs before she tackled her long, tangled hair. She left a good deal of it in the comb by the time she managed to get it into some semblance of order. She tugged at it more impatiently than normal, eager to get started on curing her jewels. She knew that she still had a little time, but was irrationally afraid that they would start rotting immediately.

When she stepped outside, still moving uncomfortably in her swaddling, she noticed that her mother had laid some new clothes out for her on the porch. She smiled a little—finally, she would get to wear her own leibo, like the other divers on her island. She recognized this particular pair—they had belonged to her grandmother. Lana pulled them on and then fastened the buttons. They were a little long—reaching to her mid-calf instead of just below her knees—but they actually fit her in the hips. She checked to make sure that no one was watching and then twirled around quickly.

When the women dove, they wore just their leibo without a shirt, but her mother had laid out something special for her celebration. It was a shirt of sheer fabric—cotton, she realized, which meant it must be quite expensive since it had to be imported—hemmed by shiny bits of seashells. She put it on and then let down her hair.

"You look beautiful, Lana."

Lana whirled, her heart pounding. Her mother stood behind her on the stairs to the porch. Her arms were crossed, and she was laughing.

"How ... how long have you been standing there?"

Leilani smiled. "They're a little long for you, but I don't suppose you'll mind. Your grandmother was taller."

Lana put her hands in the deep pockets and imagined filling them with mandagah jewels. The pants were that peculiar shade of white only achieved by constant use under the harsh island sun.

"Thank you," she said.

Her mother shrugged. "They're your birthright. Now, why don't you go and cure that jewel? If you do it now, it should be finished by tomorrow."

Lana nodded and went back inside to get her shoes. She brushed some of the sand off her feet before she entered her room—sand tended to fill the room like floodwater unless she was careful. She shut her curtains and made absolutely sure her mother was still outside before moving her pillow and taking the red jewel from underneath it.

Her hand trembled as she picked it up. She could hardly believe what had happened just a few hours ago—her decision to hide it already weighed heavily. She put both jewels in her deep pockets, tied on her sandals, and ran outside. The quicker she finished curing them, the quicker she could forget that the entire incident had ever happened.

She ran over the hot sand to the shed where they kept the curing supplies. Her father sat inside, diligently working on one of his tortoise shell lutes. She groaned inwardly. How was she going to get him to leave?

He looked up as she approached and smiled. "You look beautiful, Lana. Just like your mother did that day."

Lana blushed. "Please, Papa!"

"I guess you want to cure your jewel, don't you? Well, I'll leave you in peace. Just let me finish stringing this."

Lana watched as he delicately pulled the shiny cured mandagah tail hair over the length of the tortoise shell. Making and playing instruments was her father's passion—any time he could spare from fishing was spent in this shed. On the days when Eala, one of the older divers, opened her large house to sell palm wine, he spent hours playing for her customers in the makeshift village watering hole. Lana's mother supported Kapa's passion for music, but Lana sometimes got the sense that Leilani wished her husband could have pursued a more profitable hobby. But Leilani always harvested the mandagah tail hairs that Kapa used to string his instruments. Once cured, they produced a sound finer than any other material. He sold a few every year during trading season, but they hardly earned enough money to justify all the time he spent making them. For her part, Lana didn't mind at all, because her father used his instruments to make beautiful music.

Kapa ran his fingers experimentally over the strings. He closed his eyes as he listened to them reverberate inside the tortoise shell and smiled a little in satisfaction. Later he would place the sliders over the strings that would produce a wider range of notes.

He stood up. "I'm going over to Eala's for a while."

"I'll see you tonight, right?"

He smiled. "Of course, how could I miss it? Congratulations on today, Lana. We are both ... your mother and I ... incredibly proud of you."

Lana fiddled with her ear. "Silly parents. Now get going."

Kapa laughed and left the shed.

Lana shut the door carefully before she pulled out the two jewels. She laid them on a piece of dry canvas that she had spread out on the worktable. Then she hauled out a sack of heavy curing salt from one of the lower cabinets. Salt was best for curing mandagah jewels, but it had to be used carefully, because it was the worst of bad luck to drop any salt on the sand. After all, mandagah were freshwater fish, and even the smallest bit of salt could kill them. Kohaku, who had come to their little island from the great Kulanui on Essel, would call that sort of thinking "rustic superstition," but Lana was still superstitious enough to be careful. After all, it wasn't as though Kohaku would have to know. She cringed at the thought of his glare of withering condescension directed towards her. She thought he liked her—maybe even respected her. Well, she hoped, anyway. She bit back a sudden smile and shook her head. She hoped.

Balancing the heavy bag precariously on one knee, Lana used her left hand to scoop out a handful of salt. That ought to be enough for both jewels. The rough white crystals were still cupped in her hand when she lost her balance and bumped into the worktable.

She watched in horror as the red jewel began to roll off the canvas. If it hit the sand, the rotting process would start immediately, and she might not be able to salvage it. With a silent cry, she tossed her handful of salt to the sand and caught the jewel just before it rolled off the table.

"Oh Kai ... water spirit, please, please don't pay any attention to this. It was just an accident. Please don't make the water salty!"

She couldn't be sure if the spirit had heard her, but she couldn't let the salt linger on the sand any longer than necessary. She struggled to put the heavy salt bag back in the cupboard under the table, and then scooped up as many of the white crystals as she could separate. The rest she muttered a prayer over and used her foot to bury.

Lana's heart was pounding and she looked around frantically, half afraid that her mother had seen what she had done. No one was there. Her secrets were safe. Her breathing began to return to normal. Besides, Kohaku was probably right; there was no way spilling salt could actually make the water salty. It probably was just a silly superstition.

Lana finished burying both jewels beneath the salt without any further mishaps. Then she pushed up the roof so that the sun could shine down on the salt-covered jewels and finish the curing the process. Covered as they were, she figured that she didn't have to move the red one to a special place—her parents would never touch her jewel without her permission.

Offering one last silent prayer to the water spirit, Lana left the shed.

It was, to Lana's relief, a gentle sunset—unlike the violently red dawn that had greeted her dive. The other women—those who had never wanted to become divers, or those who hadn't passed the test—had spent all day preparing the feast for Lana's celebration. She was suddenly embarrassed that they would have gone through so much trouble on her behalf, but she could hardly object to it—such celebration was only tradition.

There had been shouts of congratulations and a few toasts—even this early in the evening, the palm wine was flowing freely—when Lana first entered the gathering. Okilani and a few of the other elders greeted her and led her to the area near the large bonfire, where only the elders and the divers were allowed to sit. She felt dazed as she squinted her eyes against its heat. Was she really an adult now? She still felt as much like a child as she ever had. Her parents still treated her the same way. Would she marry now, and start a family of her own? She was still young and didn't have to if she didn't feel ready, but yesterday it hadn't even been a possibility. She knew all about sex, of course. Her mother hadn't thought it proper to leave her daughter ignorant and, in any case—her parents engaged in it frequently and their house was not large. The prospect of it didn't scare her so much as the thought of being so beholden to another person. She had seen the way her parents looked at each other. Their fortunes were connected so tightly they had ceased to exist as entirely separate people. In an abstract way, Lana might want a husband and a family, but thinking of it now, she realized that they would bind her as irrevocably as this morning's discovery. Would it be worth it? Someone handed her a plate heaped high with roasted fish, boiled vegetables, and rice sweetened with ginger root and coconut milk. Lana stared at it blankly.

"It isn't poisoned, dear," said an old woman Lana thought she recognized.

"Oh … I'm sorry …"

"You haven't eaten all day, have you?"

Lana shook her head mutely.

The old lady clucked, revealing a sturdy tongue in a mouth lacking about half its teeth. "You're all the same, poor dears. After you come up with your first jewels. Too stunned to even enjoy the food."

Lana visibly shook herself and then smiled. "You're right, I should eat. Enjoy myself."

The lady nodded. "And if you're still feeling nervous, you ought to smoke some of that." The lady gestured to the pipe filled with amant weed that was being passed around the circle. Lana had never tried it before. It hadn't even occurred to her that she would be allowed to, now.

"Maybe … maybe I will."

"Well then, eat up."

Lana picked up a spoon and put some food in her mouth. She stared at the old woman again. She seemed familiar, but Lana couldn't figure where she might have seen her before.

"It's good. Thank you."

The lady chuckled and waved her hand in he air. "It's nothing, nothing. So long as you're enjoying yourself, Lana, that's all I care about."

Lana smiled nervously. Why was this woman addressing her so familiarly?

"Those leibo, they're too big on you, you know. You're a bit shorter than the rest of the family, I suppose. They fit me perfectly."

"Um … do I know—"

"That was some discovery of yours, this morning, wasn't it? I don't blame you for keeping it a secret. There aren't many of us who would be willingly marked like that. But that color … and given to you so freely by a dying mandagah. You may be marked despite what you've done, dear. There may be nothing you can do about it. Perhaps you might have been better off hiding your first blood after all. Too late now, of course …"

Lana's hands were shaking so badly that she heard her spoon rattling on the wooden plate.

"Who … are you? How did you know that? Please don't tell anyone …"

The lady smiled. Was it Lana's imagination, or had the gaps in her teeth disappeared? "Oh, don't worry about me, Lana. I'm just here to wish you luck. And you may need it, at that. You may need it."

Lana looked around frantically to see if anyone else had heard their conversation.

"Listen—" She turned back and stopped short.

The old woman had disappeared.

The hand she then felt on her shoulder nearly made Lana drop her food altogether.

"Oh ... Okilani. It's you."

Lana didn't dare ask if Okilani had seen the old woman. Instead, she tried to smooth her features into some semblance of a normal expression. Okilani sat down beside her on the reed mat and gave her a penetrating gaze before she spoke.

"It was just a spirit, Lana," she said quietly. "A benign one. No need to be so afraid."

Lana put the food down. She felt like throwing up the spoonful she had eaten.

"You ... you heard, Okilani?" She could barely keep the terror from her voice.

The elder turned to her and patted her hand. "No. I only sensed its presence. It came for you, after all—I wasn't meant to see it, or hear what it said."

"Oh." Lana's voice was a reedy whisper.

Okilani narrowed her eyes and Lana looked away quickly.

"A spirit?" she asked falteringly. "How is that possible?"

"We're especially close to the outer death shrine. I'm sure you noticed that it was visible today. Sometimes spirits with particularly strong wills can come back for a short time on special occasions. Did you recognize it?"

Lana considered for a second. "She seemed familiar, but I don't remember ever seeing her before. But she commented on my leibo ... they were too big, she said. Said that I was short for my family. They had fit her perfectly."

"Why, it was your grandmother, then. Your mother told me those leibo had been hers."

"My grandmother?"

"You never met her, after all. She died before you were born. She probably came to wish you luck."

"That's ... that's what she said."

Okilani stood up and looked back at Lana. "Then you probably need it."

As her grandmother's spirit had predicted, Lana felt much better once she smoked some of the amant weed. It made her cough painfully at first, but the other adults just laughed and gave her something to drink. She didn't even realize at first that it was palm wine they placed in her hands. Between the wine and the amant, she felt little more than a slight twinge of anxiety when she thought of the strange encounter with the spirit.

That amant weed was wonderful, Lana decided as she reclined on a mat by the fire. It made everything seem clearer, somehow. She looked at the moon, so bright and massive in the sky it drowned the light of all but the brightest stars. Something flickered in the corner of her eye and she turned to it. For a second she caught a faint glimpse of her grandmother, her form insubstantial and wavering by the fire. She looked younger this time, but still recognizable. The spirit winked at Lana and then raised her hand in a farewell.

Lana frowned a little and then waved back. The spirit wouldn't tell anyone Lana's secret, but her warning worried her a bit, even past the amant weed and palm wine. Her grandmother disappeared. Lana stared at the place where she had been for a few moments and then lay back down on the mat.

"Lana?"

She sat bolt upright, looking around again for her grandmother again, but it was only Kali, who had snuck up to the adult area by the fire. Lana wondered if the others would make Kali leave, but it seemed that they were too preoccupied to notice or bother.

"What is it?" Lana asked. "Here, sit down. I don't think anyone will care."

Kali smiled and sat. "Wow, Lana. I can't believe that you get to sit here now. Do you feel like an adult?"

Lana shook her head. "Not really ... but it's nice to be close to the fire, I guess. And I like the amant."

Kali looked wistful. "That sounds great to me. I almost wish that I had been training as a diver, too. I'm a year older than you and I still have to sit with the babies!"

Lana smiled. "Better find yourself a husband quickly, then."

"Don't be ridiculous. Who would I marry now? Kohaku? But I couldn't do that, could I—you'd have to kill me for stealing your one true love." Kali looked at Lana's furious blush and started laughing.

"What ... what are you talking about? Kohaku is our teacher!"

"Don't tell me. I know that. *You're* the one who's always staring at him like a fish."

"I do not!"

"Well, you like him, don't you?"

Lana looked away without saying anything.

Kali put her arm around Lana's shoulders. "Don't worry, I won't tell anyone. But perhaps, just to make sure, you could let me try a little of that amant ..."

Lana smiled a little. "Sure. Just try not to be too obvious, okay?"

Actually, Kali coughed so much that Aya came over to see what was the matter. She didn't seem to mind that Lana had given Kali some amant. Afterward, they both sat in companionable silence as Kapa played a traditional song on one of his harps. Lana was almost moved to tears—her father was, in his own way, saying goodbye to the little girl he had raised.

Yaela, the very first mandagah diver, supposedly composed the song a thousand years ago, before humans had bound any of the three great spirits—death, fire, and water. When the capricious nature of the water spirit had threatened to destroy all of the mandagah fish, Yaela had left the island and offered herself as the sacrifice that allowed the water spirit to be bound—imprisoned and thus controlled. On the inner water shrine, the prison that still held the great spirit, officiates left offerings in her memory. "Yaela's Lament" was the song the legendary diver had written just before she left to be sacrificed—saying goodbye to the great ocean and

mandagah fish that were her first love. Although a female traditionally sang the song, her father's light falsetto commanded it as
well as any woman singer Lana had ever heard:

Starlight's sweet dance on sand below
A dance for none, for none will it wait
What joy tomorrow? I cannot know
But I'll dive again, beyond the gate

This dawn, no jewel lies in my hand
And I've given all my love too late
Oh, for one more morning in the sand
Ere I meet my love beyond the gate

Come dawn's red gaze I must leave here
And the leaving some may think is fate
But within my heart, love battles fear
For I do not know what lies beyond the gate

Lana walked back home slowly beside her parents. She felt a
little dizzy, but she wasn't sure if it was because of the amant, the
palm wine, or her excitement. Perhaps all three? She looked up at
the sky and made her fingers form a circle right above her eye, so
it looked as though she had captured the moon within her hands.
Giddy laughter left her lips almost involuntarily. Her mother
looked at her, opened her mouth, and then shook her head.

"Hurry up, Lana," she said. "You still have school tomorrow,
remember."

That night, after her parents had gone to sleep, Lana snuck out of
the house—as she had done many times before—to dance beneath
the moon. She wasn't sure why she enjoyed doing this so much,
except that it made her feel close to something both beautiful and
intangible. She heard her father singing "Yaela's Lament" in her head
as she twirled in the moonlight. At first she felt joyful—reveling

in how marvelous the day had been, and how strange. But as she continued to dance, she felt almost sick with the knowledge that from now on her life would be irreversibly different. She felt tears come into her eyes and abruptly stopped dancing. What would happen tomorrow? She thought about the red mandagah jewel and more tears sprang to her eyes. Her grandmother might have been right—maybe she was marked despite herself. She couldn't know what it meant, but at this moment it felt like the worst of omens.

Lana fell to her knees in the sand and felt some of the water from the receding tide seep into her leibo.

"Great Kai," she whispered. "Please let everything be okay."

She looked out at the ocean to see if there would be any response to her prayer. The waves continued breaking gently on the shore. Nothing changed.

Then Lana realized that even now, in the moonlight, she could still see the outline of the death island.

· 2 ·

LANA MADE HER THIRD FULL CIRCLE OVER THE REEF that morning, straining her eyes for the slightest sign of movement over the sandy ocean floor. The other women swimming around her were doing the same, and she knew that the pockets of their leibo were as empty of mandagah jewels as her own. Lana had sensed something was wrong back on the morning of her initiation. She had only seen one fish—and that one was dying. In the six months since, the situation had grown progressively worse. The divers had consulted the elders and performed rituals of supplication to the water spirit, but nothing had helped. Lana couldn't shake the nervous feeling that had settled in her stomach like mildew. The day after her initiation, she had taken her cured jewels and hidden them in her clothes chest—maybe if she never looked at them again, she would be able to pretend that nothing had ever changed. But of course she couldn't. Many of the divers went days without harvesting a thing. Lana had become one of the most productive of the divers, but even she only harvested about one jewel each day. Two years ago, that might have been grounds for removing her privileges as a diver. Back then, ten jewels had been an average harvest. Today, it would be a miracle.

A brief billow of sand on the bottom caught her eye and she pushed herself farther under the water. She smiled—it was a mandagah fish. It began to swim sluggishly away from her, but when she grabbed its tail, it stopped struggling immediately. Had she somehow found another dying fish? She turned it around. Its eye ridges were still a healthy pink, not the dull gray of the one from her initiation, but it stared at her in that same disconcerting way. She reached with her other hand to pry open its mouth, but its lips wouldn't part. She tried stroking its belly to relax it, but it still refused to open its mouth. Her vision began to go white around the edges—she knew she should surface, but she didn't want to relinquish her find.

Then, without warning, the fish poked its sharp tail-hairs into her arm and wiggled out of her grip with a huge burst of energy. But instead of fleeing, it swam closer to her face. She floated, stupefied, as the fish kissed her forehead and dropped the jewel from its mouth. She reached her hand out and caught it, staring as the fish swam away. She stuffed the jewel in the pocket of her leibo and kicked up off the bottom.

Her hand trembled as she examined her find on the surface, but to her extraordinary relief it was just a white jewel. An unusual color, but not anything that would mark her. She would just have to hope that no one had seen the fish's strange behavior.

For months she had been having recurring dreams about the dying mandagah fish from her initiation. In the dreams, it would be crying—although she knew, of course, that mandagah couldn't cry—and it would always say "Goodbye, Lana. I'm bound to cross the gate." She would touch her finger to its lips and then to her forehead—just like she had done that morning—and then she would wake up. And now a second fish had willingly given her an unusual jewel. She knew the events of the past six months must be important, but she had no idea why, and because of the way she had hidden what happened during her initiation, she was too afraid to ask one of the elders. Her mother and another diver surfaced nearby.

"Did you find something, Lana?" her mother asked, swimming closer.

Lana nodded, and hoped that her face didn't show her agitation. She held the jewel out silently.

Leilani and the other diver looked at each other. "That's amazing, Lana. Neither of us found a thing. You really do have a gift for diving."

Lana blushed. "Just beginner's luck, I guess. Anyway, can you take this for now, Mama? I've got to get to school."

Her mother took the jewel and put it in her pocket. "Sure. Hurry up—you might be late again."

Lana nodded and swam back to shore.

She had to run back home to get a shirt and grab her slate before sprinting to school. Although women on her island often went all day without shirts, at school it was required. Kohaku seemed to think that wearing shirts was more "cultured," whatever that meant. She usually changed out of her wet leibo, but this morning she didn't even have time for that. Their classroom was in one of the ancient kukui trees that grew on the east side of her island. She was almost five minutes late before she finally climbed up the ladder for class. Kali had saved the seat next to her, and Lana went straight to it, trying to make as little noise as possible. Of course, since her initiation she had been late to class nearly every day, so no one paid much attention anymore.

"You find anything today?" Kali whispered as Lana knelt on the mat.

Lana nodded. "Just one. It was white."

"Wow. You really are good, you know. I heard Eala hasn't found anything in more than a week."

"You too? I've just been lucky, that's all."

"Lana, Kali!" Kohaku slammed his book shut with enough force that both of their heads snapped up. "If your conversation is so much more interesting than this class, perhaps you would prefer to continue it outside?"

Lana's heart pounded painfully. She hated it when Kohaku rebuked her like this. She and Kali shook their heads mutely. Kohaku looked at Lana for a moment, smiled a little, and continued with his lecture.

Today was geography. Though she had always dreamed of traveling when she got older, Lana found it difficult to stay awake. Her mandagah fish dreams had been keeping her up at night, and she and the other women had taken to doing longer and more demanding dives in the effort to find even the few jewels they had been able to harvest. She struggled to suppress her yawns as Kohaku patiently discussed the relationship of the inner spirit temples to the outer shrines. Although she missed a good deal of what he said because she kept nodding off, she gathered that Kohaku was talking about the climate of the islands being connected to the outer shrines. The duty of the hereditary guardians of the outer shrines was to keep the minor spirits within the cycle of their islands. This kept them away from the inner islands so they couldn't strengthen the great spirits bound there, and help them to break free. The concentration of minor spirits made the outer islands much warmer. Her island was always warm, but all of the islands got colder the closer they were to the center.

She fell asleep after that, and Kali had to wake her up for lunch break.

They climbed higher into the tree, as they always did during lunch, where they had a great view of the ocean. On clear days they could see the outline of the death shrine, although lately that sight had just made Lana feel like caterpillars were crawling in the pit of her stomach. The two girls perched in the branches and opened the lunches that they had brought from home.

"I thought I was going to die in there, the way he kept rattling on about the spirits and the temples!" Kali leaned back on her branch and stretched out with a grimace.

"I don't know. It seemed pretty interesting to me."

"*You* were the one who fell asleep."

"I've been ... kind of tired lately. Besides, don't you think it's so fascinating—the ice-mountains on the inner islands, the huge volcano on Essel ..."

Kali shrugged. "I don't know. I guess. Sometimes I just can't wait to get away from this place. It feels so stagnant here, like nothing interesting could ever happen."

Lana might have agreed six months ago, but now she couldn't help but think that things were already changing, in a way that nobody wanted.

Lana peeled away an orange rind and tossed it into the grove.

"Okay, Kali. Let's make a pact."

"For what?"

"To go away together. To see all sorts of things we could never see on this island and then come back and tell everyone about it."

"But you're a diver."

"I'm not an elder, I can leave the island if I want. What do you think?"

Kali placed the last orange wedge in her mouth and chewed slowly. "You know, Lana ... you're the kind of person who can do things the rest of us can't, but assumes that there's nothing special about you."

Lana suddenly felt nervous again, but covered it with a smile. "Come on—do you want to travel with me or not?"

Kali stared at the ocean. "If you want me to go with you ... if I can. Why not?"

At the end of the day's lessons, Kohaku told Lana to stay behind after school. She loitered in the classroom as everyone cleared out, worrying. She felt terrible for falling asleep in class earlier and prayed that he wouldn't rebuke her for it. She watched him bustle about the classroom, picking up broken bits of writing gum and straightening the precious readers that he had brought all the way from Essel. She wondered if he ever regretted coming here—she knew their way of life must seem so primitive to him. She gathered that he was here looking for material to make his name in the great Kulanui in Essel. Maybe that meant he was using them, but Lana didn't mind as long as he taught her about the world. It was hard not to love someone who had shared so much of his knowledge with her. He was the very first teacher her island had ever had from the Kulanui, having come here because he had wanted to do his field study on a remote island near the outer shrines. She loved his exotic looks—his long reddish hair, his slim build, and his fashionable clothes.

"Lana."

Her heart started pounding. She had been so intent on studying him that his voice surprised her.

"Yes?"

Kohaku smiled. "No need to look so scared. It's nothing bad. Here, sit down." He gestured to a chair next to his desk. After a surprised moment, she sat down.

"What did you want to talk to me about?"

"You are a very promising student, Lana. I've given this very serious consideration, and I would like you to ask you to come back to Essel with me when I leave in two months and pursue your studies there. I hate the thought of you wasting away on a backwater island like this with your kind of talent. You could do great things, Lana. I see it in you."

Lana's mouth opened, but her vocal chords didn't seem to be working. What was with everyone today?

"But ..." her voice came out in a whisper and she cleared her throat. "But, I'm a diver."

Funny how she now used the same excuse that she had so easily brushed off earlier that day.

Kohaku frowned. "I know your island's traditions are important to you, Lana, but you have to understand the kinds of opportunities you would have on Essel. Do you want to live your whole life on this island without ever exploring your intellect?"

Lana felt panicked. On one hand, Kohaku was offering her the exact kind of opportunity to see the world that she had always wanted—and, even more extraordinarily, to do it with him. On the other, she knew that something was wrong on her island. She couldn't just abandon everyone before whatever was happening became clearer.

She shook her head. "I'm sorry ... I just don't know. I don't think I can leave right now."

Kohaku put his hand over hers and stared earnestly into her eyes. "Don't say no yet, Lana. You still have some time. Just think about what I've said, okay?"

Lana couldn't have said anything had she wanted to. She nodded.

"Well, then. Your parents are probably expecting you home by now. See you tomorrow."

Lana fled the classroom and scrambled down the tree before she allowed herself to relax. Her entire body was trembling. He had held her hand. He had stared into her eyes. He wanted her to go away with him. It was the happiest day of her life.

She really did love Kohaku. She had realized it one morning less than a month after he arrived. He had been telling them about the great Essel wars that lasted for a century after the wind spirit broke free, and she had been suddenly gripped with astonishment that anyone could know so much, yet think so little of it. Even the most knowledgeable women on her island confined it to useful subjects, like diving or fishing or farming and trading. What possible purpose did the history of five century-old wars serve? He was so different from every other man in her experience—his clothes and manner of speech were only the most obvious. Sometimes she felt like just being in his presence was itself a trip across the earth.

But now she felt agonized by the decision he had asked her to make. She couldn't tell anyone about their conversation—not Kali or her parents—because she was afraid of what they would say. She loved diving, no matter how dismissive Kohaku was of "rustic traditions." Besides, the rainy season was fast approaching, and then it would be virtually impossible to dive for the greater part of three months. She felt responsible, since she had so rapidly become one of the better divers, to find as many jewels as she could before the rains.

During a sunset dive two weeks after her conversation with Kohaku, Lana was having little luck finding any fish at all. Tayi, one of the other divers, was combing the water with her, and they were swimming much farther out than normal and diving deeper than Okilani would have approved. They were about thirty feet underwater when a large eel slipped out from one of the reefs beside them. Its deep green skin and large mouth looked a little sinister, and Tayi hid behind Lana's back as it swam by.

"It looks like Uncle Oha," Tayi said, using the hand signals all divers knew. Uncle Oha was a large man who spent most of his evenings drinking himself into a stupor at Eala's, but Lana felt warmly toward him because he loved listening to Kapa's music.

The comparison was so appropriate that Lana burst out laughing. She started to panic when the burning water accidentally filled her lungs. She gnawed her lip and kicked to the surface, where the water was darker than it should have been, and cloudy. She floated while she hacked up what felt like half the ocean. What kind of a fool was she to laugh during a dive? The water left a funny taste in her mouth, though, and she realized that it was burning her throat more than it should. What on earth was that taste?

Panic settled in her stomach, a fear so strong she knew she would never get it to leave.

The water tasted, ever so faintly, of salt.

The next day the rains started and the dives were called off. In fact, by the middle of the day the students were all sent home from school as well—they had to help their parents prepare their houses for the rains. Lana climbed on top of the roof with her father to cover the thatch with a stronger resin and larger palm fronds from the forest. They were soaked through by the time they came back inside, but at least the roof had stopped leaking. Her mother made them change their clothes before they sat down to dinner.

It was a strange, silent meal. The only noise was the insistent sound of rain drumming against the roof of the house. In a few weeks, the whole island would start to flood, and people would have to take barges just to get from one house to another. She usually loved this time of year, but now all she could think of was the salty-tasting water. She stuffed the food into her mouth, but hardly tasted any of it.

"Lana, aren't you going to say something?" Her mother sounded impatient.

"Say what?"

"Like maybe thanking your mother for taking the trouble to cook your favorite dish?" her father said.

Lana looked down at her plate and saw with vague surprise that her mother had indeed made her favorite dish—day-roasted grouper in a sour pineapple sauce. She hadn't even noticed.

"Sorry, Mama. Thank you for making it." She turned back to the food, and struggled to find an interest.

Her mother and father exchanged a worried glance. "Are you feeling okay, Lana?" Leilani asked.

Lana nodded.

"Has … something been bothering you lately? What happened?"

For a brief moment, her mother's question seemed inviting. Should she unburden herself and tell them what had been chasing her thoughts in circles? But she had hardly sorted it out enough herself to tell her parents. It would only worry them unnecessarily. She was an adult now, after all. If spilling the salt those months ago had caused this problem, she had to deal with it herself.

She forced a smile. "Nothing's wrong. I'm just a little tired, that's all. I think I'll go back to my room to rest, if you don't mind."

"You're sure you don't want any more to eat?"

"No, I'm fine."

Lana stood up and went back to her room.

Leilani and Kapa sat in silence after she left.

"I really thought she'd like the grouper," Leilani said, finally.

Kapa looked at his wife. She was biting her lower lip and a line had formed between her eyebrows. It was uncharacteristic of her to get so upset over food, but he knew how she had hoped to help Lana past her inexplicably dour mood.

He reached across the table and touched her hand gently. "It's okay, Lei. She's growing up. She can't tell her parents everything anymore."

Leilani stared at the table. "I know … it's just … I can't help but feel that something is tearing her away from us. Something happened to her that morning, that day she was initiated. I don't know, but whatever happened … she's changed, Kapa."

Kapa had felt the same thing, but he didn't say so.

Minutes later Lana came running out of her bedroom with her sandals on and reached for her father's waterproof fishing coat, hanging in the entrance.

"Where are you going?" Kapa asked.

"I'll be back soon. Don't worry."

Lana ran out the door before either of them could say anything else.

"Kapa …"

He hugged her. "She'll be okay, Lei," he said softly. "She's just growing up." But he didn't really believe that himself.

Lana ran through the driving rain, splashing through sandy puddles that went to her mid-calf. She had to find Okilani. She had lain on her bed for a few minutes, thinking about her discovery, when she had been overcome with the terrible sensation that the salty water, and thus the smaller numbers of mandagah fish, were all her fault. After all, hadn't she spilled all that salt on the sand six months ago? Hadn't she hidden the red jewel? This must be her punishment. Kohaku must have been wrong about salt being a rustic superstition—why else would the water, which had been fresh for thousands of years, only have turned salty after she broke the taboo? She didn't mind the stinging rain. It served as a distraction from her thoughts.

Okilani's house was all the way on the other side of the island, and in the rain it took her nearly an hour to get there. As the head elder, she lived in one of the ancient kukui trees—an even larger version of the one that held the schoolhouse. The rope ladder was flapping in the wind, but at least Okilani hadn't pulled it up for the night. Lana didn't know how she could have gotten the elder's attention in this weather. She climbed it and tossed herself on the landing. Despite the waterproof coat, the rain had soaked her through nearly half an hour ago. Now she was beginning to shiver. She pounded on the wooden door, forcefully enough for Okilani to hear her over the wind.

The door opened and Lana fell inside. Okilani shut the door behind her—already the floor was covered in puddles of rainwater. She sat shivering on the floor.

"Lana?" Okilani's face was unsurprised. "I had thought you might come here. Let's dry you off."

Okilani left and came back a few moments later with two large towels. Lana wrapped them around herself gratefully and tried to stop shivering.

"Well, come on, get away from the door at least. That's the coldest part of the house."

Lana nodded and stood up. She walked with Okilani to another room that had shelves lined with books and comfortable-looking cushions on the floor. She took off her wet sandals before stepping inside. The room was warm—there were hot ashes in metal braziers on the floor, which she was careful to avoid.

"Sit down," Okilani said, gesturing to one of the cushions. She sat down next to Lana. "Now, I imagine what brought you pounding on my door in the middle of a rainstorm was important, so we can skip formalities. What happened?"

Now that she was sitting in Okilani's house, she began to wonder if she had not overreacted. How salty had the water been, after all? And how could spilling the salt possibly have caused it? She frowned and fought back her doubts. She knew as well as every other diver on her island that the mandagah were dying, and yesterday she had just discovered why.

She clenched her fists. "I'm sorry for barging in like this ... I thought it was important. Yesterday I discovered ... I mean, by accident, of course, but ..."

"What is it, Lana?"

"The water ... it's salty. Tayi and I couldn't find any mandagah fish and were swimming much farther out than normal and she made me laugh and when I came back up to cough, I realized that the water was salty. And see ..." Lana blurted, unable to stop herself, "I think it may be my fault, because on my initiation, when I was curing the jewel, I accidentally dropped some salt. I said a prayer and I tried to clean it up, but maybe ..."

"Are you *sure* you tasted salt, Lana?"

Lana cringed and stared at the floor. "I'm sorry," she said.

Okilani's eyes were grim but she still tried to smile reassuringly. "Don't worry, it's not your fault. I had suspected that might be what's happening, but the salt is still undetectable close to the island. Something like this ... it has nothing to do with whether or not you dropped the salt. This is something much bigger. I can't say I understand it yet, but I have sensed a change.

"Our way of life may be ending, Lana. If the water continues to get salty, then all the mandagah will die."

Despite the warmth of the room, Lana began to shiver again. Could the situation really be that serious? "But ... how could that possibly happen? The mandagah have lived here for thousands of years!"

Okilani shrugged. "The spirits are restless. We may be at the beginning of some sort of upheaval. But I'm just an elder, not a diviner. I can't tell you what will happen to us."

Lana felt like crying. Once again, divers would be forced to give up the ocean. Even now, in Okilani's warm room, she could smell the seaweed and the fishy bilge from the boats docked near her house. She wondered how all that could possibly end. She thought of Yaela, forced to leave the sea forever to offer herself as a sacrifice.

All the years she had sung that song, she had never imagined that one day the words would describe her.

Okilani's voice broke the long silence. "We may be able to save a few of them," she said.

Lana looked at her. "How?"

"Tomorrow … we have to harvest the fish themselves, not the jewels. We still have the freshwater lake at the center of the island. A few of the mandagah may just be able to survive there. Maybe, in time, the water will return to normal and we can take them back to the sea."

"Will that work?"

"Who can say? But I think we should try."

Okilani stared at Lana for a few long minutes. "Is there anything else you wanted to tell me, Lana?" she asked.

Lana stared at the glowing embers and tried not to cry as she kept her silence.

The next morning, the divers assembled on the beach a few minutes before dawn and waited for Okilani to explain what she had decided to do the night before. Everyone's face wore the same mixture of fear and determination. Even the men had come to the beach that morning. They would risk bringing their boats out in the driving rains to help the women harvest the fish. The shore was lined with tubs filled with freshwater to hold the mandagah while they were transported to the lake. Okilani had to shout to be heard over the wind, rain, and the waves pounding on the shore. They had to be crazy to dive in weather like this, Lana thought. Still, she felt brave standing beside her mother. She was aware, though she didn't want to be, that this might be her last dive.

The waves were so huge that all the divers had to take their air before they got near the surf. After she dove, it was hard to see because the heavy waves had turned up so much of the bottom, making her feel as though she were swimming through an impenetrable cloud of sand. Still, she and her mother made sure to stay close to each other while they searched for mandagah. The fish were so big that they could only bring one at a time to the surface. She and her mother were the first two divers to find any. They handed the fish to the men waiting on the boats and then dove back under, looking for more. Again and again they dove, often not finding anything. Okilani told them to stop around midday, when the rain had grown so fierce they could hardly see even on the surface. Despite all of their efforts, they had collected only about one hundred fish. Lana tried not to feel disappointed, but she knew everyone else felt it too. How badly had the numbers of mandagah dwindled while she and the other divers refused to notice?

Everyone helped carry the fish to the lake. Lana insisted on carrying a tub herself although it dragged at her shoulder muscles and she was already exhausted from the morning dives. By afternoon the sky had grown dark as twilight.

"Mama?" Lana said softly, when she and the other divers had taken temporary refuge in the schoolhouse.

"Mm-hmm?" Her mother was leaning against the wall with her eyes closed.

"There's something I ought to tell you … about my initiation. The mandagah was dying. It gave me two jewels. I don't know what it means …"

Her mother snorted abruptly and her eyes flew open. "I'm sorry, Lana, were you saying something?"

Lana turned her head away. "No. Nothing important," she said.

There was an impromptu party at Eala's that night. Lana's father and a few other musicians played determinedly upbeat music. Kohaku had come, but he sat by himself in a corner of the room, taking notes. He was always like that, Lana knew—an observer rather than a participant. For all Kohaku was fascinated by her island, Lana always got the sense that he considered himself above them. Lana smoked a great deal of amant weed and danced around giddily with Kali. On a strange level, she felt happier than she had in weeks, if only because she felt she was *doing* something about the things that had been worrying her for so long. Of course, there was still Kohaku's proposal, but the amant was doing a great deal to help her forget about that.

Later that night, after she had stuffed herself full of food, she and Kali were dozing against each other in one corner. Kohaku, whose walk was unsteady (although Lana hadn't noticed him consuming much palm wine), staggered over to them and sat down.

"Enjoying yourself, Lana?"

Lana stared at him. There was an uncharacteristically sarcastic bite to his words. She wondered what was wrong. "I guess so," she said. "It looks like you are, too."

"Yes, well. Perhaps I did imbibe a bit too much in the spirit of things." He suppressed a burp. "Have you thought about what we discussed, Lana? I'm thinking of going back to Essel a little early. All this rain, the disaster with the mandagah fish … not very good for the research, you know? I'll probably leave in a week or two. I'd like you to come back with me."

Kali opened her eyes and yawned. She looked at Kohaku and then Lana, and seemed a little startled at their grim expressions.

"Are you two okay?"

Kohaku ignored her. "Well, Lana? I need an answer."

No, it was too soon—he couldn't force her to decide now. There were too many aspects she hadn't even considered, like convincing her mother to let her leave the island in the company of an outsider. Lana put her hands to her suddenly queasy stomach and avoided meeting Kohaku's challenging gaze. She had thought she would have more time. Things had been so hectic lately … and now with the mandagah and the rains, how on earth could she leave the island now? How could she leave her parents, Kali, Okilani, and all the other people she loved here? It would be too much like abandoning everything she loved.

She shook her head. "I'm sorry, Kohaku. I just can't now. Maybe in a few years I could leave, but not now."

He looked as if he wanted to say something harsh, but just nodded. "May I ask why?" he said after a moment.

"Things are changing. I can feel it. If I left now ... if I left now, it would feel too much like running away."

Kohaku stood up. "Maybe one day you'll realize what you've just wasted."

He walked out of the room and into the pouring rain. Lana felt like crying.

"Lana?" Kali shook her by the shoulders. "What on earth was that all about?"

"Kohaku asked me to come back with him to study at the Kulanui on Essel."

Kali gasped. "Really? That's incredible. But ... you said no, didn't you? Why?"

Lana felt a funny sensation in her chest, something that hurt too much to breathe around. Had she really just said no to Kohaku, to the chance to leave with him, be with him?

"Well ... if I had gone to Essel with him, I couldn't have kept the pact."

"The pact?"

"Remember? We both have to be around if we're going to travel the world together."

Kali laughed and hugged her. "You're crazy, you know."

Lana silently agreed.

Over the next two weeks, the rains pounded the island relentlessly. The ground wasn't visible over most of the island anymore. The men poled barges from house to house, checking on the older people and making sure the supports were sturdy. Even the oldest on the island said that they had never been through a rainy season like this one. Okilani looked grim, and when pressed would say only that the intense rains were part of greater changes to come. The feeling that had lodged in Lana's chest that night at Eala's wouldn't go away. And in the middle of everything, when Lana's life was changing so much she hardly recognized it, Kohaku left to return to Essel. She hated him a little for that, though she knew he felt no loyalty to her people or her island, and there was no real reason he should. To him, they were little more than unusual creatures worthy of study. Yet, he had offered Lana an opportunity for more than that, and she hated herself a little for refusing him. Was she stupid, she wondered that awful night after his barge left the island and she cried herself to sleep. He didn't love her, she knew that, but he had offered her a chance to see the world. Maybe she would always regret her decision, yet even when she thought about it now, she didn't know how she could have made the other choice. Because she couldn't abandon her island at a time like this? That's what she had told him. But that was too easy, wasn't it? Maybe the truth was harder. Maybe she was a coward, too afraid of what she didn't know.

Her father had been acting strangely, too. Because their shed had long since flooded and his supplies had been moved into their house, he sat in the main room all day long, making his instruments. He worked on them with a single-minded intensity that Lana had never seen before. Part of it was that he couldn't take out the boat to fish with the rains falling so heavily, but there was something stranger in his fixation. She knew that her parents were fighting—they rarely touched each other anymore, and her mother would often stare at her father while he made his instruments, looking as though she were about to cry. Then one day, when Lana was given a ride back from Kali's house earlier than normal, she overheard them arguing.

"It's all you do, these days. Cure the tails, string the instruments, play the instruments, tune the instruments. You never pay any attention to me anymore. Me or Lana."

Kapa shrugged. "There's nothing else to do on this damn island, Lei! Not with these rains. And after they end, it'll be back to the same thing—catching fish, bringing them back, waking up early the next morning. Don't you think I wanted to do something more with my life? At least when I'm making these instruments, I feel like that. Just a little."

Leilani chewed her tongue. "How can you say that, Kapa? You are doing something with your life ... just like your father did and his father. You were born on this island, your life is on it. Do you hate it so much?"

Kapa looked at his wife and his expression softened. He walked over to her. "I don't hate it, Lei. But I don't want to waste my entire life here either. Since these rains came, since the mandagah have started dying … I've been thinking that there's nothing left for us, anyway. I've been thinking … I've been thinking that we should leave. I could sell my instruments on Essel. We could start a different life."

Leilani wrenched herself away from him. Lana had never seen her mother look so angry before.

"You expect me to abandon my home, my life, for some crazy dream you have of selling your instruments? How can we leave when things are like this? It would be running away."

"Fine. Let's run away, then! It would be like running away from nothing."

Lana couldn't stand hearing anymore. She pushed the door open all the way and stalked inside. Her parents stared at her, surprised.

"How … how long have you been standing there, Lana?" Leilani asked.

Lana just shook her head and walked into her room. "Mama's right," she said finally. "I don't want to run away, either."

She pulled back the curtains and rolled out her sleeping mat.

"Why does everything have to change?" she whispered to herself as she sat shivering on the floor.

Three weeks later, the rains hadn't even paused. If anything, they had gotten stronger. Lana stared out her window, and barely registered the familiar wash of dread. The sun should have begun drying up her island by now. The houses, though designed for floods, wouldn't be able to hold up much longer in this kind of deluge. What if the rains never stopped and her island remained flooded forever? Okilani was right—something was happening. Something to do with the water spirit, maybe, but what?

It was Kali's birthday. Lana had promised to visit, but she wondered how her parents would feel about her leaving in this kind of rain. The water had gotten too deep and choppy for all but the largest barges to work, but her family owned a small canoe that ought to get her there.

She walked into the main room, and her father glanced up from his instrument.

"You're not planning on going somewhere, are you?" he said.

"It's Kali's birthday. I promised I'd visit."

"How are you going to get there? Swimming?"

"That little boat of ours."

He frowned, then shrugged. "Just don't tell your mother. She'll be upset."

Lana glanced at the kitchen where her mother was cooking. "All right. I'll be back soon."

She tied her sandals and then put on her cloak. The boat was perched on the roof, tied down with rope that her father had fastened when the rains first started. She scrambled up the side of the house, almost slipping several times. The wood was soaked and slippery. The waterlogged knots were impossible to untie, so she reached into the pocket of her leibo and pulled out a small knife that she kept for diving emergencies. She cut one of the ropes and then let the boat slide off the roof and into the water. Then she positioned herself right above the tethered boat and slid down the roof herself. Once she was sitting in it fairly comfortably, she cut the second rope and took the paddle.

It was slow going—it took her nearly forty-five minutes to reach Kali's house. She was soaked through by the time she began to see the brown blob of the house through the rain. It looked strange, though. More lopsided than she remembered. She paddled closer. It looked as though one of the supports had crumbled in the rain. Her chest tightened—was Kali's family okay? It must have happened recently, because as of last night she hadn't heard any news of people's houses collapsing. As she moved closer, she saw two figures huddled on the roof of the side that hadn't fallen. Lana felt a little relief—at least they had all gotten out.

Then she realized that she couldn't see Kali.

She paddled faster until she was about ten feet away from the house. Kali's parents were so agitated that she had to shout and wave her arms to get their attention.

"Hey! What happened? Where's Kali?"

"The whole thing went down a few minutes ago. We can't find her!" her father called. "We're afraid she got caught somewhere."

The terror that had settled in Lana's stomach threatened to make her whole body numb.

"She was in the house?"

He held his wife while she began to sob. She wasn't a diver. They had probably tried looking for Kali and couldn't dive deeply enough.

Lana pulled off her coat and shirt and took a deep breath. Then she jumped into the water. It was hard to see through the sediment and broken wood from the collapsed house, but she pushed her way through it ruthlessly, looking for any sign of her friend. She swam around the ruined supports, but didn't find a thing. Her hands were shaking. Where on earth would Kali be? She tried to picture their house in her mind. The kitchen was toward the right side—the part that hadn't collapsed. Kali's room was on the left side. Toward the back. Lana made her way to where the room might have fallen.

There too, all she saw was a mess of scattered debris. Had Kali gotten pinned underneath it? She blew out the pressure in her ears and dove to the muddy bottom and looked up. In the middle of the mess of the collapse, she caught a glimpse of Kali's brown hair. It seemed bright, as though it was caught on a piece of sunlight. Had it stopped raining? Lana swam as close to her friend as she could. Kali was pinned underneath two large wooden beams. Lana bit her tongue to keep from crying out. Was she still alive? She shook Kali's limp hand and was incredibly relieved when it tightened a little around her own. How long had she been pinned here?

Four minutes? Kali opened her eyes. They were frantic, but she seemed to smile a little when she saw Lana. Lana shook her head, trying to tell her to relax. She gripped the first beam—roughly as thick as her waist—and struggled to lift it. Although it should have been lighter under the water, it would hardly budge. She glanced at Kali. Her eyes looked familiar, and Lana realized it was because they reminded her of the eyes of the dying mandagah fish from her initiation. Renewed panic gave Lana the energy she needed to shove the beam off of Kali's body. She watched it fall and then felt her friend grip her hand. Kali's face was twisted in a grimace, as though she could barely suppress the pain. Lana's own thoughts felt burned through with fear. Was her best friend really going to die? She bit on her lip until she tasted blood, and started struggling with the second piece of wood. Kali suddenly gripped Lana's hand so hard she felt her bones grind against each other.

She had the sudden impression that Kali wanted to say something, but of course she couldn't speak underwater. Instead, she bent Lana's head closer to hers, and kissed her gently on the forehead.

How had she known? Then Kali gasped, and Lana realized that she had finally given into the temptation to suck water in the place of air. Lana pushed the second log off of Kali in one mighty heave and picked up her friend's limp form. She struggled through the maze of supports, back to the surface.

It wasn't raining anymore, she noticed vaguely, even as she struggled to hold Kali's limp body above the water. She heard some cries and a splash behind her. Someone pulled Kali from her grip and onto a barge. She treaded water next to it, staring helplessly as Kali's father and one of the other men tried to breathe life back into her body. Was she dead? Lana didn't want to believe it, but she had understood that gesture. Yet how could Kali possibly have known? Lana was terrified—so scared that she could taste bile in her throat—that she had been given Kali's dying blessing. She heard Kali's mother, still on the roof, wailing. Her father was crying, too, but silent tears that seemed to fall from his eyes without him noticing.

The second man who had been blowing air into her mouth stopped, and laid her head back down on the barge. Kali's mother let out a sound that made Lana's brain shiver. She jumped into the water. The water swelled and a little spilled over the top of the barge. Kali's hair floated and turned a strange, beautiful iridescent burgundy. Lana looked at the sky.

The sun had come out.

They held her funeral that same day at sunset—one of the first real sunsets in weeks. Already the water level was beginning to recede. It was as though Kali's death had been a sacrifice of appeasement to the water spirit. Maybe now things would go back to normal.

She hadn't managed to cry yet. Not when they had told her that her best friend was dead, when she already knew. Not when her parents had finally heard the news and her mother had hugged her tightly. Not when she had tried to explain to Kali's mother why it had taken her too long—just seconds too long—to remove the logs that were pinning her daughter below the surface. Not even when she thought of how Kali had kissed her forehead right before she died.

They held the funeral high in the great, sacred tree of the kukui groves. It was a place of high honor—normally, only elders and divers had funerals held there. Lana appreciated, vaguely, the honor they were giving Kali, who had been neither. But Lana knew how long Kali had stayed alive under the water. If she had wanted to be a diver, she would have been a fine one.

Everyone who could leave their houses had come. They climbed up the tree silently, wearing their best clothes. Lana hadn't changed. She climbed the tree without a shirt, wearing the same leibo and sandals she had worn when she dove in after Kali earlier in the day. Every person brought a covered lamp, and as the crowd grew the great tree began to look mystically illuminated, as though there were hundreds of spirits gathering among them to see Kali away.

Okilani and the other seven elders stood on the platform built in the middle of the upper regions of the tree. Kali's body lay there as well, naked except for three large leaves covering her torso. Lana had a good view because people seemed eager to let her through to the closest branches. She wondered what they had heard about her dive. She wondered if they blamed her for Kali's death.

Her hands started trembling on the branches and she forced herself to stop. Okilani glanced at her from the platform with an expression of pure pity. Lana found herself growing angry. Why did everyone seem to pity her? She didn't deserve it. If anything, she deserved their blame. She hadn't been able to save Kali …

Okilani raised her hands and pounded her staff three times on the platform.

"Tonight, we gather for the sending of Kali bei'Maiu. By rights, today should have been a celebration of her year beginning, but circumstances have proved otherwise. The changes that have affected us all have now taken one of us away. If there are any words of comfort I can offer tonight, it is that Kali, whose gentle spirit we all loved, will be in a place far away from the great changes I sense coming. Changes that may alter our way of life forever."

Lana stared at Kali's face. What would she think of this? Would she find it funny, that everyone was according her such respect? She didn't really look dead. She looked like she would get up at any minute and sneak away with Lana, to go off and giggle in one of the tall trees while they ate oranges and threw away the peels. Could it really all be over?

The elders moved around Kali's body so that Okilani stood by her head. The high elder took off her necklace and unstrung one of her jewels—the orange one, Lana saw. She placed it in the center of one of the palm fronds that covered Kali's body. Aya was next. She pulled a beautifully colored white jewel from her necklace and placed it on the second leaf. Lai'i, another elder, placed a blue one on the third leaf.

Lana had only seen one of these rituals before in her life, when she was much younger. She stared, fascinated despite herself.

When the jewels had been placed, the elders held hands and bowed their heads over her body. They chanted in unison, but Lana couldn't understand what they were saying. It sounded like her language, but some ancient, unfamiliar version of it. Lana felt a strange sense of a presence gathering as they chanted, and the air smelled thick, like it was about to rain. When she glanced at the sky, however, it was clear—the wisps of clouds she could see above the tree branches hardly looked like they could threaten any rain. She looked back at the elders. Their chanting grew more intense, and now Lana was sure she sensed something. It was a strange kind of power—it smelled like the sea, but also like the earth. If she had revealed the red jewel and they had initiated her into these rites, she may have known what they were doing. But as it was she could only sit and watch. It felt, though ... it felt as though they were calling an earth spirit. Maybe even the spirit of this tree. Earth spirits were one of the wild ones—the ones that humans had never tried to capture and control.

With a shout, Okilani broke the circle, picked up her staff and pointed it at Kali's body. The air began to shimmer—like it does when you stare through the heat of a fire—and then Kali's body burst into flames.

The flames were pure white, and they didn't spread to the wooden platform although there was nothing separating it from her body. Lana's fingers tightened around the branch she was holding. Kali was dead.

"It's not your fault, Lana."

Lana felt tears spring to her eyes. "It is. If I moved a little faster, I could have saved you." Then Lana realized who she was talking to. Kali was bathed in the crackling white light from the fire, but she still wore the clothes Lana had last seen her in.

"You're ..." her voice came out in little more than a whisper.

"I'm leaving soon. It wasn't your fault, Lana. The house had half-crushed me. I wouldn't have survived. I knew that."

Tears were streaming down Lana's face, and she wiped them away furiously. "Is that why ... you ..."

Kali smiled. "You're special, Lana. The mandagah see it, and now I've seen it too. There's something about you. Something that eases death."

Lana was pretty sure that this was a quality she didn't need, but she just nodded.

"You're marked," Kali said. She seemed to be fading. "I can see that now. It will be true for the rest of your life—but watch out for those who can see it. They'll want to find out why. They'll want to use you for it." Her voice even sounded distant.

"K-Kali, please don't go!"

Kali looked sad, but shook her head. "I have to. There's no-where else."

"What about our pact?"

"Keep it for me, Lana."

Kali waved, and then floated up the tree until she was in the highest branches. The sun sank below the horizon and she disappeared.

Lana looked back at the fire. It had gone out. There weren't even ashes to indicate that Kali's body had been there—only the three mandagah jewels, untouched.

People stared at Lana as she and her parents made their way down the tree. They knew she had been visited by Kali's spirit—they had heard her side of the conversation, after all. Lana tried not to look at Kali's parents, but she felt their accusing stares anyway. Why had Kali visited Lana and not her own parents? She didn't really know, but she felt guilty all the same. Kapa had tethered the canoe to the bottom of the tree. The three of them climbed inside and Kapa began to paddle home.

Tears slid out of Lana's eyes and she couldn't seem to stop them. To her shame, some of the tears were for herself. Even if she had doubted it before, now she knew she was marked, and in a way she had never wanted. Something about her "eased death?" The very idea terrified her. How had this happened? All she had ever wanted to do was dive for mandagah fish and then travel with Kali. She had planned to find the Kulanui when she was older and learn all the magnificent useless things Kohaku so prized. How had all of her dreams been so ruined?

Her father broke the silence. "I think we should leave," he said in a quiet but clear voice.

Lana stared at his back through her tears. She felt her mother's hands tighten on her shoulders. Although she knew that she should still be supporting her mother on this issue, she found that she couldn't summon the energy. Suddenly, she realized that she didn't care anymore if they left or stayed.

"I already told you," her mother said, "I won't leave. It's too much like running away."

Her father turned around angrily. "Kali is dead. Do you want to wait for Lana's turn? Life on this island is dying, Lei. Even Okilani sees it. The skies might have parted now, but who knows what this terrible flooding has done to the island? It's not safe to be here anymore, and without the mandagah fish, I don't know why we would."

"But this is my *home* ..." her mother sounded desperate.

"Then make another home, with me in Essel. Don't you love me enough to do that, Lei?"

When her mother just buried her head in her hands without replying, Lana was shocked enough to stop crying herself. What was happening to her family?

Kapa said nothing more as they slowly made their way home.

Leilani left an hour after they had returned home. Kapa refused to stop arguing that they should leave the island, and finally she had stormed out in disgust. It was a beautiful warm and clear night anyway, and she was relieved to be away from her frustrated husband. At first she was simply paddling aimlessly, but eventually she realized that she had made her way near Okilani's house. She smiled a little, despite everything. Somehow she always ended up here when her life started to overwhelm her. She pulled up to the base of the tree, tethered the boat, and climbed up the ladder. As she knocked on the door, she thought of traveling to a place where there weren't any ancient kukui trees with houses built into them and felt her chest constrict. How could Kapa ever consider leaving this place?

Okilani opened the door.

"Oh, Leilani. I thought I had heard someone in a boat. Come in."

Leilani walked into the familiar house. She had been here countless times before to drink tea and talk with her mentor. She had always loved those moments.

"It's a beautiful night, isn't it," Okilani said as they walked through the house. "Why don't we sit on the roof?"

Leilani smiled and nodded. Okilani first went to the kitchen and took a pot of simmering tea off the fire and brought it up the stairs with two clay teacups. Okilani insisted on pouring them each a cup and settling into the chairs before she let Leilani speak.

"So, what brings you here tonight? You look too worried for a social call."

Leilani laughed. "You know me well."

"I've known you since you were born, Lei. And tonight you look the way you did when your mother died. What's wrong?"

Leilani took a long sip of the tea, ignoring the way it burned her tongue.

"It's Kapa. He says he wants to leave the island and sell his instruments on Essel. He says that things have gotten too dangerous here and our way of life is dying. Without the mandagah fish, he says, there's no point in staying. And now poor Kali ... it just seemed to make him want to leave even more."

"And how do you feel?" Okilani was staring up at the moon, sipping her tea.

"I know I can't leave. I'm a diver and I have a duty to this island. Leaving now would just be running away, wouldn't it?"

Okilani sighed. "Lei, I know this may be a hard thing for you to hear—and it's a hard thing for me to say—but I think it might actually be a good idea for you to leave. When these waters recede, I'm afraid we're going to discover that the only mandagah left are the ones we saved in the lake. There won't be *any* diving. Even the regular fish trade will be slow. Things are changing, and in a way, you may be safer on Essel. I can't leave—my soul as an elder is bound to this place. But you *can* leave, Lei. Let Kapa follow his dream, and let Lana put some distance between herself and what happened today."

Leilani stared into her cup, her hands trembling. "But … but this is my home. I love this island."

"If you can stand to stay here and watch as it's slowly destroyed, stay. But something is happening to the spirits, and those things always affect the outer islands first. You're usually the rational one, Lei, but this time Kapa may be thinking more clearly."

They sat in near silence for an hour afterwards, while Leilani sipped lukewarm tea and thought of what Okilani had said. Leaving would be the most painful thing she had ever done, but perhaps there really was nothing left for her and Kapa to do but move on. And Lana … she didn't even want to think of what had happened to her daughter today. She was terrified that the haunted expression would never leave her face.

Finally, Leilani stood up, and the elder looked at her calmly.

"What have you decided?" Okilani asked.

"Since the binding, my mother's mothers have lived here. But I think … I must be the one who leaves."

Okilani stood up and embraced her. "I wish you luck, my daughter. If we never meet again, perhaps your soul will find its way back here and find mine, still tied to the land."

Leilani bit her tongue to keep back the tears.

"Goodbye, earth-mother," she said, using the elder's formal title.

"Goodbye, Leilani."

As Leilani walked down the stairs, she was overcome with

the saddest sensation that she would never hear Okilani's voice again.

When her parents told Lana the next morning that they would be leaving the island, she could hardly summon the energy to feel anything at all. Without Kali or the mandagah, what was there to stay for, anyway? Of course, she loved the great trees in the grove and the smell of her island after a rainstorm, but none of those memories made her fight to stay. She would be traveling, then. Keeping her side of the pact with Kali. And seeing Essel, after all. She knew that she wouldn't seek out Kohaku. Her dreams of him seemed so childish and impossible, now. As though he had ever seen her as anything but a native of above-average intelligence. The only person besides her parents who had ever loved her had just died. What was a childish crush beside that?

They packed all day, and the smell of the waterproof resin they had spread on the heavy canvas to protect their belongings made the house reek. It was a silent, somber affair. Even Kapa didn't seem very enthusiastic. That evening he left them to exchange his fishing boat for a barge roomy enough for the three of them and their belongings. Her mother packed everything with a look of fierce determination, as though she refused to doubt her decision. Lana stared at her mother and wondered what had made her change her mind.

That night, after most of the packing was finished, she and her parents went to Eala's, so that they could give some kind of goodbye to the people they had grown up with and known so long. Everyone stared at Lana as she came in. Some people gave her tentative smiles; others turned away abruptly and stared at their drinks. Lana stared back at them, distanced from all the tension in the room. What did it matter, anyway? Tomorrow she and her parents would leave this place and she would probably never see any of them again—these people who knew what had happened to Kali, who knew that she had been visited by her ghost. Her father didn't seem to notice the tension. He was in his element here at Eala's. Today his grin was especially wide as he made his way to the center of the room, where he always sat to play his songs. He took requests that night, and a few others played with him. He looked happy there, and Lana could tell by the look in his eyes that he was dreaming of doing this every day in the city. Her mother looked vaguely ill and, after one last worried glance at her daughter, sat near Kapa and stared into space.

Some of the tension in the room seemed to penetrate Lana's gray haze of indifference. Suddenly feeling awkward and inexpressibly sad, she moved away from her parents and sat near the kitchen in the darkest corner of the room. There was a pitcher of palm wine at the table, nearly untouched by whoever had ordered it. Lana stared at it, vaguely registering the boisterous music her father and his friends were playing. It seemed incredibly inappropriate, somehow. Kali was dead. Lana hadn't been able to move the logs that crushed her friend. They would never be able to keep the pact. A tear seeped out of her eye and was soon absorbed by the wooden table.

She poured herself a glass of palm wine. In the smoky torchlight, its natural golden hue looked luminescent. It looked like liquid fire, something that could burn all thought and emotion from inside her. Though she had never enjoyed the taste of it before, she relished the burning sensation as she poured it down her throat, finishing the cup in nearly one gulp. It felt nice, sitting in her belly like that. She filled her glass again and drank it all. Everything seemed to be going a bit fuzzy around the edges. The light looked brighter and her father's happy music didn't bother her so much anymore. Kali would have loved this. They could have danced together after drinking too much palm wine and then gone running on the beach. Lana always loved doing things like that with Kali.

She poured herself another glass and couldn't help but cry when it seared her throat.

It took Leilani a good two hours before she noticed that her daughter was quietly drinking herself into a stupor in a corner. She was passed out on the table, in fact, by the time Leilani thought to check on her. Suddenly panicked, she rushed to Lana's side and held her head up. Her daughter's eyes opened and she stared at Leilani as though she was trying to determine who precisely she was.

"Mama?" she said.

"Iolana! What are you doing?" Leilani moved the near-empty pitcher from Lana's fumbling reach.

She blinked up at Leilani for a few moments before answering. "Drinking," she said.

"I can see that. Why would you drink this much?"

"I'm an adult. An adult ... you can't stop me."

Leilani suddenly wanted to cry at the despair in her daughter's voice. What had happened to them all? "Lana, baby, I know you are. But why did you drink so much?"

Lana shrugged. "It burned. I thought ... maybe it would burn it all away."

Leilani closed her eyes for a second, and wished for the strength to help her daughter. "Lana, you can't take it away like this. It will just come back, and hurt more than ever. Trust me, I know."

Lana stared at the table for a while, as though intensely fascinated with its rough wooden surface, pitted by years of use.

"Is it my fault, Mama?" she said.

"Is what your fault?" Leilani asked, painfully aware that she already knew the answer.

"Kali ... that she died. She said it wasn't, but ..." Tears were sliding down her cheeks but she didn't seem to be aware of them.

"No, Lana. It wasn't your fault. You did everything you could."

"She said I ease death. I don't want to ease death! I don't want to be marked!"

Leilani looked at Lana in shock. She hadn't told them what Kali had spoken to her about during her passing. *Was* her daughter marked? Terror gripped her at the thought. It made sense—too much, in fact. She had always felt that something was special about Lana. But in times like these ... being marked could hardly mean

Lana would have an easy life. If she was marked, there was no way Leilani could ever protect her.

She shook her head. She could do nothing about that now. She put her arm around Lana's shoulders and helped her out of the chair.

"Come on, let's go home."

Lana overslept the next morning and woke up with a splitting headache. She staggered into the main room, and saw that it was bare except for the pile of neatly packed items in the center of the floor.

"Your room is all that's left to pack up, Lana," Kapa said.

She tried to think of some appropriate response to that, but ended up running outside and vomiting. After her mother had settled her stomach with some unidentifiable, but warm, drink and some breakfast, Lana managed to pull herself together enough to help pack her stuff. She took her two special mandagah jewels out of her chest. From now on, she supposed, she would have to keep them close by, for all they terrified her. Until her family settled down again, she had to make sure they were never lost. However much she had lost the morning Kali died, these jewels were the best reminders she would ever have of her old life. Nothing could change how much she loved diving, even if that path was closed to her now. For a moment, as she held the red jewel in her palm, she contemplated drawing back the curtains and showing it to her parents. But her mother had made a decision, and telling her now would only put their plans in question. Maybe one day, in some future she could hardly imagine, it would be possible to tell them. But for now … she put the jewels into a smaller bag and stuffed that in her pocket.

An hour later, they had loaded everything onto the barge and were ready to leave the only home she had ever known. It looked empty and soulless without their possessions—there was nothing left to remind her of her childhood, of her life there before her initiation.

"Are you coming, Lana?" her father asked by the door.

"Kapa! This may be the last time she'll ever see it again."

Lana turned around and looked between her parents. Her chest ached, but it had ached steadily ever since Kali died, and she knew that there was nothing she could do about any of it.

"It's all right," she said. "I'm ready. We can go."

They left the island a little before noon, when the sun was bright enough to reflect off the floodwater in gold sparkles that made them all squint to see. Her father poled the barge slowly—the water had receded, but since they lived so close to the shore, it was still easy to maneuver onto the waterways that connected the islands.

There was no one outside. The water was still except for the ripples from their barge. Lana sat in the back and stared silently at the kukui groves. The majestic trees were slowly fading into the distance as she looked—her last view of her home. She thought of how she and Kali had sat in their high branches only months ago, thinking of Kohaku and their future. She wondered what would happen to her now—what did being marked mean? Was she destined to be miserable for the rest of her life?

Her mother knelt behind her and put her hand on her shoulder. Lana looked back at her for a moment, and then relaxed. At least she still had her mother. They watched the kukui groves together after that, and stared together at the distant, proud figure of Okilani, standing high in the branches of her tree as though it was her duty to witness their departure. Lana felt her mother's hand tighten on her shoulder. Would they ever see the elder again?

She thought of the jewels in her pocket. Did Okilani know she was marked? It was too late to ask her now. Her mother looked as though she wanted to cry, but was keeping the tears back by sheer force of will. Lana turned away and found her eyes drawn out to the ocean. The death shrine was silhouetted against the edge of the ocean, as clearly visible as she had ever seen it.

They slept on the barge for the next two weeks. She spent her nights shivering helplessly under thin blankets, wondering how much colder it could possibly get on the inner islands. Her parents had agreed that her father should go ahead with his instruments and supplies to Essel first, while they stayed behind in Okika City, the major port town on the eastern side of Okika Island. The city-island of Essel was at least two weeks away by clipper from Okika. When they first pulled into the docks, Lana was amazed at the lack of sand. Narrow, cramped city streets butted right against the water, filled with more people than she had ever seen in her life, and everywhere she heard people shouting. Leilani looked dismayed as well, staring at the loud, dirty scene. And this was a *small* city? What on earth was Essel like? How could her father survive in a place like that?

Lana supposed that she and her mother would have to find work somewhere, because her father would be taking most of their savings with him to Essel. When he had settled in they would be able to join him. It had sounded like a fine plan sitting on the barge on the way here, but now that she saw the kind of place they would have to live in, she wondered if they would have been better off staying on the island, no matter what kind of changes Okilani sensed coming.

By that evening, Kapa had found them a place to stay—a small but fairly clean room on the top floor of a boarding house near the docks of the Eastern harbor. The smell of the salt water and dead fish was strong, and the wind blew it straight into the room, which probably made it cheaper than it would have been otherwise.

Some of the despair that Lana had been feeling for the past few days changed into acute anxiety. She tried not to show it for the sake of her father, but she knew that Leilani felt it as well. She needed a chance to catch her breath, to adjust to what her life had become. She needed it, but she knew better than to expect it.

"Good luck, Papa," Lana said after they had moved their belongings into the small room.

He looked at her and then they hugged tightly. "Don't worry. In a month or two you'll be able to come to Essel, too. Everything will be fine."

Lana smiled, because she knew that he expected it, but she doubted her father's assurance. Here, they were all out of their depth. She loved her gentle father, but she couldn't imagine how he or any of them would handle life on Essel.

Leilani hugged her husband tightly. Her body was shaking, but she seemed to have managed to keep the tears back. Lana turned tactfully away and walked to the window as they said their good-byes. The sun was setting over the harbor and the huge fishing vessels—larger than any she had ever seen—were all coming into port. Brawny sailors wearing strange, weather-stained clothing hauled huge nets of helplessly flopping fish off the boats and onto large carts. She saw women walking around as well, wearing brightly dyed loose pants and matching button-down shirts that flapped around their knees. They wore heavy socks with their sandals that would have been entirely too hot on her island, but seemed to be standard dress here. Lana was wearing a shirt, but it barely covered her belly button, and people had been staring at her and Leilani as they walked through the streets. Kohaku had told her that women on the inner islands rarely showed their breasts or wore short pants. On very formal occasions, he had said, women might wear a sheer top, but it was generally seen as a rustic practice. Just one more thing she would have to adjust to.

"See you soon, Lana. I love you."

She turned away from the window. "Goodbye, Papa."

She and her mother stared at each other when he shut the door. Somehow they would have to survive. Somehow.

· 3 ·

KOHAKU'S JOURNEY BACK TO ESSEL was plagued with the most extraordinary bad luck, such that he finally saw the familiar spire of the Kulanui towering above the rest of the town a full three weeks after he had planned to arrive. Between unseasonable rains, unexpected schedule changes, and leaking boats, Kohaku had begun to wonder whether he would ever get home at all. Finally away from the hated ship, he waited in line beside the bustling docks for a street vendor who was selling sticks of rounded sweet potato dumplings. They were ten kaneka each now—fully double what they had sold for when he left a year ago. The dripping sugar that burned his tongue tasted of home, though, and he found he didn't mind the price very much at all. He downed five on the spot and then waited in line yet again so he could order ten more to bring home to his sister, Emea. Her frequent illnesses made it difficult for her to get out much. She probably hadn't had a chance to eat sweet potato dumplings since Kohaku had left for the outer islands. The thought made him lose his appetite—maybe he shouldn't have left her alone, no matter how forcefully she had insisted that he go.

But still, he could hardly wait to see her again. The frustration he had felt at Lana's rejection of his incredibly generous offer had rankled him during his journey home, but now it seemed to dissipate with the thought of his sister. Really, what had he expected from someone raised on such an anachronistic backwater? Lana might be intelligent, but it took a particularly strong character to overcome such a crippling background. He had offered to rescue her, but she hadn't been smart enough to want rescuing. But Emea would have liked her, he thought unexpectedly, and felt a moment of pure regret for opportunities lost, different roads taken. He hurried down the familiar seashell-lined streets, completing what was usually an hour-long walk in forty minutes. He lived with his sister on the middle floor of a boarding house right at the foot of the great volcano, Nui'ahi. It was an awe-inspiring sight at dawn, with the bright orange sun coming up behind the smoking top.

He took the stairs two at a time but slowed before he opened the door. Emea was sitting by the window, in the special seat he had built for her before he left. Some embroidery rested on her knee, but her hands were idle and she stared into space with an air of almost inexpressible sadness. At that moment, her golden hair seemed brighter than the sun itself. Once again, Kohaku found himself stunned by the beauty of the sister their mother had died giving birth to sixteen years before.

She turned abruptly when his shadow fell on her. Her frown of surprise widened into a smile that seemed to cover her whole face, and she ran to him.

"You're back early," she signed, using the language they had created together so that she could have some way of communicating.

"There were some disasters on the island," Kohaku signed. "It was impossible to conduct any more research, so I decided to leave. I wanted to get back sooner ..." He paused and looked at her. "It's been such a long time," he said. "How have you been?"

For the next twenty minutes, Emea's hands moved so quickly Kohaku had a hard time following what she was saying. She must have been starved for conversation. She could communicate a little with the landlady who sometimes kept her company, but the only person who really knew her language, since their father died three years before, was Kohaku. Emea had been deaf since a nearly fatal fever when she was five years old, and it hurt him to know how isolated she was from other human beings because she couldn't hear. Men would admire her in the streets when she took walks with him, but the looks on their faces when they realized she was deaf often made him want to keep her inside forever, just to protect her from that sort of pain. He had debated for months whether or not to leave for the outer islands for his research, but finally she had told him to go, that she would be all right on her own.

"I'm sorry," Kohaku said abruptly. "I shouldn't have left you here. You were too lonely."

Emea looked surprised. For a girl who was still so young, sometimes she acted much older. "I can't always tie you down like this, Kohaku," she said. "I have to learn to take care of myself."

But Kohaku thought he saw traces of bags under her eyes, and her skin was paler than it had been before. "Were you sick while I was away?"

She looked down and shook her head. He lifted her face back up by the chin.

"There's no use lying, Emea. I can just ask Palau."

"A little," she said. "I had a fever and a cough. The doctor said I should keep away from the docks … I walked down there sometimes, hoping to see you coming back. I'm mostly better now, though."

He hugged her tightly.

"I'm sorry, Emea," he said out loud, because he knew she couldn't hear him. "I promise … from now on, I'll be here for you."

Lana's mother found work. There was a sailors' hookah lounge a few blocks from their boarding house, and they hired her to be a hostess. Lana's employment search took nearly a week because she was too young for hostess work and too unskilled to do anything else. A laundry service in the richer northeast part of the city finally took her on to do manual labor in the steaming laundry vats. After a week, Lana gathered that the job was so horrible no one person managed to stay in it very long. She dyed and scrubbed a seemingly endless supply of clothes, using harsh lye soap in water just a few degrees below scalding. Despite the gloves she wore her hands felt raw and sore by the end of the day, and the fumes made her eyes water and her throat hurt. Her only companion most days was the supervisor, an older woman with a bad back who had quite possibly been doing the same work since she was Lana's age. The thought terrified her. How could anyone possibly live like this her entire life? She came home late every night, with barely enough energy to stuff some food down her throat before she went to sleep.

Her mother saw how tired she was, but Lana never told her exactly what her work entailed. She knew Leilani's job was hard enough without having to worry about her daughter. They both just had to make do until Kapa could send for them—they had to eat, after all, and the room cost money. Also, they had both bought second-hand clothes, which had consumed most of their small store of money. Their outer island clothes looked inappropriate here. Lana wasn't particularly fond of the way the dulled mother-of-pearl buttons up the front of the long shirt constricted her torso, but she absolutely refused to wear the heavy socks everyone here seemed to favor. It was still warm enough outside to go without them, and she had no intention of giving in until she had to—never mind the stares she got on the street.

One night nearly three weeks after they had arrived, Lana was trudging back home on a quiet, rosestone-paved side street in one of the richest parts of the city when she saw two people hurrying toward her. The council guards sometimes gave her trouble for her dirty, lye-stained clothing in this part of town, so she ducked into an alley and pressed herself against the rough-faced wall.

"They told me you could birth a stone," Lana heard one woman say quietly, "and still keep the mother alive. You won't get a kala till afterwards, so it had best be true."

The other woman—whose faded clothes seemed out of place next to her companion's exquisitely dyed crimson cloak—snorted contemptuously.

"Threats won't do you much good. I'm here because I choose to be, but I can leave just as easily and let your daughter die. I'll have a hundred kala before, six hundred kala after."

The well-dressed woman clicked her tongue. "Seven hundred? It seems a little much for a one-armed midwife …"

"How about for your daughter's life?" The voice had a hard-edged humor to it that fascinated Lana.

The other woman looked around nervously. "Fine. If you save her, I'll give you what you want."

Lana saw her pull a pink hundred-kala coin out of her pocket and hand it to the midwife. Lana nearly salivated looking at it—that coin would let her and her mother eat fish and rice every day for the next two weeks. They entered a large house across from where Lana was hidden. Defying all common sense, her exhaustion forgotten, Lana crept across the street and sidled through the narrow alley, picking her way through piles of refuse. Through the thick sandstone walls, she could hear a woman shrieking and the unintelligible words of someone trying to calm her.

The woman shrieked again, this time so loudly that a raven, sorting through the midden heap, looked up in surprise and then flew away. Lana suddenly began to wish that she hadn't run so impetuously into the alley—or at least that she had worn some socks. She didn't want to even think about what liquid exactly was seeping between her toes. Still—the woman was making the oddest noises now, some strange cross between a gulp and a moan that sent shivers up her spine. She crept closer, avoiding as much of the refuse as she could. Up ahead, in the garden, she thought she saw dimly flickering lamplight, as though through a shuttered window. A short wall, reaching up to about her shoulders, separated the refuse-filled alley from the meticulously clean garden. Lana scrambled up over it and, without looking down, dropped on the other side. Instead of encountering solid ground, however, she fell with a splash into a pond. Luckily most of the noise was covered up a moment later, when the girl screamed again. The sound was much louder in the garden.

"Put out the incense." The preemptory voice of the midwife cut through the room. For a moment, the subdued, worried voices and even the woman's gulping moans stopped in what Lana imagined to be surprise.

"We couldn't possibly." It was the voice of the well-dressed woman Lana had seen on the street. "Perhaps you are unfamiliar with civilized customs, witch, but that incense is burning to pacify the death spirit—so it doesn't visit my niece tonight."

The midwife didn't sound offended at the insult. In fact, she seemed amused. "Of the two of us, I think I have the most reason to know what will and will not pacify the death spirit. But as you like it—either you keep your incense, and I leave, or you put it out and I stay. Perhaps in the morning you'll see how well your incense kept the death spirit away."

The silence in the room was broken only by the pregnant woman's gasping moans. It stretched on for nearly a minute, and then the well-dressed lady must have nodded, because the midwife began giving orders again.

"Ignorant fools," the midwife said. Lana, trying to maneuver herself out of the waist-deep pond, looked up just in time to see her flickering silhouette through the latticed rice paper shutters. Abruptly, the woman turned and slid them back. Lana ducked quickly into the water, and then turned to stare at the woman standing in the open window. The one-armed midwife's nearly black eyes darted over the rippling surface of the pond as if she had seen her. Lana held her breath—not as large a one as she would have liked, but enough—and prayed that she would leave the window. The midwife had the oddest intensity in her eyes, as though she was almost afraid, but the corners of her mouth were smiling. A lao-lao fish, of the most expensive iridescent kind, swam close to Lana's rock-steady arm and began nibbling at it. It splashed its soft white light carelessly around the pond, and Lana could feel her heart thundering. The woman looked abruptly down at the water, at the exact spot where Lana was hiding. Her empty right sleeve terrified Lana for some reason that she could not fathom. For one bright, painful moment, Lana thought that the woman had seen her—that she would tell the owner of this house and Lana would be arrested and tossed into the notoriously accident-prone dockside jails. But the woman just nodded slightly and turned around.

Lana waited until lack of air burned her lungs and made her vision go hazy. Then, very slowly, she raised her head out of the water. From where she crouched, she had a fairly good view of the low bed where a gasping, sweaty, and disturbingly bloody pregnant girl was struggling to give birth. The one-armed midwife held a glass filled with some gray-green mixture to the girl's mouth and gently forced her to drink it. A great deal dribbled from the sides of her mouth, but she seemed to get some of it down.

"Tell me, lady," the girl said, her voice trembling and hardly audible. "If I die here, will my baby die too? Can you at least save my baby?"

The woman put her arm gently on the girl's swollen, heaving stomach. "I will save the baby," she said. "And I will save you. Perhaps no one else could promise you that, child, but because I am here, I swear to keep death away tonight."

The girl's eyes grew wider, but she seemed to believe the woman, because she visibly relaxed. Lana was surprised. What powers did this midwife have that she could make such a rash promise? Because, Lana could tell, those had not been empty words of comfort—the midwife had been quite serious when she swore she would save the girl's life. But when Lana looked at that girl—so thin, apart from her swollen stomach—and saw how much blood she had already lost, she wondered how anyone could possibly keep death away from her.

From the time she was born, Lana had been marked as a diver. She had never considered herself as anything else, and so she had never actually seen another woman give birth. Other girls from her island learned midwifery, and cooking, but not the divers. So Lana had the strangest sense that night that she was being given a glimpse of a new and different world. Perhaps it was more mundane than the one she had been trained for, but it still held a strange kind of fascination.

The pregnant girl lived. An hour before dawn, when both she and the midwife were covered in sweat and panting with exhaustion, she gave birth to a female baby. After they cleaned her, Lana saw that she had a head full of hair—an odd shade of reddish burgundy that reminded Lana suddenly, painfully, of how Kali's hair had looked the day she died, after the sun came out.

"What will you name her?" the midwife asked.

She and the new mother were the only two people awake in the room. The girl's aunt and the two servants who had been helping with the delivery had fallen into an exhausted sleep. After all the noise of the past few hours, the world suddenly felt very quiet.

"My aunt ... she thinks I should name her Hiapelo ... after my mother. But I don't know ..." She gently stroked the baby's head. "She has such unusual hair, doesn't she?"

"Kali," Lana whispered.

She realized what she had done too late. The midwife turned her head toward the window, but instead of getting up to look, she simply nodded and faced the girl again.

"Kali is a pretty name, I think," the midwife said.

Lana's legs, already shivering uncontrollably from standing in the water for so many hours, started to buckle.

The girl looked up. "Kali? It's nice ... rustic, I think. Kali ..." She looked back down at her baby and then closed her eyes. Lana waited to make sure that she was still breathing and then stood up slowly. It would be dawn in an hour, and suddenly she could not bear to think how much her mother must be worrying. With a last glance at the strange tableau through the window, she climbed back over the alley wall.

Hours after Lana should have been home, Leilani pulled on her jacket and walked all the way to the northeast quarter, banged on the door of the owner of the launderer's, and demanded to know where her daughter was. She had left just after seven, as usual, the ruffled man had angrily told her. No, she hadn't looked any different than normal, and would she please take her petty domestic troubles elsewhere so he could kindly get some rest?

She had trudged home in silence, praying that Lana would be waiting for her when she returned, but somehow knowing that she wouldn't. She paced the floor for hours afterward, debating whether she should call the council guards. But would those guardians of the wealthy help her at all, or simply ignore her—or worse, find some pretext to arrest her? She worked herself into such a state of worried exhaustion that she fell asleep despite herself a few hours before dawn. When she awoke, it was to the unmistakable sound of old, groaning wood. Someone was coming up the stairs. Lana appeared in the doorway moments later, soaked to the skin and shivering. She was smiling slightly, as though she was hardly aware of the expression, but Leilani thought she saw tear tracks on her damp cheeks.

She'd had a furious barrage of questions prepared for when she managed to find her daughter again, but seeing her shivering in the doorway, looking so bewildered and inexplicably elated, she found she couldn't say any of them. Instead she stood up and fetched a towel.

"You smell like fish," Leilani said as she wrapped the warm, faded rag around Lana's shoulders.

"I was standing in a pond," Lana said, as though that explained everything.

Leilani sighed. "Take off your clothes and lie down. If you go to sleep now you might get an hour of rest before you have to go back to work."

Lana never told her mother about that night, but in the days that followed she found herself growing gloomy and distracted. She lost her appetite. Working at the launderer's sapped all of her energy, and the fumes irritated her throat so badly that sometimes it hurt to eat. Leilani was so exhausted after work herself that she rarely noticed how little Lana was eating. Which was just as well, as far as Lana was concerned. There was something bothering her mother—she could tell that much, but Leilani refused to speak about it. She would come home close to midnight, her eyes red and puffy. Lana worried about her, but in a distant sort of way. There were so many more things to worry about, these days—it was easier to work mindlessly, and forget about her other problems.

Kapa wrote them a letter, finally, that arrived two weeks after the night Lana spent in the garden pond. It came on market day—the only day off either of them had all week, when people traditionally went to the bustling market fair at the Eastern docks. They were both exhausted, however, with barely enough energy to talk to each other, let alone explore the market for items they couldn't possibly afford. Leilani slowly stood up when someone knocked on the door.

It was the landlady, holding a thick, folded letter.

"This just came on one of the trade ships. From Essel," she said.

A look of barely suppressed excitement came over Leilani's face. She thanked the woman profusely and took the letter in shaking hands.

The pitying look the lady gave her mother just before she closed the door made Lana inexplicably nervous. *Had* her mother been acting strangely lately? She just looked tired to Lana, but maybe there were other signs that she had been ignoring.

Leilani sat back on the floor and broke the seal.

"Is it Papa?" Lana asked.

Leilani gave her a tight smile and nodded. Despite her rush of excitement, part of Lana couldn't help but wonder if even being all together again would solve their problems. It would never be like it was back on the island, and in her heart, that's what she wished for the most, however childishly. But even "not as good as before" was better than now, with her endless, painful labor over the vats. They had been here for two months, and already the island seemed like a fairy tale of someone else's life. She had her memories of happiness, but the sensation was impossible to access—as though the steam and lye had burned it away.

"What … what does he say?" Lana asked, vainly trying to keep her voice calm.

The paper crackled as her mother's hands started shaking uncontrollably. She rested them on the floor and put her head between her knees. When she lifted her head a moment later, she looked as though she wanted to cry, but her eyes were dry. Lana's breathing grew rough.

"We have to stay, he says. At least two more months."

So there would be no escape from the vats tomorrow.

Two more months.

The old lady hadn't come in for the past week. Lana stooped over the huge stone basin for dark-colored clothes and stirred it with a wooden paddle twice her size. She was more profoundly exhausted than she had ever been in her life. Even the smallest movement of her back sent daggers of pain shooting down her legs, but she hardly noticed that anymore. She worked in a strange haze, forgetting to eat, unable to think—concentrating only on getting through the next second. Lana took the paddle out of the water and settled it against the wall. She staggered back from the tub a little and tried to straighten her back. The effort made tears spring to her eyes, and she collapsed against the nearest wall. What was wrong with her? Her back had never hurt this much before. She started to hobble to the bleach vat, but had to stop when a sudden coughing fit overcame her. This sort of thing had happened before, but she was usually able to control them. This time, however, the coughs were deep and explosive, searing her lungs and her throat until she was doubled over with the pain of it. Globs of rose-colored phlegm fell from her mouth onto the tightly packed dirt floor. The old woman was gone. There was no one else around to hear her call for help, but she struggled to yell anyway, sinking to her knees with the effort. Her head pounded each time she coughed, and the viscous, salty mucus coming from her mouth began to look bright red. She collapsed, watching the blood-streaked phlegm sink into the earth as her world went dark.

A boy, out of breath and clutching his hat in his hands, appeared on the dusty wooden step outside the lounge. He was too young to be a customer, Leilani thought as she tapped the used ashes out of the hookah pipes. She wondered if he might be a young sailor, but his hands weren't rough enough. Even at that age, a few months out at sea made all sailors develop a set of unmistakable calluses. She stared at him curiously as Heluma, one of the other hostesses, approached him.

"What do you want, boy?" she asked, wiping her forehead with a rag.

He fidgeted with his hat a little. "I have a message. I was told a woman with a daughter who works at the launderer's up in the northeast district should be here."

"Hey, Lei, isn't that you?" Heluma said, but Leilani had already stumbled up from her chair and ran toward the boy.

"What happened to Lana?" she asked. Her heart was beating frantically.

"She collapsed in front of one of the vats. The doctor told me to fetch her mother."

Leilani closed her eyes briefly, then turned to Heluma. "Tell the boss what happened. I have to go."

Heluma nodded and put a reassuring hand on her shoulder. "Don't worry about it."

Leilani nodded and then ran back inside to get her bag.

"I'm sure she'll be okay, Lei," Heluma said before Leilani left.

Leilani didn't say anything, but she prayed as she followed the boy through the narrow city streets.

The doctor, a stout man in the traditional gray embroidered robes of his profession, made her sit down and take some tea before he would discuss Lana's condition. She waited impatiently—she had seen Lana sleeping on a cot in the infirmary, but still worry gnawed at her stomach.

"To be perfectly straightforward, your daughter is very sick." His voice and manner were calm, as though he were discussing something of significantly less importance. Leilani's breath caught in her throat. "I don't know how long this condition has persisted, but she is clearly exhausted and the chemicals at the vats have irritated her throat and lungs to a point near poisoning. She has, at the moment, a dangerously high fever."

"Is she dying?" Leilani's throat felt strangled as the words left her mouth.

He pursed his lips. "I've seen much worse cases come through. There is a medicine I could provide that would probably guarantee it—especially regarding the situation with her lungs and throat—but it's quite expensive. I get it exclusively from a trader on Kalakoas and it is very difficult to come by." He looked at Leilani's second-hand attire appraisingly. "I'm afraid it may be above your means," he said.

She felt pins of anger in her chest. "Don't make assumptions. How much is it?"

He raised his eyebrows. "A week's supply, in her condition, would cost around a thousand kala."

Leilani felt herself shaking and tried to stop. A thousand kala was more than she made in a month at the lounge. Barely that much money remained from the small stash that she had brought with her from her home island. But this man seemed to be telling her that Lana was dying. She would simply have to find some way to get the money, no matter how difficult it was. For now, at least, she could pay for the first week.

"I'll come with the money later this evening, for the first week's supply." Her voice shook as she said it, but she knew it couldn't be helped.

The man looked surprised but nodded after a brief moment.

"As you will. For now, let's get your daughter home."

Some men from the infirmary carried Lana home on a piece of heavy canvas stretched between two poles. As they neared the docks, one of the men tripped over something in the road, and Lana nearly tumbled off.

"Be careful!" Leilani snapped. The man muttered an apology and adjusted his grip on the wood. Beside him, a woman in a heavy yellow cloak whom Leilani hadn't noticed before bent over and picked something up from among the littered seashells on the main road.

"I think this is hers," she said. Her gravelly voice made Leilani oddly uncomfortable. She leaned in closer to see what the woman held. To her surprise, she recognized the bright azure mandagah jewel that Lana had harvested during her initiation. Why had she been carrying that with her? Leilani had always thought that she kept the jewel in her trunk.

Leilani forced a smile. "Why, thank you." She took the jewel back and put it in her pocket.

"I hope your daughter recovers. It takes a special person to harvest a jewel like that."

The woman's tone was almost acquisitive, but her smile was sincere enough. Leilani forced herself to be civil. "Oh," she said. "Are you a diver?"

The woman gave a dry chuckle and shook her head. "No, no. Just a connoisseur."

And with that, the woman gave Leilani a brusque nod and seemed to melt back into the crowd. She stood still for a confused moment, and then, shaking her head, followed the men back to her apartment. She ran up the stairs when they reached the boarding house and rolled out a sleeping mat. She tried to make it as comfortable as possible, but she was painfully aware of its insufficiency. How could she have allowed this to happen to her daughter? Tears ached in her throat, but she forced them down. One of the men picked Lana up and settled her in the bed. After the men had left, she allowed herself to cry for half an hour. Then, she put a pitcher of water and a glass by the bed and went to get the money. Clutching the bit of twine heavy with strung-together stone coins, she left to give away all of their savings for a chance to save her daughter's life.

Lana came to very gradually. The bed felt familiar, but she couldn't remember how she had gotten home.

"Mama?" she said. Her voice was a scratchy whisper, and even that small sound made her throat feel as though some animal was clawing at it. What had happened? Suddenly, she remembered the coughing fit and collapsing on the floor. She felt horrible, like she might pass out again at any moment. She lifted her head a little to see if her mother was there and then fell back on the pillow, exhausted. She was alone. Her mother had left some water by the bed for her, but she wasn't sure if she had the energy to drink it. I must be sick, she thought. She certainly felt sick, but for some reason it hadn't seemed like a possibility before. She had just begun to drift off again when her mother opened the door.

Her face was pale and her back was unnaturally straight, as though she might collapse if she relaxed it. Lana wondered what had happened. Leilani looked at her and then ran to the bed.

"You're awake! How do you feel?" She set a small bag down on the floor and pulled the covers up over Lana. "Do you want some water?"

Lana let her mother tip some water down her throat and leaned back against her pillow when she had had enough. When had she ever felt this weak? She didn't recognize her own body, and she hated her helplessness. Ever since they had left the island, everything in her life had gone careening out of control, and she didn't know how to get it back again.

"Mama," she began to say, but Leilani shushed her.

"You don't have to say anything. I know it hurts. Here, I bought you some medicine that will help. You'll get better soon, Lana. I promise."

Her mother was scared. This realization ought to frighten her,

Lana thought, but instead she found it comforting. Her mother was no longer the infallible goddess of her youth—she was human, and scared, and trying to hide it, and Lana loved her. Leilani stood up and took out a judicious amount of a dried green herb from the bag and used it to brew tea. She poured a cup, waited until it had cooled enough, and then sat patiently beside Lana again.

"You have to drink all of it. It probably won't taste very good, though, so I'm sorry."

Lana shook her head and drank the whole thing obediently, even when it hurt her throat to swallow. The warmth briefly stopped her shivers, and made her feel sleepy.

"Mama," she said again as Leilani gently smoothed her hair away from her forehead. "I'll be all right."

Two tears, unmistakable, streaked their way down her mother's cheeks. "I'm sure you will, Lana. You should sleep."

So she did.

The man had been propositioning Leilani for weeks. It started with broad winks and suggestive hand gestures that had become progressively vulgar as time went on. Heluma, she knew, did the occasional sexual favor for extra cash, but the idea had always been repugnant to Leilani. She wanted nothing to do with the weather-beaten, self-assured merchant, no matter how many expensive chains he wore around his neck. As her supply of the precious medicine dwindled, however, and she was faced with the impossible prospect of finding a thousand extra kala, she began to consider it. She forced herself past her own nausea to smile at the merchant as she served him sour palm wine, or refilled his hookah bowl with mid-grade amant. Sometimes, she even brushed his shoulder suggestively with her arm as she left. He responded to her slightly less frosty behavior with even more obscene propositions.

"I want you in my bed, Lei," he growled the night before she ran out of the medicine. He was on his third bowl of amant. He was impeccably dressed, as usual, but the way his slicked-back graying hair shone in the lamplight made her feel nauseous. Heluma clearly thought he was a good prospect—unhandsome, but not unappealing, and clearly wealthy. But Leilani felt ill at even the thought of going to bed with him. "Why d'you think I've been coming to this crummy place every night for the past three weeks? I've got plenty enough money to frequent more high-class establishments." He rattled his chains suggestively.

Leilani was thinking of Lana, who was getting better enough to talk for a few sentences without coughing. What would happen if she ran out of the medicine?

"For a price," she said.

He looked at her appraisingly. "Now that's what I like to hear. How much? You've kept me away for so long, I'll pay anything."

"A thousand kala," she said, and could hardly believe her audacity when the amount left her mouth. What humble hostess in a third-rate sailor establishment could possibly hope for such a large amount?

He looked surprised as well, but then narrowed his eyes. "You have guts, Lei, I'll tell you that. You think you're worth so much? Well, for a thousand kala it would have to be the whole night. You'll have to do whatever I want."

The back of Leilani's mouth filled with the taste of vomit, but he had agreed. A thousand kala. She could buy enough medicine for another week. She nodded. "My shift is over in an hour."

He smiled. "This will be a night to remember." He took a long pull on the pipe and blew the smoke into her face.

He took her to an inn with clean sheets and a proprietor who looked the other way when rich guests with anonymous partners booked rooms. He took his time with her, kissing and touching her far more gently than she would have expected. At first, she went through the motions numbly and struggled not to be sick. But then, unexpectedly, she felt herself respond physically to his caresses, even while she cursed him in her mind. It seemed to her like the worst sort of betrayal—it was one thing for her to give her body to another man, but to *enjoy* it? Her moans occurred somewhere halfway between pleasure and grief. It seemed to go on forever, no matter how she tried to speed it along. She felt crushed by him, horrified by both his and her own desire. Before tonight, she had only been with one man in her entire life, a man she was completely in love with. Was this how sex was for most women? Pleasure without love? How could she ever tell Kapa of what she was doing, of what she'd had to do—even if it was for the sake of their daughter? She felt as if she were dying when he finished, despite the fact that she had taken every necessary precaution earlier.

He came at her all night long. All she wanted to do was leave, melt away, and she couldn't because he was on top of her again, and she couldn't even tell which one of them was gasping in pleasure. And then, finally, it was all over. Sated at last, he rolled onto the other side of the bed. She shook him awake.

"The money," she said. Her voice was flat.

His cold gray eyes looked amused. He levered himself upright, reached into his purse, and tossed the coins on the bed.

"You were all right. I figured you'd have more stamina, though," he said as he collapsed on the bed again. She struggled into her clothes and put the money in her pocket.

Outside the building, she ducked into an alley and vomited violently. Then she went to find the doctor.

· 4 ·

THE WOMAN HAD SETTLED HERSELF in an abandoned stall in the Alley, one of the less-than-savory market streets near the Eastern harbor. The previous occupant, a taxidermist of chimeras and exotic creatures, had succumbed to the bloody cough that was spreading relentlessly among the less respectable denizens of the docks. A few blocks from her stall in the Alley was Opona Street, where the better-patronized vendors hawked their more respectable wares, from bolts of brightly colored silk worth thousands of kala each to increasingly rare mandagah jewels. Those wishing for items of a less decorous nature went to the Alley. Fortune-tellers and apothecaries, prostitutes and bear-baiters— they crowded the wide, dirty street, clamoring for business with pitches as vulgar as they were amusing. Which made it an ideal location for the one-armed woman to set up shop. Indeed, she caused barely a ripple among those whose job it was, unofficially of course, to monitor the Alley. Just another self-styled fortune-teller plying her trade—strange about her arm, perhaps, but not worth any undue commentary. So long as she paid her tithe to the Alley Master, she was free to do as she pleased. If her business was especially slow, it was far more logical to blame it on the weather or her location than on halfhearted salesmanship. After all, why would she go through the trouble of setting up a stall if she had no interest in turning a profit?

The one-armed woman did, of course, intend to turn a profit, but perhaps not the kind that her neighbors expected. It had taken some time for to find the girl again after that night, but after a bit of judicious inquiry the woman—who, for the past several years of her search, had taken to calling herself Akua—had found the girl's mother. Leilani's exotic good looks had attracted the interest of several men who frequented her hookah lounge (the same kind of men, it turned out, who frequented the Alley). Her accent was that of the outer islands, and her dark skin and proud bearing made many speculate that she had been one of the legendary mandagah divers. She had a daughter, one young sailor had told Akua as she felt his skull—a young girl who worked the vats at a laundry and nearly died of the bloody cough. She might have a husband too, but if so, he wasn't around to disapprove of the way his wife had been raising money of late—prostituting herself to the highest bidder. That little fact, tossed her way so offhandedly as a trivial piece of gossip, had piqued Akua's interest. She now understood that Leilani was a desperate woman, and desperate people were easy to exploit: you only had to give them what they wanted.

Akua's scrying had told her to come here to Okika City in the first place, but scryings were unreliable. She had been truly surprised (for the first time in many years) when she had chanced upon the young girl that night and discovered just how suitable she would be. She was quiet and she held herself closely, but the one-armed woman could, nevertheless, sense the untapped depths within her. Some great power had marked this girl, but she was still too young and naïve to know how to protect herself.

She was a treasure hidden in plain sight: an innocent holder of unknowable power. Soon, Akua would have her.

Leilani pulled the conical straw hat farther over her head and hurried through the rain. The light drizzle of the past few days had turned into a nearly respectable downpour—something she might have enjoyed from the relative comfort of her apartment, but which made her curse now. The offices of the city doctor were in the governing district, a half-hour walk from the Eastern harbor. Since

Lana had become ill, Leilani had learned that there were dockside healers who would probably charge far less for their services, but she had seen too many people by the docks die of the cough to trust them. No matter how much it cost her, she had to take care of Lana. She reached the octagonal brick-and-granite building several minutes later, and walked around to the garden side, where a few still-burning lamps made strange shadows dance on the wet grass. She walked to the oak door and knocked three times. Almost immediately, she heard heavy footsteps and then the door opened.

The familiar smell and warmth of the place enveloped her as the doctor ushered her inside. It smelled of clean sheets and the nose-clearing tang of healing balms, all mixed with the sweetness of fresh-cut orchids—an acknowledgment of the doctor's patronage by the council as an officially sanctioned healer. Most of the staff had gone home by this time, and the hallway was empty as he led her to the relatively small room where they stored their medicines.

"How's the child?" he asked as he lit the lamps on the wall.

Leilani sighed. "Better. She's still weak though—I worry that she's going to overexert herself from boredom."

He fingered the various jars and sachets of dried herbs before he alighted on one. He pulled the rough homespun cloth bag off the shelf and carefully tilted some of its contents into another, smaller one.

"This should do for another week," he said, handing the bag to her. "If there's any change in her condition, let me know and I'll do what I can …" he trailed off when she reached into her pocket and pulled out a money purse.

"Here," she said, untying the strings and carefully counting out ten plum-sized, rose-colored coins into his palm. "This week's thousand," she said. There was a slight breathiness to her voice, but otherwise she gave no outward appearance of agitation.

Still, the doctor looked at her sadly, almost pityingly, and Leilani cringed. Ever since this ordeal had first begun he had looked at her this way, but today it was somehow more damning. But what else could she do, after all? Let her daughter die?

After a tense moment, he handed three of the coins back to her. "I gave you less this week. You don't owe so much."

Leilani stared at him. She knew how much he had given her. He knew it too, but for whatever reason, he had decided to pretend otherwise. She felt a brief surge of anger—she had the money, after all—but it passed away quickly. It was merely a gesture of kindness—born out of pity perhaps, but who was she to refuse it? After an instant's struggle, she pocketed the coins.

"Leilani," he said just before she turned to leave. "Please … be careful. Women with lesser hearts than yours have found this city's hard edge fatal."

Leilani tightened her lips and nodded. Throat aching, she turned around and walked as quickly as she could toward the door, heedless of etiquette or even safety.

Kapa, she thought to herself, when she had exited into the blanketing rain. *When will I see you again? When will this all be over?*

Despite the rain beading on her face, Lana had raised the resin-coated paper covering the window and rested her elbows on the sill. She watched the frothy gray waves lap against the docks, making the moored ships creak and groan like tortured souls. She sighed and used her finger to smear the beads of water on the stone sill into the pictograph for "help" without really thinking. She shook her head and wiped it away with her sleeve. It was cold—but she was always cold lately, and she wondered if the chill would ever leave her bones. The gray sky was growing dark without an accompanying sunset. She had loved the rain back on her island, but here it was merely depressing—no cacophony of thunder and rain, only a desultory drizzle that went on for days and seeped into her soul like fog. How could anyone live here? Even the harbor water was too foul and cold to swim in. She longed to kick her legs against the water and tunnel far beneath the surface, to hold that precious breath of air as long as possible while exploring like a fish. Instead, she was stuck in this tiny apartment with cracked floorboards and peeling whitewash.

Below, a woman dressed in the bright purple and pink of one of the council member's houses hurried down the dock to a fish stall and commenced haggling. She was probably a housekeeper or a cook's assistant, sent out to buy dinner for that evening. Lana's stomach began to growl as she thought of the delicacies that family probably took as commonplace. Today was her birthday, but even if they could have afforded it, she was too weak to go out and haggle for food in this rain. Ever since she had collapsed five weeks ago, she had steadily improved, but even a few laps up and down their tiny apartment exhausted her. Much as she longed to work and help ease the strain that never seemed to leave her mother's eyes, she knew she still wasn't well enough. Something had been bothering Leilani lately, but every time Lana asked her about it she just shook her head and changed the subject. Sometimes she came back home late with bruises on her face and arms, but she would never say how she got them. Lana was scared for her mother, but she felt utterly powerless to help her.

Heavy pellets of rain splattered against her face. Lana shivered and went to get a quilt to wrap around her body. It was nearly dark outside, and when she looked back down at the docks the only light came from the wavering street lamps lining the harbor. Minutes later, she finally saw her mother's unmistakable worn gray coat moving through the streets just below their boarding house. But instead of going inside, she headed toward the docks where the fisherwomen were closing their stalls. Lana stared. Where had her mother found the money to buy them fish? She was further shocked when she saw her mother purchase one the size of her arm. It must have cost nearly a hundred kala! Had Leilani been saving up for special treat on her birthday? Lana would have jumped up and down if she hadn't been so tired.

Her mother, burdened by her heavy load, slowly made her way home from the docks. Before she could reach the boarding house, a strange man wearing a sailor's scarf almost casually hooked her arm and dragged her around to face him. At first Lana was just confused, but her shivering redoubled when she realized that her mother was struggling to get away from him. He laughed and then pulled so hard on Leilani's elbow that she cried out. Who was this man? Why wasn't anybody helping her mother? Leilani spat in his face. He slapped her.

Lana dropped the quilt from around her shoulders and hurried to put on her shoes. Her legs wouldn't move quite as quickly as she wanted them to, but she made her way down the wooden stairs and past the landlady within a minute. Outside, she had to squint to see past the rain, but it wasn't hard to find her mother.

"Let go of me, Keisano," Leilani was saying shrilly, trying to wrench herself from his grip.

"You didn't say that last night when you needed the money," he said, placing one hand very deliberately on her mother's buttock and squeezing.

On one level it didn't make any sense at all, but on another it felt like the confirmation of a terrible nightmare. Shivering in the rain and resisting the urge to cough, Lana knew she had to do something before she lost all of her energy and her nerve.

Before she could really think about it, she ran behind the tall, horrible man and hauled him away from her mother by the waist. Leilani looked stunned, and hadn't found her voice when the man broke free of Lana's grip and rounded on her angrily.

He was very drunk, but unfortunately, it just seemed to make him angrier rather than unsteady.

"Bitch," he growled, and swung his fist into Lana's cheek. She didn't even have time to react. Rain drummed on her forehead, and wet mud from the gravel road seeped into her back. How had she gotten there? She tried to get up, but her limbs felt like jelly. Her jaw throbbed. Distantly, she heard a cacophony of shouts and footsteps—had the townspeople finally decided to help them? Then her mother was kneeling next to her and holding her head in her lap, telling her that everything was going to be okay.

And even through her haze of pain and burgeoning weakness, Lana heard the emptiness behind her mother's words.

Leilani didn't think she would ever get over the mingled fear and pride she had felt when she saw Lana fling herself on Keisano—a strong and dangerously drunk man nearly twice her size—with the ferocity of a tiger. And she also didn't think there was a punishment anywhere in the islands suitable for someone who would hit a sick girl hard enough to dislocate her jaw. Certainly not whatever slap on the wrist Keisano would get from the dockside courts.

But her next days turned into unhinged hours sitting beside Lana's sleeping mat, heating bricks on the stove, wiping her forehead, and helping her drink as much of the medicinal tea as she could get down. Upon hearing what had happened—and the sensational character of the tale had helped it travel quickly—the doctor had come to visit Leilani personally, to give her more of the medicine and to straighten Lana's jaw. He told Leilani, much to her relief, that the relapse wasn't as serious as it could have been and that Lana would recover much more quickly this time. It was a relief, but sitting here by her bedside hour after hour it was hard to believe. The owner of the hookah lounge had turned her away that first morning, saying that she knew what it was like to have daughters and not to worry about her salary for the next week. The doctor wouldn't take any payment for his services, either. Leilani didn't quite know what to make of such charity—it was against her nature to take handouts, but then, she had never been so desperate.

Leilani woke the second morning after the incident to discover that Lana was already awake and leaning against the apartment wall, huddled in her blankets.

"You shouldn't be up," Leilani said.

Lana shook her head. "I'm tired of lying down." Her words were slightly distorted because she still couldn't open her mouth very wide. The doctor had said that most of the pain and the swelling would go away within a week.

"Why aren't you at work?" Lana asked, almost sullenly.

"They let me off this week so I could take care of you."

Lana looked at her, a terrible pain in her eyes that made Leilani want to cry. "I suppose you have enough money saved up, after all," she said, very deliberately.

The words hit Leilani with a physical force. She had prayed that Lana hadn't understood Keisano that night.

"Lana, I ..."

"I'm right, aren't I? That man ... that sailor. You slept with him? And others ... many others? For how long?"

The question startled her into an answer. "Five weeks."

Her daughter closed her eyes. "Since I got sick, then."

Leilani felt a brief surge of anger. "Of course only since then! I did this to pay for your medicine—to save your life!"

Lana's brittle laugh turned into a coughing fit and Leilani helped her lie back down. "I was hoping ... that was why," she said softly. "Isn't it funny, Mama? Would you have believed any of this a year ago? How much we've changed?"

"We haven't changed, Lana. The world has changed around us, but nothing will ever change how much I love you. Ever."

Leilani stood and walked to the stove. Behind her, Lana stirred.

"I love you too, Mama," she said. And then, more softly, "Thank you."

Leilani walked slowly through the Alley, looking at the seemingly endless parade of bizarre items in each stall and enjoying the unusually pleasant day. The salty air and warm breeze drifting with the scent of orchids lulled her mind into complacency, made her think that they would survive this ordeal after all. She was expecting a letter from Kapa on the next merchant ship—maybe they would be able to join him soon, and everything would be all right again. She passed a fortune tellers' stall and paused, drawn by the curious sight of brightly colored books that looked to be freshly printed.

She fingered an embossed red leather cover, titled *The Adventures of Pirate Lo.* The one below it was blue—a more staid account of the era of spirit binding.

"Fresh from Essel," said the strangely grating voice of the woman behind the stall. Leilani froze for a moment, filled with inexplicable unease. Where had she heard that voice before? She looked up. The woman's right sleeve was empty, she saw, and the brief feeling that she had met this woman before faded. Surely she would have remembered a one-armed fortune teller. She shivered and shifted her eyes away from the empty sleeve. Most such people were merely victims of tragic accidents, but Leilani had lived most of her life on the outer islands, and she knew enough about the spirits to understand the darker side of sacrifice. The hardness in this woman's brown eyes made Leilani wary. Still, she hid her discomfort and nodded amiably. She was only browsing, after all.

"They would be perfect for a sick little girl, too weak to go out but bored being alone."

Leilani looked up sharply and fought the urge to run away. The book fell numbly from her fingers. "How did you … ?"

The woman laughed and waved her hand self-deprecatingly. Her long brown hair was pulled into a large braided bun at the back of her neck, a severe style that did nothing for her already plain face. "Fortune teller," she said, tapping the sign with her finger. "It's my job to know things ordinary people wouldn't."

Or aren't supposed to know, Leilani thought. But she shook her head and smiled politely. "Thanks just the same. I've no desire to have my fortune read."

The lady looked at her appraisingly. "Then how about your prayers answered?"

Despite herself, Leilani was intrigued. "What do you mean?"

"Come." She gestured to the area curtained off in back of her stall. "I can explain in there."

Leilani hesitated. "I have no money."

"Money isn't always useful. Come sit with me over tea. If you don't think I've offered you what you've always wanted, then you're free to go without paying a kala. If you want it … we'll negotiate."

Leilani knew she should decline, but something in those hard brown eyes beckoned her. She was feeling hopeful today, more hopeful than she'd felt in months; maybe this strange woman *could* help.

The only light in the in the stall filtered in through the heavy curtains and fell in such a way as to cast the one-armed woman's face in almost complete shadow. Dust kicked up from the black tablecloth floated in the bars of light, swirling lazily into almost-shapes. It tickled Leilani's nose and she fought the urge to sneeze. The woman reached under the table and pulled out a crudely made wooden bowl, darkened and pockmarked with age. Then she took a pitcher of water and poured until the bowl was half-filled.

"What do you most wish to see?" the woman asked her, looking up.

"Kapa," Leilani said without thinking. "My husband, I mean. I want to know how he is."

The woman gave a tight-lipped smile. "Show me your hand," she said. Reluctantly, Leilani held out her left hand. The woman reached into the pocket of her loose trousers and removed a knife. She dipped the blade in the clear water and then, before Leilani could object or even cry out, sliced it precisely across Leilani's palm. A stream of blood dripped into the bowl. It stung, but the sudden rush of power filling the room was immediately palpable. It was similar to power Leilani had sometimes felt around Okilani, but somehow darker—like this woman commanded far more reluctant forces than the native earth spirits of her island. The dust motes froze in the light and the temperature in the room dropped.

"Say the name of the one you wish to see and look in the bowl. Close your hand when you wish to see no more."

Okilani would tell her to refuse, she knew. But recklessness kept her hand above the water.

"Kapa," she said eagerly, and looked in the bowl.

The water swirled and then deepened, until she could see nothing else but strangely shifting shapes in foggy water. Then they solidified into an image of a man sitting on a street corner, huddled in a threadbare high-collared coat that had once been brown. His hair hung past his shoulders in lanky strips and he was playing a sad little tune on a tortoiseshell harp. It was very cold there, and the fingers that slid up and down the shiny strings were cracked and bleeding. He didn't seem to notice, however. In fact, the only time he seemed to be aware of anything other than the music was when the occasional passersby dropped a blue-veined half-kala coin into his sack. Two stunned tears slid off Leilani's cheeks into the water and she saw Kapa look up at the clear sky, as though something had hit him.

"I don't understand ..." she whispered.

"Sad, isn't it?" The woman wasn't looking in the bowl, but she seemed to know what Leilani saw. "It's the fate of most who go to Essel with such dreams."

Leilani shook her head. "But in his letters ... he said he was setting up a shop, that there was a market. What happened? Why didn't he tell me?"

"In Essel the guild determines who sets up shop and who doesn't. He probably spent most of his money on the trip and had none to pay the guild. They have very ... inventive punishments for those who don't respect their monopoly."

"Oh Kapa," she whispered at the water, as though he could hear her. "What are we going to do?" She longed to run a comb through his matted hair, to hug him and promise that she would never leave him again. But he continued playing, his whole body except his hands shivering with cold.

"I don't want to see this anymore," she said, her voice trembling.

The woman ran her hand quickly above the water and the image wavered. Then she gently closed Leilani's fingers over her palm and moved it away from the water. Kapa faded, leaving only murky water in an old bowl, faintly illuminated by the dying light outside. Slowly, Leilani lifted her head to look in the woman's eyes. There was satisfaction buried somewhere within those dark depths. *I should have run when I had the chance,* Leilani thought. What she had seen had firmly ensnared her, and this strange and dangerous woman knew it.

"Who are you?" she asked.

"Call me Akua."

She shuddered. "Why did you show me this?"

The woman smiled a little. "It was your choice. I never forced you into any of it."

"What do you want from me?" she asked.

"I want to answer your prayers."

Leilani's heart was pounding with fear but she could not force herself to leave. She no longer felt any geas—there was no other power in this room right now beside the very human one of manipulation. And this woman, whoever she was, had manipulated Leilani like a marionette.

"How?" Leilani said, finally.

The smile stretched across Akua's face. The woman reached into her pocket again and this time pulled out a large leather coin purse. She untied its strings and dumped its contents—dozens of large, pink hundred-kala coins—onto the table. Leilani's mouth nearly dropped open. How could this backstreet fortune-teller have so much money?

"This is about 10,000 kala—almost exactly enough to pay for your passage to Essel, purchase some decent lodgings there, and pay the musicians' guild to set up a shop. You would be back together with your husband and he would be able to pursue his dream." The woman picked up each round stone coin and dropped them with precision back into the bag.

Each thunk reverberated in Leilani's brain and made it

difficult for her to think. Could this woman be serious? Then she realized what had been missing from the woman's scenario.

"What about my daughter, Lana?" she asked. "She's sick and the medicine's … expensive."

The coins stopped dropping. "Ah. Lana. As I said, money is not worth everything. For some time now, I have needed an apprentice … a vessel to receive my knowledge. I believe that your daughter would be quite suitable."

Leilani's formless fear turned into dread. "But—"

The woman waved her hand peremptorily. "Hear me out. Your daughter is sick, but not as sick as she once was. She needs a place outside this city to rest and build her strength. If she studies with me, she will learn an art that would make her sought after by the most powerful people in the islands. She would have far more in life than she could hope for as the daughter of a starving musician. You will be investing in your daughter's future. And it's not as though I would take her away forever; she can visit you during the spirit solstice. And what do I ask in return for such largess?" She leaned over the table, her eyes gleaming in the low light. "Merely that you wear this necklace, and that you never, ever take it off." From around her own neck Akua removed a leather cord. At its bottom swung a three-toothed key: the ancient symbol of the death spirit, carved delicately out of bone.

Leilani stared at the white charm swaying back and forth before her eyes and for a horrifying moment she almost took it. This was no small obligation the woman was asking, no matter how off-handedly she phrased the request. What bond this necklace would form between them she had no way of knowing, but she knew unmistakably that she would not like it.

With as much willpower as she had ever exerted, Leilani stood on shaky legs and walked to the curtains.

"I cannot do this," she said over her shoulder as she walked out.

As she hurried home, she tried to clear her head of the image of the woman sitting quietly at the dark table, her eyes cold and inscrutable.

That, Akua thought with some satisfaction, had gone fairly well. Considering Leilani's previous eagerness, she had been half expecting her to agree on the spot. But the seeds had been planted and she had no reason to worry about the outcome. Soon enough, Leilani would come back to the one-armed woman, prepared to give her exactly what she wanted.

She only had to wait.

Her mother was unusually agitated that evening, and no amount of prodding could get her to say why. Lana worried that she'd had another bad experience with one of her ... clients, again, but nothing in her demeanor suggested physical violence. In an effort to cheer her, Lana gave Leilani the latest letter from Kapa, which had arrived while she was out. Although reading Kapa's letters usually calmed her mother, Leilani seemed, if anything, even more agitated after she read it.

"Why not just join the storyteller's guild!" she shouted. She stalked to the stove, looking almost as though she wanted to toss it in.

"But Mama, he said that he should be able to send for us soon. Isn't that what we've been waiting for?"

Leilani looked at her and then, inexplicably, began to cry.

Lana crawled over to where her mother had sunk to the floor. "What's wrong?"

Leilani merely shook her head and sat down at the end of Lana's sleeping mat. She began to cry in earnest, deep choking sobs that made Lana want to cry too without really knowing why. What on earth was going on? She sat up and crawled over to her mother and put a careful hand on her shaking shoulders. She was terrified, for she had never seen her mother weep like this before. Only the direst circumstances would make her release herself like this in front of Lana.

After an uncertain moment Lana stood up and walked to the kitchen to get a handkerchief. She put her head between her knees to catch her breath while her mother wiped her face and blew her nose. The worst of it seemed to be subsiding.

"Lana," her mother said, dabbing her puffy eyes with the cloth. "How are you feeling?"

"Better," she said truthfully. "My jaw only hurts when I eat now."

Leilani closed her eyes. "No, I mean, how do you feel about this city? Does it … I mean, do you feel that you can't … get better here?"

Lana tried to choose her words judiciously. "Well, I'm sure I'll get better when Papa sends for us. He says he's found a really nice place for us to stay, so I bet it's warmer, and that it doesn't always stink of dead fish."

To her confusion, Lana's answer seemed to make Leilani even more upset. "Oh great Kai, help me," she said softly. She turned to Lana. "What if I told you that maybe you wouldn't come back to live with me and your father? What if you went to a different place, to be apprenticed, to learn a trade that will … that will make you sought after by the highest in society? We would still see each other sometimes, once a year …" Leilani started sobbing again, and Lana found tears on her own cheeks as well. "How would that be, Lana?" she said, her voice an octave higher than normal. Lana hugged her mother tightly.

"I would miss you."

"I would … I would miss you too."

"Would this be like what you did with those men … something we don't want to do, that we do anyway to survive?"

Leilani was silent for a long time. "Yes, Lana," she said finally. "It would be just like that."

"Then I think I could do it, Mama. For you. I think I'm strong enough."

Leilani raised her head slowly and looked at Lana. "I knew the moment I first looked in your eyes that I had given birth to the strongest daughter of the islands."

It took a long time for Leilani to write the letter to Kapa. She didn't know how to explain what had happened without telling him things that she never wanted to remember again. Eventually, she resigned herself to confessing everything. She just hoped that he forgave her when she arrived. Lana had spent the past two days painstakingly packing their meager belongings. She had to rest every few minutes, but she attacked it like a duty and refused to stop. Leilani left her dozing against the wall and went to the docks to post her letter. She took her time, for she knew that she would have to visit the one-armed woman again today, and the very thought shot dread through her heart. She knew that she had sold her daughter—perhaps for Lana's own good, but she had sold her nonetheless—and they would never truly be a family again. As slowly as she could she meandered from the docks to the Alley. She stopped to look at the wares of nearly every vendor, even things she would normally have been revolted by—pickled loon's legs, for example. Sooner than she hoped, however, she found herself at the fortune-teller's stall. The books were gone, as well as the sign, but the dark curtains still hung over the entrance to the back room. Had the woman left?

"I see you came back."

The woman's grating voice behind her made Leilani jump and she turned around slowly, trembling. "Have you reconsidered, then?" Akua asked. No, Leilani thought, but she nodded her head. The woman smiled broadly. "I'm glad. Come back here with me and we will finish the bargain."

She led the way through the curtains and Leilani followed, wishing that she had the strength to refuse this offer. What strange use did this woman have for Lana? *I should leave,* she thought, but she stayed where she was.

"First," the woman said, "the necklace." She took the key

charm from its place on the table—had she actually laid it there in anticipation?—and held it out. "If you ever take it off, I will know—and your daughter's safety is forfeit. This is the only thing I ask of you."

With trembling hands, Leilani pulled the necklace over her head and tucked it under her shirt. It felt cold and harmless on her skin, but she knew that it now bound her to the witch-woman irrevocably. She wondered, too late probably, exactly how much power that woman had gained when she sacrificed her arm.

"Well, then, the money." She reached into her pocket and pulled out the leather purse. Leilani snatched it and let its weight fall into her pocket.

"You don't want to count it?" she asked, with mocking humor. Leilani merely shook her head. She itched to get out of here.

"And finally, the small matter of your daughter. Is she able to travel? My house is by a lake in the countryside some two days away from here by river. We would travel by river boat, of course, to make it easier for her."

Leilani nodded reluctantly. "She's getting better, but there's a medicine she needs … leaves, boiled into tea at least twice a day. Will you do that?"

"Of course. I'll always have my apprentice's best interests at heart—never worry about that. As you can see, I'm packing up shop." She smiled suddenly. "This has been quite a successful trip. Could your daughter leave with me tomorrow?"

Leilani made her eyes hard. She would show this woman whatever small reserves of strength she had left. "If that's what you want."

Akua's expression softened slightly in a way that would have seemed on anyone else like a moment of regret. "It is," she said. "Could you meet me at the northern gates tomorrow at midday? We'll take a carriage from there to the river port."

She had less than a day left with Lana, then. Leilani nodded curtly. "We will be there," she said. Much as she had a few days earlier, she left the stall before the other woman could say anything else.

Lana stood before the dilapidated pink stone walls of the northern gate in a new outfit of marbleized blue pants and a knee-length buttoned top with two slits up the sides. In her bag were a new pair of shoes, a head scarf, a heavy coat, and a sheaf of expensive paper with sealing wax—all gifts from her mother. Leilani gripped her hand tightly, but otherwise displayed no outward emotion.

It was a clear, chilly, windy day, and passersby did not pause to look at them as they hurried about their business. Only one green-clad official stood near the open gate, itemizing the contents of merchant carts. After a cursory glance at the two of them he ignored them entirely.

Lana wondered what this witch-woman looked like. It was strange knowing that she was to be apprenticed to a witch—buried under the pain of being separated from her mother was a certain kind of excitement. Maybe now she would learn to control the powers that she had merely touched before. This would be different from Okilani's power, of course. The wild earth spirit alone gave that power to those it chose as elders. Witches, on the other hand, used sacrifice to bind power to them that would otherwise not be given. Perhaps if she had stayed on the island and shown Okilani the red mandagah jewel, she would have been chosen anyway. But it was too late now to regret that decision.

At almost precisely the point when the sun reached its zenith, Lana heard the clatter of carriage wheels over the seashell-lined main road. She turned around, heart in her throat. The male driver pulled the sober gray carriage to a halt right before the gate. The door opened and a plainly dressed woman, brown hair pulled into a bun that highlighted her strangely pale face, stepped lightly onto the street. Lana knew without looking that her right arm would be missing. It was the one-armed midwife from that night nearly two months ago. Lana's hands trembled, excitement warring with terror. Far more than she had on that night, this strange woman emanated power and knowledge. Lana glanced up at her mother, but though Leilani's face was set in hard, determined lines, she seemed unaware of the strength Lana felt rolling off this woman in waves.

The woman caught her eye and smiled very slowly. It was friendly, conspiratorial, and Lana could not help but smile back, even though she felt inexplicably guilty about it.

"Hello, Lana. I trust you know who I am."

Her rough voice made Lana feel wary and hopeful at once. Her mother, however, stood rigidly beside her.

"I'm to be your apprentice," Lana said, feeling awkwardly polite.

"You may call me Akua. Does that suit you?" When Lana nodded she turned to her mother. "Say your goodbyes, then. We don't want to miss the boat."

Leilani knelt down beside Lana, and held her shoulders tightly. Her eyes were red-rimmed from crying last night, but no tears escaped them now. "You know I love you, Lana. This may be painful now, but soon you'll be used to your new life and it won't be so bad. I just hope that you'll always remember me and your father—"

"Of course I will, Mama!" Lana found herself crying again.

"Shh, let me finish. You have to leave soon. I'm going to tell you something that my mother once told me: listen to what they have to say, learn what makes sense, but never ever accept anything without thinking it through first. You understand, Lana? This woman will have a lot to teach you, but never lose yourself. The Lana I raised knows right from wrong."

Lana threw her arms around her mother's shoulders and hugged her tightly, heedless of people watching.

"I'll see you in a year," she whispered in Lana's hair, and then slowly let her go. "Now leave," she said, her voice husky with unshed tears. "Before I start crying again."

Before she lost her nerve entirely, Lana clutched her bag and climbed inside the carriage.

Leilani handed a medicine bag to the one-armed woman. "Promise me you'll take care of her," she said.

Akua took the bag. "I promise," she said. Then she climbed back into the carriage and slid the door shut.

The image of her mother standing alone by that gate, rigid as a statue, stayed with Lana for the rest of her life.

There were no cabins to speak of on the riverboat. The ten or so passengers either purchased hammocks or rolled out their own sleeping mats on the narrow deck. Either way, they all slept under the stars. Lana was leaning against the rail near their hammocks, looking with dry, sad eyes at the reflected silver moonlight on the water. The boat had anchored for the night and was swaying gently in the current.

"Have you ever been on a river at night?" Akua asked, suddenly beside her.

Her grating voice no longer startled Lana. "I've never been on a river. There were none on my island. Just ocean and sand."

"It's been very long since I've been near the outer islands, but that sounds familiar."

Akua's voice was openly friendly—not demanding that Lana participate, but welcoming if she wanted to. Despite herself, she found that she liked the witch-woman.

"You'll be in for a treat, then, if you've never seen the liha'wai dance."

"Liha'wai? What's that?" Lana asked, turning her attention away from the water.

"River nits. Strange creatures that come out at night ... entirely for their own purposes, whatever those might be. But they make a beautiful display for humans anyway."

Akua fell silent and Lana turned back to the water. She could imagine swimming in it, darting back and forth like a fish with moonlight glinting off her skin. Gradually she realized that river water was indeed shimmering more than could be accounted for by the moon. Then in a sudden rush like the sound of thousands of tiny splashes, the moonlight itself seemed to fly up from the water and hover above the boat. Around her sailors and passengers alike stopped what they were doing to look. Strange, tiny silver-scaled creatures that looked a little like fish with membranous wings and long skinny webbed legs danced in the silvery light. They arched and plummeted, spun and zipped around each other so quickly they looked like blurs of illumination. A smile lit Lana's face and she stared, transfixed. How had she never known that something like this existed? She wondered if she would see miracles like this wherever she traveled, or if such wonders were far fewer than the pain she had become accustomed to. Did moments like this simply exist to convince humans to continue their largely painful lives? Or, was there was no design to it at all and it still served, unwittingly, the same purpose?

"This is their mating dance," Akua said. "All autumn long the river lights like this, and then these creatures will give birth and die. Come summer, every beautiful spark you see here will be dead."

The very imminence of their deaths, Lana realized, made their dance that much more poignant. "But next year their children will dance the same dance ... that's a kind of immortality, isn't it?"

Akua looked at her curiously, and then shrugged her shoulder. "For some, perhaps, that's sufficient."

"What other options do we have?" she asked, gazing at the liha'wai.

"Ah, Lana. There are always other options. It just depends how much you are willing to sacrifice for them."

Lana looked at Akua's empty right sleeve and wondered what option she had chosen. Then she looked back up at the dancing nits and wished her mother were here to share it with her.

· 5 ·

Emea sat with Kohaku in the back of the lecture hall, watching his hands translate what Professor Nahe was forcefully declaiming on the podium. As part of the citywide celebrations of the spirit solstice, the Kulanui was giving a series of decently well-attended lectures on the history of the spirit bindings. The room this evening was packed with studious-looking students clad in orange or green robes and a smattering of civilians drawn by Professor Nahe's reputation as a popular speaker. Kohaku wore green robes and the woven purple headband of an adjunct professor, which he had just been awarded the week before. Emea was, of course, incredibly happy for him—she would never tell him that the main reason he had finally been promoted was because Nahe had spoken for him on her behalf.

Though she had spent most of her life in a silent world after the fever that stole her hearing, Emea found it amusing to try to imagine what Nahe's voice sounded like, up there on the podium. His mouth was firm, but she knew that it could be achingly soft and pliable under her lips. His eyes raked the crowd, and for the briefest of moments they rested on her, leaving her breathless. She turned back to Kohaku, terrified that he had noticed, but he was still signing, seemingly unaware of Emea's wandering attention.

Ever since Kohaku had returned from the outer islands two years ago, she had lived in terror that he would discover her relationship with Nahe. Kohaku would never understand how much she loved Nahe. He would demand that she never see him again, and she couldn't bear to have to pick between them. It wasn't that her brother would begrudge giving her to any man; the problem was that Nahe was already married. Kohaku would never let her become a lowly second wife. To be perfectly honest, Emea herself knew she would be unhappy in such a situation, much as she loved Nahe. So she kept her relationship a secret and never thought too far into the future—for now, it was enough just being with him, and having her brother back.

She refocused her attention on Kohaku's hands, since he would find it suspicious if she didn't pay attention to what was being said when she had practically begged him to attend the lecture. Nahe was speaking of the great fire spirit, Essel's ancient patron. Nui'ahi, the great volcano, was held in check because of the fire spirit's binding, and in return the spirit held ultimate control over the greatest nation-state of the islands. Every fifteen years, any who dared could undertake the great pilgrimage to the inner fire shrine, where the fire spirit itself would pick the next Mo'i, Essel's supreme ruler. The time of the next trial was looming—in three years Ehae, the current Mo'i, would step down and a new one would be chosen. With the recent rumors of possibly spirit-caused disasters on the outer islands, people were anticipating this pilgrimage more than any in recent memory. Ehae's son, now fifteen years old, was expected to be a supplicant, but history had taught them all that there was no telling who the fire spirit would pick. And those it didn't pick, of course, served as freely given sacrifices. It was a common adage of the great pilgrimage: many venture, but only one returns. The power and the prestige that went with becoming Mo'i were such that many were willing to take the risk, although Emea herself could never understand it.

She preferred less drastic measures of honoring—or at least propitiating—the great fire spirit. Before her fever, her father had always taken both of them to the local temple at sundown on the last day of the solar month. They, along with a diminishing but determined few from their city, would burn thick candles and beg the fire spirit for forgiveness and temperance in the face of its thousand-year imprisonment. According to Nahe, worship of the fire spirit had been drastically different before the binding. Now, priests were mainly concerned about the strength of the bonds and worked to reduce anything that might weaken them. Fear—not respect, and certainly not love—motivated modern religious observance. Yet, in the remote and shadowy days before the bindings, respect and love for the spirits had apparently been normal. Without any clear knowledge of sacrifice, or of the great geas, the primitive people worshipped and honored and prayed to be spared. Nui'ahi, Nahe said, erupted no less than five times in one century, an image that made Emea shudder with a mix of horror and guilty pleasure. To see the sentinel in full rage ... it would have been a truly awesome sight.

Before she was really prepared, Nahe's speech ended. He caught her eye just before he left and signaled discreetly for her to find him outside. Emea looked frantically at Kohaku, but thankfully he was adjusting his headband and hadn't noticed.

"I have to ... ah, use the facilities. Wait here, I'll be right back," she said.

Kohaku nodded absently, already focused on chatting with a high-ranking professor two rows away. Outside the lecture hall, she felt the jarring impact of her wooden heels on the hard inlaid marble of the corridor. Covered lamps in sconces on the walls wavered as she ran past, making her shadow dance. She dashed up a rounded flight of stairs and then through another smaller corridor that ended in two closed doors. One, however, was open very slightly, letting in a thread of the chill night breeze. Emea forced herself to approach it slowly. She brushed back her hair and closed her eyes briefly before pulling the knob with shaking hands. Nahe was sitting on the edge of their hidden balcony, his graying hair pulled back into a short ponytail save for three loose braids around his temples. A fashion for a younger man, but the brashness suited him. The harsh planes of his face were not softened in the moonlight, but Emea had always found him beautiful. He turned to face her when she stepped onto the balcony and closed the door behind her. A smile played around his lips.

"I couldn't stand to see you sitting there with him, pretending that you didn't even know me," he signaled. His hands were clumsier than Kohaku's, but he could sign well enough for her to understand him.

Emea shrugged. "What else could I do? It's so hard to see you sometimes. Your wife can't know about us, and neither can my brother."

"Ah, my wife. She knows more than I give her credit for, I think. But still, in my position, it wouldn't do for us to be found out."

Emea hated when Nahe spoke like this—so … callously. Times like these she wondered if he could possibly understand how much she loved him. To dispel her doubts she shook her head and hugged him fiercely. He returned the gesture after a moment and then lowered his head to kiss her.

His passion was enough to eradicate any niggling doubts, and she gave herself up to it for a few heady moments before she gasped and broke away.

"I must go back," she said. "Kohaku is waiting for me."

He stared at her for a long moment, and Emea wished for the thousandth time that she could be with him openly. She had half-hoped that he would beg her to stay, or at least make some show of regret, but he merely shrugged.

"Go back to your sycophant of a brother then," he said, and then turned back toward the moonlit sky.

Emea tried very hard not to cry when she closed the door behind her, but she wasn't entirely successful.

Dear Lana,
You'll be pleased to hear that your father's shop is getting some recognition from people in very high places. A council member on the musician's guild who is training a young bow-harp virtuoso to play before the Mo'i on her birthday next month came by today to test some of your father's

instruments. As you can imagine, Kapa was nearly delirious. Instruments made with his own hands played before the Mo'i! After two years in Essel, his dreams are beginning to come true.

As for me, I still help out in the shop most of the time, but I have recently found another small occupation. This will probably sound as strange to you as it did to me at first, but I have begun to teach swimming lessons to rich families' children. Can you believe that most people in this city die without ever touching the water for any purpose besides bathing? We, of course, learned for necessity, but as my students will probably never have to dive for their livelihoods, they are learning it for their own amusement. I also seem to have a certain exotic cachet, since I was once a mandagah diver. Their skin is all so pale here, and no wonder—I remember complaining about the weather on Okika, but it is a hundred times colder in Essel. Sometimes I almost wish that volcano would erupt, just so I could be truly warm once before I die. No, I'm kidding, Lana, don't worry—it may be cold here, but I'm not that desperate yet. Lucky for me, though the air is cold, the water is mostly warm. I train the kids in a lake heated by underground vents—sometimes it's so hot I have to get out and cool down!

As always, I miss you and I wish you could be here with us, so that we could be a proper family again. It was so wonderful seeing you during the holidays—I couldn't believe how much older you looked. I guess that's what happens in a year. And I love the mirror you gave me, although Kapa has threatened to take it away if I keep looking at myself so often. I guess I just can't get over the novelty of seeing my face in something other than water. I never knew that I had a mole below my right eye! For some reason that keeps astounding me, although I'm sure you're now laughing over what a country bumpkin you have for a mother! Oh, and needless to say, Kapa loved the tortoiseshells. He's working on them

*right now, in fact. I have to stop writing or I'll be late for my
swimming class. Please write back when you can.*
          With all my love,
          Mama

Lana smiled and carefully put the letter in the box where she
kept all her correspondence with her parents. She wished that she
could have heard her mother when she noticed that mole under her
eye, or her father when he threatened to take away the mirror. Her
mother wrote as often as she could, but letters were no substitute
for their companionship. Lana's life usually stayed busy enough
that her homesickness was limited to times like these, when she was
alone in her room reading her mother's letters. Though her mother
had been kind in saying how mature she looked, Lana knew she
had grown less than an inch since they left Okika. Her shoes still
fit her perfectly, and the pants of the outfit her mother had bought
just before they left were only marginally shorter. Akua said it was
possible that the illness had stunted her growth. In any case, she
was beginning to accept that she would never get much taller.

Instead of sleeping mats, Akua's house had strange raised beds
that were much harder than what she was used to, but she appreciated them in winter. She stretched out on hers and sighed,
grateful for the unusual respite in the middle of the day. Akua
was out gathering herbs and other ingredients for a medicinal potion she planned to teach Lana this evening. She had told Lana
to sweep out the cabin while she was away, but that had not been
very time consuming, and she had taken the opportunity to read
her mother's letter in private.

Akua's house was old, made of rough pink stone that held in
the heat during the cold winters. It was the only residence on this
side of the huge lake, and the villagers on the other side never
ventured here. Akua said that they were superstitious about her
powers and so kept a wide berth. It sometimes made Lana feel
strange to go weeks on end without seeing a soul other than the
one-armed witch, but usually she enjoyed the solitude. Unlike

any of the villagers' homes, Akua's house, old as it was, did have real glass windows. They were thick and warped, however, so you couldn't see through them like those in Okika's wealthiest houses. The old pink house was nestled in a curve of the lake, so that the glassy silver water surrounded it on three sides. In the mornings the mist was sometimes so thick you could hardly see your hand in front of your face, so Akua had tied a rope from the door of the house to the woodpile out back so Lana wouldn't get lost bringing in fuel for the morning fire. By now, however, the morning mist had long since cleared, and it was warm enough that she might be able to go for a quick afternoon swim.

That, by far, was what she loved most about living with Akua. She had missed diving with a nearly physical ache since leaving her island. The water around the docks in Okika, and in all the major towns, in fact, was too murky to see in, let alone swim. But this lake was a treasure: as the big-city merchants had not yet deemed it worthy of commercial purpose, it was still pristine and beautiful. It wasn't quite as nice as diving on her island before the disasters, but she knew it was probably the closest she would ever get again.

Lana didn't bother to put on her sandals before she walked out-side. Akua knew she dived, of course, but Lana preferred to do so slightly farther away from the house, when she was hidden by the reeds and could pretend that she was all alone in some magical marshland hidden from any human encroachment. She walked to a more distant part of the lake than usual, since the sun was so warm and the air smelled so dense and heady. The sun, nearly directly overhead, glinted on the glassy surface of the lake and was reflected in muted, mottled green and gray on the water plants. Eventually, she came to a small lagoon, almost entirely enclosed by large, broad-leaved trees. Here, the surface of the water was dotted with late-blooming purple lotuses. Smiling, Lana shed her clothes and stepped into the water. She pulled a half-opened flower from its leaf and braided it into her hair right behind her ear. She caught a glimpse of her reflection on the rippled surface of the water and laughed. Her mother was right, she did look a little more mature—her face had filled out to the point where she thought she almost looked pretty.

Lana took a deep, practiced breath and dove under the water. At first, it had been strange to dive with no need to look for mandagah, but she had learned to simply enjoy how beautiful and different the world looked underwater. A blue-scaled fish bigger than her arm looked at her curiously and then wriggled behind some nearby lotus roots. Lana moved languidly through the water, peeking under stones and periodically clearing her ears. As she moved to a part of the lake much deeper than anywhere she had ventured before, she caught a glimpse of something—a flash of silver, a sudden spray of light—in the corner of her eye. The lake's water sprite. She had seen it before when she dove in the deeper water. The other times it had merely observed her, but for some reason today it decided to approach. As it headed toward her, she could make out a strange face, so pale that she could see every pulsing vein beneath it. The sprite was no more than three feet tall and clothed in a strange green cloth that looked like seaweed. Its hair was white and hung around its head like a nimbus. Lana had never seen a water sprite before; they rarely showed themselves to humans. She panicked when she remembered the lotus flower that she had twined in her hair. Was it angry with her for taking it without permission? The creature stopped a few feet away from her and narrowed its silver, opaque, iris-less eyes at her. It reached with an impossibly narrow hand for the flower in her hair before pausing, hand poised.

"I know you," it said, the words curiously audible below the water. The sprite had the voice of a boy.

Lana was rapidly running out of air and she tried to signal this to the creature. After a brief moment he nodded and grabbed her hand. With a speed so great that she was afraid her arm might be ripped from its socket, the sprite drew her above water and onto a grassy bank beside a part of the lake she didn't recognize. She gulped air for a few moments until her vision stabilized. The sprite was seated a few feet away from her, on what looked like a lotus made of silvery water that rippled in the breeze. She had never seen anything like it before—it was beautiful, but on another level profoundly disturbing. Water shouldn't be able to form shapes like that, but clearly this sprite didn't follow the same laws as humans. Between his pale fingers he was twirling the purple lotus flower that had been in her hair. After a moment, he looked at her again. The strange effect of his opaque silver eyes was even stronger above the water and she couldn't control the sudden thumping of her heart.

"I know you," he repeated. Even his voice sounded like water, slow and drippy.

Lana took a deep breath. "How ... do you know me?" she asked.

He tossed the flower into the air. It glowed brightly and then melted, pouring in a steady purple stream back in the lake. "The witch took you to the island. She needed a stronger geas, that time ... I didn't think she should bring you. You are marked by a sacred creature of the water—you should have had no part in it. Ah ... but she is too powerful, that woman. Even I can't see her mind."

The creature's alien eyes had a kind of wistfulness. Something in his words sounded oddly familiar. She concentrated on that familiarity like an itch that needed to be scratched, and suddenly a jumble of forgotten memories forced their way through her consciousness. She had been sick and dead tired on her first evening in Akua's house, and the witch had given her more of the draught than normal. Lana hadn't even questioned what was in the tea, but it made her feel unusually sleepy and lethargic, so she had drunk less than she should have. What followed was hazy—and as she had woken up the next morning in her bed with her sleeping clothes on, she had dismissed it as a dream. She remembered seeing a look of pure avarice on Akua's face just before she hefted Lana's slight frame over her shoulder and walked out to the lake. Lana must have passed out sometime after that, because her next memory was one of being in the water, encased in a shimmering bubble of air being pulled like a chariot by the water sprite.

"You shouldn't take her there," she remembered his slow, drippy voice saying through her haze. They were above the water again, floating without getting wet right before an ancient stone staircase that ascended from the water onto a tiny island. The island was almost entirely covered by a shrine of the old style—like the pictures she saw in school of the difficult days before the spirit bindings. It had a sloped roof made with red-painted shells and a series of rounded arches around the sides. On the large wooden door (which looked much older than the rest of the structure) was an embossed carving of the three-toothed key—the ancient symbol of the death spirit.

"She belongs to the water, not to that," the creature had said again, as Akua mounted the stairs with Lana on her back.

Akua turned around to face the spirit. "She belongs to many things. And she will soon learn its power."

Then she remembered Akua opening that ancient wooden door and being overcome with a sudden terror. Of what happened after that, she had no memory at all.

Lana looked back at the sprite.

"Ah, so you remember a little. I had wondered how thoroughly she had drugged you. I tried to stop her, but I see it's too late now. The years have left their mark."

Lana's hands were shaking. "What are you talking about?" She felt like shouting. "What was that island? What was she doing?"

"Your master is in the service of the death spirit, little diver." Suddenly, the air before him started to shimmer and his water-lotus began to collapse back into the lake. He looked around in panic. Lana felt the presence of Akua's power and trembled. The shimmering air was doing something strange to the sprite's skin—he looked almost like he was bleeding water. He shouted something that sounded like the roar of a swollen river, but the strange thing attacking him didn't stop.

Why was Akua hurting this water sprite? The power Lana sensed felt like a geas; she remembered reading something in one of Akua's books about how it is occasionally possible to disperse their milder effects. Before she could think better of it, she bit sharply into her forearm, sucked and then spat her own blood onto the crouched figure of the sprite.

"A sacrifice from my body as recompense for his transgression," she gasped, heart pounding. She sensed a curious note of surprise, and then amusement from the power behind the geas. Lana stood there defiantly until the air stopped shimmering and the geas dissipated. The bite in her arm was still bleeding, but she hardly noticed. The sprite was sitting on its half-ruined flower, staring at her.

"Perhaps you are more than we all thought," he said, voice trembling.

"I never meant to be marked," she said.

The sprite began to sink back into the water. "Do you not wish to lay your own geas on me, for this?" He gestured toward her bloody spit, which was dripping down his cheek but somehow caught up in a tiny bubble of water.

She shook her head. How horrible, she thought, to have your entire life bound up in someone else's sacrifices. "Just ... speak to me sometimes. And maybe one day I'll find out what you're forbidden to tell me."

"Be careful, little diver. You should know better than anyone the dangers of swimming too far under the surface."

She watched as the water closed over his head, without even a ripple betraying that he had ever been there at all.

"I see you found Ino," Akua said when Lana walked into the house later, her hair still dripping.

"Who?" Lana asked, torn between fear and anger.

"The little water sprite. I had wondered if he would find you, but I hadn't expected him to approach you." Akua was sitting by the table, cutting vegetables for dinner, a task that usually fell to Lana.

"Well, why would you bind him with such a geas, then?" Lana asked. The bite on her arm was aching, and her success that afternoon made her feel a little reckless.

Akua glanced up, an appraising look in her eyes. "Caution has always served me well, Lana."

"What don't you want him to tell me? What are you hiding?"

"I'm not hiding anything, my dear. I'm merely sheltering you from knowledge that you are not quite ready for, like any good parent."

Lana thought of her mother and their hardships in Okika. Akua's motives for hiding this information from her were almost certainly quite different. But Akua couldn't know that Lana remembered some of what had happened to her that first evening. She sensed that the two of them were entering a game together, but Lana knew she was at a distinct disadvantage—not only did she not know all the rules, she also didn't know the stakes. But from the way the firelight glinted in Akua's dark eyes, Lana guessed that they were very, very high.

One evening a week later, Lana was hanging herbs on the ceiling to dry when she was startled by three loud raps on the door. Akua looked up from the book she was reading.

"Answer the door, Lana," she said.

The person knocked again and a man's muffled voice begged to be let in. "Who is it?" she asked Akua.

"Someone who wants our help, I imagine. Why don't you open the door and find out?"

Lana walked to the door slowly, wondering who it could be. They rarely had visitors, as the villagers generally avoided them.

Outside shivering in the light drizzle stood a man at least a foot taller than she, with weary bags under his eyes and a desperate, determined expression on his face.

"I ... I need the services of the lakeside witch," he said, teeth chattering.

Lana looked back at Akua, who merely nodded. "Come inside, at least," Lana said.

The man looked a little alarmed, but walked over the threshold.

Lana shut the door as he took off his dripping hat and faced Akua, still sitting placidly in her chair.

"Please, I beg of you, help my wife ... she's been in labor these past ten hours and we're afraid ... she might ..." he trailed off. Lana was caught off guard by the grief in his eyes. She supposed it was to be expected that a husband would be upset when his wife was dying, but spending so much time with Akua seemed to have made her forget what normal human emotion looked like. After Akua's habitual reserve, such overt emotion seemed almost ... gaudy—though it shamed her to admit it.

Akua's face, of course, remained impassive. "What will you give me for my services?" she asked.

"I'm a simple man," he said. "But I will give you all of our savings, everything, if you'll come."

Akua smiled slightly. "Keep your money. I'm sure your wife and child will need it. No, from you I request something different: a sacrifice, freely given."

The man blanched and for a second Lana was afraid he might vomit. She felt a little sick to her stomach, as well. What was Akua doing? It seemed too cruel to force a man as desperate as this into sacrificing himself.

"Sacrifice," he said as though he were forcing the word past his throat. "Like Apano?"

"He got what he wanted, didn't he?

"What will my sacrifice be?" he asked after a long pause.

Akua glanced at Lana briefly and then shook her head. "That can be decided later. Suffice it to say, it will be reasonable. Do you accept?"

The man closed his eyes and nodded. "For the sake of my wife and child."

Akua levered herself up from the chair. "Get my things, Lana. And don't forget the surgery, we may need it."

Most of what she learned from Akua actually had nothing much to do with the real workings of power. Akua always told her that power should be understood, respected, and used rarely—for all power required sacrifice, and that could never be given too freely. Instead, she taught Lana healing and midwifery. Every so often—usually a few months after the end of the spirit solstice—a woman from the village, cloaked and terrified, would beg Akua for a special draught to rid herself of an unwanted pregnancy and sometimes a charm to prevent one. These did require a minor geas to work well, and Akua had taught Lana how to make them. Anyone who could master those subtleties, she told her, would be sought after by queens and prostitutes alike. Lana had begun to learn the secrets of midwifery, but that skill was considerably more complicated, and this birth especially so.

The woman had already lost an amazing amount of blood. The bed sheets were drenched in it, making her sallow face look even paler. She was sweating and moaning, and seemed to be floating in a state somewhere between consciousness and death.

"How long has she been like this?" Lana asked the man quietly, as Akua removed the sheets and prepared to examine her.

"She first passed out a few hours ago," he said.

Akua looked up at the two of them. "She's very close to death," she said. "We have to hurry. Lana, I want you to boil the knives in water and prepare a draught to help stop her bleeding. It needs to be very strong—you can use him for the sacrifice, if you want."

The very thought made Lana's stomach clench and she shook her head. It wouldn't require a very large sacrifice, after all. In the corner of the cottage with a stove she grabbed two pots and dipped both of them in the barrel of well water his wife kept by the door. Lana had memorized in detail the recipe for the draught to stop bleeding, although she had never made it with a sacrifice before. The herbs themselves were enough in most situations, though clearly not now. She worked quickly, ignoring the man's worried presence behind her, and finished in fifteen minutes. She carefully fished a knife out of the boiling water and held it above her hand.

"A sacrifice of my body, freely given," she said and ran the knife over her palm. As the blood dripped into the bubbling water she sensed the anticipatory presence of the power around her. Her heart pounded with fear and reluctant pleasure—this was always what she loved most about calling on power, that moment when anything could happen, and the result was ultimately in her control.

She recited the traditional geas carefully:

As the blood that flows
through our bodies
is staunched, goes back to the earth,
so I bind the earth to act in kind.

The reaction was instantaneous. Though it was a relatively minor geas, the power she felt flow into the draught might just have been enough to save that woman's life. She poured the finished brew carefully into a pewter flask and brought it, along with Akua's boiled instruments, to the woman's bedside. The man looked terrified at the sight of the knives.

"You aren't going to hurt her, are you?" he said. "You swore—"

"I keep my word," Akua said sharply. "Your wife is near death. You'd do well to stop talking and let me save her."

He offered no more objections. Akua took the hot draught from Lana, smelled it and looked at her with slightly raised eyebrows.

"You used your own, I see," she said.

Lana shrugged, a little defiantly. "Self-sacrifice is more powerful."

"His would have been perfectly adequate, Lana. But, as you choose. It's well done—thoughtful of you to put in so much bitterwort."

"For the pain," Lana said. "I thought you may ... cut the baby out. She'll need it."

Akua smiled and turned back to the woman writhing deliriously on the bed. She held the draught to her lips and calmly, gently even, made her drink the entire contents. Lana wiped where it dribbled out of her mouth with a clean cloth. When the woman finished she seemed to relax a little, and sunk into a deeper faint.

"The baby's head is facing the wrong direction and the birthing-cord is wrapped around its neck," Akua said. The man, kneeling by his wife's side and holding her hand, cringed but kept silent. "If we let her deliver it, the baby will be strangled and she'll probably die. So you guessed correctly, Lana. We have to cut."

Lana stared—she had been amazed when Akua had told her such things were possible, but she had never expected to assist such an operation. "Have you done this before?" Lana asked.

The look in Akua's eyes was distant, but frighteningly intense. "Once," she said. "But then I had both my arms. I will tell you what to do, Lana, but today you must do it."

Lana was too stunned to even protest. She felt numb as she prepared herself—swabbing the woman's swollen belly with alcohol, setting up the instruments.

"What do I do now?" Lana asked, forcing her hands to stop trembling.

"Take the small knife," Akua said. "Make a vertical cut from her navel about two handspans long."

Lana took the knife and lowered it to the woman's stomach. She felt the man's eyes boring into her side, but she refused to look at him. She couldn't afford to see his terror now.

"Don't cut deep," Akua said. "You can't cut the baby."

Lana took a deep breath and lowered the knife. More blood slid down the woman's too-pale skin as she cut as carefully as she could. She felt like she had entered a trance. The blood didn't affect her anymore, and she was barely aware of anyone else's presence except this woman and her baby. When she finished making the cut she pulled the skin apart slightly at Akua's instruction and saw the thinner membrane of the woman's womb. Akua told her to make another vertical cut, this time with an even smaller knife. She slid her hands inside the exposed womb. The baby was there, and alive. She felt its tiny heart beating below her searching hands. She found the birthing-cord and, as carefully as she could, unwound it from around its neck. The woman began gasping again, and Akua went to her side and muttered a few quick words. She calmed down, but Lana could tell that she had very little time left.

"Pull the baby out, Lana," Akua said. "I'll help push from here."

Lana nodded and tried to get a firm grip on his body. She pulled him out gently, head first. His upper body was still covered in part of the caul, but when she pulled it off he took a few experimental gasps of air before crying.

The rest of the process was messy—clearing out the afterbirth, carefully stitching her skin closed—but Lana barely noticed. She glowed with the knowledge that she had saved two lives that night.

· · ·

Manuku hated the column of air in the center of the 'Ana's tower. He struggled to ignore it while he swept and dusted, but he always found himself sneaking sidelong glances and then wishing that he hadn't. Dark things swirled inside that column—light that passed through it came out distorted and twisted. The air felt colder there—though it was, of course, always frigid on the island. His family had served the inner death shrine since right after the great 'Ana's spirit binding. He alone was trusted with sweeping the Honored One's now-abandoned chambers.

She was said to be immortal, the 'Ana, legendary binder of the death spirit. His great-grandfather had cleaned these chambers when there had been a body occupying them, but she had disappeared over a century ago. No one knew where—and in fact, only Manuku, his young daughter, and the High Priest himself knew that she was gone at all. And unless something went terribly wrong, it was unlikely that anyone else would ever find out.

Manuku's family possessed a certain genetic trait that had made them very valuable to the 'Ana and the priests on the island:

almost all were born deaf. The hand-language they spoke had been passed down for generations, and now probably resembled archaic speech more closely than the modern tongue everyone else spoke today. Other than his own family, only the High Priest could speak their sign language, which effectively stopped any information about the 'Ana from leaving the island. It was forbidden for any of Manuku's family to learn to write. Of course, he had never wanted to learn the complicated system of pictographs regardless. His life was simple. Every day he cleaned the great altar of whatever might have been left of the offerings from the night before and helped to train his daughter to succeed him. Once a week, he climbed the interminable steps to the 'Ana's chamber and wished that he might somehow be relieved of this burden.

When he was a boy, his father had warned him about that column of air. He told Manuku that the column went straight through the earth to the binding chamber itself, where the restless spirit remained imprisoned. If you looked into it too deeply, his father had said, the death spirit would show you many things—some lies, some truths, but almost always things you would wish you had never seen. His father died in a freak accident when Manuku was sixteen. A spark from the great fire in the offering chamber caught on the ancient altar cloth and the blaze went up so quickly his father had no time to escape. He had been burned over most of his body before they managed to put it out. He died two days later, telling Manuku with his ruined hands that he had seen his own death years ago, in the column. Yet that wasn't what still haunted Manuku about that day.

"I saw the 'Ana," he had said while Manuku struggled not to cry. "She was fighting the death spirit, but it was too powerful. It broke free. As she died it exploded onto the world ..." His father gasped and then briefly held Manuku's hand in a near-painful grip. "Never forget who we guard, Manuku. In this very island is the embodiment of death. Never forget what would happen if it breaks free ... and it *wants* to break free, Manuku."

Manuku often thought about his father when he cleaned the

'Ana's chambers. He wondered if what his father saw had merely been more of the death spirit's lies, or if it had been as real as his vision of his own death. Today, the column of air was a dense, roiling cloud of half-formed shapes, as though the death spirit was more excited than usual. When he glanced at it against his better judgment, the vague shapes he saw there disturbed him, but he never looked at it long enough to be sure. He cleaned the dusty, echoing chamber with his eyes half-closed, airing out the bedding on the balcony and cleaning dust from the closets, all of which opened on the left side. He was wiping off the hand mirror when he caught a glimpse of an unusually clear image in the column behind him. Though he knew he should put it down and leave, he found his eyes riveted to the reflected image. A young girl was sitting in a boat. Despite the rain hat pulled down over her face, he could still tell that her gaze had a certain flashing strength—this, combined with skin darker than Manuku had ever seen before, made the girl's looks striking, but not unappealing. She was speaking with a strange creature nearly as pale as she was dark, with blue-veined skin and hair that shimmered hypnotically. Though he had never seen one before, he knew that he must be looking at some kind of lesser spirit. He had no idea who the girl was, but anyone who could converse so freely with spirits had to be very powerful. Suddenly, the image shifted. Now he saw the binding chamber, which he recognized immediately though he had only been there once in his life. The girl was older now, and those strong eyes had gone hard and inexpressibly sad. She stood in charred clothes before the worn, gray-flecked stone at the base of the column of air. Jammed upright in the stone—the hardest known to man—was a yellowed, broken shard of bone. Beyond the column was another woman with skin just as dark as the girl's, being held by a manifestation of the death spirit itself. The girl brought a white flute to her lips. When she began to play, both the stone and the bone inside it shattered, and the freed death spirit roared up the column of air ...

Manuku dropped the mirror. He didn't bother to check whether it had broken before he turned and fled.

. . .

Lana pulled her reed hat lower over her face and watched the water dribble in the puddle at the bottom of her boat. The day was overcast and the dense mist that covered the lake showed no signs of clearing. Lana sighed and grabbed the oars again. At least she wasn't likely to get lost—she had traveled this route so many times that she could find her way to the village merely by following the patterns of the reeds. When the mist was this thick, she liked to play at creating silly geas out of great puffs of air. A deep breath wasn't much of a sacrifice, but the air sprites seemed willing enough to take it in exchange for visions of mandagah swimming through the mist, or snakes slithering through her hair. Today, vaporous butterflies landed on her ears and fluttered on the top of her oars. But they dissolved when the boat rocked violently and two exquisitely thin, pale, webbed hands gripped the edge. Soon she saw Ino's unmistakable face, and his white hair seemed to shimmer hypnotically even in the fog's intense gloom. He did not leave the lake entirely, but instead floated with his head resting on his arms, draped over the side of her boat and dripping water in a steady stream. Lana felt too listless to even be mildly surprised.

"Something has changed, little diver," he said in the slippery, wet voice that she had grown used to.

"Has it?" she said. She knew by now that she had to be careful with Ino, especially when he was trying to tell her something important. Akua's geas was sensitive and clever, but in the delicate game they had been playing for the past few months, one of Lana's chief advantages was the meager dribble of half-formed hints she received from the water sprite. Despite her growing feeling that Akua was hiding something important from her, Lana had decided to trust the witch. She couldn't stand the implications of doubting her—not after she had finally settled into this life. She felt wary, she reasoned, because she hated to be kept in the dark by anyone, not because she felt that Akua would ever seriously harm her.

The sprite spat some water just past her face and for a fleeting moment she saw it form in the shape of a key, pointing toward the center of the lake. It splashed into the water on the other side of the boat with a brief ripple. "The lakeside storm is getting more powerful. For each favor, there is a sacrifice. With each sacrifice, its goal is more attainable."

Lana stared for a long time into Ino's unblinking silver eyes. Finally, she nodded. "I'll take care to avoid the storm," she said.

Ino smiled sadly. "But you can't, little diver," he said. "You can only make yourself powerful enough to meet it."

He dropped back over the side of her boat. Lana ignored her shiver of fear and grabbed the oars again. It was another slow-going hour before she made it to the village.

The ship manager's office for the tiny harbor on the tributary doubled as a post station. Trade boats on their way to Okika City had stopped by there this morning, and Lana hoped that a letter from her parents had come with the delivery. Most of the people she passed on the muddy street were hunkered under their straw hats and barely spared her a glance. She was grateful—her association with Akua made them wary at the best of times, and she hadn't been back since she helped deliver that woman's baby. Noela, the wife of the dock manager, looked a little surprised when Lana walked inside the cramped front office and took off her hat, but her welcoming smile was only slightly more strained than usual.

"Lana! It's been so long, hasn't it? Here, let me see if anything came from Essel for you." She jumped off of the stool where she had been writing precise notes in her open ledger and took three steps to a large reed basket where the week's mail was sorted. She thumbed through them rapidly and then pulled out a set of papers, folded twice, tied with string and sealed with clear wax.

Noela stood up and handed Lana the letter. "Looks like it's

from your mother. Let's see … that's about thirty kaneka." After rummaging around in her pockets, Lana found the change and dropped the cheap stone coins into the box on the desk.

She had stuffed the letter inside her pockets and was putting on her rain hat when Noela cleared her throat nervously.

"Listen … maybe someone should tell you this, Lana. No one around here really wants the witch coming back, not after what happened to Saulo. I don't think anyone will touch you—everyone knows you're a nice girl. But be careful, okay? If anyone gives you trouble, just get out of their way."

Lana stared at the older woman. Saulo? She must be referring to the man whose wife Lana had saved, but what had Akua done to him? Unable to think of any appropriate response, Lana thanked her and ran back outside. The rain had stopped and the sun was showing some signs of peeking through and clearing away the persistent fog—not as dense in the village as it was on her side of the lake, but maddening enough. Lana absentmindedly un-fastened her hat and walked slowly through the streets, unable to avoid the mud that splashed onto her homespun socks and straw sandals. Conversations stopped as she walked by, and Lana grew uncomfortably aware of people's eyes on her back. Mindless village busybodies, Akua called them, preoccupied with other people's lives because they can't find enough interest in their own. Lana had laughed at the time, and then felt a little guilty after. But as the whispers grew louder, Lana thought that Akua had been right. She fumed inwardly—it was only natural for them to associate her with Akua, but couldn't they see that she had no effect on her mentor's actions? A man, a simple fisherman by his clothes and smell, bumped into her as they crossed paths and spat at her feet. Noela's warning suddenly took on ominous overtones—Lana wanted to get out of the town as quickly as pos-sible. Still, she had some shopping to do before she could get back in her waiting boat. With no other defense, Lana raised her chin and held her shoulders back, daring any of the whispering people lining the streets to openly insult her. She had nearly made it to the general store unmolested when a sudden unnatural hush followed by the brief gurgle of a baby giggling made her turn around slowly. She recognized the woman immediately, although she looked considerably healthier than the pale, delirious expectant mother of two months ago. Tied to her back with a green and blue cloth—colors of good luck for a child of difficult birth—was an infant, blinking sleepily at his mother. She lightly kissed someone who stood in the entrance of one of the stores, and then stepped out into the street. After a moment, the man standing in the doorway called her name. She turned around. For a second her eyes caught hold of Lana's, but they left without the light of recognition. Of course, how could she recognize her? Though Lana had placed her own hands inside that woman's womb, they had never actually met. The thought made her feel inexpressibly sad—ever since Kali died, she had felt distant from people. Even the ones closest to her. The man stepped out onto the street, and she saw that he was walking with crutches. She felt another shock of recognition as he handed the woman a rain hat—it was Saulo. After the woman had gone on her way, he turned around and saw Lana. They stared at each other for a tense moment, and almost against her will Lana looked down to see what he had sacrificed for his wife and child.

His left foot was wrapped in bandages, but even so it was easy to tell that it was half gone.

Lana tasted bile and for a second she was afraid she might faint into the mud. Her vision was half-white when she sank to her knees with tears stinging her eyes. When Akua had talked about a sacrifice, she had never even imagined something on such a scale. Lana looked back up at the man, who was staring at her with a hard, unreadable expression.

She suddenly felt a harsh tug at her braid as a man much taller than her forced her up from the ground. "Should I get the bitch for you, Saulo?" the man asked, tugging on her braid so hard that Lana was forced to stand on her tiptoes. Although she gasped in pain, she found herself curiously unable to speak.

Saulo shook his head. "It's not her fault. Leave the girl alone—she saved my wife and my baby."

The man reluctantly released her braid, but Lana still felt too horrified to move. Saulo gave her one last glance before making his slow way back inside the shop.

"Tell your master," the other man said, spinning Lana around to face him. He had a bulk to match his height, and she realized he had been using far less than his full strength to pull her from the ground. "Her favors come at too high a price. It's a cruel fate, Saulo's—for a cobbler to lose his foot."

The man stalked away. Lana swallowed, though her mouth had gone almost completely dry. Rather than think about the implications of what she had just seen—and risk being sick in the middle of these incredibly unsympathetic villagers—she walked the few yards to the general store.

There was no one inside but blind Apano, shelling green peas while humming an old tune quietly to himself. She and Apano had struck up an odd friendship since the first time she had visited the village—he was one of the few people she had met who had been born, like her, in the outer islands. His island had been near the outer fire shrine, where the salty water meant there hadn't been any divers, but talking to him still made her feel almost like she was home again. He was the only other person she had ever told about Kali. He wasn't that old, actually—probably only fifty—but he had lost his sight years earlier. The rumor was that Akua herself had blinded him in return for orchestrating the death of the pirate who had killed his parents when he was a teenager. Since Apano knew she was Akua's apprentice and had never shown her the slightest bit of resentment, Lana had always dismissed it as a rumor. Now she wasn't so sure.

"Lana?" he said, raising his head. "Is that you?"

Lana smiled. "How on earth can you tell, Apano? I haven't been here for months."

Apano opened another pod and let the peas drop into the pot

between his legs. "I can't tell everybody, but I can always tell you. You feel different."

Lana sat next to him. "I saw Saulo today," she said.

Apano's hands slowed, but didn't stop shelling the peas. "He's holding up pretty well, considering. Probably because he's got his wife and baby boy to be thankful for."

To her surprise, Lana felt hot tears begin to slip from her eyes and onto her clenched fists. "I didn't know, Apa," she said softly.

He tossed away the pea pod. His hands were strong and darkened with freckles from long years of making the journeys between the islands. She had always found them comforting, and today it was a relief when he put them over her own.

"I know you didn't, child. She is very careful around you. Her sacrifices may be painful, but she always gives what she promises."

"Did … did you get what she promised?"

Apano gave a brief, bitter smile that was unlike anything she had ever seen cross his usually gentle features. "Yes. I did."

Apano's daughter came rushing inside the store, her face flushed with excitement. "Dad, you won't believe this, but I heard that apprentice girl had the nerve to come back here after—" Her expression when she saw Lana was almost comical, but Lana didn't laugh.

"We have a guest, Kaila," Apano said mildly.

"What … what do you want?" she asked after a brief moment. Her stomach was bulging with a pregnancy Lana hadn't noticed when she was last here two months ago. In fact, she looked like she was bearing twins, which would be hard on a woman with such a small frame.

Lana stood up. "Five pounds of sugar, five pounds of salt, and a small jar of honey. Then you can talk about me all you want."

The woman looked as though she wanted to say something else, but turned around and began filling up bags. Lana noticed that though she couldn't have been more than five months into her pregnancy, she moved like she was near term. Kaila handed her the bags and avoided meeting her eyes when Lana paid. As Lana was tying her purchases securely to her back, she decided to take a risk.

"It might be a hard birth," she said. "It looks like you have twins. If things start looking serious, you could … send for me. I won't ask you for any sacrifices."

Kaila looked up sharply at Lana and put her hands over her belly protectively.

"Get out! I don't want you or your witch's help. Get out!" she rushed at Lana and pushed her back against the doorframe.

"Kaila, enough!" Apano's voice held such force that both of them froze and stared at him. "Lana was only offering to help. Give her back her money and apologize. Even if you feel sorry for Saulo, you can damn well do better than to pick on a girl who's just as much of a victim."

Kaila looked at Lana angrily, but she handed her back the money and muttered a half-hearted apology.

"Be careful, child," Apano told Lana as she was leaving. "Never think you can't end up on the wrong side of a sacrifice yourself."

Lana was drenched by the time she arrived back at the cottage—the skies had opened up just as she was over the center of the lake, and only Ino's help had managed to keep the small boat from flooding. She thought she might never stop shivering if she didn't get out of her wet clothes immediately, but she still hesitated a moment before the door. What she had experienced at the village made her feel tainted, and yet how could she confront Akua with it? Part of her wanted to scream at her mentor for doing something so cold-hearted, but another, weaker, part of her only wanted to forget about it. After all, she couldn't do anything to help. It had always been clear who had the power in her relationship with Akua. If Akua kicked her out, where could she go? Her parents? But wasn't her mother the one who had given her away in the first place? Lana shook her head firmly. Leilani hadn't had a choice. Her mother would never have done it if she'd had a choice. Rain pelted her, and still she did not move. In the end, Akua solved the problem by opening the door for her.

Akua was wearing a coat and a rain hat, and looked mildly amused to see Lana standing stupidly on the doorstep.

"You're back, I see," she said. "Why don't you bring the food in?"

Lana mentally shook herself and walked into the cottage. The front room was warm from the fire burning in the hearth, but she still felt cold. She should confront Akua. She *should,* but ...

"I'll be back by dusk," Akua said.

"You're going out in this weather?"

Akua glanced out the open door and sighed. Quickly, so that Lana could not follow the words or even the flow of power, Akua recited a geas. Moments later, the rain stopped. The clouds still loomed above threateningly, but she felt the strength of the geas holding them back.

Lana's heart began pounding again—not with dread, this time, but with anticipation. "There's a geas to stop the rain?" she said, wonderingly. For a giddy moment she imagined herself with such power, and the control it would finally give her over her own life.

Akua's smile was indulgent and just a little amused. "There's a geas for everything, Lana."

"Will you teach it to me? You never teach me anything like that."

Akua shook her head. "You're not strong enough. You wouldn't be able to hold it. Do you know what happens when you aren't strong enough to hold a geas, Lana?"

She shook her head mutely.

"Pray you never find out, then."

And Akua had left by the time Lana realized that she had forgotten to confront her about Saulo. She tidied up the kitchen and tried, without much success, to feel regretful.

KOHAKU CLUTCHED THE APPOINTMENT SLIP, barely able to stop himself from running out of the main hall and into the streets. Yet, happy as he was, he couldn't help but feel a certain amount of trepidation. After all his years of study, it came down to this: an hour after noon one week from today, he would know if he had achieved his dream of full professorship or if he would be forever doomed to his same lowly assistant professor status. In the four years since he had returned from his field study on the outer islands, he had slaved away at perfecting his research and sharpening his findings. A month ago he had submitted the final product to the presiding council of professors, and they had told him today that they were nearly ready to make their final decision. He had done everything in his power to make his research as compelling as possible; now all he could do was wait.

In its own way, it was something of a relief.

He hurried home and bounded up the stairs, skipping three at a time. Emea spun around when he opened the door, a quizzical smile on her face.

"Did something good happen?" she signed.

Kohaku tore off his purple headband—a little damp with his excitement—and tossed it to the ground. "In a week, I'll never have to see that lousy thing again."

Emea laughed—an oddly modulated breathy sound that Kohaku found infinitely endearing. "You were quite proud of that two years ago, you know."

"It's hardly something to be proud of now. I'm getting older—I'm ready for that professorship."

"Don't worry, I'm sure you'll get it," Emea said, and then turned from him to go back to the loom. She had dug it out of the dusty pile of their mother's belongings a few months ago and had been working at it like a woman possessed ever since. Kohaku couldn't imagine what had gotten into her—she had enjoyed occasional embroidery projects before, but he could see no reason why she would suddenly become obsessed with weaving. The cloth she was making now had an alternating pattern of horizontal deep blue and vertical checks of purple and gold. It was the latest fashionable color scheme used for the lightweight carrying cloths with which mothers tied their babies to their backs, but since Emea didn't get out very much, it was doubtful that she would be aware of it.

Kohaku watched her shuttle the loom back and forth with practiced gestures. When she had first started a few months ago she was constantly cursing and hitting the machine, but now she looked like she had been doing it for years.

He stepped in front of the shuttle and tapped her head. "Why do you do that so much now?" he asked.

She shrugged. "It's a way to pass the time. I like doing things with my hands."

"But you seem so ... focused. You sit around all day wearing these shapeless shirts—if I didn't know any better, I'd say you were gaining weight."

Emea frowned. "I'm fine, Kohaku. Leave me alone." She turned her head away from his hands and began working the loom. Kohaku considered tapping her head again but then sighed and moved out of her way. It was her business, after all. She had been acting strangely of late, but he could deal with that after the judging next week, when he had more time.

Emea pulled the letter from her pocket again, looking around surreptitiously to make sure that Kohaku had gone to his room. She had been fingering it all day, ever since the errand boy had delivered it this morning. "I grow tired of playing this game," it said in the scrawling hand she knew so well. "Why are you avoiding me? If you are not there tonight, at our usual place, I shall consider it over." As usual, it was unsigned in case a copy found its way into his wife's hands. Emea took a deep breath and touched her swelling belly. She would not be able to hide it for much longer—even Kohaku had noticed something was wrong. Letting herself get pregnant with Nahe's child was one of the most reckless things she had ever done, but she could not bring herself to regret it. She loved Nahe, after all, and though she could not be his first wife, perhaps if she gave him a child she would at least be a cared-for mistress. After all the longing of the past few years, she had begun to think she could settle for that. Still, she had avoided meeting with him this past month because she knew that he—if not Kohaku—would have been able to tell she was pregnant. She didn't know how to tell him and she was afraid of how he would react. She stayed up nights longing for him, afraid that after all these years his affection for her was finally waning. He didn't touch her the way he used to, and he spent much of their time together worrying about his wife. It was easier, most of the time, to lose herself in her loom, to find the smallest pleasure in the placement of each thread in the pattern. She was nearly done with the carrying cloth—an inch more, and then she would do the tassels. She had been afraid, at first, that using a pattern and colors so in vogue at the moment would tip off Kohaku, but she should have known that he would underestimate her own knowledge before he'd suspect her pregnancy. Though she couldn't be sure of Nahe, she knew that Kohaku would disapprove when he found out. She dreaded seeing his expression when she told him that she would be leaving and taking the lesser position of second wife to his superior at the Kulanui. He probably wouldn't even come to their ceremony, quiet though it would be. The thought of losing Kohaku, who had spent his whole life taking care of her, made her sad enough to weep, but it wasn't enough to change her mind. She knew that a second wife in Nahe's household would be little more than a servant for his first—but she thought it would be worth it, to raise her child with a veneer of respectability. And to be with Nahe. Emea's fingers stilled on the loom.

Tonight she would tell him. When she finished the carrying cloth, she would drape it over her shoulder like a sash and meet him by the steaming hot spring in a secluded corner of the fire shrine. She worked steadily for another three hours, until the early setting sun began to sink below the great volcano. A smile came unexpectedly to her face when she took the cloth from the loom—getting pregnant had been an accident, but she had rarely felt more excited in her life. The baby growing in her belly made her feel more anchored and powerful, filled with a magic all her own. She peeked inside Kohaku's room and saw that he had fallen asleep on his books. She smiled—she should have known that she wouldn't need to fabricate an excuse for him. He had stayed up all night studying yesterday. Since the rain of the past few days had turned the back streets into a mud wallow, she tied on her wooden platform clogs. Though she didn't truly need them, she also donned an oversized jacket and a rain hat— she hated the way men looked at her in the streets after sundown. Finally, she tied the carrying cloth gently around her shoulders. She fingered the blue tassels as she ran down the stairs.

Nahe was leaning carelessly against a cracked, ancient lintel that had become entwined with a creeping vine-tree whose drooping leaves caressed the top of his head. Emea took a moment to study him, reveling as much now as she did years ago in the set of his chin and his hard green eyes. She knew she would do anything for him, and the knowledge had almost ceased to scare her. The steam from the spring coiled upward lazily, condensed on the ceiling of the open pagoda, and dripped slowly back into the water. Nahe looked up suddenly, as though startled by some noise, and saw her. He nodded, but didn't smile.

"I thought you wouldn't come," he signed. "I thought you'd grown tired of me."

Emea took a tentative step toward him. "I could never ..."

"Then why have you avoided me for so long?"

She touched the edge of the cloth and fought for her resolve. "Nahe ... I have something to tell you."

He looked at her appraisingly. Before she could think better of it, she reached over and kissed him. She wondered if he seemed less enthusiastic than normal, but then forced the thought from her head. Eventually she broke it off and leaned against him, holding his arms around her belly as they stared at the nearly full moon. It looked swollen, glittering on the thousand gold and red sloped pagoda roofs of the fire shrine. New roofs were added every year when the old ones crumbled to dust—some said the shrine dated back to long before the spirit bindings, even before the founding of Essel. She waited as Nahe gently stroked her breasts and then went further down her body. She wondered if she had underestimated him, but seconds later his hands froze and she could feel his muscles tighten. He turned her around violently and Emea was shocked to see how angry he looked.

"You're pregnant?" he asked, his hand gestures even sloppier than normal.

Emea bit her tongue to keep back tears and nodded. He closed his eyes and she could see him force himself to calm down.

"It was an accident," she said, "but I was thinking that maybe ... I wouldn't mind being your second wife, Nahe. In fact, it would make me quite happy."

Nahe stared at her for a second and then started laughing. Though she couldn't hear the sound, the look on his face was enough to send shocks through her body.

"Emea, don't be ridiculous. My wife wouldn't hear of it—she owns the house and pays the servants. She might cut me off completely if I took a second wife."

Emea felt tears coursing down her cheeks, and she struggled to stop them. "But you're a famous professor. How could she own everything?"

He gave her a patronizing smile. "Dear, you don't understand anything about the world, do you? Professors get paid nothing, but my wife's fortune lets me live the life I want. I'm fond of you, but you can't expect me to give up all that to live with you and raise a child with barely any means at all. Perhaps it's time you stopped being so naïve."

At least, Emea thought bitterly, she had stopped crying. "So ... what should I do?"

Nahe shrugged. "Keep the baby, if you want, but don't expect any help from me. If you tell anyone that I'm the father, though, I'll ruin your brother. And I couldn't be seen with you after the baby is born, of course."

A white haze covered her vision. The faint sulfurous smell from the pool amplified in her nose until it smelled like carrion and she thought she would choke. "Do you mean ... that if I have the baby, I'll never see you again? Everything would be over?"

There was the faintest hint of pity in his eyes that she grasped at wildly to keep from drowning. "I would hate to do it. There just wouldn't be another choice ... though of course, you could still get rid of the child."

Emea sucked air past her closed throat. Her legs felt like water—she grabbed the tree for support. "If I get rid of the child," she said as calmly as she could, "will you stay with me?"

He nodded amiably, as though they were discussing an old table in need of replacement. "I know of a woman who sells those things. I could send someone tomorrow with a dose and it would be gone by morning."

Feeling incapable of moving her hands, she jerked her head and turned away. She imagined that he called after her as she stumbled down the ancient stairs, but he probably just watched her with his arms crossed, his expression unreadable.

An errand-boy delivered a package around noon the next day. Emea wrapped a worn shawl more tightly around her shoulders and went to the door. The boy had delivered many messages to her before, but he seemed surprised at how haggard she looked. She had woken up this morning with a fever and a cough, in addition to an unbearable ache in her chest.

Her hands were rock steady when she unwound the packing cloth to reveal a tiny wooden jar. She sniffed and nearly gagged on the smell. She had no way of knowing what he had sent her, but she was past caring. What else could she do? She loved Nahe more than anything, including her unborn child. She took the vial and walked to the window. She had dropped the carrying cloth there the night before, and when she picked it up now tears blurred her vision. Outside it was a beautiful sunny day. People were out on the drying streets, hanging decorations for the upcoming spirit solstice. It was usually her favorite time of year. She remembered when Kohaku would take her to the central pagoda in the fire temple and they would watch the fireworks explode over thousands of gently swaying paper lanterns. She had looked up to him so much then. She had thought that no one in the world could ever be as wonderful as her brother. She took the top off the wooden bottle and held it to her lips. Then she pinched her nose and forced it down her throat.

Kohaku came home a little later than usual. He had been informed that his hearing date had been moved up—he now would have only two more days to prepare. The news had made him feel so nervous he stopped by a hookah lounge frequented by Kulanui students and spent a few precious kalas to purchase and smoke some amant weed. When he opened the apartment door, he was first surprised that Emea hadn't lit any lamps. He fumbled around in the near-darkness until he found one, then he went back into the corridor so he could use a wall torch to light it. It was only that second time he walked into the apartment that he found her. She was lying on the floor by the window, passed out. As he walked closer, he saw that the dark stain on the floor was blood—the lower half of her body was covered in it.

Kohaku called her name, though he knew she couldn't hear

him, and rushed to her side. He leaned down and nearly cried out when he realized she was still breathing. What had happened to her? With all that blood he could only think that someone had attacked her, but there weren't any bruises or cuts anywhere on her body. Unable to think of anything else, he picked her up and carried her to her bed. She stirred a little when he did that, and her eyes—so dilated they looked black—stared at him uncomprehendingly.

"I'm dying," she signed when he put her on the bed. Kohaku stared at her. His heart pounded, but he poured out some water and forced her to drink it.

"What are you talking about?" he said. "What happened?"

"I got rid of the baby ... and now I'm dying ..." She started to cry and Kohaku could only stare at her helplessly. Finally, he went back to where she had fallen, and saw an open wooden vial near the smear of blood. He stooped to pick it up and smelled the lid. Though he had no medical training, he thought he detected the faintly pungent scent of hea berry—a dangerous fruit used by those who wanted to rid themselves of an unwanted pregnancy. Kohaku knew plenty of other students who'd had occasion to mention their need to find some hea berry for girls they'd impregnated.

Finally, everything snapped into place. Emea hadn't been attacked. She had overdosed on hea berry and now she was in danger of bleeding to death. A sharp groan from her bedroom sent him running back inside—the blood was beginning to soak the bed and she was writhing in pain. He could never afford a doctor—let alone convince one to come at this late hour—but there was a woman he remembered from his early days at the Kulanui who had been a sort of healer for all his friends. If she was still there, she lived half a mile away, above an herb shop. With a silent apology to Emea, he bolted out the door and down the street, managing a twenty-minute walk in about ten.

"What the hell did she take, rat poison?" Lipa asked, roughly pulling down Emea's pants.

Kohaku picked up the empty bottle he had found and showed

it to her. She sniffed it once and then put it down. "You were right. It's got hea berry in it, and some other stuff just as dangerous. Whoever made that knew the basic ingredients but not much about keeping it safe."

Lipa's dark face had a few more wrinkles than he remembered, but otherwise she was still the same competent, slightly eccentric woman he had known years ago. She had been known for her short temper and pretty smile, but she wasn't smiling now, and that scared Kohaku even more than the blood.

She slapped Emea's face. "Hey, wake up girl!" Emea opened her eyes and Lipa turned to Kohaku. "You say she's deaf? Well, ask her where the hell she got that jar."

Kohaku nodded and did the signs very carefully. Emea seemed to understand and after a second she responded.

"Nahe," she said.

At first he didn't recognize the sign—they had only used it a few times before. "What do you mean?"

"At the Kulanui," she said laboriously, as though each gesture was exhausting. "Nahe and I … lovers. I was pregnant, but he didn't want the baby. Didn't want me with the baby. Said I could get rid of it, so I did." Tears slipped out of the corners of her eyes and she shook her head violently. "So stupid …" She closed her eyes and turned her head away from him, grimacing in pain.

"Well, what did she say?" Lipa asked, stirring a dark green powder into a glass of water.

Kohaku felt a little lightheaded when he turned to her. "She was … having an affair with my superior at the Kulanui."

"And the asshole gave her this so he wouldn't have to deal with his bastard? Figures—you're not so bad, Kohaku, but I always thought you academic types were pretty damn selfish. Here, help me get this down her throat … I'm not sure it will help, but …"

Kohaku knelt awkwardly behind the bed and held Emea's head while Lipa made her drink the green liquid. A good deal of it dribbled out of the corners of her mouth and onto the sheets. The effect of such an intense color against the pallor of her skin was at once grotesque and pathetic.

As soon as she had drained the glass, Emea began hacking viciously. She turned on her side and vomited what looked like the entire contents of her stomach on the bed. She continued to heave even when there was nothing left to come up. Kohaku watched Lipa pour more water into a cup and mix it with another powder. Emea tried to refuse, but she was too weak, and eventually Lipa managed to get a little bit down her throat. Soon afterwards Emea calmed down and her breathing grew slow and even, as though she were sleeping.

Lipa, half-covered in vomit, sighed and sat down on the floor next to Kohaku.

"Damn it, Kohaku … I don't want to say this, but there's nothing much else I can do. The hea poison's entered her system. It looks like she took it hours ago—maybe if you had found her earlier, but now …" She shrugged and avoided his eyes. "Maybe someone who knows the spirit geas could help—I never learned those, too dangerous. Honestly …" she looked back up at Emea, who was groaning in her sleep, "… I think it's too late."

Too late …

His vision wobbled, and the sound of Emea's labored breathing amplified in his ears until he thought it would pierce his skull. One thought managed to ring coherently in his mind: he had killed his sister because he had not known her well enough.

She died in the morning. All night she kept deliriously signing "I'm sorry," as though she couldn't be sure that he would understand. He told her that he loved her.

"Don't blame yourself," she said, toward the end. "Tell Nahe I love him."

It was a trick of the light, but when he stared at her pale, unmoving body he imagined that her chest was still rising, that if he just tapped her on her head, she would wake up and tell him how silly he was for believing a bad dream.

But Lipa was still there, packing her things away. This night had added a few more wrinkles to her collection—the bags under her eyes almost looked like bruises. Kohaku was sure he didn't look much better.

Lipa stood in front of Kohaku with nothing but pity in her eyes. She put her hand on his shoulder. "Is there anything I can do? I'm so sorry—"

"No," Kohaku said, a little too forcefully. "I'll be fine. I know you did everything you could."

Lipa looked like she wanted to say something, but just nodded and left.

Kohaku waited in the foyer of Nahe's ostentatiously wealthy house, noting the tall clear glass windows and the life-sized, exquisitely carved fire dolls, which would be sacrificed in the upcoming spirit solstice after being honored for a year inside this house. Only the wealthiest of Essel's residents could afford such displays, but Nahe's wife had inherited a vast fortune from her father's trading business. Emea had probably naively imagined that getting pregnant would force Nahe to take her on as a second wife.

He felt curiously calm and detached—as though his real self was still frozen next to Emea's bedside, watching helplessly as she vomited her life away. Thoughts of her honed the hard edge of his anger, but they still didn't touch his grief. In fact, in some distant way, his present situation amused him—he had spent his whole time at the Kulanui looking up to Nahe and seeking his approval. Now he didn't care what Nahe thought of him.

He heard footsteps before Nahe came into view, his mouth set in a disapproving frown. He was wearing the blue and orange checkered headband of his office, and looked as though he was planning to head straight for the Kulanui.

Kohaku leaned against the wall, waiting for him to come closer.

"They tell me you wouldn't leave. You should know better than to come to my house, boy. This had better be important."

Kohaku's anger grew a few degrees colder. "Emea is dead."

Nahe looked momentarily shocked. He gripped Kohaku's elbow with surprising strength and dragged him outside the house. "What the hell are you talking about?" he whispered, taking Kohaku further down the street.

"She died this morning, after being poisoned by a medicine delivered to her yesterday afternoon. It was supposed to kill the baby, but it was too strong and it killed them both."

Nahe stopped walking and stared at Kohaku. "You're serious."

Kohaku held out the wooden jar. "You must recognize this, Nahe. Whoever made it didn't know very much about what they were doing, and whoever sent it must not have cared much about Emea's safety."

Nahe's face started turning red with anger, but his voice was still steady. "So, what do you plan to do? Arrest me for negligence? She took the damn potion."

"I could tell your wife," Kohaku said.

Nahe let out a bark of laughter. "You think she doesn't know about my infidelities? It's fine with her so long as I don't bring anyone home."

"I'm sure she wouldn't be too happy knowing you fathered a child."

"Well, I got rid of it, didn't I?"

For a second Kohaku thought his hard-won composure would crack, but he held on. "Is that it, then? You didn't care for her at all? Just before she died, she told me to tell you that she loved you. I can't believe that she would have wasted her love on such a worthless man."

"I was the only one who would have her! She couldn't even talk. I learned that hand-speak of hers—how many men do you think would have taken a half-formed girl like that? I'm sorry she's dead," he added, looking down a moment before returning Kohaku's cold stare. "But what do you expect of me?"

Kohaku felt like he was breathing underwater. "I want you to care," he said. "But in the absence of that, you could at least help me pay for her funeral."

Nahe smiled. "Ah, so it's money you're after. I should have known. But what kind of rites could a girl like her have expected, anyway? Just take her to the fire temple and be done with it—I'm sure you could afford that. If you wanted me to pay for a processional to the lip of Nui'ahi … well, don't put on airs."

Nahe patted Kohaku on the shoulder and strode off.

"I could discredit you in front of the council," Kohaku shouted at his back.

Nahe stopped and turned around slowly. "Just try it," he said, and continued walking.

"I have to say, Kohaku, this is really excellent work."

Under the leaden gray of his grief, Kohaku felt a vague sense of pride. Earning praise from Professor Bopa was a high accolade—she was notorious for her harsh tongue and even harsher pen.

"I agree. No one has ever done such a comprehensive study of the culture and practices of the outer islands. It's a great contribution." Professor Totome, the second member of the reviewing committee, scratched under his beard and smiled slightly.

Nahe, the third member, sat silently next to the other two, his face revealing nothing but mild disapproval. Kohaku tried not to look at him, instead focusing on the immediate goal of getting through the meeting.

Bopa rustled through her notes. "This one case you mention— a young girl named Lana, I think—was particularly fascinating. You say she actually refused to come to Essel because of the sense of duty she felt as a diver?"

Kohaku felt the corners of his mouth turn up slightly—it had been a long time since he had last thought of Lana. "Yes. The divers of the islands take their duty very seriously, although I didn't really understand that at the time. But I do wonder what happened to her … the reports I've heard over the past few years aren't too promising. They say the water has turned brackish and some of the islands were permanently flooded. There are rumors all the mandagah fish have died."

"So it seems quite likely you were documenting a dying way of life," Totome said. His voice was scratchy from too many years at hookah lounges, but it was friendly.

Before Kohaku could respond Nahe stood up angrily and slammed his hands on the table. "Let's stop this circus, shall we?" he said, looking at his shocked colleagues. "You'd have to be blind not to notice his shoddy documentation and lack of attention to established authorities."

Totome looked at Nahe mildly. "Keep your voice down, Nahe. Of course I noticed he didn't spend much time dealing with the sources, but I felt that his area of inquiry was sufficiently different that it was a reasonable—"

"His conclusions are also ludicrous." Nahe picked up a sheet of paper and began reading from it. " 'The islander's reverence for the mandagah fish is actually based upon an ancient link, forgotten on the inner islands, between the water spirit and these rare fish.' This goes against every established convention—"

"Don't be such a blowhard, Nahe," Bopa said. "I thought his conclusions were well-founded. What good is a Kulanui without a little debate?"

Nahe looked angry enough to hit Bopa, but she stared at him until he sat back down.

"Enough," he said quietly. "I am the head of the council, and I say that this student is unfit to enter our ranks. In fact, I declare that the sloppiness of his work makes him unfit to be in the Kulanui at all, and I hereby divest him of his rank and forbid him to further waste anyone's time with his hopeless aspirations."

Kohaku stared, but he could not even summon indignation to meet Nahe's look of triumph. Yesterday's cold, sharp-edged anger was still there, but buried under a turgid river of grief.

"You can't do that, Nahe. The council can still overrule you—"

"And what if you try and fail, Bopa? What if more side with me? What do you think will happen to you then?"

Bopa stood up abruptly and gathered her papers. "I refuse to be a part of this monkey trial," she said as she walked toward the door. "Kohaku, I'm quite sorry. I still say your work was excellent."

"And you, Totome?" Nahe asked.

Totome glanced at Kohaku and then gave an infinitesimal nod.

Nahe smiled. "You're dismissed, Kohaku. You can leave your robe and headband on the table."

Kohaku pressed the filtering cloth close to his mouth and nose. The air this close to the lip of the volcano was acrid—poisonous, if you stayed too long. The lavish expense of this funeral ceremony was due in part to the inherent dangers involved in climbing the volcano. Up ahead, priests and priestesses chanted ancient songs of supplication. They asked for his sister's spirit to be kept within the islands and they asked her not to bear the living grudges for her untimely death. Emea had always loved Nui'ahi, and after his failure to protect her, he realized it was the only thing he could do. The fee had taken all his money, even after he had sold their apartment and all their possessions. Still, there wouldn't have been enough if Lipa hadn't given him the rest. He didn't know how he would ever repay that debt, either. Four white-clad men carried his sister's body on a mat of woven reeds. Around her shoulders, contrasting with the stark white of her dress, he had tied the carrying cloth she had made so lovingly. The path was rough and filled with rocks that crumbled under his feet and made it difficult to find a purchase. The air was so foul that he thought he might vomit, but he continued, viewing it as a penance, if not a method of purging his grief.

The altitude had plugged his ears, but he didn't bother to unplug them—he liked the dampened sound. He tried to imagine what life had been like for his sister, who hadn't been able to hear since she was four. He watched the mouths of the chanters move in unison, but didn't hear what they were saying. Perhaps his sister's inability to hear had been more of a blessing than a curse—it was one less reason to feel pain. It would have been so much easier to tune out the world with one less sense for it to overload. Finally, they reached the lip of the volcano. This part of the ceremony was quick, for the whole funeral party would be in danger of passing out if they stayed much longer.

He touched her hand when they reached the top, trying not to notice how unnaturally cold and stiff it felt. His eyes fell on the blue and gold of her shawl. Not quite understanding the impulse, he untied it just before they tipped her body in the orange-gold pit of molten lava. She went directly under, and then bobbed like a cork to the surface. Her clothes caught fire, then her hair. She burned until he could no longer make out her figure, and the ash that clogged his throat might just be hers.

· 7 ·

LANA SAT BY THE OPEN WINDOW in her shift, squinting as she sewed a button back on her shirt. She hadn't acquired a new piece of clothing in nearly four years, and the wear was beginning to show. This shirt—blue with a shiny orange strip down the middle—had been a gift from her parents during her first visit to Essel four years ago. Since it still looked less shabby than her other clothes, she had planned to patch it up as best she could and wear that when she visited her parents in two weeks. But Akua had been a hard taskmaster recently and this would probably be her only chance to mend her shirt before she left. Lana glanced periodically at the stove, where the draught Akua had been making for the past three days simmered quietly. Akua had gone out earlier that morning to gather the final ingredients—although Lana could hardly believe there was anything she hadn't already used in it. The smell didn't bother her as much as it had at first, but she was still grateful for the periodic breeze. Akua had not yet told her what it was for—a familiar annoyance. She seemed to delight in tantalizing her with powerful geas and then refusing to explain their workings. Lana, it seemed, was never quite ready enough or strong enough to tackle a major working of power. As for today's potion, she felt Akua had already bound too many geas to it for her comfort—ever since the incident with Saulo two years ago, she found it difficult to trust Akua when too much power was involved.

Just as Lana was tying off the thread, Akua opened the door, a small smile on her lips and a worn canvas bag over her shoulder. A strong gust of wind made the door slam shut, but Akua didn't seem to notice. She walked over to Lana, barely sparing a glance for her draught.

"What is it?" Lana asked. She had rarely seen Akua so excited.

"You're ready," she said. She finally seemed to register that Lana was only in her shift and she waved at the shirt impatiently. "Put that on," she said. "We're going out for a few days."

Lana stared, but pulled the shirt over her head. "Akua, what are you talking about?"

"Get your mandagah jewels. I am going to teach you a technique of great power."

"Why on earth would you need ..." Lana trailed off, her heart thudding painfully. "Jewels?" she whispered.

Akua smiled gently. "I've always known, Lana. Do you think you could hide something like that from someone who's spent her whole life studying power? Go get them, then—the blue and the red."

Lana couldn't even speak. She ran up the stairs, terrified and excited with the conviction that Akua was finally going to teach her a geas of power.

Akua held out a tall earthenware cup, filled to the top with the foul-smelling draught that had been simmering on the stove for the past three days. Lana glanced briefly at Akua's serious eyes and fought her nausea. It smelled something like soured pomegranate juice, with the sweetness replaced by the stink of rotting vegetation. A layer of dung-brown foam floated atop of the liquid. Every few seconds an oily brown bubble would rise to the top and break, giving her another whiff of its rank stench.

"You want me to drink this?" Lana said, carefully breathing out of her mouth.

Akua laughed. "If you hold your nose it won't taste so bad."

"I have to drink the whole thing?" Akua nodded and she sighed. "What is it, exactly?"

"It invokes certain spirits, so that when you perform the real sacrifice over the two jewels the power will be doubled. I'll show you how to prepare it once you see what its effects are. This way your binding between the two jewels will be nearly unbreakable."

Lana wondered why that would be necessary, but she had been with Akua long enough to know that the witch never explained herself before she was ready. Shrugging her shoulders, Lana pinched her nose and tipped the noxious mixture into her mouth. Despite the fact that she couldn't breathe, the very feel of it sliding like a worm down the back of her throat nearly made her vomit. She dropped the cup on the floor, where it landed with a dull thud. The little bit of liquid remaining dripped out, but it seemed to have lost all of its viscosity and seeped through the floorboards without even leaving a damp spot. Through the silvered haze that descended over her vision, Lana watched Akua nod in satisfaction and pick up the cup. As soon as the draught entered her stomach, she became aware of the prickling sensation of incipient power, much stronger than anything she had ever invoked herself. It felt as though Akua must have tied this geas to all three of the bound spirits—water, death, and fire—an unusual and tremendously powerful technique. Lana lay sprawled on the floor, staring at the wooden ceiling beams gone nearly black with age. She had the strangest sense that she could see shapes in their shadows—the brief flick of a scaled hand, the shiny gleam of too-white teeth. She suddenly realized that she was surrounded by spirits—some leering, some laughing, some sitting stone-faced, all waiting to see why she had called them here and if she had the power to bind them. As she lay prone on the floor in a haze more profound than anything she had ever experienced with amant weed, it occurred to her that until this moment, she had never understood the real danger she courted every time she cast a geas. If she didn't prove capable of binding them, these spirits would devour her from the inside out.

Akua helped her to sit up and smoothed her hair back gently.

Lana noticed that the spirits seemed to back up at the sight of Akua. Could that be respect in their insubstantial eyes? Fear?

Akua put the two jewels in a bowl of water, where they bobbed gently. "Don't worry, Lana," she said. "One day you will command power much greater than this. They are all subject to your will, as long as you are sure of yourself."

The phantasms in the corners were laughing, but Lana focused on Akua's reassuring eyes and nodded firmly, though her head felt in danger of floating off her neck.

Akua pressed a knife into Lana's loose grip. "Use this to cut your wrist. Not too shallow, not too deep. Then read this—you'll know when." Beside the bowl Akua had placed a yellowed sheet of paper, with a single geas poem written in old-style pictographs in its middle. Lana stared at it for a few hazy moments before gripping the knife's wooden handle more firmly. She would have to be strong enough. The spirits that crowded around her—a badger whose dun-brown head was twice as big as its body, a fish with hard golden scales and eyes that dripped thick, viscous water—flickered in and out of visibility. Unlike Ino, they were not strictly bound to this world; their existence was only partially physical—until someone like her forced them to submit to a geas.

Slowly, as though the air had grown too thick to move, Lana held the sharp blade above her left wrist. She stared at the wide blue vein and imagined blood pumping through it, and then imagined that blood as power. In a brief, almost casual act of violence, Lana slashed her wrist and allowed the vein to pump its dark red contents into the bowl containing the two jewels.

Power descended like a fog into the small room. She sensed the spirits' tension, the sharp way they watched her for any weakness. She refused to look back at them. Instead, she looked at her jewels. The blood slid easily from the blue one, coloring the water beneath it, but it clung to the red, deepening its color until it seemed to glow from the inside.

"Good ... very good, Lana," Akua said softly, guarded surprise in her voice. "Now read the geas."

With difficulty, Lana tore her eyes from the gently spinning red jewel and looked back at the yellowed paper beside it.

Like womb-sisters,
like self-bound stars, these objects
even when apart
remain together.
So one's power
becomes the other's.
So one's sacrifice
serves for both.
Let the one who receives it willingly,
give willingly,
a sacrifice of fire, water—

Lana broke off abruptly and stared at Akua. Her hold over the power wavered dangerously. The last word was written in pictographs she couldn't read. They looked as though they were part of the ancient scholarly writing style she had never learned. Since speaking in the middle of a geas recitation would break it, Akua frowned a little, then dipped her finger in the bowl of bloody water and scrawled four phonetic characters on the floor. Lana nodded.

"A sacrifice of fire, water …" she stared at Akua's quickly drying scrawl, "or *make-lai*," she finished. The power sealed itself off. For a brief moment the surrounding spirits opened their mouths in what could have been a lament or simply a keen of rage—Lana couldn't hear them, but the hair on the back of her neck bristled and she shuddered. Then the room seemed to stabilize. The corners held merely shadows once again, and the haze in Lana's head was simply exhaustion. Akua stared at her, eyebrows furrowed but eyes unreadable. After a moment, her mentor plucked the two jewels—which felt somehow different, now, as though their power had mutated—out of the water and handed them to Lana.

"You know how to thread these, don't you?" she asked.

Lana nodded, too tired to speak.

"We're leaving tomorrow morning. Bore the holes by then and I'll give you some riverweed to string it on."

Lana was surprised. The supple, silver-gold strands of riverweed were rumored to be the fallen hair of sprites, and fetched notoriously high prices.

Akua stood and picked up the bowl of bloody water. She tossed its contents out the window and then poured a little more fresh water from a pitcher by the stove. She walked to a low cabinet and pulled out a small jar and a roll of bandages and walked back over to Lana, who was prostrate on the floor.

"Here," she said gently, "your arm probably hurts. You lost a bit more blood than I'd anticipated."

Once she mentioned it, Lana realized that her arm was throbbing. Red blood still oozed from the cut in a turgid flow. Akua fished a necklace—a key carved delicately out of bone—from the inside of her shirt and held it briefly. She muttered a quick geas and the blood slowed to a trickle—a masterful use of power that Lana could not help but admire. Akua then washed her cut and rubbed it with a balm that smelled of bee pollen and lichen.

"You'll have to wrap the bandage," Akua said, her slightly lined face showing signs of exhaustion. As Lana tied the linen strips around her wrist she felt an unexpected burst of affection. The witch had secrets, hidden motivations, and an undeniable streak of cruelty. But over the years Lana had come to admire her. Akua's intelligence, her flawless command of power, even the disdain she had for societal conventions had earned Lana's respect. Lana ripped the cloth with her teeth and tied it in a knot. Akua gave her a tired smile.

"You look exhausted. Why don't you just go to sleep? You'll have time to bore the holes before we get to Ialo."

Lana felt renewed surprise. Ialo was the second biggest city on Okika—a three-day journey by river. It was the last big port city on the traditional ship routes to the Eastern outer islands, the ones by the water shrine. "Why are we going to Ialo?" she asked.

"To set up shop. We'll do a bit of trading, and you can go on to Essel from there."

Lana was too exhausted to be more curious. She hauled herself off the ground and then staggered a bit as her vision went temporarily white.

"Oh, Akua?" she said, just before she climbed the stairs. "What does *make-lai* mean?"

Akua's fingers froze momentarily over the jar she was picking up. "It's a word of power in the river language. It hasn't been common for nearly 500 years."

Just before Lana went to sleep, she wondered how a word she had never heard before could sound so dirty.

The riverbanks were strewn with the gray, rotting carcasses of the liha'wai, who just months before had been dancing under the pregnant spring moon. Most of the more affluent passengers on this riverboat had pulled their brightly colored scarves across their faces, and some had even doused the cloth in heavy perfume to better hide the smell. The sight of the multicolored scarves flapping in the wind made Lana think of exotic birds. The sound of the other passengers' voices complaining about the stench blended with the imperative commands of the sailors into a cacophony, dulled by the wind rushing past her ears into something almost comforting. Despite the profusion of scarves, Lana thought the smell actually wasn't so bad—the docks in Okika had sometimes smelled far worse. It was the sight that disturbed her more—the dark, thick bodies of the flies crowding around the river nits' eyes and mouths. Some of the nits were still alive, flapping their tails and spindly legs uselessly even as the flies devoured their flesh. It was hard to see the beautiful sparks that lit the river in early spring reduced to such gruesome mortality in the harsh heat of summer. But the muddy edges of the wide river were crowded with flotillas of tiny pink dots suspended in beds of mucus. The liha'wai eggs would hatch in a few days and begin the cycle again, even as the air above them still stank of their parents' decaying bodies.

Akua had fallen asleep on her hammock, a leather-bound book shielding her eyes from the noonday sun. Lana walked over to her own hammock and fished the two jewels out of the pocket of her leibo. She didn't wear the diving pants very often anymore, since they made people look at her like she was some country bumpkin, but standing in her bare feet on the sun-shrunk boards of the riverboat, she could almost pretend she was back home. The weather would make it a cool day on her island, but at least the biting cold of the lingering winter had disappeared. Lana settled on the hammock and fished out the boring needle Akua had found for her before they left. She was nearly done with the hole in the blue jewel, and then she would start on the red. In her pocket were also two strands of the supple but improbably strong riverweed. She wondered about this strange trip as she patiently worked the needle deeper into the dense jewel. Why had Akua insisted she perform that geas, and then make necklaces out of her jewels? Akua's cryptic answers were beginning to make her feel nervous. The sensation—like being led over treacherous ground with her eyes blindfolded—was already familiar enough for her to hate it.

"Why do you want me to thread these jewels, anyway?" Lana asked softly.

To her surprise, Akua picked up the book and turned to face her. "I told you. For power."

"I know, but *how*? What did that geas do? What's in Ialo?"

Akua sighed, but the corners of her mouth lifted ruefully. "You just don't leave well enough alone, do you? We're going to Ialo to sell one of your jewels. The person who takes it will become a willing sacrifice for you to access whenever you choose, because of the power between the two jewels. They were already linked—more strongly than I had thought, actually—but the geas reinforced that bond and allowed you to take power with one through the other."

Lana's hands tingled as though she had been sitting on them for too long. "A ... willing sacrifice? But, wouldn't that hurt ...

the other person, even if they didn't know what they were accepting?"

Akua shrugged. "It's completely benign. You get the power of a willing sacrifice and the other person feels a little more tired than normal for a day."

Lana began pushing the needle back into the jewel. "Really? So how are we going to find this person?"

"We'll go to market. You'll probably understand when you see them—a happy person, someone with a lot of energy. They'll be attracted to your jewel. All you have to do is make sure that they never take it off. If they do, the connection will be broken and you won't be able to use the sacrifice when you need it."

The needle broke through the other end and Lana fished one strand of riverweed from her pocket. She threaded it through and then tied it at the top. After a moment's thought, she concentrated, then spat carefully on the knot and muttered a simple geas. The strand heated briefly and her spit sizzled. When it had burned away entirely the knot was gone, leaving a smooth, unbreakable chain.

Akua chuckled, then shook her head. "You shouldn't show off, Lana. It's bad manners."

Lana smiled and looked back at her creation. The large blue jewel was glinting in the sunlight brightly enough to shine blue streaks of refracted light onto her lap. She swung it lightly around her fingers.

"This is pretty, isn't it?" she said. "Whoever buys it will appreciate that."

In honor of the spirit solstice, the citizens of Ialo had painted their houses a dazzling range of colors—as though there had been a contest for who could create the most vivid combination. The wealthiest had found the brightest gold and silver to mix with the traditional blue, but even the more mundane reds and oranges impressed Lana. The intricate, abstract whorls of color were like nothing she had ever seen before—back on her island, they had never had the leisure to paint such incredible decorations. Of course, Ialo was a city dedicated to the water, so it made sense that its citizens made such a production of the year-end holiday. According to legend, Yaela bound the water spirit, Kai, just at the end of the rains, which meant that although the spirit solstice was intended to honor all the bound spirits, it was celebrated on the anniversary of Kai. Floating next to the giant waterfall that gave the city its name, the riverboat slowly descended through a series of locks that would eventually deposit them in the large bay below. Surrounding the bay was the city, a horseshoe-shaped profusion of colors and crowds and ships that, over the years, had expanded right into the water itself. From Lana's viewpoint, it looked as though half the market district on the western side of the city wasn't on land. Whorehouses and gambling parlors crowded alongside abandoned buildings that were slowly rotting back into the bay. They all balanced on precarious wooden stilts, with a continuous porch extending perhaps three meters in front of the buildings. In some sections these walkways had fallen away, and Lana saw that most people took barges poled by ferrymen. The market district slammed into the actual harbor, where huge ships bobbed in the calm bay, restocking and repairing damage before making the rest of the journey to the eastern islands. Across the bay from the docks the land sloped upwards and the houses abruptly gave way to huge, leafy trees. At the top of the hill sat a large building, freshly painted in every imaginable shade of blue and green. The temple faced east, toward the outer water shrine.

As they descended closer to the city, the air began to smell like spicy fried dough, which was rolled and then skewered on pinewood—an Ialo dockside delicacy.

Lana breathed deeply. "Doesn't it make you hungry?"

Akua snorted. "Hardly. You'd be better off getting some food made by cleaner hands."

"So street food is beneath you, is it?" Lana asked. She leaned over the edge of the boat and laughed.

"Maybe I'm just getting unadventurous in my old age. Try some if you want."

The boat finally fell into the bay with a little splash. Lana watched in curiosity as the sailors pulled in the canvas and maneuvered the narrow vessel into the harbor. As soon as the dockside workers caught the ropes and tied the boat down, Lana grabbed her small bag, swung it over her shoulder, and scrambled down the side of the boat on the sailor's rope rather than wait for the gangplank. The sailors seemed a little surprised, then laughed and made some joke about how children always made the best climbers. Lana clicked her tongue in annoyance—she was so short that people often made that mistake. Since Akua would probably be the last off the boat, Lana followed her nose around the barnacle-covered hulls, seeking out the food vendors. She found some a few yards away, sitting in a small, flat-bottomed boat, seemingly unperturbed when waves from an incoming ship made the burning oil sizzle on the edge of the cauldron. The older woman frying the dough smiled at Lana when she approached, her warmth undiminished by the fact that she had only three remaining teeth.

"What will it be, keika?" she asked.

Lana smiled back and ordered six dough rolls, which a younger woman in the back of the boat made nearly as fast as the old lady could fry them. Lana took the food, wrapped in cheap packing paper, and then dropped a half-kala coin into the woman's lined palm. Halfway back to the boat, Lana squatted in the shadow of a trading ship that reeked of the deep ocean and pulled out a roll. The hot oil burned her mouth and the spices made her nose run, but she closed her eyes as she ate it, like she was a penitent at a devotional. When she opened them, she was a little startled to see Akua's familiar green traveling pants. She looked up at Akua's sardonic expression, suddenly feeling embarrassed.

"Sorry I didn't wait for you," she said, sucking on the end of the pine stick.

"Far be it from me to keep you from breakfast. So, is it as good as you thought?"

Lana stood up. "It's the best thing I've ever tasted ... well, maybe except for Mama's grouper. You want one?" she said, holding out another roll. Akua shrugged and took it. She chewed for a long time after she bit into it, her expression one of intense concentration.

"Well?" Lana said.

Akua laughed. "You're always so earnest ..." she said. "It's spicy, but good. Better than I thought. So maybe there are a few things you can teach me, too." She took another bite and nodded. "Well, let's go. We should get to the market district before the noonday rush."

The two left the docks together, munching on fried dough and laughing. They looked so happy together that many people looked at them and smiled, thinking that they might be mother and daughter. The few who noticed Akua's missing right arm turned away abruptly, unaccountably chilled.

. . .

Pua walked slowly through the narrow streets on the edge of the market district, absentmindedly peeling and eating the sweet roasted chestnuts she had bought near the waterfall. She had been walking through Ialo since dawn, remembering what it had been like the first time she and her sister Makani had traveled here, more than thirty years ago. Back then the houses hadn't been crowded so close together and the market district hadn't spilled into the bay, but the spirit solstice paintings had dazzled her just as much—decorating their houses was a ritual as well as a hobby for most of the residents of this oddly devout city. She and Makani had traveled here as two would-be adventurers, leaving their small community in the outer islands to explore the world. They had been planning to see Essel, maybe even the inner islands, but they never made it past Ialo. On their way to the inn one night, they had noticed something unusual by the docks. A line of girls, conical straw hats pulled low over their faces, were holding paper lanterns that swayed in rhythm with their feet as they shuffled forward onto a barge. In the dark, the girls looked like a sedate procession of gigantic fireflies. Three water temple officiates, dressed in the blue silk robes of their rank, stood at the head of the boat, silently surveying the girls as they lined up in front of them. She and Makani stared at each other for a surprised moment, and then walked closer to the tail end of the line. In the far back, two girls were arguing fiercely with each other.

"I don't want to go," the shorter one whispered. She pulled off her hat. "I won't go. You can't make me."

"We don't have a choice, Lia. Mama will kill us if we don't go," the taller one said, but Pua thought that she sounded like she agreed with her sister.

To Pua's surprise, Makani broke away from her and walked in front of the two girls, who stopped their whispered argument abruptly.

"I'm sorry, but … what is this?" Makani asked, gesturing toward the barge.

Makani's beauty always stunned people the first time she met them. After a few moments the younger one finally found her voice. "It's … for the water shrine. The guardian. We dive in the pool shallow as a thimble and deeper than the ocean and the water guardian will pick one of us for his wife." She frowned. "But I don't want to do it!"

The older one stared at her sister in frustration. "Well, we have to. If we don't hurry up, they're going to leave without us. Oh, come on, Lia, please don't cry!"

"Do you think … what if you give us your clothes and lanterns and we go for you? We can meet here afterwards, and no one will ever know." Makani spoke breathlessly, and Pua could tell that she was determined to find some way onto that boat. Makani was like that—whenever she got an idea, it was impossible to resist her.

"But … but we're not wearing any clothes under these," the older sister said, gesturing toward their navy blue wool robes. "For the diving."

Makani nodded, and then looked around. A few of the girls in the back of the line were looking at them curiously. Pua guessed that they only had about two minutes before everyone would file onto the boat. Makani began walking purposefully away from the group, toward a large ship. After a moment's hesitation Pua and the two sisters followed her behind the hull, where they were hidden from the other's eyes.

"Quickly," Makani said as she undid the long row of buttons down her shirt. Pua smiled to herself and began undoing her own buttons—traveling with Makani was certainly interesting. The younger sister grinned and then pulled her robe off over her head.

The older sister fingered the tight weave of Makani's leibo as she put them on. "You know, I've seen these ..." she looked up suddenly. "Are you a diver?"

Makani nodded. "Or I was, anyway. How did you two get picked to do this?"

"The temple interviewed almost everybody ... I don't really know why they picked us, but when they sent us the invitation, our mother ... well, we couldn't get out of it."

Makani tied the hat under her chin and gripped the lantern. "Is there anything else we should know?"

The older sister handed Makani and Pua two tiny wooden figurines carved in the shape of a thin fish. "These are your passes. You don't have much time left. We'll meet you back here at dawn. Good luck."

Pua and Makani waved at them and then sprinted back to the procession just as the last girls were filing onto the barge. Two temple officiates standing near the back looked at them strangely, but didn't say anything. Pua stood as the barge was slowly poled across the bay, wondering what would happen inside the blue-painted walls of the water temple.

It felt as though they had descended into the bowels of the earth—the staircase to the pool continued interminably until the air became so damp Pua found herself fighting incipient claustrophobia. They finally emerged in a cave, lit eerily by their bobbing lanterns and two torches on the walls. At the opposite end of the small cave sat a massive wooden door, carved in intricate bas-relief. The officiates made them all unstrap their sandals and leave them by the staircase. The floor was damp but warm, and Pua was aware of a strange energy beneath it, almost like the tremors before an earthquake. Two people by the door hauled it open with a brass ring. The groan of the rusty hinges echoed like screams off the damp walls. When she and Makani walked through the entryway Pua felt a pang of disquiet for the first time. What were they doing here? Wouldn't the water spirit find them out? They had grown up in the shadow of the outer water shrine, though, and perhaps Makani couldn't believe that its guardian would ever do anything to hurt them.

The room they entered was at least four times the size of the antechamber, and the wavering shadows cut by their swaying lanterns even more imposing. At its center was a roughly circular pool of water with a smooth surface that reflected their faces as easily as glass. The officiates ordered them to stand around the pool. One by one, each girl removed her robe, tossed in a wooden figurine, muttered a prayer of supplication and jumped into the water. Some surfaced almost immediately, looking bewildered when the other girls helped them up. Some remained under the water for what must have seemed like an amazingly long time to people who hadn't grown up around divers. A few jumped to find that the water suddenly only splashed around their toes. Those girls blushed especially red and ran quickly back to their place in the circle. When Makani's turn came, she calmly removed her hat and robe and tossed the little figurine in the water. She sucked air into her lungs with special diver's breaths, gave Pua a tight smile, and jumped into the water. For the first three or four minutes afterwards, when the whispers began, Pua remained confident. After seven minutes, however, terror began to slowly drip into her stomach—no one could hold her breath this long, not even a diver. Makani must have drowned.

Pua let out a high-pitched wail and sank to her knees. The

water guardian had punished them for sneaking in on his ceremony and had killed her sister. She suddenly noticed the bottom
hem of an officiate's blue robe and a finger peremptorily tapping
her shoulder. Pua looked up slowly, wiping her face.

"Stand up, girl," the woman said, hauling Pua up by the arm.
"Was she your sister?"

Pua nodded silently and the woman frowned. "You don't look
familiar ... what are your names? Who interviewed you?"

Pua's heart began racing so fast she was afraid she might faint.
Behind the woman she noticed that a few girls had attempted
to jump into the pool, but the water had suddenly turned shallow. Her sister was trapped. The woman interrogating her turned
around also.

"Great Kai," she muttered and then faced Pua again. "Show me
your figurine." With trembling fingers, Pua dropped the fish into
the woman's hand. The woman stared at it for a few moments and
then clenched her fist angrily. "We sent these to the postmaster's
daughters! What did you do to them?"

Suddenly there were hands gripping her from behind and Pua
let out a helpless bleat of fear. "We ... traded. They didn't want to
go, so we traded," she said, clenching her teeth as they wrenched
her shoulder painfully.

The woman shut her eyes briefly. "You traded. If you've angered
the guardian—" She broke off when she noticed a commotion behind her. The water started to churn violently, splashing waves
on the feet of the girls surrounding it. In a sudden spray of steam
and water, Makani practically flew out of the pool, her long black
hair inexplicably dry. Rippling arms of water held her in the air
for a moment and then lowered her gently onto the pool. The tiny
figurine was strung around her neck on a strand of riverweed,
but it had been transformed from rough wood into a shimmering
opalescent white, like a mandagah jewel. Makani had an expression in her eyes Pua had never seen before—distant, but ecstatic.
She walked carefully across the water of the pool—it didn't splash

around her toes like it had before, but each step she took rippled outward. Pua raced toward her and caught her before she collapsed on the ground.

"I thought we were going to explore, Pua, but I guess we're going back," she said softly.

"That's okay," Pua said.

The next day, a boat bound for the outer islands held rather unusual cargo: Pua and the water guardian's new bride.

Thinking about how much her life had changed that one night, Pua wondered for the first time why Makani had been so sure she would travel to the water shrine with her. Then she smiled wryly—Makani had always known how much of an influence she had over her little sister. If Makani were still alive, Pua would still probably follow her wherever she went. But Makani had died five years after giving birth to little Kai, and nothing could have convinced Pua to leave him then. So she had continued on in that strange place with only a little boy and a grieving, half-human man for company. Ali'ikai and Pua had always had an understanding, and after Makani's death that understanding had deepened into something like friendship. Twenty-five years after Makani's death, Pua still sometimes felt a pain in her chest when she thought of her sister, but she knew that her grief was nothing compared to his. He had shut himself off after she died. He was distant toward everyone, even his own son. Pua had realized that if she didn't care for Kai, no one would. And so she had become "Mama Pua," and spent every day hoping that she could be as good a mother as her sister.

Pua had taken Kai to Ialo one time before the change. He had played in the streets like a normal little boy, stuffing his face with chestnuts and fried dough rolls and giggling uncontrollably at the antics of a street magician. Walking down the same streets two decades later, she still had the strangest impression that she could hear his voice calling her name, telling her about some food just up the road. But Kai was an adult now, and sometimes she wondered if he was entirely lost to her.

The reason why she had come was this: Kai, who was never angry and always unfailingly polite to everyone, had been in black rage after an argument with his father. He had begged her to go to Ialo and buy supplies and clothes that would make him look as normal as possible during his pilgrimage to the inner water shrine. Just before she left, he had confided to her that he was half-afraid the death or fire spirits had found some way to weaken their bonds—too many ominous things had changed in the past six years for the terrifying possibility to be dismissed. The wind spirit had broken free five hundred years earlier, but she remembered enough of the legendary tales of death and destruction in that event's aftermath to be very afraid. She had finished buying supplies the other day, but she knew that as soon as she returned Kai would leave, and she wasn't sure if she would ever see him again. So she spent her days walking the streets, haunted by memories.

The market district was especially crowded this morning, probably because it was the last Market Day before the beginning of the solstice. People were out buying charms and house-dolls for the new year and dragging last year's charms and dolls to the nearby temple, where they would be burned on Solstice Evening. Pua wandered aimlessly through the crowded dirt roads, stopping to look at nearly everything—including what a young man with a puckered scar over his right eye claimed were the mummified remains of a mermaid. About an hour after noon her stomach began rumbling again and she cast about for a food vendor. She realized that she had wandered into the grubbier part of market district, nearer to the docks. There were some interesting wares on display, but no food, since the vendors were afraid of light fingers. She was rounding a corner onto a road that would take her back to a busier street when she noticed a young woman displaying a necklace that glinted familiarly.

Pua stopped and then turned around slowly. The girl looked at her almost nervously, and Pua thought the expression made her look much younger. Even though she was much shorter and a bit heavier than her sister had been, something about her swarthy skin and oddly determined lips reminded Pua of Makani. Pua shook her head and looked at the necklace. To her surprise, it held an unusually large mandagah jewel—bright blue and hung on a seamless chain of riverweed.

Pua let out a small gasp and looked up at the girl. For the first time, she noticed another, older woman sitting in a chair quietly behind her, pretending to read a book while she studied Pua.

"Is that a mandagah jewel?" Pua asked the younger one. "Haven't the mandagah been killed off? I didn't even know they were still on the market."

The woman shrugged, seemingly regaining some of her composure. "It's a special jewel—harvested years ago, before the disasters."

Pua looked down and she noticed the girl's tough, worn leibo. It had been a long time since she had seen any, and she smiled softly. "You were a diver?" she asked.

"For a little while. Too little."

"My sister was a diver too," she said, but felt embarrassed when she realized that this girl could not have given it up out of choice, like Makani. She sighed. "I'm afraid I don't have nearly enough money for a beautiful jewel like that. But … you're wearing a purple sash … do you tell fortunes?"

The girl hesitated visibly and then nodded. "It doesn't always work, but if you want one I can try."

Pua laughed. "You won't make it too long out here if you're so honest. But don't worry, I'll pay you first."

The fortune-teller glanced briefly at the older woman. "Well … how about one kala?" she suggested.

The price was so ludicrously low that Pua almost objected, but then shrugged and handed her the coin. It wasn't her responsibility if this young woman had no idea of how to handle herself on the streets. Besides, her demeanor made Pua think that she had something in mind other than money, which made this encounter all the more interesting. The girl pulled a small knife from the pocket of her leibo and gestured toward Pua to sit down on a straw stool. She then took a small bowl and poured some water from a half-filled gourd into it.

"If it works," she said to Pua as she sat down, "it may not say everything you want to hear. And it isn't always accurate—the future is pretty unpredictable, even in the best of times."

Pua nodded, truly surprised at her unprofessional honesty.

The girl swished the knife in the bowl a few times, absent-mindedly slashing the water. "So, is there a part of the fortune you want me to focus on?" she asked.

Pua thought of Kai. "There is someone I ... love very much. I want to know if his mission will succeed. If I'll ever see him again."

"Well then, let's start." She spat into the water and muttered something under her breath. Suddenly the water seemed to solidify, letting the knife slice it like butter without immediately filling in the gap. It was a trick Pua had seen Kai do a thousand times, after his change, but she was shocked to see that this young woman was capable of it. Water clung to the knife. When the blade began to look blurry due to refracted light she pulled it out of the bowl and took Pua's hand.

"What's your name?" she asked softly.

"Pua ... bei'Polunu," she said, suddenly alarmed at the girl's intensity. She had never experienced a fortune quite like this before.

The girl turned Pua's palm outward and scored it with the water-encrusted knife. Water and blood mingled and poured back into the bowl. Something in the air around them had changed, just like the charge before Kai or his father said a geas.

As the water stays a step ahead of the river, so the spirit stays a step ahead of time. I ask the river-dancer to step ahead and look behind for Pua bei'Polunu.

That was definitely a geas. Its delivery was a bit less sophisticated than what she was used to, but she had never imagined that street fortune-tellers knew such techniques. The girl was silent for a long time and then she began to speak.

"Many paths cross," she said slowly, as though she was repeating something whispered in her ear. "The one you love will not finish his journey. He will return, but the future is always uncertain. Always remember: everything ends. We all will die."

Pua waited for more, but she knew it was over when the water in the bowl slopped back into its original shape. The warm breeze off the bay suddenly felt frigid. She wished that she hadn't proposed a fortune telling—she knew with a dread certainty that this was real. The girl's hesitant half-predictions had not been the words of a charlatan.

The girl sighed and tossed the knife back in the bowl. "I'm so sorry," she said. "It was so vague … it's a terrible time to tell fortunes." She looked up at Pua with a small smile. "Perhaps I should find another profession."

Pua smiled tentatively back. "Maybe you just need to learn how to make things up."

The girl laughed and reached for the necklace in her pocket. She held the beautiful blue jewel in her hand for a second and then handed it to Pua. "Here, take it. I'll give you a real good price for it—how's fifty kala? I'm traveling, actually, and if I get to Essel with that and they find out, I'll have to answer to the guild and I'd rather not have the hassle."

Pua took the necklace and fingered it gently. The riverweed was seamless. How could she give this beautiful object away for such a pittance? Even after paying off the guild, Pua knew she could get a hundred times more for this in Essel.

"It's a good luck charm, really," the girl said. "It works if you never take it off. It's especially attracted to you, for some reason—better for it to be with someone who can appreciate it than someone with a lot of money who will leave it to molder in a drawer."

"A good luck charm?" Pua said. It didn't feel very lucky, but the stone was so beautiful, and it reminded her of Makani.

"If you promise to never take it off, I'll give it to you for free."

Pua shook her head. "No, no. I'll pay you what I can. Thank you … thank you for doing this for me."

The woman looked toward the ground suddenly, avoiding Pua's eyes as she gave her the money. The necklace felt familiar, as though it had always hung around her neck.

Maybe, she thought as she walked away from that young woman who reminded her so much of her sister, maybe it really is a good luck charm.

. . .

Lana felt sick to her stomach when she watched Pua leave. Though Akua had assured her that the necklace was harmless, lying about its true nature still felt wrong. But Akua looked satisfied, and the red jewel on the second string of riverweed around her neck hummed with a strange new energy that excited her. She tried to hide her confusion as she turned to face Akua, who was sitting with a book over her chest.

"That was good," she said. "Although I wouldn't have recommended telling her real fortune—they're too messy and depressing. No one wants to hear it." Akua looked at the sun and then clucked her tongue. "Your boat leaves this evening, we should be on our way."

Lana cleaned up slowly, wondering if Pua would ever know how they were now connected.

Lana's boat cast off at sunset, riding through the narrow strip that separated the bay from the ocean before unfurling its sails and setting off for Essel. If nothing untoward occurred, she would be seeing her parents in seven days. Just before she went below to get settled in her hammock, she noticed a woman about the same age as Pua vomiting weakly over the side of the boat. Her concerned husband finally had to carry her downstairs. The scene made her think a lot about Pua and the benign effect the necklace would have on her. That woman would probably be fine once she got on land, but would it really be okay for Lana to inflict that same kind of pain on Pua, who had no idea what she had agreed to by accepting the jewel? Lana looked at a fiery sunset, nearly the same color as the mandagah jewel hidden under her shirt, and wondered if it would be right for her to use the necklace, no matter what Akua said. Akua's moral compass seemed a little off, sometimes. But then, to have so much power at her fingertips!

I shouldn't use it.

But she wasn't sure if she would, regardless.

THE EVENING BEFORE THE SPIRIT SOLSTICE, Leilani took a broom outside their small shop and swept the first leaves of the changing season from the porch. She found that she enjoyed the different seasons on Essel, even though her favorite, the hot season, was criminally short. She especially loved when the leaves changed colors—it made the city look as though it had decorated itself in a profusion of gold, orange, and red specifically for the solstice. The air was warm this evening, but it had lost the muggy edge that had kept so many of Essel's residents in their houses the past month. She hoped sales would pick up when the weather cooled, as had been the trend for the past few years. Kapa had taken the downtime to work on a new kind of percussion instrument that he planned to present to the guild in a few weeks. Leilani had continued her diving lessons and helped around the shop, ticking off the days to when Lana would come home. It ought to be any day now—Lana's last letter had said she would take a ship from Ialo within a week. Leilani had cleaned Lana's room in preparation and bought enough food for a true solstice feast.

Leilani felt oddly nervous as she swept the porch, periodically squinting at the crowds for Lana. It had been so long since she had last seen her daughter, and she supposed she was afraid of discovering how much she had changed. No matter how often they exchanged letters, nothing was an adequate substitute for living with someone—sometimes Leilani thought that she had missed her daughter's whole childhood. She could hardly believe that Lana had turned eighteen—she was a true adult, ready to find a husband and have children of her own. Leilani couldn't help but wish that they could have been a real family, but if she had any regrets, she knew she deserved the blame.

Leilani picked up the broom and headed back inside. On the threshold a familiar voice made her freeze mid-step. She turned around and saw Lana, orange and blue shirttails flying, bounding across the road toward her. They hugged fiercely for a long time, and Leilani surreptitiously wiped a few tears from her eyes before they separated.

"I was hoping you'd come back today," she said. "I bought all your favorite foods. Lana … you look so much older, somehow."

Lana laughed and tugged on her braid. "What are you talking about, Mama? I'm still as short as I was five years ago."

"Still, you look older." Leilani shook her head and smiled. "Come say hello to your father. He's in back working on his instruments."

Leilani watched Lana hug her father and wondered if she herself was getting old. She felt the same as always, though she had lately come down with these inexplicable illnesses that kept her bedridden and worried Kapa into spending more of their money than he should. The bouts of illness had been getting worse recently, but she had never told Lana about them. She was determined to stay healthy so long as her daughter was here. Reflexively, Leilani reached for the necklace that she had worn since the day the witch-woman gave it to her four years ago. The symbolism of the key had never been lost on her—she knew that the woman dealt with death, and that by accepting the trinket Leilani had brought some kind of sacrifice upon herself. Could the necklace somehow be responsible for her illnesses? The thought made her terrified for Lana. It was too late now for self-recrimination, but she still wondered whether she had done the right thing by acquiescing to the one-armed woman's request without ever really knowing what she intended.

Her face must have betrayed some of her worry, because Lana and Kapa were staring at her concernedly.

"Lei, are you all right? Is it—" Kapa cut himself off and glanced at Lana.

Leilani shook her head firmly. "I'm fine, don't worry. I'll go up and start cooking."

Lana hesitated for a moment and then followed Leilani up the stairs.

There was a certain strain around her mother's eyes that hadn't been there before, Lana thought. She had been cheerful enough when they made dinner together—a process that had taken hours because of the absurd amount of food her mother had bought—but Lana still detected a sadness in Leilani's eyes that she hadn't seen since their days in Okika. She wondered what her parents were keeping from her, in their guarded looks and abrupt changes of conversation.

Despite her concern over her mother, Lana ate until she had to loosen the drawstring on her pants. Leilani had prepared some traditional Essel solstice food like a pottage of roasted chestnuts and raisins, a drink made with yogurt and pomegranate seeds, jellied oranges, as well as foods from their island—Lana's favorite grouper sprinkled with dried seaweed, and yucca root roasted with ginger and sugarcane. When she couldn't eat anymore, Lana leaned back in her chair and groaned.

"I can't move," she said, still sipping the pomegranate yogurt.

Her mother laughed, a little too brightly. "I'm glad. You're looking too thin. What's that woman been putting you through, lately?"

The red mandagah jewel suddenly seemed to burn under Lana's shirt and she shrugged uncomfortably. "You know, charms and things. It's pretty mundane, really—I spend most of the time memorizing herbs and potions for medicines. It's not hard."

Her father suddenly put down his drink. "So, you know a lot

about illnesses now?" he asked, looking at her intently. "Like a healer?"

Her mother glanced at him and frowned, but kept silent. Lana bit her lip—the tension in the room was making her uncomfortable. "Sure," she said. "Probably more than most—Akua's a good teacher."

"Lana," her father said, avoiding Leilani's eyes. "Do you think you could make something to help your mother?"

"Kapa! We agreed—"

"I know, I know, we promised, but you're sick, Lei, and Lana can help."

"I am not—"

Lana leaned over and pounded on the table. "What are you two talking about?"

Leilani and Kapa exchanged glances. Finally Leilani sighed, as though all the energy had left her body. "Fine, then. You tell her, since you had to ruin the meal."

Her father looked like he wanted to apologize, but then just shook his head and turned to Lana. "Lei's had six fevers this past year, three just in the hot season. She doesn't know what's wrong, and she won't let me pay for a doctor to help her."

"It's too much, Kapa! Especially since I always get better on my own."

"But what if you don't next time? You don't see yourself, Lei …"

Lana felt like she had been plunged into some strange fantasy, where suddenly her parents actually discussed their problems with her, and even expected her to moderate them. She had never so acutely felt the line she had crossed between childhood and adulthood. She had supposedly crossed it five years ago, after her initiation, but she had still *felt* like a child. Until now.

"Stop it," she said quietly, staring at the table. "Papa's right. It's not good to get sick so many times in one year—it could be something more serious. I'll make something. But if it doesn't work, promise me that you'll see a doctor."

Her mother stared at her for a long time, and then finally nodded. "I'm sorry. It wasn't right of me to keep this from you. You're not a child anymore." She smiled, a little bitterly. "It's really true, isn't it?"

Leilani stood slowly and began clearing away the dishes. Her father gave some half-mumbled excuse and disappeared into his workshop. Lana stayed and helped in the kitchen, wondering why she felt so scared.

Lana prepared the potion that night after making a sunset dash to all of the apothecary shops southside of Nui'ahi. She had found, to her surprise, everything she needed, and even some things she hadn't been aware existed. She sat in the small lot outside the shop until well after the moon had risen, using the outdoor fire pit to make the slow-cooking potion. She made a mixture that one of Akua's books had said cured most fevers. Briefly, she considered using the necklace for the cooling geas, but then, in a quick spasm of guilt, slashed her palm more deeply than necessary to make up for thinking it. She didn't know which was stronger, her guilt or her curiosity, but she refused to give in to temptation. She might admire much about Akua, but she was afraid of what she might turn into if she followed her mentor's approach to sacrifice. When she finished she hauled the cauldron off the coals and poured water over them. She covered the cauldron and left the draught on the dirt right outside the door and then trudged wearily up the stairs. Her mother was sitting in the kitchen, reading by flickering lamplight. She looked up when Lana walked in and smiled wearily.

"I finished it," Lana said, pulling out another chair. "If you get sick again, drink a glass every five hours until the fever goes down."

"Thank you," she said. "I'm sorry I put you through the trouble."

"Mama ... never think I could forget how much I owe you."

Her mother squeezed her hand. "Somebody must have blessed me to have a daughter like you."

Lana left on the day after the spirit solstice, when the charms and house-luck dolls all around the city were still ablaze. The inferno at the top of the fire temple in the heart of Essel would burn for the next eight days as officiates and residents said their devotionals to the bound spirit. From the vantage of her boat, it looked as though the city was covered in smoke and flames, with the belching sentinel of Nui'ahi as its omnipresent backdrop. It looked ominous, like a picture of carnage, and not the aftermath of days of celebrations and carousing. Her ship had been sitting at the docks for more than an hour because of the unusual number of ships leaving Essel this morning. This new year marked the transition to a new Mo'i, and the number of supplicants was far greater than normal. From what Lana could tell by peering at the official ships in the harbor, at least a hundred people were all leaving today to travel to the inner fire shrine. Only one would return—the new Mo'i. She had often wondered what would compel a person to take such a risk—could so many people be so sure they would be chosen? No one knew why the fire spirit picked some over others. But as she looked at the line of supplicants—some in their teens and some who looked old enough to be great-grandparents—she wondered if desperation, not overweening self-confidence, led most of them to this decision. And was she so different? But even if life sometimes overwhelmed her, at least she hadn't yet been crushed by its weight.

Several of the supplicants looked as though they had not bathed in recent memory. She saw woman draped in ragged coats, despite the warm weather, smoothing her matted hair. Her fingers came away smeared with grease. A younger man, standing toward the back of the line, had the same kind of hollow-eyed, desperate expression, but his clothes—navy pantaloons with a white shirt and an embroidered, knee-length vest—looked respectably lived-in, as though he had not quite yet surrendered to the street. His light brown-red hair, though thinning, reminded her unexpectedly of Kohaku. She had not thought of her childhood crush in a long time, and the memories that had once been so painful now made her smile softly. The supplicant even looked like Kohaku, although his face had blurred in her memory and she could hardly trust it. It made her sad to think that this man who so resembled her first love would probably, along with all the others, be sacrificed to the fire spirit within a month. Just as her boat was finally ready to leave the harbor, the man turned around and briefly caught her eye. She thought she felt a moment of startled recognition—*could* that possibly be Kohaku?—before his eyes hardened and he looked away.

No, she thought, walking to the other side of the deck. Of course not.

Akua wasn't home. She had left a note for Lana on the table by the fireplace.

Lana,
I'm out making preparations for tonight, when I will show you the final stage of your new power. Bring the necklace. I've instructed Ino to take you to a special place in the center of the lake—don't be alarmed by anything you see there, I promise it won't hurt you.

Her name was a barely legible scrawl at the bottom of the paper. Akua's handwriting was generally indecipherable, with awkward characters squashed next to one another as they rambled across the page. Lana looked out the open door and saw Ino sitting serenely on a lotus leaf made of rippling water. He must have emerged from the lake while she was reading the letter. His liquid eyes looked somehow wary as she approached him, but she knew that there was no real way to read a water sprite's face. They simply weren't human enough.

"The witch wants me to take you to the center," he said, his voice sounding more alien than ever.

"I suppose we should go, then," she said.

Ino stared at her silently for such a long time that she began to feel uncomfortable. "Do you listen to everything she says?" he said finally. "Will you follow her blindly down the path of death? You are a diver—would you turn your back to the water?"

His words and his weird, alien anger made Lana's stomach knot. She looked at the air around him expectantly, but it remained stable. Why wasn't Akua's geas attacking him for his words? To her shame, part of her wanted it to.

"What choice do I have? The fish are gone! Akua's my teacher now. All this ... it may be sacrifice, but it's not death." She paused. "I know she's keeping things from me, Ino, but it's just ... I have to, I *want* to learn."

"You know nothing, little diver. The witch is far more than you think—you should resist her."

Lana's body tensed with anger. "So says one who has been bound by her geas for decades! Why don't *you* resist her?"

His opaque eyes seemed to soften. "At least I *know* I'm bound, Lana."

It was the first time he had ever used her name. Why did that simple fact undo all her anger?

"Why doesn't the geas attack you for saying this, Ino?"

"The witch decides," he said.

Lana stared at him—could he possibly be implying that Akua *wanted* him to say these things to her?

"If you refuse to leave," he said, "I am bound to take you to the center. Do you insist?"

Though she knew the idea of leaving was ludicrous, the strangeness of Ino's behavior almost made her consider it. Was Akua planning something dangerous? Probably. Was that reason enough to make her leave? No. Whatever this was, it was too powerful to ignore. She'd wanted Akua to teach her more powerful geas for years—she could hardly run away now that she finally had the chance.

"You should take me, Ino," she said.

The water surrounding him began to dissolve back into the lake. He held out his hand and after a moment Lana put her own inside his pale, spindly fingers.

"Then let's dive," he said, and pulled her under the water.

They were under for a long time, but the water sprite kept a bubble of air around her mouth and nose so she could breathe. He led her to the deepest parts of the lake, but curiously she never felt any pressure on her ears. The world he showed her was ethereal and terrifying, a surreal waterscape where hideously laughing faces appeared in the most unlikely locations. Even the swaying algae seemed to have glinting fish eyes and mocking coral grins. This far below, Ino's pale skin was translucent, but instead of veins she thought she saw tiny creatures, like minnows or baby fish, squirming beneath his skin. He must have sensed her sudden tension, because he turned around and smiled briefly, a sardonic grimace that made her feel even more disquieted. Still looking at her, he blew offhandedly into her face, releasing a stream of hundreds of tiny, dazzlingly bright red and gold fish. They swirled around her face and her hair for a moment before gathering together and swimming away. Lana stared at Ino, desperately trying to control her breathing and facial expression. She didn't know why he was trying to scare her, but she was determined not to let him. Seeing her frown, the smile left his face and he nodded briefly before leading her onward.

The things she saw after that were mildly unsettling, but she got the impression that the creatures of the lake were no longer putting on some kind of show for her. Perhaps ten or fifteen minutes later, he began angling upwards and Lana once again entered the more familiar parts of the lake. They emerged in an area with crystal clear water, but oddly shielded from direct sunlight by a heavy mist. In fact, even though they were mere feet away from the tiny island, she couldn't pick it out of the fog until Ino led her to a set of steps.

She called up fragments of memory from that other time she

had been here. The steps emerged from the lake itself onto the island, where an old-style temple took up most of the land. The wooden door, decorated with a key carved in bas-relief, was closed. Ino walked halfway up the steps, a film of water clinging to his pale skin.

Lana looked at him and then back at the door.

"Should I go in?" she finally asked.

"It's what she wants," he said. He settled quietly on the steps, but Lana got the impression that he was nervous being so near the temple.

"It looks like a death temple …" Lana said slowly, half to herself. "There aren't so many of those, these days."

Ino spat into the water and a fish darted away. "Perhaps you aren't so ignorant, after all."

Lana looked at the water sprite and smiled. "You know, Ino—I get it. You think this is a bad idea. I might even agree with you, but I don't see many other options and …" she shrugged, "I guess I'm curious."

Lana walked the rest of the way up the stairs and put her hand on the door, stopping just short of pushing it. "Will you wait for me?" she asked, not looking at him.

"You have my word, little diver," he said, and it was the closest thing to affection she had ever heard in that alien voice.

The temple was a simple open room, with a smooth stone floor and a few books resting on shelves inlaid on the back wall. In the center of the temple Lana saw something she could only describe as a column of air—although it was not technically a column, and it was filled with a substance Lana was fairly sure wasn't exactly air. It seemed to bore straight through the ceiling and floor with its insubstantial milky-gray mist. Within it Lana thought she could see strange shapes darting in and out of visibility—a man's face replaced by a horse's head, and then an old-style ship foundering in a storm and smashing against some rocks, the expressions of fear and agony on the faces of the passengers as they realized they were going to die—

Lana abruptly wrenched her eyes away from the column, feeling nauseated. What kind of a place was this? But she had seen that column before. Once, many years ago … She shuddered and sat abruptly on the floor, wrestling with sudden memories of a night that she had forgotten for the past four years.

Sick and rendered nearly insensible by the drugs that Akua had given her, Lana had been dragged to this temple on her first night in Akua's home. Akua stood in front of the column for a long time, holding a strange off-white-colored flute and occasionally reciting a few words in an incomprehensible language. The drugs distorted everything, but eventually Lana saw the witch put the flute to her lips and blow three brief notes. Lana grew aware of the sudden change in the air—the feeling of anticipatory power. Then, Akua had pushed Lana inside the column.

She had been terrified, but too befuddled to do anything. She felt as though she were falling through time instead of space. As she fell, she was overwhelmed with brief, confusing glimpses of a thousand people's deaths. Some were peaceful, surrounded by family, but most were sudden and painful. The sensation that she had entered the very essence of death terrified her. She saw a man dying in a horrible fire, and then a huge stone, nearly as tall as she was, with a shard of bone impossibly embedded in its middle. Whatever entity lived inside this column made her tremble with its desire; no matter what the cost, it told her, it would have that shard of bone destroyed. Just before she thought she would pass out with fear, the column of air spat her out, leaving her to huddle on the mercifully cold floor and realize that she had wet her pants.

"She will do," she had heard a voice say, and then everything faded.

Lana rocked back and forth on the floor for a long time after the memories returned, overcome with nausea as though she had just experienced it. After a while, she uncurled herself and put her hands flat on the floor. She crawled toward the back of the temple, careful to avoid glancing at the column even when she fingered the strange inscriptions carved into the blocks of stone immediately surrounding it. She stood up when she reached the few books, uncomfortably conscious of the presence at her back. She felt almost as though it was watching her.

The books here looked far older than the ones Akua kept in the cottage. Lana forgot her fear as she ran her finger curiously over their spines, picking up a thick layer of dust that she wiped absentmindedly on her pants. On a whim, she picked up a smaller volume, bound in ancient, cracking leather and filled with yellowed pages that seemed likely to crumble at any moment.

Lana sat down with her back to the wall and opened the book. On the first page she saw the older character for "observation" handwritten in inartistic but sure strokes. Something about the handwriting struck her as familiar, but she didn't quite know why. All of the characters in the book were of a far older dialect, as was the grammar, and she sometimes had to skip over whole paragraphs as incomprehensible. It read like a strange series of disjointed anecdotes and tidbits of information—an account of the choking ash rain from a minor eruption paralyzing Essel was followed by a strange geas the author had learned to let her see temporarily at night. When Lana noticed a casual reference to Yaela's recent sacrifice and binding of the water spirit, she realized with a shock how old this book must be. What she held in her hands was an account of the world before the spirit bindings—if Nui'ahi was still erupting and plagues were ravaging the cities, that meant the fire and death spirits were still unbound. A few years after this author had scribbled these observations in this book, a whole new era of civilization had begun. The thought made her feel breathless—what an incredible time in which to live! How had Akua come across such a book? She remembered Kohaku discussing the few texts that still survived from that period, and she could only imagine how much a personal account like this would be worth to the Kulanui.

After flipping through a few more pages, she noticed meticulous drawings of the outer islands, including one that wasn't often drawn on maps anymore—the wind shrine. Beneath the drawing the author had written a brief note: "Wind shrine island is too big, too far away. With no inner shrine, how long can Dahi expect to contain the spirit?"

But far more disturbing to Lana was an entry toward the back of the book.

"From an ancient witch-woman whose death I observed last night, I have learned an awesome secret, one that frightens and excites me. I realize, now, that though I have spent years searching for answers, I have been floundering in the dark until this woman revealed the secret to me. Soon, I think, I will truly understand death. She taught me a geas, one I am half-afraid to write here, despite my protections."

The next few sentences were all but unintelligible to Lana:

"… sacrifice, she warned, but the principle theorems behind this geas must be applicable to oneself as well as others. I must think on it further. For now, it will suffice to write the geas as she told me (in the traditional verse-form):

Death, the monger
Self-styled King of All
Can yet be thwarted
By those it claims to rule.
Oh, Death will come,
But not yet, not yet—
Not to those whose lives
Death cuts before their flower even fades.
I will face this Death of circumstance
Not inevitability

And take its awesome sacrifice:
To be hounded into the Inevitable.

The reciter of this geas will be hounded by the circum-
stantial death of the person they are trying to save. But the
wording, I notice, is tricky—the reciter must be hounded to
an inevitable death, which I assume means either exhaustion or old age, and not being physically slain by the death
itself. The wording makes me suspect that if that should
happen, both the reciter and the original person would die."

There were a few more entries written after this one, but Lana
had read enough. She put down the book and made the mistake of
looking up. In the column of air she saw a white mask with parallel red stripes on the cheeks that looked like a gigantic version of
the ones worn by performers during the demon holiday. Its eyeholes were filled with fire and the smiling cutout mouth somehow
seemed to be laughing. Lana scrambled up from her place on the
floor and ran out the door, slamming it shut behind her.

Ino was still sitting on the steps. He glanced up at her, looking
inexpressibly sad.

"You didn't like what you saw?" he asked.

Lana's legs felt like jelly and she sat down next to him. "I don't
really know what I saw," she said, "but no, I didn't like it."

She and Ino sat in silence as they waited for the witch-woman
to come.

At some unseen signal, Ino left her so he could lead Akua to the
temple. She came in the boat, which floated much lower in the
water than usual because of her heavy cargo. Evening had fallen.
Lana had a hard time seeing Akua's expression through the mist,
but she thought that her teacher looked almost resigned.

"So, you came," Akua said when she stepped out of the boat
and onto the steps.

"Thought you could scare me off? You said something about the necklace."

Akua nodded. "Well then. Bring that inside," she said, gesturing to a brown sack in the back of the boat. She went inside the temple as Lana staggered under the bag's weight and struggled to haul it up the stairs.

When she entered the temple and deposited the bag on the floor, she saw Akua picking up the book Lana had dropped in her haste to leave earlier. Akua stared at her appraisingly and then, without saying a word, put the book back on the shelf.

"Upend the bag," Akua said, as the door shut behind them. Lana complied and watched, amazed, as hundreds upon hundreds of linked charms spilled out. Most were made of bone, like the one around Akua's neck now, but some were carved from pieces of wood and she thought she even spotted a pair of white mandagah jewels. Each charm had its match, and she wondered why Akua would go through the trouble of making bonded charms without giving one of the pair to a willing sacrifice.

"These charms represent an immeasurable amount of power. I'm getting older, I live a relatively quiet life. I have no real need for them anymore. But your time with me is ending, Lana—I've taught you nearly all I can and I want to give you something that will help you when you're on your own."

Akua looked completely sincere as she said this, and Lana relaxed. Ino had worried her over nothing. But she was surprised at the mixture of anger and loss she felt at the thought of leaving Akua. There was so much more she had yet to learn, she was sure of it, but she supposed that Akua had never promised to turn her into a master of the spirits. She knew more than enough to support herself as a healer, now.

"But how can I use so many of these?" she asked, staring at the enormous pile in front of them.

"You can't. But that's why we're here—tonight we'll transfer their power to your red mandagah jewel. There are few self-sacrifices, even, that are more powerful."

Something about Akua's suggestion made her nervous. Some of those necklaces looked ancient, like they had stories they were desperate to tell—stories that she didn't really want to know. But Akua looked expectant, and Lana couldn't think of a reasonable way to refuse her. After all, wasn't this what she had always wanted since becoming Akua's apprentice? A chance at real power?

Finally, Lana nodded. "What do we have to do?"

At Akua's instruction, she pushed the necklaces across the floor until they were right in front of the column of air. Though Lana tried not to look, the guilty glances she stole made her think that the strange presence inside the column was more agitated than it had been before. The air was swirling maniacally, with images appearing and morphing and disappearing too quickly for Lana to even recognize them. She tried to suppress her sudden trepidation—she wished that she were outside with Ino instead of in here, performing a task she didn't understand.

"When I invoke the geas, push the necklaces into the altar. Then you and I step inside at the same time." She looked hard at Lana, who suddenly felt like she wanted to vomit. "This could be danger-ous, Lana. It's imperative while we are inside that you do every-thing I say. Do you understand?" Akua's eyes held a dark intensity that Lana had never seen there before, but she took a deep breath and nodded.

Akua straightened and pulled the bone key necklace from un-der her shirt. She gripped it and closed her eyes, but right before Lana expected her to begin the geas she opened them again and smiled ironically.

"I really like you, Lana," she said. "I wasn't expecting to, but I do. I guess that makes this harder."

Lana returned the smile. She supposed odd moments of un-expected affection had always been part of their relationship. "I like you too. I'll miss being your apprentice."

Akua's smile grew even more sardonic. She looked at Lana for an uncomfortably long moment before closing her eyes.

Like a womb-sister, like a self-bound star, I call the power of the bond.

The skin on Lana's legs and the back of her neck began to prickle and her unbound hair rippled slightly in a breeze her skin didn't feel. Akua stood there for a very long time, and it seemed that the air around them gradually grew too thick to breathe. It was heavy with power—a level of power that Lana had never felt before. This was far more than what Lana had drawn when she first bound the two mandagah jewels together. She half-expected to see spirits waiting in the shadows, but only sensed the agitated presence inside the column of air. How was it that no other spirits were summoned by this influx of power? When the time came that Lana was afraid the walls would crack with it, Akua finally ceased the flow of sacrificial energy and opened her eyes. She inclined her head toward the pile of necklaces. Feeling as though she were moving through molasses and panting with the effort, Lana pushed them all inside the column of air. They scattered, blown apart by the terrifying fury of a storm, made all the more intimidating because she couldn't hear anything at all. She was trembling when she looked back at Akua, unable to keep her hands from shaking even when she pulled the mandagah jewel out from under her shirt. Akua's lips were in a grim, determined line. The older woman gripped Lana's elbow firmly and, with a shove that didn't even allow Lana time to scream, led them both into the maelstrom.

The wind that shrieked past her sounded like a thousand people wailing in chorus. It grated at her and made her teeth ache, but she didn't dare plug her ears. There was nothing beneath her feet, but she didn't feel the same sensation of falling that she remembered from the last time she entered the column—in fact, it looked as though she and Akua were floating. The necklaces swirled madly around them, nicking Lana's skin. A particularly jagged edge of one necklace gashed her forehead right above her left eye, but before the blood could drip down, a pair of blue lips materialized out of the air and began sucking it away.

"Stop it!" Lana screamed as she swatted away the lips.

"Stop it! Stop it!" came the mocking echoes of the screams around her, each one louder than the last. The lips before her grinned and then, with a spray of spit, stuck out a bright blue tongue and vanished. Lana forced herself to breathe. She looked pleadingly at Akua, whose face seemed like it was glowing. The necklaces hadn't touched her skin at all.

The witch held up her hand and the fierce storm around them suddenly stopped. A hand emerged from the mist, covered in brown-green scales with six incredibly long tapered fingers that rolled and unrolled themselves with a thousand tiny pops. The longest of those fingers hooked around Lana's necklace and delicately held it up before her eyes. The red jewel was glowing with the intensity and heat of a burning coal, and Lana flinched away from it. The other necklaces surrounded her, each suspended on a long, tapered finger like the one holding her mandagah jewel.

A long knife appeared in the air before Akua and stabbed her viciously several times. The wind screams began again, cackling with laughter, as Lana gasped. To her surprise though, instead of collapsing, Akua frowned and waved her hand—suddenly the blood and the knife disappeared and Lana realized that she must have been looking at an illusion. Akua gripped the key necklace again and the air stilled.

> *The sacrifice of make-lai is not dying,*
> *but the tithe of another life.*
> *And this, the tithe,*
> *accepts the thousand sacrifices of make-lai*
> *for power.*

In the dead calm Akua looked hard at Lana, who gulped down air but couldn't seem to fill her lungs.

"Iolana bei'Leilani," she intoned, her voice driving shards into Lana's brain. "Do you accept the tithe? Do you accept the power? Do you accept the sacrifices?"

Lana looked around wildly, only to see a thousand grinning mouths above each of the necklaces. "Do you? Do you?" some of them screamed, while still others urged her "No, say no to the witch, Iolana bei'Leilani. Let her keep her sacrifices."

Why was Akua's expression so tense, so almost hopeful? Where were they? What would she be agreeing to? She knew enough about the ways of power to know that her answer was vital. One last chance to refuse ... but she already knew she wouldn't.

"Yes," Lana said.

The mouths screamed.

The jewel seemed to explode in front of her face. For a second in the overpowering light she thought she saw her mother, collapsed at the foot of the stairs, gasping for air as Kapa called for help. Lana passed out under a bright red explosion of pain.

The early morning sunlight filtered gently on her face through the mist. The sound of water lapping against the sides of the boat nearly lulled her back into sleep, but the sudden memory of the geas in the death temple made her grasp frantically for her necklace. The jewel was still there—it hadn't been destroyed. Then she remembered the strange vision she had seen just before passing out—of her mother nearly dying at the foot of the steps. She sat up abruptly, rocking the boat so that water splashed inside.

"What is it, Lana?" Akua asked, leaning back in the boat with a weary expression.

Lana shook her head. "My mother ..." she said slowly, "I think something's happened ..."

She leaned over the edge and saw Ino's face a few feet beneath the water. The boat stopped.

"What do you want, little diver?" he asked.

"My mother," she said, struggling to rein in her disorientation and her panic. "Show me my mother."

She sensed Akua's curiosity behind her, but didn't care. Ino spread his hands and the surface of the water above them became unnaturally smooth. Colors began to shift and, after a moment, she recognized the inside of her parents' house. The image was inside their bedroom. Her mother was lying on her sleeping mat, shivering uncontrollably despite the covers piled on top of her. Kapa was trying to force her to take the draught Lana had left with them but her mother could hardly keep her mouth open long enough to swallow it. Ino's scrying didn't let her hear anything, but she didn't need to—the vision inside the death temple had been correct. Her mother was dying.

She splashed her hand in the water. "I don't want to see anymore," she said hoarsely. Tears began to dribble down her cheeks and she couldn't stop them. What was going on? Ino looked at her sadly and then descended under the water. After a few moments, the boat began moving again.

"I have to leave," Lana said, holding her head in her hands. It still ached from whatever had happened in the temple.

"How did you bind Ino to a scrying without a geas?" Akua asked.

Lana shrugged. "I asked because I thought he might." Her smile was ironic. "Maybe I gave him the sacrifice of friendship." She raised her voice. "Ino," she said, knowing the sprite could hear her. "Take me to the village. I'm going to Essel."

She spent the money that Akua had given her on the fastest ships, but still the trip took her three days. During those long, restless, hours, she wondered if she would be too late. But surely she would sense it if her mother died? She knew she had to try to save her, but in Ino's scrying it had looked as though Leilani's illness was too far along. On the second day she remembered the terrifying geas in that ancient book in the death temple. A few hours before she arrived, she resolved to use it. Her mother had sacrificed too many things for Lana to hesitate now. Her mother didn't deserve to die so young. Lana would do whatever was necessary to save her.

Lana sprinted until her breath burned in her throat, arriving at her parents' shop in half the time it usually took her to walk from the harbor. A blue cloth on the door indicated that the shop was closed, but the door was open and Lana shoved her way through it. She ran up the stairs and halted in the doorway of her parents' room, panting. After a moment she wiped sweat from her eyes and looked up. Her father stared at her like she was a ghost, but her mother, piled under blankets just like she had seen in the scrying, didn't seem aware of her presence.

"Lana?" her father finally said, quietly.

She nodded and tried to catch her breath. "I saw ... I came to help."

He glanced at his wife and then stood up and walked toward her. "She's dying," he said. Though she had already known it, hearing the words spoken aloud made the bottom drop out of her stomach. Her throat ached.

"A doctor came this morning ... he said it was a matter of hours. Your drink was probably the only thing keeping her alive this long." A few tears dripped out of his eyes and he wiped them away angrily.

Her father looked older, she noticed, far older than he should have. His heavy eyebrows were beginning to turn gray and his eyes held a look of world-weary sadness that was painful for her to meet.

"Papa," she said, "I don't know if I'll see you again. I love you."

She hugged him and then walked to where her mother was tossing deliriously. The illness had ravaged her body—half of her hair had turned gray and her skin was ashen. Lana bit on her tongue to keep from crying out and knelt down.

"Mama," she said, smoothing back her mother's hair. "I came back."

Leilani opened her eyes, but didn't seem to recognize Lana. She muttered something incomprehensible and then sank back into unconsciousness. It was near the end—Lana only had a few minutes to perform the geas before it would be too late. Still, her hand hesitated when she went to touch the mandagah jewel around her neck. She had decided what to do, but the prospect still terrified her—to be pursued to her death by the horror she had briefly experienced inside the temple?

"If you don't, Mama will die," she said under her breath. "She'll *die*," she said louder, and stared crying.

She felt Kapa's hand on her shoulder and looked up.

"What is it, Lana?" he asked. "What—" He broke off. After a moment Lana realized that he must have seen her necklace.

"Where did you ..." He almost sounded scared.

Lana stared at his feet, tears still streaming from her eyes. "My first dive ... I found two jewels. The blue one ... and this." After a moment she dared look at his face and nearly recoiled from the horror there.

"A dying mandagah?"

She nodded.

"Why didn't you ever tell us? All this time, you were marked ..."

He sat down next to her and Lana swallowed. "Papa ... I'm going to try to save Mama. Whatever happens, don't speak or move."

She waited for his nod and then turned to Leilani.

The twin jewels of a dying spirit's last gift—I call the power of the bond.

She felt the sacrificial force flood the room and she allowed it to continue until she found it difficult to breathe and the air seemed permeated by a bright haze. It felt different than the power Akua had called in the death temple, though—stronger, and yet more tainted. Suddenly, as though she were back inside the column of air, she saw a thousand faces of death laughing at her. She had fleeting, terrifying glimpses of people dying all around her—and through it all she felt, insistently, the subtle yet horrible tie to Pua's life force. Lana's hands were trembling and she could barely push her voice past her throat, but she forced herself to recite the geas. She had called the power—there could be no turning back.

Death, the monger, she began, and tossed herself over the edge.

A hunched figure in blazingly white robes stood over her mother's body and looked down at Lana. She couldn't read its expression because it wore a mask like the one she had seen in the column of air—white with parallel red stripes across the cheeks. There was also a black dot in the center of its forehead that seemed far less like a part of the mask than an infinitely deep hole. At its waist hung a silver chain with a key weighing down the middle.

Lana forgot to breathe.

This was her mother's death.

Her mother opened her eyes and looked at Lana with comprehension for the first time. "Lana? What are you doing here?"

Lana glanced at her and shook her head silently. What would the death do now? Her father let out a wordless shriek of joy and hugged Leilani fiercely. Lana stared at them, disbelieving. Couldn't they see what had happened? Didn't they know that the death was still standing over her mother's body?

"Only you can see me, Iolana bei'Leilani," a voice said. She realized that it must be the death's, but it didn't seem to have a point of origin. "You have summoned me. No one has done so in a very, very long time. I might enjoy this game before I return to take your mother."

"You will not have her," Lana said, her fury winning out over terror.

It laughed. "That remains to be seen. Will you make the opening gambit, or should I just take you both now?"

Lana swallowed and forced herself to think. The only option available, she decided, was to run back to Akua and beg for her help—she knew almost nothing about the geas she had just recited and her ignorance would endanger her mother's life. She would have to use a geas to travel back, but even the thought of using the mandagah jewel again made her feel sick. The feeling of its power had subtly changed; it felt dirty and painful. And to think—she had wanted this. She had thought such power would buy her freedom. The irony was bitter enough to make bile rise in her throat. But she had done what was needed, and nothing could convince her to use the necklace again. Which left her with one other option: a non-regenerative self-sacrifice.

"Papa ..." she said, voice quavering. "Could you get me a knife? A nice, sharp one?"

Her father must have sensed the urgency in her voice, because he left without comment. He returned with one of his whittling knives, which would be good for what she had in mind.

"Ah, so you've decided," the thing said. "I await with anticipation." It glided across the floor from over her mother's body to stop a few feet in front of her. She realized that its body was translucent—she could still see her parents through its robe.

She watched them staring at her as she raised the knife to her ear and, with as steady a hand as she could manage, sliced off her left earlobe. She heard her mother's gasp vaguely through a haze of pain. The blood from her ear dripped onto the small piece of flesh that she kept in her cupped palm.

"The wind I hear screaming past my window has traveled to the world's far places. Take this sacrifice and carry me on the far-traveling wind to a witch named Akua."

The window behind her parents blew open.

"I love you, Mama," Lana said. Then the gust tore her from the floor and pushed her out the window, hurtling away from the smoking sentinel of Nui'ahi and back toward the one woman who could help her.

Akua was standing outside the cottage when the wind tossed Lana to the ground on the muddy embankment by the lake. The white death, which had followed her here close behind, looked at Akua for a moment and then bowed. The older woman inclined her head.

"Lana, what have you done?"

"I took my mother's death," she said. "I read about the geas and I did it."

"You did, Lana?" Akua said softly, staring at the death. "You're resourceful, aren't you? I ... I wasn't expecting this to end quite this way. But you can't survive this on your own ... come inside."

Lana picked herself up from the mud and brushed locks of sweaty brown hair from her eyes. Akua looked relatively calm, which helped reduce the sharp edge of terror Lana felt. Lana stared at the death and then scurried inside the house. It attempted to follow her in, but Akua held out her hand.

"You cannot cross this threshold. You know that."

"She's my quarry, now. You can't help her."

"She came of her own free will. This once, it is my right."

She and the death hesitated for a moment before it inclined its head and backed away from the doorway. Akua shut the door and turned around.

"We don't have much time," she said, gesturing for Lana to follow her. She walked to the pit where they hung the cauldron and told Lana to scoop out the cold ashes. Lana's hands turned black before she before she revealed a false brick bottom with a small handle. When she pulled that off she saw a small, narrow wooden box. Akua removed it carefully, brushing off the soot and dust. She pulled off the top of the case, revealing a narrow flute made of bone, about as long as her forearm. Akua stroked it once and then handed it to Lana.

"This is the single most powerful object you will ever see," she said. "I give it to you willingly, because it's probably the only thing that will keep you alive. Playing it invokes the sacrifice ... a great sacrifice."

Lana looked at her mentor's expression and suddenly realized what it must be. "Your arm?" she asked.

Akua nodded. "The greatest sacrifice." She stood up. "I can give you some time, to help you bind it this once. But after that, you must not come back here. Ever. Do you understand? I can't do anything more to help you."

The blood coming from her ear had slowed to a trickle, but the whole left side of her face ached. She was terrified and exhausted, but she had no other choice but to leave. Lana stood reluctantly and followed Akua to the doorway. The death was waiting right outside the door, its key swaying from side to side like some strange metallic appendage.

"Hand me the flute," Akua said. Lana did so and watched as Akua blew a few brief notes—a snatch of a melancholy melody—with just one hand. The rush of anticipatory power was instantaneous.

"Does death ever understand the sadness of its own existence? Could it ever understand such a song?"

It didn't sound much like a geas to Lana, but the death stilled. The corners of its mask-mouth began, impossibly, to turn up.

"Six hours," it said. "I'll give her six hours to get away. Contemplating my own melancholy, I won't even be sure where she is."

Its sarcasm was palpable and Lana wondered at the familiarity between the witch and the death. They spoke like old friends. Akua pressed the flute and a few hundred-kala coins into Lana's hand. "Be careful," she said. "Survive."

"You'd be better off saying sorry," Lana heard the death say as she ran to the lake. She jumped inside the boat and paddled as quickly as she could before she felt Ino beneath her, speeding toward the town.

She wondered why she hadn't heard Akua respond.

PART II

Place of Hidden Things

· 9 ·

EACH DAY HAD STRETCHED OUT BLEAKER THAN THE LAST after Emea died. Homeless after the lavish funeral he'd given her, Kohaku had worked odd jobs that paid enough to feed him but never enough to afford a roof. He had considered and discarded the idea of suicide a hundred times before he found himself drunk on cheap palm wine one night, climbing to the top of a giant pagoda on the east side of the fire temple complex. In a drunken haze, he contemplated almost rapturously the thought of tossing himself from its heights. But as he stood there he had noticed an unusually large gathering of people around a few bonfires in the courtyard in front of the main temple. Temple officiates were serving them food, he realized, and the smell of a solstice feast brought him back far enough to himself to realize what he was doing.

So he had climbed back down the roof and went to see what was happening. It turned out the people were supplicants, about to risk everything for a chance to become Mo'i. A group of around a hundred would leave the next morning on ships making the journey to the frigid inner islands. As he munched reflectively on a slice of still-hot currant bread, he decided to add his name to the list. If he failed, as he almost certainly would, at least he would have found an honorable way out of his misery. If he succeeded—and the thought nearly made him drop his bread with the flood of pleasure that it brought—he could take revenge on Nahe.

The next morning, just before they left, Kohaku saw a passenger who looked just like that girl Lana from the outer islands, staring at him from another ship in the harbor. It couldn't possibly be Lana, he knew, but the look in her eyes—like she was reproaching him for his decision—made him look away angrily. He could feel her staring at him for a few more minutes, but when he looked back up she had gone.

He thought about that girl a lot, after the ship left the harbor and he awaited his probable doom. She had been one of his best students, he remembered—he'd even asked her to return to the Kulanui with him, so she could continue her studies there. That all seemed so long ago now. But thinking of Lana was something to focus on, to help him forget his life of the past few months and to ignore the increasingly squalid quarters he shared with supplicants of similar social standing. Though every penitent for Mo'i was granted free and safe passage to the fire temple, the ones regarded more or less as temple fodder were given quarters even more cramped than the sailors. The current Mo'i's son and a few other upper-class adventurers had been given far more sumptuous apartments on a boat traveling ahead of theirs.

Kohaku spent most of his time on deck, huddled inside his flimsy coat and staring at the jagged icebergs that the crew exhausted themselves avoiding. If the wind was with them, they might arrive in another week. If not, it might take as long as three. Kohaku didn't really care, one way or another. He was just grateful to have a goal again—even if that goal was probably his imminent death.

One of the sailors, a tall woman with pretty green eyes, grabbed a coiled rope resting at his feet. He smiled a little at her and said a greeting. She looked around and then greeted him back before climbing the rigging. Though the crew wasn't supposed to speak to or even acknowledge the supplicants—who were to spend their time reflecting and preparing for the upcoming trial—they had grown so accustomed to his presence that they often seemed to forget. Besides, the most he ever thought about the upcoming trial was the prospect of getting a bath. They had each been promised a bath and a fresh set of clothes once they arrived at the fire shrine. It had always seemed strange to him that the stronghold of the essence of fire should be in such a frigid, lifeless place as the inner islands. Well, he supposed they weren't completely lifeless—he saw an occasional albatross flying overhead, and there were rumors among the students at the Kulanui that the islands were home to a peculiar kind of fat, flightless bird. The idea of seeing the shrine might have interested him three months ago, but he found that he had almost completely lost his desire for academic pursuits. Maybe Nahe had burned it out of him.

The woman climbed back down the rigging with a bit of frayed rope in her hand.

"Good sailing weather?" Kohaku asked her.

She looked surprised and then nodded. "We'll probably get there in four more days. The fastest it's ever been for me."

He had figured as much, but the thought of arriving so soon made him feel suddenly melancholy. He supposed that he had gotten used to the sea, even in such a short time.

The woman noticed his expression fall and put her hand to her mouth, then swore—just like any other sailor, Kohaku thought, amused. "I'm sorry," she said. From her accent, he guessed that she was from one of the rice farming islands, about halfway between Essel and the ruined wind shrine. "Guess that's why they don't want us talking to you. This is my first time, though. Some of the others have taken three ships with the supplicants. It sounds wild … all those people going and only one coming back." Her eyes suddenly focused back on him and she swore again. "Sorry—I did it again. I'm sure you don't want to be reminded … I mean …" She was blushing vibrantly as she stared at him. Maybe he was just feeling starved for affection, but he found that he enjoyed her coarse tongue. Though he had always considered his sister to be the ideal of feminine beauty, he had to admit that there was something appealing about this tall girl's wide, sturdy frame. Her dark auburn hair was pulled into a bun at the base of her neck.

He smiled. "Don't worry about it. What's your name?"

"Nahoa," she said, leaning closer toward him. Something about the position felt intimate.

He smiled at her. "If I'm still alive in six days, Nahoa, will you come back to Essel with me and be a Mo'i's first wife?" He didn't know why he said it. He felt as though some cloud had descended over both of their heads—dense enough for him to forget that he had come here to die.

She frowned at him, but the corners of her lips kept turning up. "I ... you must be crazy!" Then she swore again, unable to keep from smiling.

"Will you?" he asked.

"What kind of a question is that? I don't even know your name!"

"Kohaku," he said, wondering why he had chosen this, of all times, to feel the stirrings of happiness. "Will you?"

She looked up at the sound of a shout from the rigging. "It's ... I'm on for lookout. I have to go."

Still, she didn't move. Kohaku smiled a little bitterly. "The overwhelming odds are I'll be dead in six days. If by some miracle I'm not, would it be so bad? You seem like ... a good person. I've been needing a good person lately."

Her green eyes looked entirely guileless, like she was actually moved by an awkward proposal from a disgraced assistant professor who hadn't shaved or taken a bath in at least a month.

There was another shout from the rigging. "Later," she said as she jumped on the spiderweb of ropes. "I'll give you my answer later."

Three days later, the night before they arrived at the fire shrine, Nahoa caught Kohaku's eye when he was quietly eating dinner with the other supplicants. He made some excuse and found her on the other side of the deck, twiddling with long curly hair that she had, for some reason, released from its bun.

"I've ... well, I've decided," she said.

He found that he was actually nervous. He had made the proposal in a moment of temporary insanity, but as he had thought about it over the next few days and surreptitiously watched her interacting with the rest of the crew, he felt oddly certain that she was the one woman that he would ever want. His previous relationships had been sporadic and half-hearted—he probably hadn't even been with a woman since he began at the Kulanui. Since then he had only indulged in the occasional furtive tryst with a fellow student. As he waited, he was for some reason reminded of how he had felt those many years ago, waiting for Lana's response to his offer to study at the Kulanui. He remembered how angry—and hurt, probably—he had felt then.

She sighed. "This is dumb. I know this is dumb because I know you'll be dead in a few days and then where will I be? That's why they tell us not to talk to you, I bet. Oh damn, I have no idea what I'm getting into." She looked at him expectantly.

"Well ..." he ventured after a few moments, "what's your answer?"

"Yes. It's yes, all right? I know this is crazy." She exhaled, and then looked at him with a scowl. "But you better promise not to die or I'll be really, really pissed off."

Even her frown was endearing. It made her look about ten years younger. He smiled and touched a bit of her hair that had fallen over her shoulder.

"Did you take that down for me?" he asked.

She nodded, avoiding his eyes. "Well ... I figured I couldn't just look like I normally do, for something like this. My mother never thought it would happen for me, you know. She wasn't even that upset when I joined a ship. Thought it would give me something to do. Well, and she also said it was my best feature. My hair, I mean. Said I looked a bit like a horse with it up, but I never really cared."

"I'm glad that you said yes," Kohaku said. The air was freezing, but the moonlight looked eerily beautiful on the ice floes and he didn't feel as cold as he should. "I'm ... glad."

She didn't say anything, but put her arm around his back and they stayed like that for a very long time, staring at the icy half-moon.

The fire shrine was nestled between two massive snow-covered mountain ranges, about three hours away from the natural harbor by sled. Hairy, massive, lumbering creatures the likes of which Kohaku had never seen before drew five supply-laden sleds at a time. The animals looked gentle enough, and didn't seem to mind the snow and ice encrusting their shaggy fur. Still, the sight of those long, curved, dangerously pointed tusks peeking out from beside their impossibly long noses made him wonder how tame they could really be. They each had two riders perched inside a covered basket that he supposed served as a saddle. The first rider faced forward and gave instructions to the rider manipulating the harness and reins.

The sight of the huge, tusked beasts, as well as the sudden realization that they were hours away from probable death, had made a few of the supplicants rethink their decisions—they were being held in the back of one of the sled trains, bound by ropes and gagged. Everyone was free to make the pilgrimage, but once begun, it had to be finished. Strangely, the thought of trying to escape didn't even cross Kohaku's mind as he left the ship and shivered on the freezing volcanic rocks in the harbor. Meeting Nahoa had done something to him—it made the prospect of what he was about to do have more hope than desperation. She waved to him from the deck just before the sleds began their journey across the featureless white expanse of snow. He held in his mind the image of her face, red with cold (and maybe even tears), as they drew closer to the fire shrine. But when he thought of Emea, he felt oddly guilty. How could he have found someone who made him happy just months after his sister had died so horribly? Of course, he reminded himself, his biggest reason for coming here was to grasp at a last opportunity to take revenge on Nahe. Meeting Nahoa had just given him another reason to succeed.

Long after his hands and nose had gone numb, the sleds slowed to make their way single-file through the mountain pass that would take them to the fire shrine. Jagged mounds of ice-covered stone towered on either side of them. Ahead, Kohaku saw that the sun was already beginning to set—daylight lasted for only five or six hours here. Their passage through the mountains was silent except for the rhythmic shuffle of the beasts' feet and the occasional whispered direction from the front riders. The rest of them had been instructed to remain as silent as possible during this part of the journey—the ice and snow on the rocks was highly unstable and loud voices could set off an avalanche that would bury them all.

It was actually amusing, Kohaku thought, how silent they all were—as though they thought being buried under falling snow would be worse than the death by fire that awaited them in the shrine. Surely the thought of achieving a more peaceful death had occurred to some of the supplicants—but the silence held and the procession reached its destination safely.

The fire shrine was a huge complex built on a low plateau before a gigantic, steaming crater lake. It was constructed, of course, entirely out of the pink-veined marble that could only be quarried on this island, and was otherwise used to make the hundred-kala coin. He saw similar expressions on the faces of the other supplicants around him—trying, and failing, to decide how much money was contained in the very stone of the main building.

The shrine officiates led the supplicants up the steep staircase that took them to the bridge over the crater lake. The steam smelled of sulfur and some other element, and the water seemed to be changing colors. Kohaku wondered what would happen if anyone fell in. They followed a gravel path that took them away from the main entrance and to a relatively small building toward the back of the temple.

"This is the bath house," said an officiate slowly, enunciating his words like one would for a small child. "Ten of you are allowed inside at a time. After you all receive your garments, you will be led to a chapel where you will spend the night in silent contemplation. The trials will begin in the morning."

A murmur of sudden trepidation went through them as the twenty or so women were led away and taken to a different entrance. Kohaku was allowed inside with the second group, and he marveled at the warmth of the bath house, especially considering the temperature outside. He took off his clothes and shoes in the anteroom and walked slowly on the warm tiles of the arcade. To his left were buckets and a series of pumps with a bar of soap and a razor blade beside each. Kohaku shaved and scrubbed his body thoroughly—long after most of the other men were finished—before getting inside the steaming pool. His muscles were just beginning to unknot when an officiate directed them into a dressing chamber. They were each given simple white drawstring pants, a long-sleeved shirt, wool socks, and straw sandals before being forced back out into the frigid air. The walk to the chapel, which was deep underneath the shrine, took nearly fifteen minutes. When they arrived, the first things Kohaku noticed were the intricate mosaics covering every wall, lit beautifully by a large fire in the center of the room. He then noticed that for the first time since they began their journey, the two groups of supplicants—the rabble and those of high society—were together. After the last of the supplicants was herded inside the chapel, the officiates slammed the door and he heard the unmistakable sound of a bolt sliding home. There was no way to escape.

As the night wore on and his tailbone began to ache, Kohaku thought of Nahoa and Emea. But most of all, he thought of Nahe and the pleasure he would feel strangling that man with his own entrails.

He was called late the next day, when only a handful of supplicants remained. As the day wore on, more and more of them had to be forced outside the door, blubbering and crying. The sight would have made Kohaku sick to his stomach had he not felt oddly detached from the whole situation. Even the more respectable supplicants—those who were left, anyway—looked at the dwindling numbers of people in the room with a hard-eyed wariness, and the dates and palm wine that had been provided for them remained untouched. When a female officiate, flanked by a burly man whose purpose was clearly enforcement, tapped him on his shoulder, he barely felt anything other an odd excitement. The stairs she led him down were so deep that toward the bottom they were little more than notches hewn in stone. At the bottom was an ancient wooden door with a crude, disturbing snake carved into it.

"Do you sacrifice willingly for the fire spirit?" she asked him in a voice devoid of all inflection.

"Yes," Kohaku said.

The burly man opened the door and, with a shove, sent him staggering inside.

Kohaku's first, terrifying, impression was that he was not going to have a chance after all—they had simply tossed him in a roomful of fire to burn alive. But when he noticed that his skin still hadn't charred, he looked around more carefully. The only fire in the long rectangular room, he realized, was a huge blue-white flame in the center of a circle of ash. The walls were covered with perfect mirrors that reflected the flames to infinity, and made it seem as though they could reach out to burn him at any second.

"You haven't started wailing," said a morose voice that wasn't recognizably male or female. It seemed entirely disembodied from any source, but Kohaku assumed that it must emanate from the tower of blue fire. He tried to avoid looking at the ring of ashes surrounding it before he realized that the rest of the floor was strewn with them too.

"Ah, you must be thinking that you're surrounded by death, but that's a mistake. You're surrounded by *sacrifice*. Some more willing than others. I always hope for more unwilling supplicants, but they have trained you well. They keep their hold over me."

Trembling, Kohaku stepped closer to the fire. Sweat cooled on his skin. There was a dark object, he noticed, at the heart of the fire—like an everlasting candlewick for an everlasting flame.

"Are you going to … will I be a sacrifice?" Kohaku ventured. He didn't quite know what else to say.

"Do you want to be?" The voice sounded slightly sardonic.

"Well, I …" the sight of the flame reminded him painfully of his last sight of Emea, falling in the lava of Nui'ahi. "I wouldn't mind," he said.

The flames leapt, hot enough to singe the hair on Kohaku's arms.

It laughed. "Wrong answer."

Heat seared his closed eyelids. He thought he was going to die. But maybe that would have been a mercy.

When it was all over, after he had watched the dozens of remaining supplicants burned into pillars of ash by raging flame, they carried him up from the bowels of the shrine on a reed stretcher. At least a hundred people had gathered in the main hall to bow as he was hurried to the surgery. The priest who served as the doctor looked at his arm with an expression of barely contained surprise. Kohaku tensed when he gently examined his blackened hand, but the man did nothing more than grimace with sympathetic pain. Of course, Kohaku thought in some part of his mind that wasn't clouded with agony, no one here could possibly know what had happened.

"I'm sorry, but I'm going to have to cut off your left hand," the man said gently. "It's too badly burned."

But how will I talk to Emea? Kohaku thought frantically. Then he remembered that Emea was dead.

With effort, he nodded. The pain in his arm was beginning to make him lose all sense of time or place. "Just … give it to me afterwards … please." The man looked surprised, but he nodded. Kohaku closed his eyes—those ashes had seared their way into his hand. He didn't want to just throw them away.

"Is that really necessary?"

Kohaku's eyes flew open and he struggled to sit up. She was

seated on a chest of supplies in the corner, smiling. And that impossible voice—so dimly remembered, so immediately hateful.

Hands pressed him down, voices soothed him. It seemed that no one else could see her. Blue flames leapt in the hollows of her irises.

"Oh, keep whatever grisly tokens you want. Just try not to show it to that sailor. Well, not if you want to marry her, anyway."

Kohaku shook. In life, she had never been so callous, so biting. "Why are you—"

She stood. "Just a reminder, dear brother. Take my revenge."

Someone forced a drink down his throat and he floated gratefully into unconsciousness.

Three days later, wrapped in sumptuous down blankets edged in fur that hid the heavily bandaged, handless arm that was bound beneath his shirt, he and a much smaller team of sleds made their way back to the docks.

He was still light-headed with pain. They had wanted him to stay for much longer, but he had felt a sudden urgency to get back to Nahoa and tell her that he hadn't died after all. He had thought about her a lot as he lay in a bed softer than any he had ever felt, suffering a pain that threatened to make him delirious. The image of the tall, foul-mouthed sailor with warm eyes was far more comforting than that of his sister. Emea's voice haunted his unguarded moments. Her demands for revenge made him want to weep and wonder if he had lost his mind. The fire had tainted Emea, but Nahoa was still unsullied. He fell asleep on the ride back, only to be awakened by one of his attendants' exceedingly gentle hand on his right shoulder.

"We've arrived, my lord," he said softly.

For a second Kohaku wondered who the man was talking to. He still hadn't come to terms with the fact that he was now Mo'i—he could barely believe that he was alive and that Nahoa was going to marry him.

Careful arms helped him out of the sleigh and made sure he was steady on the ground before releasing him. He scanned the faces of the crews leaning out over the bows of the ships, but to his disappointment, he didn't see Nahoa anywhere. He followed his attendants silently, wondering where she was and if she was avoiding him because she had rethought her decision. They were about to load him into a bosun's chair before he realized that he was standing in front of a different ship.

"Wait!" he said, whirling around and staggering a little. "This is the wrong ship."

The man he was talking to looked confused. "But … it's the one that will take you to Essel, my lord. Your triumphant return."

Kohaku finally realized that this must have been the ship that took the richer supplicants to the island. Of course they would use that ship to bring the Mo'i back to Essel. But Nahoa wasn't on it, and he had to find out, one way or another, if she wanted him. For all he knew, maybe word of his disfigurement had already reached her and she was repulsed by it.

"I have to find someone in the other ship. Then we can leave." Kohaku said it calmly, because he realized that no matter how much his arm hurt, it would be an inauspicious way to start his reign as Mo'i if his own attendants thought he was insane.

The man nodded slowly and called a few others to follow him as Kohaku walked back over the rocky ground to the other ship. The crew was now talking loudly among themselves, probably speculating as to why he hadn't boarded.

"I'm looking for a sailor," Kohaku called up, ignoring the immediate snickers. "Her name is Nahoa. Is she here?"

"Yeah, she's here, but she won't leave her hammock. Says she's sick. What do you want with her?" The man who spoke looked weathered and important enough to be a captain.

"What business of it is yours?" said Kohaku's attendant angrily. "If the Mo'i wants the girl, then you'd damn well better get her!"

The captain hesitated and then shrugged and pointed to a young boy nearby. "You. Go get Nahoa."

The boy scurried off and Kohaku waited, suddenly nervous. He wished that he didn't have to do this in front of all these eyes, but he supposed that he didn't have a choice. A few minutes later, the boy came back dragging Nahoa, who was yelling out her objections to all who would listen.

"I don't see why I have to get dragged out here just to have my face shoved in the dirt! All right, I know he's dead! It doesn't mean I want to see whatever small-dicked asshole the fire spirit picked in his place." Kohaku couldn't see her face very clearly, but it sounded like she was sniffling.

"Nahoa, dear," the captain said, smiling down wryly at Kohaku's attendant, who was looking apoplectic with shock. "Perhaps you should restrain that tongue of yours in front of the Mo'i."

"I don't give a goddamn about any moy," she said as the other sailors let her through to the front of the bow. Then she looked down. "Oh," she said, softly, covering her hands with her mouth. "Is it really you? Am I ..." Kohaku suddenly worried that she would faint, but a nearby sailor seemed to notice it too and put a hand on her back.

"I didn't die," he said. "I think that was our deal."

Her eyes opened even wider and she nodded. "Yes. I mean ... I can't believe ..."

"Will you ..." Kohaku coughed uncomfortably, suddenly aware of the anticipatory silence around him. "Will you come back with me? You don't have to—"

"What happened to your arm?" she said suddenly, finally having noticed the empty left sleeve of his elaborately woven shirt.

"I burned it," he said. She had a right to know, and everyone would find out eventually, but he just couldn't bring himself to say what had happened in front of all these people.

She has such a transparent face, Kohaku thought, smiling. Concern seemed to ooze from every little nuance of her expression.

"Are you okay?" she asked.

"I will be. Will you come?"

She ran to the rope ladder and climbed down. The sound of the whispering crew grew to a roar when she ran forward and hugged him. He could tell that she was trying to be gentle, so he didn't show that it hurt. She started crying, which somehow surprised him.

"I really thought you were dead, you idiot," she said. "And now you've gone and made yourself Mo'i. What about going back to Okua and having kids? What about sailing? You've ruined everything!"

Kohaku felt suddenly worried. "You don't want to come back?" he whispered into her hair.

She broke away from him a little and smiled. "Of course I'll come back with you," she said. "I'm going to be a moy's first wife."

They held hands awkwardly as they walked together to the first ship.

"Good luck," one of the sailors yelled to them as they boarded. But even though Nahoa's presence beside him made Kohaku feel far happier than he had since Emea died, the throbbing of his arm and missing hand reminded him of what he could never truly escape.

10

L ANA PULLED THE ROPES MERCILESSLY TAUT before she knotted them around herself. A week ago she had woken up halfway out of the tree just before the knot had completely un-wound, which would have sent her plunging into the outstretched arms of the death below. After spending nearly a week without sleeping at all, she had dared to make up a geas that would let her rest in trees until sunup, but she had quickly learned that sleep-ing in trees wasn't really feasible without a rope. She had bought a good one in Ialo before booking a passage on a ship that would take her far away from human civilization. People, she had re-alized, had a habit of having unfortunate accidents—sometimes fatal—whenever she was around. She had asked the death about it, but it had responded cryptically—saying merely that it was not directly responsible. Still, when she saw a seven-year-old boy's legs get crushed under the wheels of a burro cart that she herself had narrowly avoided, she knew that she had to get as far away from other people as she could.

On the water it was easier to bind the death because it was out of its element, but sea voyages cost money and she couldn't stay there forever. So she had paid for passage aboard a small trade ship bound for the remote Kalakoa islands. She claimed that she wanted to pilgrimage to the ancient wind temple at their center, which made the crew look at her a bit strangely, but they prob-ably assumed she was an unusually devout member of some fringe religious sect and didn't ask any more questions. She bound the death over the water, but sometimes when it seemed likely to break her binding with a counter-geas, usually at night, she would play the flute softly for hours at a time. She played slow, melancholy songs that reminded her of her mother and their time on Okika. The more personally relevant the song, she had realized, the more powerful it was—the very intensity of her emotion made it like a self-sacrifice. The sailors sometimes listened wistfully themselves, and they were more forgiving of her misplaced notes than was the death, which would lean closer, its white robes flickering with scenes of destruction. As long as she played the flute, the death could not touch her—and so, over the past few months, she had often resorted to playing when she could think of no other geas to bind it. She had become a fairly competent player, in fact, though before this ordeal she had practiced the flute only a few times with her father.

Lana touched the flute now, reassuring herself that the light, smooth instrument was still in her pocket. Each night, sleep seemed a little more elusive, despite the fact that she felt more exhausted than she had ever imagined possible. It was at night that the dreams attacked her—dreams of death and pain that she could not stop. She dreamed of Kali often, sometimes as though her friend were struggling to tell her something through a barrier of water through which no sound could pass. Sometimes she just dreamed of the day Kali died, the sunlight hitting her hair as it floated on the water. Sometimes she cried, out of exhaustion and self-pity, but mostly she felt desperate and numb.

The tree she had climbed into this day had red bark and wide limbs with huge leaves. The trunk was too wide for her to tie a rope around it, so she had tied it off to the limb beneath her. She pulled her bag out from underneath her back and took out several strips of smoked and salted catfish that she had bought in the trading outpost on the edge of the island. That had been nearly a week ago. The fish pieces were beginning to smell a bit like bilge water, but she ate voraciously, barely noticing the sour aftertaste. The death was sitting on a branch below and to the right of her. She could see the tree through its translucent body, but the bark beneath it seemed to be crawling with odd, malformed insects that periodically devoured each other after vicious fights. Images were always distorted through the death's body, but she could never be sure whether she was witnessing illusion or actual destruction. Its mask-face swiveled toward her, staring with empty eyeholes as she pulled an oblong piece of bruised yellow and green fruit from her bag. She had seen some blue-furred monkeys fighting over a piece of this fruit earlier that day, which had made her decide that it probably wasn't poisonous. This was a real danger in this lush forest—nearly everywhere she looked something was bursting with multicolored fruits that she had never seen before, but she had heard too many tales of the dangers of the Kalakoa forests not to be wary. The fruit had thin skin and green, juicy pulp that made her lips pucker. She took out the large brown seed and tossed it at the death just to see what would happen. It flew straight through its body, making it ripple like water. The deformed insects beneath it scurried down the tree.

"You shouldn't do things like that," it said, suddenly a foot away from her elbow.

She stared back at it with almost perfect calm. It couldn't scare her like it once had. "Why not? You're a spirit. You're noncorporeal. It shouldn't have bothered you."

A bright red centipede nearly as wide as her thumb began crawling across her stomach. Two scaled, segmented fingers emerged from under the spirit's robe to pick it up by one end. The spirit rippled and Lana saw that the centipede now had a pair of bright blue butterfly wings by its head. The death released the creature, which flew awkwardly, tail dangling, for a few moments before a spider twice as large as her hand leapt from its web and devoured it in three economical bites.

Despite herself, Lana's heart started pounding.

"Take care," it said softly. "I could tire of this game."

"I still have the flute," she said, gripping it so tightly her palm started to sweat.

The death drifted downwards, back toward the other branch. "That's true," it said.

Lana stared at it for another moment and then began to eat the fruit.

She didn't quite know why, but over the next few days she began collecting the seeds from all the fruit she ate. It weighed down her bag considerably, and she felt the death's stare every time she did so, but she felt just a little safer with them there. The seed she'd thrown at it was the only thing she had ever known to disturb the death's equanimity.

For lack of any other destination, she had been picking her way across the barely recognizable path to the wind temple. She occasionally came across the signs of another recent human presence—the remains of a campfire, or a brief warning carved in bark of a tree about a particular fruit—but she walked alone. She bound the death with silly little geas—nursery rhymes, really—that it took its time breaking, mocking her with every word. She filled the forest with her melancholy tunes that sometimes even edged into happiness. Every so often she talked to the death, just so the sound of her own voice could cover the often vicious natural cacophony in the forest. Occasionally, it responded. When she thought about it, it frightened her how comfortable she felt—alone this way with the death.

She had stopped to pick some fruit for lunch when the death suddenly appeared before her, the corners of its mask-mouth turned up.

"A ship," it said. "A dead thing that carries the living is a ship."

Lana felt the geas dissolve around her. She groped frantically for the flute even as she stumbled away from the death. It wasn't in her pocket. She tripped on an upraised root and landed on her butt in the loamy earth. The death's empty eye sockets seemed to be glowing from some inner depth, and for a brief moment Lana thought she saw within them the image of a ship slowly sinking into a pool of flames. She couldn't breathe.

"You've run out," it said. "You lost the game."

Where the hell was the flute? Then she remembered that she had dropped it with her bag on the other side of the path before she went to climb the fruit tree. How could she have been so careless? Lana cursed herself silently and scrambled away, crawling on her back like a crab toward her pack. The death watched her progress silently for a moment and then flew forward.

It *entered* her.

She felt immovably cold, like fine old ash iced inside one of the glaciers that spread across the inner islands. Her very thoughts seemed crystallized, jagged, as though they had frozen in place. And the spot they had frozen allowed her only three words. The most important words.

Find the flute.

With whatever small part of her mind she had left, she fought the death. Though she couldn't see or hear or smell anything, she could touch, and so she inched her hands along the dirt, fighting to remember where her pack must be and where the flute must be resting on it.

She felt her breath grow so shallow in her lungs she knew she was barely breathing, but she forced herself to move. She thought of her mother.

"You can't save her," the death said, its androgynous voice crackling like fire in her head. "You can't save yourself. Give up."

She must be within reaching distance of the pack now. She bit her lip hard, taking reassurance from the pain and the metallic taste of blood. So long as she was alive, there was hope. But the cold was seeping into her bones and she knew that if she didn't move now she wouldn't be able to move at all. With a desperate lunge and a prayer to whoever saw fit to listen, she groped for her pack. She felt the worn canvas, but no flute. Had it rolled off? Panic set her lungs on fire, but she reached further.

Instead of meeting wet, vine-covered soil, her hand found the familiar shaft of whittled bone. She brought it to her lips and played a single note—one that she couldn't even hear—with as much force as she could muster. She felt the death struggle to stay inside her body before she forced it out with the terrified strength of her sound.

The first sense that returned to her was her hearing, and she had never thought such a high-pitched, scratchy sound could be so beautiful. A few monkeys in the tree above her were screeching down, as though with indignation, and she relished in that sound as well. She was alive.

When her vision cleared, she saw the death a few yards away from her, sitting cross-legged. The ground beneath its translucent body was a veritable battleground of maimed and malformed insects. Lana tried not to look. Instead she forced her shaky fingers into a song while she tried to think of yet another way to bind the death.

She had been too confident before, almost comfortable with its silent, terse companionship. Over the past few weeks she had, improbably, lost her fear of death. It had returned with a vengeance in the past few minutes, however. She had to remember that she needed to stay alive—not for herself, but for her mother. Instead of jokingly binding it with children's riddles, she needed to think of something that would keep her safer longer. She thought about it for a long time, periodically losing her train of thought in the cadences of the music and then dragging it back again. Nearly half an hour later, the corner of her eye caught on her worn canvas bag. Some of its contents had spilled when she had groped at it before, including the more than a dozen seeds that she had spent the past few days collecting.

Her fingers nearly skipped a note.

The seeds. There had to be a way to use them to bind the death. In the first few weeks of the death's chase, the thought of making up her own geas had terrified her, but soon she had realized that it would be her only means of survival. She thought about the phrasing for a few more minutes and then let the melody she was playing peter out, its final soft note ringing in her ears. This would have to work.

"Life is no more anathema to death than light is anathema to dark. They both require each other to exist. Yet, death only holds the key. It doesn't know—"

Lana broke off abruptly at the sudden shift in the death's attitude. It had gone from merely watchful to anticipatory. The grubs beneath its translucent body grew still and the banked light in its eyeholes made it look almost ... wary. She swallowed nervously and continued.

"It doesn't understand the essence of life—the only lives it can take are those that have already started living. The seed is death's paradox: death cannot take it—a mere seed can't go past the gate— but within the seed is the ultimate potential for living. A seed is the life that denies death."

The death settled back into its sitting position. Its wooden mouth began angling up into its customary mocking expression. Could it be relieved? "What do you want?" it asked.

"A day for each seed," Lana said. "A day for each life you can't yet touch."

After a moment, it nodded. "That's fifteen days."

The bindings fell into place and pulled taut. After a moment to catch her breath, Lana stood up and walked on shaky legs back to the tree. Incredibly brave or dangerously hungry, whichever she was, she realized it made no difference. She picked a fruit and tore into its sweet flesh with her teeth.

On the twelfth day, she reached the wind shrine.

It was an ancient, dilapidated structure built in an even older tree at the top of a long-dead volcano. She caught a fish that morning, after spending nearly half an hour crouched as still as she could manage in the shallow, muddy banks of the river. She roasted the strange blue and orange striped creature over the fire, ate as much as she could get down, and then packed the rest of it away in her bag for later. She spent the rest of the day climbing to the base of the tree. Most of the path had been washed away, forcing her to cling and scramble from tree to vine just to haul herself up the side. The midday rains began while she was halfway up, and for several moments she was terrified that it would wash her right back down the hill with the mud. The warm, earthy smell of the steam rising from the mud and the innumerable calls of frogs, birds, insects, and monkeys piercing through the rain patter made her feel inexplicably nervous, even though these were the normal sounds of the forest. The wind temple had been an arbitrary destination—a place to go that she knew was far from human contact. But what would she find when she got there? The path had lost all signs of recent human habitation a few days ago, but was it possible a caretaker still lived up in that ancient tree? After all that had happened to her, she didn't like the idea of walking into the unknown. Her life was frightening enough already without losing the little bit of control over it she still had left.

Still, what was she supposed to do? Turn around?

She reached the base of the enormous tree a few hours later, just when the rains began to stop. She took the water skin out of her bag and drained half of it in nearly three gulps. She panted as she put it down and wiped her mouth. She wanted to drink the whole thing, but that wouldn't be smart this far away from the river. She had no guaranteed freshwater source up here.

"Are you going to visit the spirit?" The death was floating a few feet above her. It was the first time it had spoken to her in days.

Lana looked at it as she caught her breath. "No reason not to," she said finally. "Although I doubt that it will deign to reveal itself to me."

It didn't respond and Lana stood up. She walked around the base slowly, noting in amazement that it was more than fourteen feet in diameter. She had never seen a tree so big in her life. On the opposite end from the trail, Lana saw that a series of steps so steep as to form a virtual ladder spiraled up the tree and ended right at the rickety wooden platform of the temple. Lana sincerely hoped that someone had been here sometime in the past century. After the wind spirit had broken free five hundred years ago and wreaked its bloody revenge, most of the wind temples had been burned and the ashes pounded into the earth. This one's inhospitable location was probably the only thing that had saved it from the same fate. Carved in the bark just beside the first step was a symbol that Lana knew was supposed to represent a jagged knife edge, but she had always thought it looked more like a sideways lightning bolt.

She stared up the spiraling staircase again and felt her trepidation intensify. She had never been afraid of heights, but she knew that if she climbed this tree, falling would be a real possibility. Still, curiosity gripped her when she looked at the half-hidden temple. She wanted to find out what was there—to do something, finally, besides just run. Before she could rethink her decision, Lana approached the first step and began, gingerly, to climb to the top.

The wood was strong, but the steps had been carved unevenly and she lost her balance a few times before hauling herself over the platform. Even back when the wind spirit had first been bound, how could anyone have dared make the trip here? Perhaps people had been more devoted back then, more faithful. Although she hadn't seen it from the ground, the platform opened directly into the shrine itself. There were no walls to speak of—it was entirely open to the elements. The floorboards, she noticed as she gingerly walked inside, were still drying from the rain. Any item that might have indicated this place was something more than an empty shell of a tree house had been nailed down. With good reason, she thought, considering the strong wind that blew the smells of the forest below to her nostrils. The death floated outside the temple, beside the staircase that had led her here. Looking around, she saw no overt signs of habitation aside from an unnatural cleanness to the place. The nervousness that had plagued her during her trip up the tree began to fall away. This shrine felt oddly peaceful. She walked forward until she was nearly at the unguarded edge of the structure. At her feet she saw a broken blade nailed into the wood and she wondered how it remained unrusted after centuries of pelting rains.

An odd clicking noise behind her made the hairs rise on the back of her neck. She whirled around, only to come face to face with a massive bird-eating spider, nearly the size of her head. Though she knew it was impossible, something in the way it clicked its mandibles together made her feel as though it was grinning. Lana screamed and stepped backwards, only to scream again when she realized that she was toppling over the edge. She managed to grab at the planks of wood before she went down.

She hung there with sweaty fingers for several moments, mind bubbling with fear while she tried to figure out what to do. The boards themselves began to vibrate with the impact of someone moving slowly across them. Lana thought she heard a woman's voice muttering something. Out of the corner of her eye, she saw the death waiting below her. She cursed silently and hoped whatever was walking toward her was benign.

"Help!" she screamed. "I'm going to fall!"

The pace of the steps didn't increase. "Hold on, hold on," she heard a voice say. It sounded rough and quavering, like that of an old woman. Lana almost forgot her fear in disbelief. How could she have not noticed another person in this small temple?

"… get so few visitors, these days, I always forget to put out the security rope," the woman was muttering. Lana's fingers were beginning to weaken and she prayed silently that the woman would finish her slow trek across the temple floor. A few moments later, Lana saw a rope end fall to her right side and she grabbed it gratefully. She hauled herself up over the edge of the temple and lay on the still-damp floorboards, panting and shaking.

"My, my," said an old woman, leaning over her on a gnarled branch of a cane. "You should have called for help sooner. It wouldn't do to have all my visitors falling out of the tree, now would it?" She let out a highly inappropriate chuckle.

Lana forced herself to sit up and look at the woman. She was even older than Lana had suspected—her craggy face and wispy white hair made her look at least ninety. How could such an old woman survive in this kind of place?

Lana thought she heard a clicking sound and she looked up frantically for the spider, but it had disappeared. She only saw its massive web, covering half the ceiling. She shuddered. She didn't want to think about where the spider could be.

"So what brings you here, my dear? I haven't had a real visitor for … why, it must be these past thirty years. And you look like you have a problem a bit larger than normal." She gestured toward the death, waiting beyond the temple boundaries, its mask at its most unreadable.

Lana's eyes trailed to the woman's stick, which had a design vaguely reminiscent of a spider carved into its head. This woman radiated a subtle power, and Lana wondered if she could possibly help her.

"I need help … to stay alive," Lana said slowly, looking into the woman's surprisingly sharp black eyes. "I don't know how much longer I can do it on my own. It's not just my own life I'm guarding. I have to save my mother."

"I suspected as much." The old woman's voice suddenly sounded far less crotchety. "But it's been many, many years since I even heard of such a geas. You're a young girl. You must have trained with someone who knew the old ways. Yes, someone …" The woman gave her an appraising stare and then shuffled to the back of the temple, where she opened a rough-hewn wooden cupboard. After a moment's deliberation, she removed a long, narrow bottle made of glass with a cork stopper and walked back to where Lana was sitting.

"You should make a supplication directly to the wind spirit," she said, sitting down with a creak of bones. "It hasn't been done in five hundred years, but you don't look to me like you have better options. Besides, I think it wants to see you."

The woman winked and bit into the cork.

"It ... wants to see me?" Lana asked, suddenly nervous again. How could the wind spirit even know who she was?

"Just a hunch," said the woman indistinctly. After a moment's more of wrestling with it, her remarkably strong teeth managed to yank out the cork. Wind rushed out of the bottle with a sound like a mournful lament, howling briefly around the room before leaving through the open sides.

The old woman sighed wistfully. "I really did like that one. I was keeping it for a special occasion. Ah well. You can't keep them bottled up forever. So, do you agree?"

The change of subject was so abrupt it took Lana a few moments to even understand what she was asking. "Well ... how do I bind that when I make the pilgrimage?" Lana asked, gesturing toward the death spirit.

"Oh, don't worry. So long as you're on the pilgrimage, you're under the jurisdiction of the wind spirit. Only the spirit itself will have the power to kill you."

Lana hoped that was reassuring. "I'll go, I guess. I don't really know what else to do."

The woman smiled briefly at her, and then licked her finger to test the wind. "Just a light breeze," she muttered to herself. "Iolana, do you know how to call a wind?"

Lana's breathing grew shallow. How did the woman know her name? After a moment she shook her head silently.

"Sailors used to do it, back before the wind spirit broke free. Now only a few of us can. Those chosen by the wind. But I think you could learn, if you wanted to."

"How?" Lana asked. It was almost surprising how, after everything, her natural curiosity could still be piqued. But then, Akua had always taught her that even the most minor knowledge was its own kind of power. And Lana knew she was in too deep to refuse whatever help was offered.

"Have you ever heard the way the wind howls at night? The way it rattles doors and shrieks and moans? The wind is a melancholy, powerful spirit. No geas can call it, though they can bind it. Calling it is a different sort of skill—to call the wind, you must feel its melancholy in your soul and match it."

"With the flute?" she asked, after a moment's thought.

The woman's face broke out in a bright grin, revealing a full set of teeth. "That would be brilliant. More appropriate than you know. Yes, try it now, with the flute. If you call a wind, I'll bottle it."

Lana sat with the flute poised above her lips for a long time as she tried to get the image of what she wanted to convey just right in her head. The woman had told her to match the wind's melancholy, not simply imitate it. When she finally thought she was ready, she began to play. The notes dipped and swirled like no other melody she had ever played—in fact, they didn't sound very much like a melody at all, and yet they were somehow still musically cohesive. She did her best to echo the wind's melancholy, playing in its silent and violent places alike until she had created something both sad and powerful. She felt the wind enter the temple, softly at first, and then more strongly, until it seemed to be playing with her. It howled past her ears with a shriek that was almost joyous. She played until the wind was merely another whisper in her ear, and then the woman had corked the bottle.

The woman was staring at her with a strange, almost shocked expression. "You may just survive. You're followed by more than you know, and yet … you may just survive."

Lana's smile was half-derisive, half-sincere. "At least I'm a quick study."

The woman nodded, bemused, and handed Lana the slim glass bottle. It looked empty, but she could feel tremors against the fingers that gripped it. "Keep this with you at all times. Go to the wind island, and get the tribespeople there to take you to the ruins on the mesa. Uncork the bottle. The spirit will come to you."

Lana took the bottle from the woman. "I understand enough to know I don't know a thing," Lana said, impulsively, as she slid the bottle inside her pack. The top stuck out. "But … I'm grateful for this."

"A thousand drips will fill a bucket," she said, which Lana supposed was better comfort than none. She then rose with a speed Lana thought should be impossible for a woman her age. "You must leave now. It's time I had my dinner and you should leave this hill by sundown."

Lana walked back to the porch. "But wait," she said just as she put her foot back on the first step. "Who are you?"

The woman smiled. "Caretaker of this humble temple, servant to the wind spirit, and … an acquaintance of a mutual friend. Now go."

The dismissal had no sting to it. Lana nodded and began climbing back down the tree. She froze a few steps down when she thought she heard the unmistakable cry of a bird in its death throes. A sharp clicking, like that of a bird-eating spider, followed it. Lana shivered and climbed down the rest of the tree as quickly as she could.

The few traders at the outpost looked shocked when she staggered back in fifteen days later, covered with mud and considerably thinner than she had been a month earlier. They told her that a ship wouldn't be arriving for another three days, and Lana, so exhausted her teeth hurt, decided she could risk staying in town and relying upon the kindness of a medicine trader's wife who had been among the ones to witness her arrival in the settlement. She was a thin woman, baked brown by the sun and a difficult life. Her eyebrows were thin blond lines across her forehead, and her hair was light blond streaked with white. She could have been anywhere between thirty and fifty—the salty air and the sun out here had a way of preserving people. She opened the door of a tidy two-room house made of birch wood. The logs had been dried and sealed carefully, but Lana guessed that they couldn't have been more than two years old. In fact, most of the houses in the traders' village looked relatively new.

The woman paused in the entrance and took off her shoes. "It's all the rain," she said, half apologetically. "It gets so you don't know what you're bringing in. I hope you don't mind."

Her Essel accent made Lana wonder what had brought her to this isolated place. "Don't worry," she said. She bent down to untie the laces of her sandals and tried to ignore the sudden sharp pain when she reopened a cut on her back. She stood up and looked behind her to make sure that the death hadn't crossed the threshold. It waited like a sentinel outside the door, mask expressionless. That had been her first geas—it couldn't cross the threshold of a place that Lana herself had been invited into. Even though it was also bound by her pilgrimage, the thought of it looking into this woman's house made her nervous.

"Can I shut the door?" Lana asked, carefully polite.

"Oh, of course." The woman opened the larder and began pulling out some food while Lana closed the door. It would be good to spend a few days without the death as her constant companion.

"Why don't you go and wash up? We don't have much—just a pump and a bucket outside, but I thought you might want to get rid of all that grime ..."

Lana smiled ruefully at the slightly appalled look in the woman's eyes. She could only imagine how grubby she must look. It had been months since she had last seen her own reflection in something clearer than a muddy puddle. "I would love that," she said.

The water was lukewarm and the pump squeaked in a way that made the space between her shoulder blades shiver, but she spent more than half an hour scrubbing herself before she felt clean. After she had dumped the last bucket over her head, she sat silently on the rough wooden floor of the bathing room. Water dripped between the slats of the fresh timber and disappeared into the ground below. Nearby, a monkey let out a great bellow and birds shrieked in response. It was hard to forget how much closer—and how much *stronger*—the forest was than this spare enclave.

The whole time she had been evading the death, she had hardly even thought of bathing, so how could something so simple and mundane make her feel so bereft? It was as though all of the strain and weariness of the past two months—months when she'd had no time to think of anything but how to survive till the next morning—had finally caught up to her. And if two months had taken her so close to her limit, she didn't know how she could even survive the year. She felt her eyes well with tears. She didn't regret her decision to save her mother, but she had never felt so desperately helpless before. She couldn't stay alive on her own much longer, and she *hated* how useless that made her feel. The wind spirit had to help her. If it didn't ...

Lana shook her head firmly and drew another bucket of water. She splashed her face and then dumped the rest of it over her head. When she was sure that the tears had stopped, she opened the door. Next to a towel, the woman had replaced Lana's mud-caked clothes with clean ones. The sober gray pants were too long and the shirt came all the way down to her mid-calves, but she had never appreciated such soft, clean cloth more in her life. She had nearly forgotten what it felt like not to be wet.

When she walked back inside the house, the woman clapped her hands in approval. "What an improvement!" she said. "Still too thin, but at least not as desperate as when you staggered in. I can't imagine what you were thinking, tramping off into the forest to see the wind temple. We all thought you must have died. Here, sit down."

She ushered Lana to a table like the one her family had used back on her island—low to the ground, surrounded by legless chairs with cushions. The woman had set out what looked like leftovers from the previous day's meal—cold tea and fermented disks of pan bread with a spicy, thick bean soup. Lana practically fell on the food, with only a last shred of manners preventing her from stuffing most of the bread in her mouth at once.

"Thank you so much," Lana said, when she had finished everything. "I don't deserve your kindness, but thank you."

The woman smiled, which made her look younger. "I have a daughter about your age. I don't get to see her much ... not since

Tapamahe moved out here to make his fortune. It's nice to have someone else to feed in the house. Especially since it looks like you need it."

Lana leaned back in her chair and looked at the ceiling. The pale beams reflected light from the open window.

"How long have you been here?" Lana asked. "The house looks new."

"We moved here from Essel about five years ago, but we've had to rebuild the house twice since then."

Lana stared at her, shocked. "*Twice?* What on earth happened? Fire?"

She shook her head. "It's the winds. The old timers say that the Kalakoas have been plagued by them ever since the wind spirit broke free. I don't know about that, but every rainy season the sea starts to swell and huge storms rip right through here. You've never felt anything like it—a wind that can just destroy everything in its path. I wept so hard the first time it tore down my house. But you just learn to clear out quickly and be grateful for your life. The first year we came here, the winds were so horrible that we actually sent … well, I mean …"

The woman, who had seemed lost in her story, looked abruptly embarrassed.

"You actually sent what?"

The woman looked around and then leaned forward over the table. "Well, I suppose it won't hurt to tell you. You're leaving in a few days, after all." She spoke in an almost-whisper, like she was afraid of someone overhearing. "We sent the spirit a sacrifice. It was horrible … everyone over sixteen had to put their name in the lottery. We picked this other trader's wife, she had just recovered from the forest sickness. They tied her up and took her into the forest and came back twenty days later without her. They said they had given her to the spider crone up in the wind temple. I really wanted to leave after that, but Tapamahe said we should stay. The storms got better for the next few years, but her husband … I swear he died of a broken heart. He stopped eating, sleeping, talking ... and one day he just wandered off into the forest and never came back. It's this place, you know." She looked through the window briefly and held her shoulders as though she was cold. "It sucks everything out of you if you stay too long. It sucks away your life."

Lana felt sick to her stomach. That poor woman ... she couldn't have been a willing sacrifice. Did these people know how cheaply they had sold one of their own? For a few paltry seasons of mildly better weather? But maybe in this hard place they felt it was worth it.

"Anyway," the woman said, "that's why we were so surprised when you came back. They said the last time someone came back alive from visiting the spider crone was about a hundred years ago."

Lana's throat suddenly felt very dry. She poured herself another glass of tea and drank it in one pull. Outside the window, Lana thought she heard the telltale click of a bird-eating spider. But when she looked, it was only the death.

The wind shrine lay on the outermost western edge of the islands—at least three weeks away from the Kalakoas by a fast boat with a favorable wind, making no stops. Of course, there had been no such boat for nearly five hundred years, and Lana was forced to make her painfully slow way by hopping from one successively small harbor to the next. Since people always greeted mention of the wind spirit with a kind of distant reserve, Lana avoided telling anyone her destination. Nearly a month after she left the Kalakoas, she arrived at the last island with a half-decent harbor on the western rim. Though it was technically part of the rice islands, the residents mostly fished and farmed sugar cane. After the boat docked, she wandered a few miles up the coast until she found the fishing harbor.

Since it was midday, all of the boats were still out except one. A small man about her father's age had hauled a boat halfway out of the water and was patching a hole in its rudder. The small sailboat looked old but sturdy and Lana couldn't help but compare this man's diligence with her father's. Back on their island, Kapa probably would have used the breached rudder as an excuse to stay at home and work on his instruments. She hadn't realized it as much as a child, but now she understood how ill-suited her father had been for the life of a fisherman. The man looked up when she approached. She answered his slight frown with a smile, grateful again to the woman on the Kalakoas for letting her keep the clean clothes. Her own had been ruined in the forest, and Lana had learned that half the trick of getting passage to unusual places was looking respectable. That and having money. Unfortunately, she had only about two hundred kala left. She hoped that would be enough.

"Having trouble with your boat?" she said, when she was close enough to be heard without yelling.

The man shrugged. "A bit. My fool of a nephew wasn't careful at low tide and ran aground. Took a hefty chunk out of the rudder, so I've had to miss a full day and a half's catch fixing it."

"That must be a hardship. How much money have you lost, then?"

"Oh, about thirty or forty kala, I'd say. What's it to you?" Sensing a deal, he had put down his hammer and was looking at her intently.

"How would you like to make up that money plus some once you fix that rudder? I need a boat to take me to the wind island." Lana said it matter-of-factly, knowing that her own confidence would help convince him to make the treacherous journey.

He sucked in air and it whistled through a gap in his front teeth. "What business do you have in that miserable place? The wind tribes ... they're barbarians. They eat animal flesh, you know—the hearts, even, while they're still beating. And they don't speak any decent tongue. I've heard that the wind whistling through the ruins can drive a man mad. It's not a safe place, let alone for a woman traveling by herself."

Lana tried to keep her voice confident. "Be that as it may, I'm determined to go, and I will pay you well for your trouble."

"Well, if it's like that ... how much will you pay? It's a two-day journey and I would need the money for the missing catch on my return. Oh, and I won't dock my boat—they say that the wind tribes claim ownership of anything that touches on their land. They're not human, I tell you. They'll send winds that can drown you if you anger them."

Lana bit her lip. She didn't know what she would do if he wanted more money than she had. "A hundred and sixty kala," Lana said finally.

The man let out a bark of laughter. "You're crazy. I need at least two hundred to cover my losses."

Lana hesitated. "How about a hundred and eighty?"

He looked at her hard. "You look like you're at the end of your tether, honey. Your clothes aren't too shabby, but your eyes still look desperate. I don't know what you're planning to do on that wind island, but I have a feeling I'd be better off not getting involved with it. Still, I'd hate to turn away someone in need. Two hundred kala. No less."

Lana nodded.

She waited a few feet away from him on the dock when he put the final touches to his patched rudder. He said they would set sail first thing tomorrow morning at high tide. Lana lied and told him she would stay the night in town at the inn and left before the first boats returned from their day at sea. She didn't want to be responsible for any fatal accidents. The death floated beside her as she walked further up the coastline. She stopped when she reached a deserted beach, a stretch of white sand covered with decaying brown lines of washed-up seaweed. She stared at the encroaching waves as the sun went down over the ocean. The death was silent beside her. Was it just her loneliness that made its presence something she occasionally even enjoyed? Or was it some more fundamental affinity? *You ease death ...*

"Tell me," she said when the pink sky had deepened to purple, "what happens after we die? Where do we go?"

The death looked at her, its mouth hole in a neutral line. Still, Lana sensed some surprise.

"Why do you ask? Have you decided to give up, so close to the wind?"

Lana shook her head. "No, of course not. You know me better than that."

The corners of its mouth turned up slightly. "Perhaps I do, after all."

"I was just wondering, I guess. Everyone's so afraid of death, but just because no one really knows what happens. Is it good? Is it horrible?"

The death turned its mask away from her. "I cannot say."

Like all spirits, it was bound to total honesty and something in its wording struck her as strange. "Why won't you tell me?" she asked. "You'll still get me in the end, either way. Why the secrecy?"

"It's simply the way it is. Those of the living cannot see beyond the gate."

Lana shrugged and looked back out at the ocean. "What's behind your mask, then?" she asked, after a few silent minutes.

"My, you're full of questions tonight, aren't you? Do you really want to see?"

Its mocking tone made her wary, but she nodded her head. "Sure," she said.

With taunting slowness, the death revealed its long segmented fingers and pulled off the mask.

Lana had a brief, sickening impression of a face made up entirely of a grinning maw filled with shiny oversized teeth. Then its face seemed to morph in a few nauseating lurches into that of a young girl. Lana gasped. She knew that diffident smile and long, auburn hair. It was Kali. It morphed again, still Kali, but dead, just as she had looked after Lana pulled her out of the wreckage of her house. Even though there was no light at all on the beach, somehow the death had mimicked the red hue of her hair with the sun hitting it perfectly.

"Have you forgotten about me, Lana?" It wasn't her voice, it was the death's hideously accurate parody of it.

"Stop! Stop it now!" Lana screamed, squeezing her eyes shut.

"But I thought you wanted to see me, Lana."

Angrily, frantically, she reached inside her pocket and pulled out the flute. Almost without thinking, she funneled her anger and sadness into calling a wind. Far more quickly than the last time, it ripped in from the ocean, howling with the strength of Lana's fury and slamming into the death. Though she had never seen it affected by the weather before, the death was pushed backwards, and Lana vaguely saw a hand-shaped depression of air wrap around its throat.

"She is mine for now, Death. Do not torment her." The mournful voice was the wind, howling in her ears.

"She asked," the death said in a strangled shout. Its face looked different yet again—now gray and sagging like a cadaver.

"Do not torment her," it said again. "Remember your place."

After a moment, the death nodded and then replaced its mask. The wind spirit's insubstantial body suddenly appeared before Lana. She felt a hand caress her cheek.

"I await you, pilgrim."

With a howl that sent shivers through her marrow, the wind whipped back out to sea.

After a few moments of disbelieving silence, the death appeared barely two inches from her face.

"You can go running to the wind, for now, but you will be mine again soon. And when you are, don't think I'll forget this. Don't think you'll find avoiding me as easy as before."

Lana turned her head away from it and curled into the sand and algae, trying as hard as she could not to think at all.

They made good time to the island in the little fishing boat, despite the fact that the fisherman insisted on stopping twice to lay out nets and see what he could catch. Lana suspected that the favorable winds were no accident, but she of course said nothing. She tried to ignore the death's silent, brooding presence during their journey, but she felt scared when she thought of what might happen when she no longer had the wind spirit's protection.

The man laid anchor about fifteen feet away from the ruined harbor, where the water was still too deep for her to stand.

"This is as far as I go," he said.

Lana nodded absently and turned back to look at the island before her. The wind island looked huge—perhaps even bigger than Okika. The fisherman had told her that the wind island used to be part of a much larger landmass, but most of it had been flooded two thousand years ago, before the water spirit had been bound. Seeing the utterly foreign landscape before her now, she could believe his tale—she had never seen anything like it before in her life. Impossibly tall, craggy red rocks with flat tops jutted from the earth as though they had been punched out with a fist. The entire island appeared to be covered in red-brown dust, and the only plants she could see were a few short, stunted bushes more prickle than green. The sun's heat felt like a kiln, without any of the comforting wet humidity that she was used to. The harbor looked completely deserted, but she thought she saw a few plumes of smoke off in the distance. She would have to talk to one of those wind tribes soon—hope that they would lead her to the ruins and not simply murder her on the spot.

"You leaving or coming back with me? I'm not staying here any longer." The fisherman had settled himself against the mast, crossing his arms.

Lana shook her head. "I'm sorry. Here, take this." She reached into her purse and pulled out the second of her large, pink-veined hundred-kala coins. He practically snatched it from her hand and then held it up to the light. Apparently satisfied, he pocketed the money.

"Well then, get going. You should have no problem getting to the harbor. I can't say I'll be sorry to see you go. You've got a damn weird feeling about you, girl … like the worst kind of bad luck. The wind was perfect the whole way here and I kept expecting it to turn."

Lana could find nothing to say. She knew his words, however inhospitable, were justified—far more than he even suspected. Without saying another word, Lana put her bag on her head and then lowered herself into the water with her other hand. The death floated above her, avoiding the touch of the crystal-clear water. She paddled the fifteen feet to the harbor, careful to keep her pack dry. She couldn't afford to get her food wet. She climbed out of the water on a crumbling stone staircase and looked back. The man had already turned his boat around.

Lana slung the bag over her shoulder again and shielded her eyes from the glaring sun. She could barely make out a wisp of smoke coming from behind a series of sharply jutting rocks a few miles away. *Find the wind tribes and get them to take you to the ruins on the mesa*: those had been the spider crone's instructions. She just hoped they would listen to her.

Many hours later, when the sun was just beginning its final descent below the horizon, Lana managed to clamber to the top of the dusty crag of rock separating her from the plume of smoke. She swept what looked like the remainders of a very large nest from a tiny crevice and sat down inside it. The rock felt cool against her wet cheek and her breathing began to return slowly to normal. She had nearly finished the contents of her water skin, and she knew that she wouldn't be able to last another day in the baking sun without finding some freshwater source. Unfortunately, even from this vantage point she saw only an endless expanse of dusty red stone. How was it possible for any place in the islands to be so devoid of water? Lana couldn't remember ever being so thirsty. Far below her was an encampment of a wind tribe, their squat lodgings nestled against the rocks and spreading perhaps forty yards beyond them. Lana guessed that it probably housed about three hundred people. It looked semi-permanent, with a convenient rock outcropping serving as a stable for their oversized horses and burros. The houses themselves looked like tents, but instead of cloth they used painted hide. She couldn't make out people's faces from so far away, but she could see their fires—increasing with the sinking sun—and people laughing and sharing food around them. Children ran half-naked by the horses, and shrieked as they wrestled slobbering, furry creatures with long snouts and frighteningly large teeth. She thought they might be wolves, although they bore only a distant resemblance to the illustrations that she had seen so long ago in Kohaku's books.

Lana sighed. They didn't look violent, but she knew that these people would not take kindly to some stranger appearing in their camp, even at the request of the wind spirit. She also worried about what kinds of accidents might befall the tribe while she stayed with them. The death spirit had been relatively passive recently, but she didn't dare trust that. It had followed her silently the entire way here and was now sitting, completely translucent, a few feet in front of her.

"Will you go down," it said quietly, "or are you too afraid? Do you forfeit the wind spirit's protection, then? Dubious though it might be, I would have thought you would prefer it to me."

She sensed a mocking smile in its voice, but its mask remained impassive. Lana shook her head. "I'm going down. I just have to … think about what to say. How I should approach them." A sudden breeze ripped through her thin clothes and she shivered. How could it get so cold so quickly? The dust kicked up by the breeze clogged her nose and she sneezed violently. "Great Kai, I'm thirsty," she said, half to herself. "I bet they have some water down there."

The death suddenly leaned forward and a strange light in its normally dark eyes grew brighter. She glanced at it sharply moments before she felt strong hands reach roughly under her armpits and haul her upright. She couldn't see her attacker, but she could smell him—a hard odor of earth and sweat and horseflesh. He was holding a strong walking stick to her throat with enough pressure to make it very hard to breathe. Actually, she realized moments later, she had been assaulted by two men. As one of them kept the stranglehold on her throat the other walked in front of her. His round, dust-red face was surprisingly young, but he looked at her with the determined bravado of a boy intending to prove himself a man. He wore a pair of low-slung hide pants and a short, open vest without any buttons.

The one behind her growled something in her ear. The words were incomprehensible, but they terrified her all the same. She heard a breathy bleat of terror and realized it was her own voice. The one before her, brandishing a carved stick that looked heavy enough to crack her bones with one blow, rattled off something else in the same tongue. She shook her head frantically—she would have said something, but the stick was still too heavy across her throat.

The one she could see made a brief gesture to the one behind her and the pressure on her neck eased slightly. Lana gulped air and then began to cough violently on the dust.

"Who ... are you?" said the boy in front of her slowly, his accent just barely intelligible. "What your business is? Eggs ... eggs ...." He trailed off, looking desperately at the man behind her for help.

"Steal," said the man, with an even thicker accent. "Come to steal eggs of ..." he paused and then said another incomprehensible word that sounded like *hrevech*. He pulled the stick hard across her neck again. "Answer," he said.

Lana nodded frantically and the pressure eased. "My name is Lana ... Iolana. I am here to see the wind spirit ... I need to go to the ruins on the mesa."

The boys looked at each other. The young one said something but the one holding her made a dismissive sound. "Hrevech," the first one said again. "Steal eggs?"

"I don't know anything about eggs. I don't know what a ... hrevech is." She noticed that the boy in front of her had a leather sack attached to his hip that she now guessed was filled with the precious eggs. He narrowed his eyes at her before kneeling in front of the crevice she had cleared the old nest out of earlier. He picked up a few of the dried twigs and pieces of animal hair littering the stones nearby and said something to the other one.

"Old," the boy told her, standing up. "No eggs."

Suddenly, she heard a grating screech echo off the rock. The man holding her abruptly let go and she stumbled forward.

"Hrevech!" he shouted. They were no longer paying any attention to her—he and the boy were waving their sticks in the air and shouting. Lana looked up and gasped. Circling in the sky above them was the largest bird she had ever seen. It looked vaguely like an oversized hawk with a wingspan at least twice Lana's height, except its eyes and its beak were disproportionately large. It had a blue-gold underbelly and dusty red feathers on top with fluffy, stark white feathers on its face. Her breath caught in her throat. *How beautiful.*

It seemed to Lana that her erstwhile captors were trying to catch the creature's attention for some reason. The bird—a hrevech, she assumed—flew closer to them. Lana's heart started pounding when she glanced in its eyes—she didn't trust their alien, predatory intelligence. When the bird began circling less than ten feet away from them, the older one—a man, perhaps, but certainly no older than she—grabbed her summarily by the elbow and hauled her farther down the slope. With another screech so powerful Lana was afraid her ears would bleed, the bird swooped down. Lana screamed and cowered against the stone, but the bird pulled up barely two feet from her head and began circling around the crevice, almost protectively. The boys looked back and saw the same thing. They exchanged a few terse words and then the younger one began to sing.

His singing voice was rough and his words incomprehensible, but his wavering pitch held a certain determined power that she had heard before. When she felt the beginnings of a strong wind, she realized why his disjointed notes had sounded oddly familiar: he was calling a wind. The wind began to howl and blow around them, but he still sang, even when Lana could no longer hear him. Suddenly the wind grew so strong that she realized she was in danger of tumbling off the edge of the rock. Before she could find an outcropping to grab onto, a particularly strong gust punched her in the stomach and she tumbled into open air.

She didn't even have time to gasp.

I should have hit those rocks, she thought. But the two boys, still on either side of her, didn't look surprised at all. Was the younger one, still singing, somehow using the wind to make them fall at an angle? Just before they should have smashed into the red dust at the bottom of the cliffs, the wind suddenly gusted with enough force to pop her ears and buoyed them so they landed with barely a thump on the dry earth.

Lana dug her hands in the soil and drew several long, shuddering breaths that rasped in her throat. She had spent months courting death, but she had never felt so close to it. She didn't even mind the dust—at least it was earth. At least she wasn't falling.

After a few minutes she felt someone tap her shoulder. She looked up to see that she was surrounded by red-faced people, looking at each other and talking in quick whispers. Her older captor had disappeared, but the younger one was standing protectively beside her, arguing with the gathered crowd. As they went back and forth, Lana attempted to brush some of the dust from her pants and stood up shakily. She wasn't sure if it was fear, thirst, or exhaustion, but though she knew she was on solid ground, everything she saw seemed to be wobbling. She took a deep breath and stared at her feet.

"Iolana," the boy said carefully. She looked at him. "They say 'why is she here?' You said ... before ... you wish to see the great wild spirit of wind, correct? You wish us to help you to the ruins?"

Lana nodded wearily. "Yes," she said. "That's it. I'm on a pilgrimage."

He nodded and turned back to the crowd. They spoke for a few more minutes, this time with considerably less emotional fervor. Lana took this as a good sign. Finally, they seemed to reach some agreement and the people wandered off, back to tend the fires that had dwindled in their absence and the food that was sticking to the pots.

"They say you are intruder. I say … great spirit wants you some reason. We must help. They say take to … leader." He paused and smiled reassuringly. "No worry. Good man, leader. Will help."

Lana smiled back and tried not to notice the death behind him, so opaque it almost looked corporeal.

The boy—whose name was Yechtak, he told her—led her to a large tent set up in the shadows of the cliff face. She wondered why their encampment would crowd so close to large outcroppings of rocks—was it possible they needed to defend themselves? The flaps of the tent were covered in dark maze-like designs that reminded her, in their intricacy, of some of the house decorations in Ialo during the spirit solstice. With one final reassuring smile, Yechtak pulled back the tent flap and led her inside.

The room was very dark despite the fire burning in a pit dug in the center. There was a hole up top for the smoke to escape through, but most of it seemed to linger in the room itself, making Lana's already irritated throat hurt. The only person in the tent was an old man sitting by the fire on a single cushion without even a support for his back.

Yechtak called out a greeting and the man turned his face to him, smiling. Almost immediately, though, the smile left his face and he looked toward Lana. She shuddered. Yechtak gestured for her to sit on the other side of the fire. As she lowered herself through the haze of smoke, Lana realized why the old man's gaze seemed so strange: his eyes had been gouged out. This had happened a very long time ago, judging by the weathered and creased scars. As with Akua's arm, she had no doubt that this man's mutilation had been intentional and self-inflicted. She knew that she was in the presence of great power.

The room began swaying again.

"You come with dangerous guests, Yechtak," Erlun said.

Yechtak thought Iolana looked tired and sick, not dangerous. Was even Erlun threatened by the presence of this young Binder?

He shook his head. "We found her in an old hrevech nesting cave. If she had stayed the night there, she might have become baby food. We probably saved her life."

Erlun smiled. "Saved her life? Perhaps. But it certainly wasn't selflessness that led you to call a nesting hrevech nearly down on your heads. Now you can go up and steal the eggs when you want without searching for another nest, of course."

Yechtak blushed and stared into the fire. "Well … it *was* a good opportunity. But, anyway, I don't see how she can be dangerous when she screams at just the sight of a hrevech."

Erlun made a clucking noise with his tongue. "Fear is not always a sign of weakness, Yechtak. Remember that. In some, fear is a sign of ignorance. And besides, you did not listen carefully enough. I said you came with dangerous *guests.* You have brought more than one creature to my fire this evening."

Yechtak looked around. "What do you mean? There's no one but me, you and the girl."

"You do not have the eyes to see my fourth guest, but I do, and I tell you that it is dangerous. And yet, I suspect that for now it will not harm us. This girl knows what she has brought with her, but she comes regardless, which indicates either great carelessness or great need. Which is it? Ask her."

Yechtak turned to the girl, whose wide, weary eyes seemed to trap him. He blinked for a few moments and then began to laboriously translate Erlun's question with his limited command of the Binder language. The girl's eyes, impossibly, widened further as he asked his question, and the glance she gave Erlun spoke volumes of guilt and pain. She reached to her throat to fondle a large red bead that hung from a chain in what seemed like a reflexive gesture. Who was this woman? He had seen mothers who had lost sons to the plains battles give looks like that. Could she have lost a child?

"I … I apologize for coming," she said after a few silent moments. "But I came in desperation … in great need. I must go to the ruins on the mesa. I must find the wind spirit. I was summoned because perhaps, the wind spirit can help me evade this unwelcome guest and help me save someone ... someone very dear to me."

Yechtak translated Iolana's response much faster than he had translated Erlun's question. The old man smiled gently at her and nodded. Yechtak felt a ball of nervousness in his stomach that he had not even been aware of begin to unwind. He had not wanted this oddly appealing girl to justify Erlun's fears.

"She tells the truth, Yechtak. She carries a wind jar—the wild god desires her and I must do its bidding. Tell her that we will help her reach the ruins on the mesa. One of us will guide her there."

Yechtak's eyes were drawn to the old man's bare chest, where he could barely make out the intricate tattoo—the only record their tribe had of the safe path to the ruins. Each of the shamans in the six wind tribes had that tattoo given to them upon their ascension to power. And each of the shamans had sacrificed something in turn for the knowledge.

"You will take her?" he asked. "But, Erlun, do you think you could make such a journey ..."

Erlun shook his head gently but something in his countenance made Yechtak snap his mouth shut.

"No, son. I know I cannot make such a journey. Someone else must be her guide—someone who I can trust with the map. You were the one who found her. It seems appropriate that you should be her guide. This will be your own special initiation into manhood. And perhaps, one day, you may even take my place."

Yechtak bit his cheek to keep his face from showing undue emotion, but he wasn't sure how successful he was. To be entrusted with the shaman's map ... it made his head spin. His mother would be so proud. No plains-battle manhood for him; his would be an initiation far more important and dangerous.

Erlun laughed and put his hands closer to the fire. "Well, tell her, why don't you? You can preen later."

Yechtak blushed again—a very unmanly habit that he would have to break—and began his awkward translation.

Lana found herself warming to the strange blind man, even though it was impossible to relax with the death hovering at the edge of the room. She should have had the foresight to make sure the old man invited her inside, but it was too late now. The death's recent silence put her on edge—made her think that it would hurt someone else out of frustration. Of course, it was silly for her to ascribe a human emotion to such an alien presence. She was grateful when Yechtak told her that he would guide her to the ruins on the mesa, although she didn't quite understand the pride in his voice.

A woman wearing a simple homespun skirt and buckskin top decorated with red and white beads entered the tent quietly. She was carrying a large basket that she placed down right beside the fire. Inside, Lana saw slabs of bloody meat and carefully cleaned wooden skewers. The smell of congealing blood this close was overpowering and she felt herself growing dizzy again. Why had this woman brought the flesh of slaughtered animals inside a tent, anyway? She glanced up at Yechtak by way of a question, but the unmistakable expression on his face made her understand.

This was supposed to be *food*. She had heard the wind tribes ate the flesh of slaughtered animals, but she hadn't imagined that it would be in such quantities, without any normal food to temper it. The woman smiled at both the old man and Yechtak and made what sounded like polite conversation with them while she skewered the meat and placed the sticks on holders suspended above the fire. This vaguely reminded Lana of how her mother made grouper, except the smell of roasting meat, with the blood and fat dripping into the fire with sizzles and pops, nearly made her want to vomit. Of course, she knew that she could hardly afford to refuse these people's hospitality after they had agreed to escort her all the way to the ruins. Once three slabs of meat were sizzling above the fire, the woman took the blood-soaked basket and left the tent. She returned a few minutes later with three smaller baskets, each one half-filled with warm, golden-brown bread and a clay jug of water. To her surprise, Lana loved the bread, even with the smell of roasting flesh in her nostrils. It was sweet and made with a grain she had never tasted before. Although she was thirsty, she only sipped at the water—she didn't know when she would have more. She watched in dismay as the woman smiled and pushed a huge slab of meat off the spit and into her basket.

After the woman left, Yechtak and the old man dug into their food as though they were the wolves she had seen in the encampment earlier. Neither of them seemed to mind the way the blood in the uncooked center ran down their chins and mingled with the melted fat. Lana ate all of her bread and then began, reluctantly, to eat the meat. She had no excuse for wasting these people's food. It was chewy and even the parts that weren't bloody still tasted of animal. Beside her, Yechtak had sucked the marrow out of the bone and was looking as though he was actually still hungry. As surreptitiously as she could, Lana took the basket out of his hands and put hers in its place. He looked at her gratefully and began devouring it. So long as someone ate the meat, she didn't feel so bad about being rude. And despite the lingering queasiness in her stomach, the bread had finally satisfied the hunger that had been gnawing at her for the past few days.

After he finished eating, Yechtak rocked the old man—who had fallen asleep—gently by the shoulder. They talked for a few minutes and then he turned back to Lana.

"Tomorrow ... we have ceremony. The next day, I will lead you to ruins?"

Lana nodded. "That's good," she said.

When she followed him out of the tent she felt the old man's gaze on her back, but the death didn't linger there. As always, it followed her.

The next day, Lana felt torn between wanting to continue her journey and being grateful for the chance to stop and catch her breath. The beautiful red rocks and the cloudless sky looked brighter to her the next morning, as though her eyes could now register their actual hues. After Yechtak's mother served her a simple breakfast of bread and some kind of boiled vegetable, Lana found herself wandering around the camp. Most people smiled at her and some called out greetings, but they generally ignored her presence after a few seconds, returning to whatever tasks they had been doing. She began to feel like a ghost—or even like the death itself, silently observing people's lives, but unable to directly participate in them. Eventually she wandered to the far edge of the camp, where women chattered to each other as they sat in a circle grinding flour on large stone slabs with round stone pestles. Among the workers, she recognized the same woman who had brought her food the previous evening. She smiled at Lana and beckoned for her to come closer. In the middle of their circle was heaped a pile of the strangest grain she had ever seen. They were each about a foot long and covered in gold, orange or red berries that the women sawed off with knives before mashing in their bowls. The woman quietly handed Lana a stone slab, a pestle, and a basket already filled with berries. Curious, Lana sat next to her and began grinding the grain into coarse flour. The slab had a trough worn into the middle of it, precisely the width of the stone. After some initial covert glances, the other women ignored her and she fell easily into their rhythm. One of the older women raised her voice in a high, ululating chant. Lana paused and shook out her wrist, sore from the unaccustomed work. The women around her began hitting their pestles in unison and responded to the elder's call in rough harmony. As she didn't know the words, she stayed silent, but she swayed in rhythm and smiled at the comforting familiarity of it. Back on her island, she and the other divers had never been made to do these kinds of domestic chores, but she recalled the harvesting songs of the women who climbed the hills before the start of the rainy season to harvest the taro and manioc that grew there. In some ways, these strange people were far more familiar to her than the jaded citizens of cities like Okika and Essel.

Hours later, when the sun was beginning to sink behind the

dusty red rocks to the west, Lana heard the dry screech of a hrevech echo in the valley. The women looked at each other and then, silently, began to put away the day's work. The pounded grain they packed in tightly woven baskets and the remaining husks they stored in a small cave in the rock face. Through an evening sun bright enough to make her shade her eyes, Lana saw the wheeling figures of the hrevech settle down on rocky promontories. The women were oddly subdued as they walked back toward the main part of camp. In fact, everything was eerily quiet—all of the tents looked deserted. Even the wolves and horses had fallen silent. She wondered where everyone had gone, but when she tried to ask someone, the woman closest to her made a quiet shushing noise and gestured for Lana to keep walking. They walked until they left the outer edge of the camp and arrived at a range of large rocks a couple of hundred yards away. In dead silence and fading daylight, the women climbed up the worn path in the rocks one by one. The death stayed close by Lana, silent and brooding. It had been like this ever since she came to the wind island, and she was beginning to wonder if such close proximity to the stronghold of another spirit's power made it uncomfortable. If so, she thought, that knowledge might be a potent foundation for a geas. The climbing wasn't very difficult, but small rocks had gotten inside her sandals and cut the bottom of her feet. She had to pause every few minutes to kick them out, much to the annoyance of the women below her. Eventually she saw a large natural amphitheater, separated from the climbing path by a narrow passage that could fit two people abreast. Inside the huge flat space, surrounded on all sides by higher rocks, she saw a massive bonfire and hundreds of men and boys—what looked to be every single male in the tribe. The women, however, barely paused, climbing perhaps thirty feet above the amphitheater before emerging on relatively level ground. Hundreds of other women had already gathered there. Some sat, some stood, but no one spoke. They had a very clear view of the men below. The women let her near the edge of the rocks, and as she got closer, she recognized Yechtak, wearing only a loincloth, standing by the fire with the old shaman. He glanced up at Lana, but another woman clamped down on her hand when she tried to wave. This must be his initiation, Lana realized. She had expected it to be something like her own test when she had become a diver, but all of this felt far more intense. There was no sense of expectant happiness here—only worried anticipation.

Slowly, Lana lowered herself to the rocks and waited for the sun to finish its descent. Like all the other women, she could only wait and see what would happen.

Yechtak saw Iolana's attempt to wave at him and a nearby woman's rush to stop her from breaking the taboo. Of course Iolana had no way of knowing that communication between men and women during an initiation was forbidden, and her innocent gesture helped to ease his nervousness. She was a strange person, he thought, but he liked her. She had a habit of looking into space and quietly speaking—not as though she were talking to herself, but as though she could see someone he couldn't. He recalled Erlun's cryptic remarks about his bringing two guests the night before and wondered what kind of burden this woman carried. Tomorrow they would begin their journey together, and maybe he would be able to find out.

Soon after the last of the women arrived, Erlun raised his hand to signal the beginning of the ceremony. On the opposite side of the fire, Gervach pounded the lead drum into the ensuing silence. Moments later, the other drums began filling in the rhythm, slowly increasing their tempo until the whole amphitheater rang with the sound. In the distance, Yechtak heard the lonely call of a hrevech and the answering sigh of the wind.

Although Erlun, as shaman, was the ultimate leader of the tribe, Gervach's position as war chief made him nearly as powerful. In war councils, Gervach's opinion was tacitly understood to be final, but initiations like these were entirely under the shaman's jurisdiction. And a good thing, too—Gervach knew as well as anyone what this initiation meant, and he had been angling for years to have his son succeed Erlun after his death. Over Gervach's angry pounding, the shaman began chanting, a deep throaty sound that made the hair on Yechtak's arms shiver.

Erlun's two assistants took Yechtak by his shoulders and pushed him gently to the ground. He lay with his bare back on the cold, hard stone, staring up past the bonfire to the sky. The stars shone like hard, scattered bits of light, and the moon itself was barely a sliver. His heart was nearly pounding in time with the drums, but he tried to control his breathing. Erlun lit a torch in the fire and held it a foot from Yechtak's face.

"Who do you serve above all?" Erlun asked. The drums had stopped.

Yechtak watched the hypnotic motion of the torch as Erlun passed its searing heat over his chest and tried to remember his response. "The wild wind," he said, finally.

"Why?"

"To atone," Yechtak said. He wondered if the heat from the torch was burning his skin. "We are the descendants of the ancient guardians. We must honor the wild wind by repenting for its imprisonment."

Erlun nodded and handed the torch to an assistant. Yechtak stifled his sigh of relief. The shaman's blind eyes fixed on his face. "The path to the ruins is the spirit's closest secret," he said softly. "Do you swear to guard it well, my son? For all of our sakes?"

"I swear."

The drums began again, faster than before. His hands guided by an assistant, Erlun took up the special hrevech-bone tattoo quill and heavy wooden hammer. He began his chant again, an ancient hymn of honor to the wind spirit, as he dipped the quill in the deep black ink made with charred nuts. A man's hands held Yechtak's shoulders firmly, but he struggled not to squirm or wince when Erlun's hands came down with surprising sureness on his chest. The needles pierced his skin and the ink bled into the wounds as Erlun hammered on the sharp quills. Though Erlun had not been able to see the pattern on his chest for decades, he still knew its shape intimately, and no one else was permitted to transmit such a sacred design. The pain was horrible. Yechtak bit his tongue and stared into the fire, willing himself to be strong. After long minutes had passed, he found himself getting light-headed with the pain. The drums and Erlun's chants wavered in his ears and he turned abruptly away from the fire. He had to find something else to focus on. Looking up at the silent, shadowy figures of the women, he saw Iolana sitting with her legs over the ledge, staring down at him. He felt stronger looking at her, and the pain of the quills relentlessly pounding into his chest didn't seem so unbearable anymore. After half an hour, it was over. Someone put a wet cloth over his chest to soak up the blood and excess ink. Erlun, looking exhausted and far feebler than Yechtak had ever seen him, leaned forward when the drums fell silent. Beads of sweat dripped from his nose onto Yechtak's face.

"I wonder," he said, his voice low and raspy. "If I should have done this. I have changed your life forever ... just for that one Binder. I sense it ... a new path stretches ahead of you, and it is painful. Will you hate me for it later?"

"Never," Yechtak said in a strangled whisper. "I could never ..."

Erlun smiled softly and patted his shoulder. "Of course, we all have choice. If you turn away now, I won't blame you. And yet ..." He turned his face briefly away from Yechtak's and looked up to where some of the women still watched. Iolana was staring down at them, the light of the bonfire making the frizzy edges of her long, dark hair look like a bright halo around her head. Erlun looked back at him. "I somehow think you will stick to the path, no matter the dangers. She is dangerous, my son. She knows nothing of our ways, our language, and yet the wind spirit wishes to see her. That alone says enough, but I sense it. It's not just the burden she carries. She has more power than she realizes, and that is dangerous. Do your duty, but no more. Do not let her trap you."

Yechtak looked into Erlun's earnest, sad face and shuddered. "I won't. I promise."

Another man put a hand on the shaman's shoulder and helped

him stand. Conversation burst like an air bubble, a loud and un-intelligible stream of noise that Yechtak simply let wash over him. What was it about that girl that could scare Erlun so much? Even though Yechtak barely knew anything about her, it was his duty to lead her safely to the ruins. Tomorrow, his real initiation would begin.

They walked on foot, leading a stubborn burro that carried all of their supplies and water. For the first few days of their journey, Lana had wished almost continuously for a straw rain hat that could at least keep the worst of the sun from her face. Now, two weeks after setting out, she was beginning to get used to the pounding sun. They generally avoided walking in the grueling hour or two of high noon, spending it in the shade of rocks, if they could find them, or huddled beside the stoically uncomfortable burro if they couldn't. Yechtak was a nice companion, and his command of her language improved drastically over the days. He had learned it originally from his father, he said, who had spent some time on other islands when he was younger.

He fell unusually silent after mentioning his father, and Lana didn't press him. Instead, she diverted her attention by marveling at the subtle changes in landscape that she had been noticing over the past few days. While the land where Yechtak's tribe was camped had been virtually devoid of all plant life except for the occasional stunted scrub bush, the ground here was far moister, sprinkled with brightly colored wildflowers and an occasional tree. These trees had white bark with high, leafy branches that spread out like a paper umbrella. Up a hill in the distance grazed a herd of animals that looked something like deer, only larger and with fur of mottled blue and yellow patches. Several yards beyond them a similar creature nearly twice their size watched the herd protectively, occasionally waving his dangerously sharp tusks at the few other tusked creatures who tried to get within striking distance of the others.

"What are those?" she asked, pointing to the strange animals.

Yechtak seemed to snap out of whatever dream had been holding him. "Oh, the dveri. They are Ofek's this year, so I cannot touch them. Besides, there are only two of us, and wasting any part of a dveri is a crime. It would bring another war on our tribe."

Lana's stomach felt queasy at just the thought of eating such beautiful creatures, but she didn't comment, instead latching onto the implications of what Yechtak had just said. "Another war? With the other wind tribes? You *fight* each other?"

"Of course. How else could we decide who gets the dveri herds and the maize fields and the camps closest to the river? Do your people not war on each other?"

Lana spied a bright blue flower at her feet and knelt to pick it. "Not really," she said, braiding it into her hair. "There hasn't been a major war since the wind spirit broke free. Some of the islands have disputes with the others, but nothing ever gets very violent … I guess we don't think it's really worth it."

Yechtak looked amazed, but after a moment he nodded. "Yes, of course, your people are Binders. Though it is evil, binding does create ease among humans. It makes them … dependent on each other. Binders don't like war. For people like us, the true people, there is no ease, no other way besides war."

She thought about what he said the rest of that day, even as they set up camp on a small hill from which she had her first view of the swift-flowing river. Perhaps Yechtak was right—in a land with as few natural resources as this, perhaps war among humans was inevitable. But was it truly impossible for people to cooperate without the looming threat of a millennia-enslaved spirit breaking its bonds and wreaking revenge? Would the world really collapse if they all broke free?

The death sat near her by the fire. In its robes, she saw hundreds of men slaughtering each other for the sake of a field of maize.

A week later, most of it spent walking down-river while avoiding contact with the other wind tribes, they arrived at the entrance to the maze. Yechtak called it something else, a name that was unpronounceable even by the standards of his tongue, but it was quite simply a maze. The way through it had apparently been inscribed on his chest the night of his initiation. Even though it was relatively close to the river, the huge rocky outcropping looked nearly as barren as the place where Yechtak's tribe had been forced to camp. It stretched on for miles, and the peaks surrounding it were so high and jagged that the only way inside was through the tiny passage at its base near the river. Yechtak took the burro's lead and Lana followed behind, making her careful way through the labyrinth of crumbling stone and blocked passages. It was hot, dirty work, punctuated by long pauses in which Yechtak checked the tattoo on his chest before choosing the best path. They had to stop earlier than they usually did, because the high rocks on either side of them cast long shadows that made it impossible to navigate the treacherous footing.

Yechtak said that they didn't have to worry about either dangerous predators or the other wind tribes here, so they set up camp virtually where they stopped walking. The wind began howling after night fell, but the surrounding rocks protected them from the brunt of it. Lana shivered and pulled her blanket closer around her shoulders. The burro snorted and shuffled its feet nervously, looking around as though trying to discover the source of the unearthly moans. Yechtak said something softly in his own language and then began tracing the dark pattern on his chest without actually looking at it.

"How much longer till we reach the ruins?" Lana asked, pitching her voice so she could be heard over the screaming wind.

"Two days, I think," he said. "We have finished the most difficult part." He reached into the fire with a long stick and rolled out one large, soot-covered brown egg. They had been eating hrevech eggs ever since Yechtak found an unattended nest three days before. Even though Yechtak complained loudly about the lack of meat, Lana was secretly grateful for their plain fare. The eggs, in fact, were a surprising treat, because she hadn't expected to like them. Back on her island, they had never eaten anything other than fish eggs, and even after she left, she had only eaten eggs from sparrows and the occasional chicken. Yechtak took the egg, cracked it open against a nearby stone, and gave the larger half to Lana. Even though it had been sitting in the fire for nearly half an hour, the yolk was still a little soupy. She dipped the end of a stale piece of bread inside it and began eating silently, wishing that the wind would sound a little less threatening. Above her she heard the dull clack of falling rocks dislodged by the wind.

She yawned and looked up, surprised to see that Yechtak was staring at her intently.

"What is it?" she asked, tossing the empty half-shell further down the path.

He shook his head. "It is nothing. You should sleep ... tomorrow will as well be hard."

She thought of pressing him—his eyes seemed so distant and troubled—but instead she nodded and lay down a few feet from the fire. She had almost drifted off when Yechtak's quiet voice startled her awake again.

"Do you remember how I told you before ... about our wars?"

"I remember," Lana said, her voice a scratchy whisper.

"I ... did not tell you everything. The wars are not just for life ... for water and maize. They are for manhood. Boys wish to be men, to be brave, so they fight wars. My mother says ... she says they are games. Deadly games. My father died in those games, then my brother. Now I'm all she has left. I am seventeen—most fight before this age, but my mother begged me not to. And I stayed a boy, to be with her. Erlun is wise, he must have known why I stayed in my mother's tent, so he sent me with you, so I can be a man without the games. The Binding is evil and yet ... without war I would still have my father. My brother ..."

His voice trailed off into silence. Lana sat frozen, wondering if she should say something, or if she even had the right. She had spent the past few months so wrapped up in desperation and self-pity that she had barely given a thought to all the things she still did have. Unlike Yechtak, she still had both of her parents. In the end, she didn't say anything. Yechtak remained silent, and her own thoughts lulled her back into a dreamless sleep.

Something had fallen on top of her.

She opened her eyes abruptly and bit back a curse of frustration when she realized that she could hardly see anything: it was still dark and the fire had dwindled to a few glowing coals.

The thing on top of her moved and she realized it was Yechtak. His face was close to hers now, and she could feel his heavy, wet breath on her cheek.

"I am sorry," he said softly, incomprehensibly. "But I want ... I mean, I would like very much ..." His words were slurred and confused, as though he had just woken.

"Would you kiss me, Iolana?"

Lana tried to hide her shock. "Yechtak, why—"

He closed his mouth over hers. She felt his rough tongue and tasted the sour tang of his saliva. For a moment, she stopped struggling in her shock. Unbidden, an image came to her mind of her mother, back when they were in Okika, with bruises on her arms and face from the men she slept with. She thought of that horrible sailor in the rain who had dislocated her jaw. Was Yechtak no better than those leering, violent men? What was he doing to her?

She freed one of her hands and began pounding on his back, shrieking as well as she could with her mouth covered. She didn't want this ...

Just as suddenly as he had fallen on top of her, he broke off the kiss and backed away. Lana closed her eyes, trying to calm her high-pitched wheezing. Minutes later, unsure of what else to do, she looked back up at him. Tears were running from his wide open eyes and his hands were shaking.

"I did not deserve this," he whispered, touching his tattoo gently. "Erlun trusted me too much. I am not a man, just a boy ..."

His sobs echoed off the rocks, filled with such wrenching pain that her heart opened to him despite herself. Tentatively, she reached over and touched his shoulder. He reacted to her gesture violently, taking his head out of his arms and shaking her off as though she had some deadly disease.

"Do not touch me," he said. "You cannot. My ... my love is too strong. I cannot control."

Lana gripped her elbows and looked away, trying to push away her shock and figure out what to do. But before she could decide, a large rock crashed to the ground with a deafening noise a few yards away. The burro brayed frantically and began tugging at its lead rope, which was attached to a nearby rock. With a sudden snap, it broke and the burro took off down the path, in the direction of an even louder rock fall. Lana glanced at Yechtak, but he simply looked stricken. She knew, however, that if that burro escaped with all their supplies, they were both doomed. She scrambled upright and took off after it, holding the blanket over her head to keep the falling pebbles from hitting her face. Behind her, she heard the roar of more falling rocks, but she ignored it. The burro had stopped its frantic run and was cowering in the shelter of an overhanging rock. She walked toward it slowly, amazed by the sudden, dead silence. The wind had abruptly ceased howling and the last of the rocks had fallen. The burro came to her almost gratefully and she stroked its head while she waited for her breathing to steady.

She knew almost before she turned around that she was boxed in. That noise behind her had been too large for anything besides an avalanche. By the light of the first streaks of dawn, Lana saw the huge pile of broken red rocks hazily through the whorls of dislodged dust. Her legs could barely hold her up when she walked closer to it, leading the reluctant burro by the broken rope.

"Yechtak," she called as loudly as she could, "are you all right?"

After Lana had almost convinced herself that he was either dead or lying unconscious, she heard him clear his throat. "I am all right. This is best. We are separated."

"Don't be crazy!" Lana shouted. "I have all the supplies! What are you going to do without water? How can I get to the ruins without you?"

"I have some water with me. I will go another way and meet you there. Your way is simple. Follow the path until you reach a white stone shaped like a bird. There will be a tunnel. Follow the tunnel until you reach the mesa."

She heard his footsteps walking away from her. She stayed for a long time calling his name, but he never responded.

She and the burro could just barely fit in the cave beside the bird-shaped stone. The statue was weathered and pockmarked, but the folded wings and open beak were still unmistakable, and she had breathed a sigh of relief when she saw it. She didn't know what she would do if she got lost in this maze. The death seemed to grow more insubstantial as they walked through the crumbling stone passageway, but it still followed her silently. The violent images that she was accustomed to seeing in its robe had vanished as well, making her think that this close to the wind's stronghold, the death must be losing its power. The thought cheered her even as she wondered what awaited her on the other end of the tunnel. Would the wind spirit help her, or had it simply called her here on a cruel whim? The tunnel widened and the path turned into a series of shallow steps that continued for an interminably long time. The tunnel was dark, but the death itself let off a cold glow by which it seemed both she and the burro could see. She lost all sense of time as she trudged up the stairs, her dusty sweat soaking her clothes. She was hardly aware of when they emerged at the top, except that the brighter light made her squint.

"Your protection is almost ended," the death said quietly. "You'll be mine soon."

Lana didn't even bother responding—she was too close to her goal, too close to surrendering herself to yet another spirit to think about the one already dogging her. Even though they had been destroyed five hundred years ago, and ever since subjected to the worst ravages of time and weather, the ruins on the mesa still had more than enough power to enthrall. Gigantic spires of deep red stone climbed to the sky even as their foundations crumbled beneath them. Toward the center of the mesa, what must have once been the main building was now reduced to piles of rubble, though even these were still commanding due to their sheer size. She wondered how anyone could have hauled so much stone to build such a massive structure in this remote wasteland of a place. It must have been very grand a thousand years ago. She, however, could not help but reflect on the irony of the scores of people who must have sweated and toiled to build a structure dedicated to the glory of a failed binding.

Even though there was no discernable breeze on the mesa, her hair fluttered and the burro shuffled nervously. She climbed with it over a few scattered piles of rocks—some of which looked like they might be the smashed remains of statues—and tied what was left of its rope to a post sticking out from a ruined wall. She just hoped that the burro wouldn't bolt, no matter what happened to her. Even if she didn't succeed, Yechtak would still need the supplies to get back home. She looked back over the mesa and saw that its dead center was occupied by a tall circular platform, strangely undamaged given the destruction around it. It seemed like the ideal place to wait for the power she had come to meet.

Trying to ignore the fear that suddenly gripped her innards, she pulled the glass wind jar from her pack and, after a moment's thought, slung the bag over one shoulder. She would regret being without her blanket or water when it grew dark. She gave the burro one last pat on its head and started walking toward the center of the ruins.

"I can't go any farther," the death said when she reached the base of the platform. A ladder of step-sized holes had been bored into the stone at regular intervals. She took her hands from the holes and looked back at the death.

"Then stay," she said. "I'm sure you won't be parted from me for long."

She took a great pleasure in climbing up the rock before it had a chance to respond.

After she clambered over the top, she sat silently for about ten minutes, reveling in the view and the simple pleasure of feeling *alone* again. Soon, she would be at the mercy of yet another spirit, but for now, her time was her own. Geas were strange, weren't they? They were as much about surrender as control. She hadn't understood that when she was still with Akua, but she did now. Terror and hope, bound in one irresistible package.

Then she picked up the glass jar and pulled out the cork.

The wind that she had called with the spider-crone back in the Kalakoas came roaring over the mesa. For a few heady moments she smelled the rich, damp aroma of loamy earth and air teeming with all kinds of life. What a difference from this arid, nearly barren place. Instead of gradually fading away, the wind picked up even more fervor and intensity, blowing around the platform until it was like a wall on all sides. A large, vaguely human shape, made entirely from frantically pulsing wind and swirling red dust, flew forward until it was a few feet away from her. She was shivering uncontrollably, but she forced herself to stare into its hideously malleable face.

"I have come," Lana said to it. "A solitary pilgrim to beg help from the one that broke free."

The dust in the wind's makeshift body seemed to glow. "And why should I grant help to a descendent of the Binders? Dare you think I owe you something?" Though she could barely hear her own voice, the wind's words pierced her ears and made her shivering even more pronounced.

"Spirits never owe," she said, squinting against the dust swirling around her face. "Humans sacrifice, and spirits grant. I only ask that you allow me the chance to sacrifice. Did you not call me here? Do you not know why I come, instead of resigning myself to the death that chases me?"

The wind's laugh was so piercing that her knees nearly buckled. "I do, of course. I know you are Iolana bei'Leilani and you come on behalf of your mother, who knows more than you think of what you have done for her. But perhaps I did not call you here to help you. What if I only called you here to see who this girl was, she who has caused such ripples among the ones that remain bound?"

"I have come," Lana said with a lot more bravery than she felt. "What do you see?"

"A young, naïve sapling who understands only a small part of the danger that chases her. You don't see what you are involved in, sapling, do you?"

"I understand that I must save my mother. But I don't know enough, I don't have enough power ... you think I don't understand those things? That's why I came halfway across the world to find you."

The wind laughed again, and this time Lana was forced to sink to one knee. "Ah, desperate, but not entirely stupid. But my time for vengeance has long passed, and I would be a fool to kill a girl that death itself regards as important enough to chase. You might keep it bound just yet, for all your naïveté."

Lana could hardly contain her shock. "You mean ... you want the spirits bound, even though ..."

"The binding is hideous. It forced me into to a shape against all my nature. All the spirits rebel against it, but only I broke free. I have existed in the world before death was bound and after ... and I prefer the world after. So, it seems I owe you Binders something, after all. I agree to grant your request."

The wind's pseudo-body suddenly broke apart and dust swirled around her, getting caught in her nose and making her sneeze violently. The sounds of the wind began to increase in force.

"Do you know the sacrifice of the wind?" the dust screamed.

Lana thought back to the days when Kohaku had taught her about the spirit bindings. She could almost hear his voice in her head. "Time ..." she said slowly, "Time and pain."

The wind decreased to a mild breeze. It reformed in its vaguely human shape before her and smiled. "Good," it said. Very slowly, it leaned forward and caressed the back of her head. Then it kissed her lips. Its kiss was smooth and dry—miles away from the hot desperation of Yechtak's mouth two days earlier. This time, however, she didn't dare struggle. She let it kiss her and stayed silent even when it pulled away, wondering why her body felt so charged with power.

"You cannot speak," it whispered, "or open your mouth to scream until the third rising of the sun. If you speak, the death will take you. If you leave this altar, the death will take you. On the third dawn, you will have the gift I grant you: You will become a black angel. So long as you fly, the death will not be able to take you."

Lana stared at the wind spirit, but did not even dare gasp. A black angel? There had only been two in known history, and both had presaged great destruction. In fact, the second black angel had given herself as the sacrifice that allowed the wind spirit to free itself. With another bone-shuddering laugh, the wind faded from the promontory and Lana found herself alone again.

So she had bet, and she had lost.

A pain greater than any she had ever known flared along her back. She dug her palms into the stone, bit her lip, and waited.

The death could not step onto the promontory, but it could circle around it, taunting and tormenting her when it knew that she was powerless to even voice a retort. It would call out to her with Kali's voice, begging Lana to save her and then blaming her for her death. Lana cried, but she did not speak and she did not move.

Slowly, the wings were beginning to burst from her skin. Blood ran down her back, soaking into her pants and shirt. When she realized that part of the agony was being caused by her shirt constricting the growing wings, she roughly tore two holes into the worn fabric. By the time the first sun rose, the baby feathers and growing bone structure stuck out perhaps two feet from her body. Occasionally, she heard the wind, but it was always as a faint whisper, as though it were merely checking on her. The death, on the other hand, was implacable.

The wet blood baked onto her skin in the blistering sun. Flies landed on her back and buzzed around her ears. She barely had the energy to shake them off, and touching her back to brush them away made her want to vomit. About once an hour, she allowed a trickle from her water skin to wet her lips. Even though she desperately wanted more, she knew that she would have to ration the relatively small amount over the next two days. Survival was all that mattered, the only real meaning that could enter her mind as the sun made its way across the sky.

I won't let you die, Mama, she repeated silently to herself as the monstrous black wings ravaged her back. *I won't.*

The second night, Lana dreamt of water. Everything else she forgot when she awoke, but she was left with a penetrating sense of terror and a conviction that she had, somehow, been drowning. Had her wings dragged her under? That seemed to trigger a memory, but then it vanished under a renewed onslaught of pain. *Of course,* she thought, *how could an angel ever swim?*

She felt the urge to scream so strongly that she was forced to stuff her fist into her mouth until she could calm down. It hadn't even occurred to her before, but the undeniable reality made her want to toss herself off the edge of the platform and let the death have its way with her.

She would never be able to dive again. A creature of the water, she had now bound herself permanently to the wind. She was becoming a paradox, a character in tales parents told their children: not an angel, but a waterbird.

Long ago (her father always said, when he had minutes to spare and she begged him for the story) before humans existed and the islands were just the blackened offspring of the union between earth and fire, a strange creature lived beneath the sea. It had no name, for it was merely one of thousands of half-spirits that existed in those days.

What did it look like? (she would ask) The purest, most beautiful mandagah fish (her father said), with eyes like green jewels and skin that flashed and swirled with different colors. And large, larger even than he.

This creature was the least of its kind, yet it longed to be the greatest. And not within the confines of its people and traditions, but in a grander, far more dangerous way. This creature decided that to be the greatest of its kind, it must leave the water.

So it approached the great Kai in its coral palace.

"Kai," it asked, "can you grant my desire? Can you give me wings to escape the water?"

The Kai shook its great head. "I have not the power to change your nature, water creature. Return home, accept your fate."

But the creature refused to give up. It approached the earth spirit, just now entering its half-slumber.

"I also have not the power, water creature," it answered. "Return home, accept your fate."

So the creature, stubborn and determined, approached the wind. "Oh master of air," it asked, "please, do you have the power to release me from this water?"

"Only one power can change your nature, water creature, and I have it not."

"Which power is this, great wind? How have I never heard of it?"

The wind laughed. "Ah, you have heard of it. The power that transforms movement to stillness, presence to absence, something to nothing. Have you never felt it?"

The creature understood. "Death?"

"If you have the courage to face it."

So the creature searched for death, but it was harder to find in those days of spirits great and small.

After many years of searching, the creature found the death by its side.

"Death," he said, "you alone have the power to change my nature. Can you give me wings to leave the water?"

"Why not step through the gate? That is the truest change."

The creature was afraid. "I do not long to die, Death."

So Death decided to grant the creature's sincerest wish. Its body transformed from that of a great fish into something between two states—a waterbird.

At first the waterbird was happy. But it discovered that it could no longer swim.

Why not, Papa?

Because its body had too much bird for the water (he said).

It called for the death, but it did not return. So it crawled, so slowly the journey lasted years, to the surface. Here, it thought, finally I'll be great. But on the surface, it could fly, but it couldn't breathe.

Why not, Papa?

Because fish can't breathe out of water, Lana, like you can't breathe underwater.

"Death," it gasped as it died. "Come here, take it back. I don't want to be this half-thing anymore."

"But I gave you exactly what you desired, waterbird."

"Please save me!"

At the sight of the creature's distress, Death relented. "I cannot change you back," it said, "but I can give you a halfway place for your halfway body."

And so the death took the waterbird to the netherworld between death and life, where it guards and lives to this very day.

Why was the waterbird so stupid, Papa?

We all long for things we shouldn't have, Lana. Thankfully, most of us never get them.

The third night, Lana began vomiting. She didn't know how much blood she had lost by now, but the slickness on her back and her persistent dizziness did not reassure her. All she had to do was make it through one more dawn. Yet the hours had never stretched so long before, and the pain had reached a pitch that was almost unendurable in this enforced silence. Her throat itched with the need to scream, to weep. She could feel new muscles forming in her back, strong enough to move the huge black wings that had now grown as tall as she.

"Lana ... I'm dying," said the death to her, using her mother's voice. "Please come. Please come and save me."

Lana grabbed a handful of rocks and hurled them at the death. They sailed through its body and landed on the ruins below. She longed to scream at it, but instead she bit on her already bloody lip and closed her eyes. She was stronger than all this—they would see how strong she could be. Her strength would be equal to what she had lost. The light from the half moon shone harshly tonight, illuminating nearly the entire mesa. She heard the rough scratching of something scrambling over the rocks to her left, but she ignored it, assuming that it was one of the small rodents that lived in the ruins. When she heard a gasp, however, she turned her head.

It was Yechtak. He had climbed to the top of one of the mounds of rocks near the burro. His eyes were wide, but he had clamped his hands over his mouth as though he did not dare speak. Perhaps he knew she was bound to silence. The wind briefly swirled around him and then faded away again. They stared at each other for a long moment before something like resolution settled on his face.

In the last few hours before dawn, Yechtak sang the wind in his rough untrained voice, giving her a measure of peace through the beauty of his own sorrow.

The first light of dawn hit the mesa, turning the sky a clean pink instead of the blood red sunrise she remembered from all those years ago, when she had completed an entirely different sort of ordeal. The pain in her back subsided to a dull throbbing—the wings had finished growing. She had given the sacrifice of the wind. For all the good it had done her.

Her joints screaming in protest, she forced herself to stand up. The new muscles in her back seemed to know how to fold the wings so their tips merely brushed the ground. The stones around her were littered with night-black feathers. Wind ruffled her hair gently, and the spirit gradually emerged before her in its semi-corporeal form.

"You have succeeded, pilgrim. You have become my black angel." Its voice was gentle, almost respectful. "I can no longer protect you here. You must go."

Lana wondered if the itching in her throat was a scream or a swear. She had wanted help, but not this. It was too much sacrifice, too much pain.

"These wings … are a curse." Her voice was rough, barely audible.

The wind didn't deny it. "A necessary one. They will keep you alive that much longer."

Lana nodded slowly and picked up her bag, containing only a blanket, an empty water skin, and her now-useless leibo. As she straightened, she heard Yechtak's warning shout and was then suddenly overcome with the death's invasive presence. This was worse than the time in the forest—she was much weaker, and it was far more determined. She started to slip away and then, just as abruptly, found herself kneeling on the floor of the altar, panting and alive. Wind screeched and pounded in her ears.

"You must fly, Lana. Take my gift and leave!" Desperation was palpable in its voice, and when she turned around, she understood why: it was fighting the death spirit. She had no time left.

Stretching out her wings experimentally, she let off a wild, defiant yell and threw herself from the top of the promontory. At first she fell, but then a gust of wind buoyed her up and she pumped her wings—tentatively at first, and then desperately. And then she was rising, floating up and manipulating gusts of wind with an instinct she barely understood. She turned around and saw Yechtak, singing as he scrambled higher on the rocks, and she realized that the favorable winds were his doing.

"Goodbye, Yechtak," she shouted. Moments later, both he and the mesa vanished out of sight.

Yechtak waited for a long time on the rock pile, until the curious howling wind on the sacred altar had stopped and he sensed the wild spirit itself coming closer to him. He held his breath and waited as it formed itself out of the wind.

"Do you realize what you just witnessed, my son?" asked the wind.

Yechtak nodded. He could hardly believe it, but he knew. "I saw ... she became a black angel."

"Yes. And you love her, even so?"

He nodded again. "I will always."

"Then I have a duty for you, a sacred task that only you can perform. Will you accept it? Will you do what none of your people have been asked for centuries?"

He thought of Erlun's trust in him and how he had broken it so quickly. He would not break it this time. This time, he vowed, he would be strong enough. "I accept," he said. "What do you wish me to do?"

"Leave this island, and tell the world what you have seen. Be the black angel's herald ... and perhaps the destruction to come won't give death so much strength."

Then the wind left him and he was alone.

At first only the stones themselves, the ancient red sentinels older even than the wild wind, witnessed the passage of the black angel. For her, they stirred themselves, and watched her ungainly first flight out of the ruins and over the plains. *Poor girl,* they thought, remembering the other, the one who flew like an eagle and not a just-born fledgling, the one who had returned and let her blood splash across the stones of the mesa so that the wild wind would be free. To the stones, it did not seem like so very long ago. They wondered how this one, too, would die.

She passed out of sight of the mesa and the wondering rock, her wingstrokes stronger now, her command of the air more sure. The dveri were the first mortal creatures to see her, and at the sight the females huddled close to the river. A great black, wheeling hrevech, they thought her—for they did not know how else to view such massive wings that blotted even the sunlight. No vicious beak or chilling caw, but nothing about the majestic figure suggested anything human. They were slow to edge away from the lake, even after its shadow dwindled to a speck. They were small; its splendor was predatory and frightening. They had never seen anything quite like it before.

Only a few children from Ofek's tribe noticed the angel, and they pointed at the sky in startled and excited shrieks that caused their dogs to bark and their caretaker to shush them. It was heading towards they ocean, they saw, a great black-winged god shot like a slingshot from the wild spirit's ruins.

"Nana! Nana!" they shouted, squinting their eyes against the bright dawn sun and just barely making out a human figure beneath those impossibly large wings.

With a sigh, Nana looked up from her beading and prepared to humor them.

Her eyes were not what they had been, but she saw what had captured the children's attention readily enough. Her dveri bone beads fell with a series of tiny smacks into the mud below.

She said a prayer, and then another. The creature she was all too afraid she recognized vanished over the ocean, with not even a feather to mark her passage.

. . .

The sudden flash of light from inside the column was so bright that Manuku stumbled backwards and landed on the hard marble floors of the 'Ana's room. Unable to stop himself, he grabbed the mirror and looked to see what had happened.

It was the girl again. He could tell that much even before the light cleared and he could see the image. Since that day four years ago when he had dared to look into the column with the 'Ana's mirror, he had seen her often. The death spirit seemed obsessed with her, especially during the past year. But this was easily the most agitated he had ever seen it. The image he saw in the column made him grip the handle of the mirror until the scalloped edges bit painfully into his skin.

She had wings. Unspeakably massive black wings that the girl was using to fly over the ocean. He thought that it must be one of the spirit's lies, but the shock and the anger that seemed to vibrate off the image told him that it was true. But how? How could any human fly? There was blood on her face, he saw, and she was crying as she beat through the air, as if it hurt her to do so.

The image suddenly changed. He saw the binding chamber, and he knew that this was the scene the death had shown him a hundred times over the last four years. He hated watching it and knew he should put down the mirror and leave, but the same curiosity that had stayed his hand so many times before kept him watching now as well. It was slightly different this time, he realized. The girl had never had wings before. Then he saw that she was holding him, and the expression on her face was so vicious that he winced. He saw the glint of a blade and then she was stabbing it into him over and over again until blood covered the front of her shirt and he could no longer even see his own face.

Manuku smashed the mirror.

11

KAI STOOD UP TO HIS KNEES IN THE MUDDY CREEK that had once been the mighty Moka river. He let the water soak through his pants and the sediment settle over his feet, though he could have stayed perfectly dry if he chose. On the muddy banks to his left and right, stranded fish flopped and drowned beneath the harsh sun. Their desperate need to survive, the frantic pounding of their hearts as they slowly slipped towards death assailed his mind like a thousand tiny hammers. His head ached, but he refused to shut them out entirely. He was Kaleakai, the almost-water guardian, and even these dying river fish took some comfort in that. They hadn't made it to the tributary in time for spawning. There shouldn't have been a need to—the Moka dwindled to this degree rarely, and even then only in the high dry season. These fish had thought they had plenty of time to find a mate, to lay their eggs, to die in the cool waters upstream.

And they should have.

Aware of the futility, but unable to stop himself, Kai touched the waterbird feather in his hair and called a geas. Moments later, water coursed over his arms as though from nowhere, a torrential rush that washed all the flapping fish from the banks and into the muddy river. He forced himself to stop when all the frantic voices of their deaths had turned into sighs of contentment, the reassertion of purpose. Kai looked down at the river—it had risen barely an inch, and even that had exhausted him so he felt dizzy where he stood. Slowly, he climbed up the slippery bank and onto the tall brown grass at the river's edge. A few hundred yards across from the river, a series of rice paddies lay abandoned. The drought had dried up more than the river—back in the last village he had seen dozens of refugee farmers in line at the well. He had no idea where they would go now. He sighed and sat up, swatting at the flies that had found him in the absence of dying fish.

He needed to make it to the country inn by nightfall, but he realized he wasn't looking forward to braving human company again. He had never understood quite how alien he appeared to most people until he had left on this journey. Pua had never treated him differently and his father was ... well, his father. He knew he had powers no human could touch, but those differences had never made him feel like some sort of chimera—until now.

Of course, he thought, standing up and stretching, he wasn't very good at talking to people. Back at the village, the refugees had pointed to his hair and skin and whispered to each other in increasingly loud voices. Finally, one middle-aged man, his skin brown from the sun, had walked up to him.

"Are you a guardian?" he asked, a little belligerently.

Kai realized he didn't even know the answer. For two weeks he'd avoided the thought of going home and receiving his father's tears. Two weeks while his father waited in the antechamber of death.

"Yes," he said, inadequately.

The whispers from the crowd behind him grew into sounds of outright shock. The man looked angry. "Did you bring the drought with you? We all know it's the spirits. Something's happened."

"It isn't me, or the water spirit," Kai said, although he supposed he couldn't be entirely sure of the latter. "I'm trying to discover the cause of your drought. Events like this are happening throughout the islands. I think you must be right, it must be the spirits."

The man seemed a little surprised at Kai's honesty. "Well ... what spirits, then? We offered sacrifices," he gestured behind him. "You can see how well they worked."

Kai hid his horror at the thought of what these farmers' back-garden sacrifices might have entailed—needless death, mangled geas, almost-useless bindings—and attempted to claim that he didn't know anything else.

"There's only two left, though," the farmer said, cutting through his babble of words. "Only two it could be."

Fire and death. The words had chased themselves through his thoughts ever since he had left the water shrine, and all throughout his long walk down the Moka river road. He hadn't even reached the inner temples, and already he had seen more than enough to convince him of his worst fears. The spirits weren't just *trying* to break free—*one of them had already weakened its bonds.* The knowledge was enough to terrify the hardiest guardian. Droughts along the Moka, far worse than any for centuries; brackish water and wholesale mandagah deaths in the islands around the death shrine; contagious fevers, of a virulence no doctor had ever encountered, engulfing whole trading villages in the Kalakoas; tide pools on some outer islands mysteriously glowing right before volcano eruptions ... something was happening, something un-precedented for at least half a millennium. Kai's father had refused to consider the possibility. If it had nothing to do with the water spirit, it was none of his concern. Sometimes it seemed that his father really didn't care if millions of people died, like when the wind spirit had broken free. And people thought of *him* as alien— Kai shook his head at the irony. They would quake in fear at the sight of his father's cold, fey, utterly inhuman countenance. Or they would have, before Ali'ikai had chosen death.

Fire or death. He had drafted a letter to the new Mo'i of Essel, and he had high hopes that it might yield some results. After all, the Mo'i had just recently been selected by the fire spirit itself. He, more than anyone, might have a clue as to the strength of its bonds. Kai had also written a letter to the death guardian, but he didn't have much hope. By all accounts, Lono made Kai's father look like the soul of human charity. And yet so much of these occurrences suggested the last-bound spirit. But perhaps that was just his prejudice—of the four original bindings, only the death Binder had survived the process. The infamous 'Ana, who supposedly still lived in her tower on the inner island. No one knew how she had bound it; the depth of the mysteries surrounding that most famous of geas had fascinated scholars for centuries. Kai had always wondered how they could trust such a mysterious binding. And after what he had seen on this journey, he couldn't help his suspicions.

He arrived at the inn just as the sun was setting behind the bamboo groves around the Moka River. He had expelled the water from his clothes, but the dirt clung to them, and he knew he hardly resembled a distinguished guest. The expression of disdain on the face of the proprietor who opened the door to the tall gates revealed this quite eloquently, but her expression changed when she saw his face.

"Oh, your honor," she said, smiling widely, "we were expecting you."

"Of course," Kai said, disliking her instantly. But the grounds of the inn were lovely, and no one here would be so boorish as to stare and whisper.

"I trust you had a nice journey, sir?" she asked, without any obvious irony.

Fire or death? "Lovely."

He cast his mind up to a flock of cranes that had just emerged in a frantic tangle from the reeds by the river. Their calls echoed across the empty fields. He felt their panic and caught a hazy image of a great thing tearing across the sky. He pulled away and shook his head. Something big was coming. Something that reeked of death.

But he supposed that he already knew that.

. . .

There was an old saying that Nahoa had been hearing a lot recently: "The Mo'i's house is a place of hidden things." Now, nearly three months after she had married Kohaku, she knew it only painted half the picture. It wasn't just his house that kept things hidden, it was his heart, too. On the ship during their long ride home, everything had seemed like a dream. He had been so open and relaxed and gentle around her, and she had settled naturally into the role of caretaker. He had needed it at first—he had been incredibly weak and awkward in the days just after he lost his hand. But even after he began to heal, he seemed to expect the same level of devotion from her, demanding that she help him undress and pick out his clothes, even though the house had many servants. To be honest, though, she didn't mind—even though in public he acted like the soul of authority, she saw him in his most desperate moments of insecurity. She knew how much he needed her. Sometimes he would wake up late in the middle of the night, sweating and shaking. Sometimes he seemed to be furiously arguing with someone, but of course there was no one else in the room. Mostly, he just begged her, "Has it happened yet?" Usually, she would soothe him and say "no," but one night she actually pressed him.

"Has *what* happened yet? What are you talking about?"

He looked at her, his eyes glazed over as if he were still half-dreaming. "The dying," he said quietly.

She didn't ask him anything else after that.

It scared her, how little she knew about him and yet how deeply she cared about him. He would vanish for days at a time, and when he returned would behave as though his absence had never happened. He ignored her questions about where he had been so completely that she eventually just gave up asking.

He had been gone for two days now. Whenever he disappeared, the servants would avoid meeting her eyes and protest—far too loudly—that they new nothing of "His Honor." Sometimes, the pressure of being such a stranger in this sprawling labyrinth of a house made her want to open a window and scream. It would have been okay if she had Kohaku to share it with, but over the months he had only grown more distant. Three years ago, when she had left a house with too many children and too little space to become a sailor, she had thought she could never get enough of solitude. Now it wore at her bones until she cried, helpless and alone in the Mo'i's vast quarters.

Still in her sleeping clothes even though it was well past noon, Nahoa paced in circles around the room, unmindful of the tears that fell in a slow drip from her eyes. Her nose began to run and she looked around for something to blow it with. The room was a mess, she realized with mild surprise. Rumpled bed linen was strewn across the floor. Two days' worth of uneaten food trays were stashed in every corner and dirty clothes covered most of the floor space. What in hell had she been doing for the past two days anyway? It was mostly a blur—she remembered calling for amant weed and a pipe the first night she realized Kohaku wasn't coming back home. She must have been wandering in a forgetful amant-induced haze ever since.

"You have to pull yourself out of this," she muttered. She thought about her mother, and how depressed she had been after their father died. She had sat around for days after the funeral, refusing to eat or sleep or cook for her seven children. As the oldest, Nahoa was forced to take on her responsibilities, and for the first time she had gained a real appreciation of the work her mother went through, willingly, every day. This experience had also made Nahoa suspect that she never wanted children. And then, a month after her mother had fallen into her depression, she abruptly levered herself up from her chair and, quite matter-of-factly, began making dinner. She never smiled quite as much, afterward, but she seemed to have recovered.

"Your father wouldn't have wanted me to die for him," her mother said one day years later, when Nahoa asked her. "And I still had all of you. So I decided that the best thing to do was keep busy. The pain doesn't go away, exactly, but … it's easier to ignore."

That, Nahoa realized, was exactly what she had to do. She blew her nose on a nearby bedsheet and tossed it into the center of the room with the other dirty clothes. Then she straightened up the bed and piled the food trays on top of one another—pausing to eat some cold bread pudding and fried spiced tubers from the night before. Of course, she knew that she didn't have to do this. In fact, the maids would probably be appalled, but she hardly cared. After the main rooms had been cleared, she decided to get started on the wardrobes. Kohaku's, to her surprise, had a huge pile of dirty clothes on the floor. She had assumed the maids cleaned it, but perhaps he had given instructions for it not to be disturbed. She slowly sifted through the pile, smelling the clothes and deciding that most had to be cleaned. They had a strange, musty smell about them—damp and almost metallic. A shirt at the bottom of the pile was by far the dirtiest—stiff and crackly with some hardened substance. She brought it out into the light to see the stain more clearly.

She let out a brief scream of surprise before swiftly stifling it.

The shirt was covered with blood.

After her initial frenzied panic subsided, she became aware of two things. First, that the blood—still a little damp on the inside—could not possibly be Kohaku's. Second, that since she didn't have the guts to confront him with it, she had to find some way to get rid of the shirt before one of the maids discovered it. Unsure of what else to do, she put the shirt inside a sacrifice bag and called for one of her maids to help her get ready to go out. She would have to go to the temple. She had been there a lot recently, to be free momentarily of this house and its frustrations. She wondered if she was gaining a reputation in the city for being a strange religious recluse.

"It's good to see you getting back to your old self, my lady," said Malie, her maid, as she helped her into her clothes. "You've kept too much to yourself lately. If I may, I don't think all of this isolation is very healthy."

Nahoa sighed. "You're right. It's hell." She tried to curb her language in formal situations, but around Malie she felt more comfortable. "But what can I do? I might be first wife, but there's no one around for me to talk to."

Malie pulled Nahoa's hair into a bun and then began wrapping a beautifully woven scarf of gold, white, and orange around her head.

"Well, you know," she said as she fastened it with a few judiciously placed pins. "Ka Nui, the cook—his sixtieth birthday is today and he's having this big celebration in the kitchens tonight. There should be plenty of food and music ... I mean, please don't be offended, I'm not trying to be presumptuous, but I thought if you want—"

"I'd love to go!" Nahoa could hardly stand the rush of grateful anticipation.

Malie smiled. "There, see? That was easy. Now take this and I'll call a carriage." She handed Nahoa a cloak dyed in orange and gold to match the rest of her outfit. It had taken Nahoa a long time to get used to cloaks, since they were mainly an affectation of the rich, but she found—to her embarrassment—that she rather liked the elaborate clothes Malie picked out for her to wear. She had an eye for flattering styles and colors.

Minutes later, she was escorted to her carriage. They spent nearly half an hour negotiating muddy streets—which had been drenched by days of late-winter rains—before reaching the fire temple. A phalanx of temple officiates, carrying large, resin-coated paper umbrellas, scurried out to greet her. They held these over her head as she climbed out of the carriage and began walking up the white marble stairs.

"How kind of my lady to honor us with another visit. Might I ask where you wish to go today?" It was the old head nun, her eyes looking positively beady below the white stubble on her shaved head. Despite the chilly weather, she wore nothing but a faded red wrap around her legs.

"To the high sacrificial fire," Nahoa said tersely. Over her many visits to the temple, Nahoa had grown to hate the head nun. She didn't quite know why, but something about the way she would stare until Nahoa was forced to turn around and meet her eyes, or the overly solicitous way she asked about very private aspects of her life, made Nahoa thoroughly distrust her.

They walked through the main hall of the temple and climbed the stairs to a chamber on the left, where none but the most important visitors were allowed. The nun opened the door to an octagonal room with small fires burning in niches on all eight sides. In the center of the chamber roared a massive bonfire that was never allowed to go out except on solstice eve. Nahoa sat in front of it cross-legged and pulled back the hood of her cloak.

"You have an offering for the great fire?" asked the nun, uncomfortably close to her ear. To Nahoa's dismay, she had settled herself directly to her right.

Nahoa simply nodded and gripped the white sacrifice bag carefully.

"May I ask you what—"

"No, you may not," Nahoa snapped.

The nun's lips crept infinitesimally upward. "I apologize. I forgot my place." But she looked decidedly unapologetic.

Your breasts look like desiccated plums, Nahoa thought to herself. Firmly ignoring the nun, so as not to encourage her further, Nahoa stared into the fire. She longed to get rid of the filthy thing in her lap, but she hesitated. The fire spirit had selected Kohaku to be Mo'i, but would it condone … ?

She couldn't finish the sentence, even to herself. Yet, what else could it be, with all that blood? She wished she could believe that it was the blood of some animal or something else entirely innocent, but she knew it wasn't true. It was human blood, and any human who had lost so much of it was either dead or dying.

Suddenly, she couldn't handle touching it any longer. With an averted gaze, she tossed her burden into the fire. It crackled and hissed as it burned, and for a brief moment the air filled with the pungent smell of burning blood. Before it dissipated, Nahoa caught the nun's sharp look and bit back a curse.

She bowed her head and began mumbling the prayers she half-remembered from her childhood. Eventually, she just fell silent, willing the old hag to leave her alone.

"How have you been feeling lately?" Her oily whisper made Nahoa shudder involuntarily.

"I'm fine," she said.

"Oh? Your appetite hasn't changed at all then? And how about mornings, my dear? You never feel sick in the morning?"

Panic gripped her. For the past three days she had vomited violently into the chamber pot in the morning, only to have her nausea clear up later in the day.

"I feel fine, I told you." Nahoa knew her tone was less than convincing.

The nun nodded slowly. "I see. Well, the changes should be happening soon enough. It's still relatively early, after all."

"*What's* relatively early?" Nahoa hissed, painfully aware of the guards at the door. She was terrified that she knew what this horrible woman was referring to.

"Why, don't you know? I've heard that you're already three weeks late, but you asked for the rags anyway. Now, isn't that a funny thing for a Mo'i's first wife to do? I'd almost think you were trying to hide it, that you were scared, that you didn't know what to do." She leaned in so close that Nahoa could feel her hot breath on her ear. "Are you afraid of him, Nahoa? Do you regret marrying the one-hand Mo'i? Are you afraid of bearing his child?"

Nahoa slapped her. She didn't flinch. "I love him."

"Yes, but do you trust him?"

"I don't have to listen to this," Nahoa said, standing up. "I'm leaving."

"We can protect you here, my lady. You and the child."

Nahoa put her hands to her ears and stalked out the door.

That night at the cook's party, Nahoa struggled to forget what the head nun had told her. At first everyone had treated her with awkward deference, but after the wine and amant loosened them up, they were very welcoming. She laughed and danced and stuffed her face like she had back on the ship. She found that she had a taste for pickled carrots and rice, even though she hadn't enjoyed them since she was a child. Still, the nun's words were never far from her mind. Much as she hated to admit it, the old hag had been right: she was pregnant, and she had been denying it to herself out of fear. She simply wasn't sure who it was she had married, and her misgivings had doubled since her discovery of the bloody shirt. She didn't believe Kohaku would ever hurt her, but his unpredictability was terrifying.

She wondered if she should just try to get rid of the baby, but she had seen enough disasters back in her village to make her wary. After all, who could she trust? She was the Mo'i's first wife, and if she entrusted her need to anyone, she could never be sure if the potion she drank was to eliminate the baby or them both. Many women desperately envied her position, and wouldn't hesitate to get rid of her if given the chance.

Malie plopped down beside her on the bench, her face flushed from dancing.

"Are you tired, my lady?" she asked. "Would you like me to take you back upstairs?"

Nahoa forced a smile and shook her head. "No, I'd like to stay here. I'm not a very good dancer, that's all."

Malie looked at her critically. "Maybe it wasn't wise for you to come, in your condition. You should sleep for the—"

Nahoa's knuckles went white as she gripped the table, but she was spared hearing the end of Malie's sentence. Two drunk, laughing men careened into the bench, sending something fluttering into her lap. As Malie stood up to berate them for their bad manners, Nahoa looked down.

It was some sort of pamphlet, printed on cheap, rough paper and bound with twine. "The left hand of freedom," she read on the cover. "A reasonable and incontrovertible argument for the ruling of this great city by its own people through direct and unbiased elections." Elections? Could this writer possibly be arguing for the elimination of the Mo'i? But didn't they know that it would be impossible to control the fire spirit and Nui'ahi without the trials? She flipped to the first page.

"As the disappearances continue without any effort made by authorities to track down those responsible, the argument that they are in some sinister manner connected with our tyrannous Mo'i, Kohaku One-hand, grows more plausible daily. How can this brazen violation of our laws be tolerated? Because the Mo'i—he whom the law ought to first govern—is considered above the law. Let us be free of these centuries-old superstitions. Let us cease our fear of the fire god and the sleeping Nui'ahi! Who of my readers truly believes the sleeping giant will awaken without a Mo'i? Who truly believes—"

Malie snatched the pamphlet from her lap and handed it to the taller of the two men with a sharply reproving look. He smiled awkwardly at Nahoa before tucking it into his pocket. Nahoa couldn't help but notice the crusted dirt beneath his fingernails and his dirt-smeared breeches. A gardener?

"Deepest apologies, my lady," he said. Under his thin veneer of friendliness, she thought she heard deep unease. "That was just a bit of rubbish I'd been meaning to throw out. Hope I didn't offend ..."

Nahoa shook her head. It was obvious the man was lying, but she didn't know what to make of the situation. "Of course not," she said.

"So go on, then," Malie said angrily at the two men. "You've imposed on my lady enough already."

They backed away awkwardly. It occurred to her that four months ago she would have been one of them—there would have been no awkward gulf of status. They would have willingly shown her that pamphlet and perhaps even explained what it meant. By marrying Kohaku, she had irrevocably separated herself from her old life.

A part of the wall by the massive stoves began to detach itself, a movement that made the musicians suddenly stop playing and everyone else grow still. The wall slid into the piece above it and a teenaged boy with lopsided ears emerged.

The boy grinned a little. "One-hand has returned. No more disappearances for a few days, at least."

The tall man with dirt-crusted fingernails took a few long strides toward the boy and hauled him the rest of the way out of the hole. "We have a guest," he said softly, pointing to Nahoa. "You see? Our friend Malie saw fit to bring her to our small get-together."

It sounded like an accusation.

"Come, my lady," Malie said, standing up. "You should get some rest. I think you've been through more than enough."

For all her exalted position, Nahoa had never felt more power-less. They didn't want her here. She nodded silently and avoided the hundred eyes that followed her as she walked from the room.

She knew that Kohaku was in their rooms even though she couldn't see him anywhere. He was probably up in the aerie—he spent a lot of time there recently, especially after his nightmares. She slowly climbed the circular stairs that began in the middle of the front parlor, traveling through a dark hole before emerging into the delicate glassed-in bubble that formed the aerie. Kohaku was there, as she had suspected, looking out over the city.

"You again?" he said, his voice so bleak it shocked her. Before, at least, he had always been happy to see her. Nahoa's heart squeezed.

"I ... I'm sorry—"

Kohaku abruptly turned around. He looked surprised. "Oh, Nahoa. I didn't know it was you."

He smiled a little and walked over to embrace her. Who else did he think would come up here? The same person he spoke to at night, when he thought she was asleep? She kissed his chin, breathing in his smell of fresh rosemary-scented soap. His hair hung damply down his neck. She wondered why he had bathed before he saw her—had he needed to wash off someone else's blood?

"I missed you," he said softly.

"Where the hell were you? I didn't know what to do, I was so lonely …"

He kissed her, moving his hand slowly under her shirt. She had known he wouldn't answer. She abandoned her confusion and sense of betrayal and surrendered herself to him, allowing him to apologize in the only way he was able. Their lovemaking no longer contained the innocent joy of the first few weeks after their marriage, but they still had passion … they still had love. She didn't understand why, but she knew that she loved him more than reason. If whatever horror he had become involved with eventually overcame him, she wondered whether she would be dragged down too. Would she destroy herself for the sake of his love?

With a muffled groan, he exploded inside of her, gripping her waist like a man about to fall from a cliff.

"I'm pregnant," she said as they lay in bed together. "I think … I think it would be better if I got rid of it, but I don't know—"

"No!"

His strangled bark made her words stop unformed in her throat. She looked over at him, surprised to see his expression of horrified misery.

"Not you too," he said, more softly this time, gripping her hand. Two tears fell from his eyes onto her neck. "I couldn't live … not if it happened to you too."

"If what happened? Kohaku, what the hell … ?"

He lay back down beside her, staying silent for so long she was actually startled when he began to speak again. "I haven't told you much of my past, have I? I'm sorry for that—I just never wanted to burden you with it. I … I once had a sister. She was beautiful and pure and utterly selfless—but she was naïve, and I didn't watch her closely enough. If I had … maybe if I had …" He gulped air like he was fighting back tears. After a brief moment, he continued. "For years, without my knowledge, she had been carrying on an affair with a man named Nahe, one of the most senior professors in the Kulanui. She was in love with him, but he was only using her. One day, she got pregnant. Instead of taking responsibility for the child, he gave her something he said would get rid of it. She was dead the next morning. Afterwards, just to cover his own tracks, he had me thrown out of the Kulanui ... so I wandered the streets, and then I decided to sacrifice myself to the fire spirit and just end it all. You know the rest, I think."

Nahoa caressed his cheek with a trembling hand and planted a soft kiss on his forehead. "It's okay," she whispered through her tight throat, "I won't do anything. I'll keep the baby, I promise."

She fell asleep curled up against him, his hand on her belly.

The next day, after heaving a good portion of her dinner into the chamber pot, she discovered that Kohaku was gone—not on some mysterious errand, but apparently inspecting a section of the southeastern docks that had flooded after a storm two weeks ago. Kohaku's confession last night had made her see his recent actions in an entirely different light. He was tortured by far more than she had realized. And yet, she sensed that he had gained a sense of catharsis by telling her about his past. Perhaps if she could learn more about what he had been doing so secretly, she would be able to ease his pain even more. She could not help but think that his desire not to burden her with his problems had led to all of the confusion between them. She idly stuffed herself on the overwhelming portions heaped on her breakfast tray while she thought of what to do. In fact, she was so busy thinking that she ended up polishing everything off, even though she could hardly countenance it. Her stomach felt full, but twenty minutes later she suddenly had a desperate, uncontrollable craving for rice and pickled carrots. She was wondering if she should send down to the kitchen for some when the obvious solution to their troubles hit her. Of course! She remembered how the boy had emerged from that strange hidden door in the kitchen the night before, saying that Kohaku had "returned." If there was any information to be had about what her husband was doing, she would probably find it in there. Of course, she could hardly go exploring with so many eyes on her, so she called down to the kitchen anyway. She would wait until night, after the kitchen had shut down and she could (she hoped) sneak around unnoticed.

She whiled away the time eating and reading the basic history texts that Kohaku had given her a month before. Kohaku was still an academic at heart, and he wouldn't hear of his wife not increasing her knowledge of the world. Malie interrupted her later that evening with a pot of hot tea and a steaming dinner. The cook had thoughtfully included an extra helping of pickled carrots—along with pickled beets, mushrooms, and loquats. She gestured for Malie to sit with her and share some of the food.

"I suppose the kitchen is closed now, right?" she said when she had finished.

Malie looked surprised. "You're still hungry, my lady? I could probably go down and fetch something myself ..."

Nahoa shook her head. "Oh no, I was just wondering. Don't worry." So now would be a good time to leave. She looked at Malie's maid uniform—plain purple five-button shirt and pants, cut shorter than fashionable to make it easier to do dirty jobs. She would look a lot less conspicuous wearing something like that rather than her own clothes.

"Malie, would you mind if I borrowed your uniform for the evening? I can give you something of mine ... I'll return it soon, I promise."

Her maid raised her eyebrows. "Why would you want this old thing, my lady?"

"For some private business." Nahoa usually avoided putting on airs, especially around the servants, but she didn't want Malie asking more questions. "Would you allow me?"

"Of course. Whenever you're done with it, just call me again." Her tones were perfectly respectful, but her eyes looked like they were laughing. Nahoa ignored the hint of mockery and gratefully exchanged clothes with the maid. Since Nahoa was at least three inches taller, the sleeves and pants looked ludicrously short, but at least she wouldn't look so conspicuous. In fact, Malie looked far better suited to her clothes than Nahoa herself. She helped Nahoa pull out the pins that held together the elaborate bun on the top of her head and then brushed out her long hair. They would have to leave the room together, and when Nahoa was finished, she would find the maid so they could exchange clothes before returning. If all went smoothly, no one else would know she had left at all. When they were ready, they opened the doors and walked quickly down the hall, Malie leading the way down unfamiliar servant corridors until she judged them safe.

"Just go further down this hall and take the second set of stairs to your right. That will take you to the kitchens," she said.

Nahoa stared at her, about to stammer some confused denial, but Malie put her finger to her lips and walked in the other direction before she could say anything. Nahoa bit her tongue. How did her maid always seem to know so much? Three flights down the staircase Malie had directed her to, Nahoa emerged in a corner of the dark kitchen. There were only a few lamps still lit on the walls—probably to help guide servants searching for a midnight snack. She searched near the stoves until she reached the place where the boy had emerged. She felt all along for a seam and finally found it, roughly four feet above the ground. After a brief struggle, she managed to slide the panel up with her palms. She peered inside the now-revealed hole, seeing nothing but darkness. Well, something obviously had to be on the other side. Since she hadn't brought a light with her, she would have to trust it. Taking a deep breath, she squeezed herself inside the hole and slid the panel shut behind her. She crawled on her belly for about ten minutes in the sharply downward-sloping tunnel before emerging into a wider hallway that was scarcely brighter lit than the kitchen. There was a door at the end of the corridor and some light spilling beneath it. Not quite knowing what she had expected to find, she walked forward. Her trepidation increased tenfold as she got closer—what would Kohaku do if he found out that she had done this? What if she found out something she didn't want to know? From behind the door she heard the sound of harsh, labored breathing. Her heart pounded loudly, but before she could let sudden fear drown her resolve, she cracked open the door.

There were two lamps on the walls, and she squinted in the unexpected light. The room was very small—perhaps five by five feet with ancient stone walls and a damp floor. There was someone inside the room—the breathing had grown harsher and faster when she opened the door, interspersed with panicked whimpers. She opened the door all the way and stepped inside.

A man was suspended from the ceiling by ropes wrapped around his shoulders and waist. His clothes and the floor below him were saturated with blood, some slick and fresh, but most crusted and dry. It stank like he was rotting alive, and perhaps he was. His feet had been cut off—but only one stump had been bandaged, very crudely. His left hand was also gone, though his right gesticulated frantically at her. She wondered at first why the only noises that came from his mouth were strangled, inarticulate gasps, before she noticed the blood that pooled with the spit rolling down his chin. His tongue had been cut out as well.

She knelt on the slick floor and vomited so violently that her stomach began to cramp. She wept as she purged herself. She knew who had done this. After all, she had even found the bloody shirt. It was amazing that this man was still alive, after all the blood he had lost. She stood up slowly and forced herself to look at his mangled body again, feeling light-headed.

"I'm so sorry," she said. How inane, though. How inadequate.

But why would Kohaku do something like this to another human being? Why not just kill him outright, instead of keeping him here in a state of constant agony? What could anyone possibly do to deserve this?

"Who are you?" she asked, though she knew he couldn't answer.

She realized that his hand gestures had a certain repetitive quality to them—as though he were trying to tell her something.

In fact, they reminded her of the hand language that Kohaku had playfully taught her in their first few months together.

"Please," she thought she saw him sign, over and over again.

"Please do what?" she asked.

"Kill me, kill me, kill me ..."

It took every ounce of determination she had not to vomit again. When she looked back at him, she nearly fled from the desperation in his eyes. There was a potion, he told her, that Kohaku kept tantalizingly close, in a hidden compartment just outside the door. It would kill him in less than an hour. Nahoa didn't even try to talk him out of it—who would want that kind of life, even if he did survive his injuries? So she did the only humane thing she could think of and searched for the compartment. She found it fairly easily—a part of the wall you had to push in to pull out. A simple wooden jar, filled with a dark, foul-smelling fluid. She went back to the man and handed it to him. She wished there was a way to cut him down, but she saw nothing to stand on anywhere around her, and he was suspended too high. His hand froze when he saw the jar, and then he began to laugh.

She wasn't even quite sure what he was doing at first—the sounds coming from his mangled throat sounded like no laugh she had ever heard before. He began crying and shaking, but still his mouth twisted in the bitterest smile that she had ever seen. Then, without preamble, he pulled the cork of the bottle off with his teeth and swallowed the entire potion.

"Who are you?" Nahoa asked again, without quite knowing why.

He signed something, but she didn't know the gestures. "I don't understand," she said carefully. "Do you know the syllables?"

His head lolled forward and for a moment she was afraid that he was gone already, but then his hand began to move. "Na," she read. His gestures were getting sloppy—probably the first effects of the poison. "He."

Nahe. The man who had destroyed Kohaku's life.

It took him a long time to die, but Nahoa forced herself to watch—to witness the end of a man who had spent what was probably the last three months of his life in total agony. He died clutching the jar of poison, his mouth twisted in the same bitter smile he had worn ever since he saw it. Barely aware of her own actions, she closed the door and crawled back up the secret passage. She didn't bother to switch clothes back with Malie. She barely thought at all, making her way back to their quarters like a homing pigeon. Servants stared at her as she passed them in the hall, but she barely acknowledged their existence. She had to practically crawl up the steps to the aerie, her legs had grown so weak beneath her. She wondered if she would faint, and then resolved not to do so until she had confronted Kohaku. But he didn't even notice her when she came in. He was facing Nui'ahi again, but looking down, completely absorbed in something he held in his lap. She walked closer and peered over his shoulder.

She swore loudly, and Kohaku started at the sound of her voice. What he held was a hand. A hand so charred and blackened it should have fallen to ashes, but something held it together. At first she wondered if it was somehow Nahe's before she realized the obvious truth. It was his. Kohaku had, for some reason, kept the hand that he lost.

Kohaku swung around, looking almost murderous at being interrupted. His expression changed when he saw her, though. On his face she saw surprise followed closely by horror.

"All that blood ... are you—"

"It's not mine, Kohaku," she said evenly.

His eyes widened.

The ground beneath their feet began to tremble slightly, as it had a few times this year, and Nahoa stumbled. This close to a volcano, such tremors were inevitable, but Kohaku's reaction went far beyond the bounds of reason. He dropped the hand and its box on the floor and pressed himself against the glass of the aerie.

"No," he whispered.

Had she ever understood him? Even at the very beginning, that solemn night on the ship, had their connection been as much an illusion as the moon on the water? She married him for escape, for adventure, for love. She wasn't sure why she stayed.

When he realized that it had just been a little tremor, Kohaku sighed and sat on the edge of a chair. His whole body trembled. Even now, even knowing what he had done, Nahoa still wanted to comfort him. He had gone through so much, and that man had killed his sister and destroyed his life. She couldn't entirely blame Kohaku for what he had done, but she also knew she could never condone it. How could she live with him, knowing he was capable of such calculated violence?

"I ... I'm leaving, Kohaku," she said. Her voice seemed to break him out of his trance. "I saw it. I saw that room ... and don't pretend that you didn't do it or you don't know what I'm talking about. I know it was Nahe and I gave him the poison. He's dead now—you won't be able to hurt him any more."

Kohaku stood and tried to hug her, but she held out her hand to stop him. She couldn't break now. "Nahoa," he said desperately, "You know it was Nahe. Don't you know what he did to me? *He killed my sister!* I didn't have a choice." His voice broke and Nahoa started to cry. "How can you blame me ... if you leave, you'll take away the only thing left that means anything to me."

She shook her head. "Maybe I can't blame you. I've never been good at judging people, but ... nothing makes sense anymore. I just ... you've changed, Kohaku. I'm afraid."

"I would never, ever do anything to hurt you. You must know that. Tell me you know that."

Nahoa sobbed involuntarily and nodded. "I know. But could you promise to never do it again? No more killing?" *No more talk-*

ing to air in the middle of the night, no more staring at the charred remains of your hand?

He hesitated. "Nahoa, I can't—"

"Then I have to leave." She hugged him briefly, but fiercely. "I love you, Kohaku," she whispered. She turned away and fled down the stairs.

"That nun from the fire temple—you must be the one who told her I was pregnant."

Malie rubbed the sleep from her eyes. For the first time since Nahoa had met her, she looked—if not precisely afraid—then less than supremely confident. Eventually, she just nodded.

"You work for her, then? Your scheme ... it was probably to get me to flee to the fire temple so you could use that as leverage with the Mo'i, wasn't it?"

Malie didn't respond, but her silence told Nahoa all she needed to know.

"Well, you've got your wish. Take me there now. Tell the old bat that I want her protection." She felt like her skin was the only thing keeping her from crumbling.

· 12 ·

SOMEWHERE OVER THE COAST of the easternmost rice island, Lana realized that she had to stop. In a few more minutes she would be in danger of passing out and simply plummeting to the earth. A few hours after she began her mad flight, the death had caught up with her, and she thought she heard something like amusement in its voice, past the frustration.

"You keep surprising me, you know. You fight a losing battle, but a worthy one."

Lana's back felt like it was ripping apart, but she managed to reply, "Just trying to stay half a step ahead."

But that had been hours ago, when she was still riding the initial exhilaration of her new powers of flight, and before her exhaustion threatened to help the death fulfill its mission. Warily, she circled closer to the ground and saw that she was over a very rural area, with nothing but a turgid river and rice paddies for miles on either side of her. In the distance she thought that she saw a large house and she angled for that, hoping whoever lived might invite her over the threshold. As she got closer she saw that the building was not so much a house as a villa—a place where well-to-do travelers could get away from city life, or those just passing through could spend an idyllic evening. Sobs caught in her throat. This kind of place was the least likely to take in a dirty, smelly vagabond with no money. Her presence would probably offend the guests. But she was too exhausted to think of another geas and she knew that she would never be able to sleep in a tree with her back in its current state.

Which meant that she had to try. If no one invited her over the threshold ...

She pulled the large black blanket from her bag. She would have to use it as a cloak—better they think her a hunchback than some freak of nature. Then she pulled out the flute, and sounded the first shaky notes before she lowered herself to the ground.

"Threshold," she said quietly. Her nose was running uncontrollably, battered by the cold air above. "Wait until they invite me over the threshold."

The death gestured toward the bamboo gate graciously. "You know they won't let you in."

Lana shook her head and stuffed the flute back in her bag. Then she pulled the blanket around her shoulders and made sure that it covered the wings.

"Is someone there?" she called, amazed at how weak her voice sounded. "Could someone come to the gate?"

She heard footsteps and then a woman just a little taller than she opened the door. She was wearing the demure dress of a household servant, but she held herself with authority.

The woman clicked her tongue. "I'm sorry, we don't give to beggars here. You'll have to try the town. It's a day's walk. Good day."

Lana stuck her hand in the door before the woman could close it. "Please," she gasped. Everything was going white around the edges and she sunk involuntarily to her knees. "Please just invite me over the threshold. I'll sleep in your garden, I'll do whatever you want, just please ... I'll die if you don't."

"As I said, we don't take in beggars here. And certainly not hunchbacks who haven't bothered to bathe in weeks. Now please, leave!"

In the corner of her eye, Lana saw the death creeping closer. The set of its shoulders radiated triumph and its mask mouth was curved in a smile.

Lana realized she was weeping. "In the name of everything you have ever loved, please let me in. I have nowhere else to go …"

She heard a series of rushed whispers from inside the courtyard and the woman turned to look behind her for a moment.

"Oh, now look what you've done!" she hissed.

"Is something wrong?" a male voice asked. It was deep and melodious, filled with strange undercurrents that reminded her of the ocean.

"Nothing you need concern yourself with," the woman said. "Would you like some more rice wine?"

"Who are you talking to?" he asked again. Lana wondered if she should call out to him, but her voice seemed to have failed her. She was lying prone on the ground without really knowing how she got there.

"Just some hunchback beggar, your honor. She seems to have collapsed, but I'll get some help to toss her out. We wouldn't want anyone to disturb your stay with us."

"Collapsed? Why don't you help her, then?"

The woman's frown deepened, but the man summarily pushed her aside and opened the gate fully.

The face that belonged to the beautiful voice was the strangest she had ever seen. His hair was not so much white as clear, hanging down a little past his shoulders and catching and reflecting whatever colors surrounded him—now mostly green and blue. His eyes, set in his pale face, reminded her more of Ino's than anything recognizably human. Though she had caught a glimpse of deep blue irises when he first opened the door, as soon as he looked at her his irises disappeared. His eyes became like a peek into the deep ocean, rippling with reflected light and the hint of a deeper movement beneath.

"Who are you?" he asked softly. "Do you wish to come in?"

"You must invite me over the threshold," she said. "The geas. If you don't, it will get me." The wall between her thoughts and her words seemed to have broken down. She didn't know why she told this man things he couldn't possibly understand, but she desperately wanted him to believe her.

He looked over to where she had gestured and his eyes abruptly regained their irises—this time starburst violet.

"What have you done to be chased by such a thing?" he whispered.

"My mother ... to save my mother." She started coughing—it was getting very hard for her to breathe. To her surprise the man wrapped his arm around her shoulders and held her.

"Leave her alone," he said in a voice as imperious as an old-style king.

The death laughed. "She is mine, she made the sacrifice. Who are you to deny me? The would-be guardian who rejected his heritage?"

The muscles in his throat tightened. "My father has chosen death. I will return to the shrine. I claim this girl as the right of the water guardian. You can't take her from me."

"Yes I can. While she is still here, I can. You have to bind me."

The man's eyes looked like windows into the water of a deep-sea trench. He reached up to right side of his face where a blue feather had been braided into his hair. He touched the feather, which began to glow with palpable, alien power. She realized he must be invoking a sacrifice for a geas.

"As death always stands on the wrong side of the gate, so you will always stand on the wrong side of mine. Death and water have always been opposed—so long as this girl stays with me, you cannot touch her."

The death's robes faded away until it was merely a mask and a swinging key, floating disembodied above the grass. The man nodded and then put his other arm under her legs and picked her up. She closed her eyes, but she still felt the stares of people as he walked back through the courtyard.

"What's your name?" he asked her, as though there was no one else listening.

"Lana," she said. It had been a long time since someone had used her diminutive. "Yours?"

"Kaleakai," he said. "But most just call me Kai."

He had known she wasn't a hunchback just from the feel of her shoulders, but as he carried her through the silent, gawking crowd of servers and guests, he wondered exactly what her large cloak was hiding. She was definitely wounded—blood dripped steadily from underneath her pants leg onto the ground, and she looked like she had passed out in his arms. Her mouth had gone slack and her expressive eyes were closed. Every time he looked at her he felt a jolt that nearly destroyed his composure. She was dirty and she smelled, but he thought that he had never seen a more oddly compelling woman in his life. Her accent was of the outer islands, and for once the reminder of home wasn't unpleasant. She must have been a diver, one of the last of her kind. The red jewel that hung from her neck on a cord of riverweed was incalculably rare.

The innkeeper who had opened the gate seemed to break out of her stupor and ran in front of him.

"Your honor, I assure you, if you wish it, that we can accommodate this girl for the night, but surely you don't plan to …" she seemed to have a distaste for even uttering the words.

"See to it that the tub is filled in my bathing room. I'll also need several buckets of extra hot water and some bandages. Just knock and leave it in front of the door. There's no need to come in."

The woman looked absolutely paralyzed with shock for one moment and then nodded her head jerkily. She had been careful to give him the most sumptuous rooms at the inn—even though he was an unconventional guest, he was still an important one. His rooms were located off the main building and included his own personal garden, complete with a miniature waterfall and carefully cultivated lilies. It couldn't compare with anything back at the water shrine, but it did make him feel more at home than anything else had on his journey. He slid the door to his rooms open awkwardly with his foot and then closed it after he set Lana down on the bed.

She groaned when he did that and rolled over on her stomach, still apparently unconscious. Unsure of what else to do, he pulled off her cloak.

Blood. And black wings.

He had saved a black angel.

Lana came to on her stomach in a bathtub, with someone washing the blood off her back with achingly slow gentleness. She wondered, idly, who it could be and then remembered the strange man with the eyes that looked like the ocean: Kai. She was in the same room with the water guardian. She opened her eyes and realized that she was naked, and then realized that this fact didn't bother her nearly as much as it should have.

"You're awake," he said. His smile made her want to melt into the water. "I've washed off your back, but if you're not too exhausted, perhaps you should do the rest."

Lana nodded and took the sponge from him. Before she could even thank him, he pushed the soap and the buckets of water closer to her and closed the door discreetly behind him. Pain and the added encumbrance of the wings—draped awkwardly outside of the tub—made her take much longer than usual, but eventually she had scrubbed every part of her body pink and her hair until it couldn't possibly smell anymore. She wondered why he hadn't said anything yet about the wings. He must have had some reaction—probably disgust and revulsion that he was too kind to let show. A few minutes later he knocked gently on the door and she told him to come in. He covered her with a towel and then carried her into his room—a spacious suite with a raised bed and a veritable feast laid out on a table by the door.

He laid her stomach down on the bed and took out some bandages and balm. She held the sheets tightly as he wrapped them around her back, gritting her teeth against the pain. Her new flying muscles burned as well, but the gentle pressure of his hands seemed to ease their tension.

"Why are you doing this?" she asked when he had almost finished.

"Because you need help." His eyes had gone opaque-blue again, beautiful enough to drown in.

"Do you help everyone who needs it, then?" she said.

He looked away and she could tell that her words had hit a nerve. "No," he said finally, sadly. "I don't suppose I do. But I thought, perhaps I could atone for it by helping you. I might be the only one who can."

Lana sighed and paused for a moment to enjoy the feel of his hands on her back. "You know what I am, don't you? You know what it means?"

"I know. I don't care. I saved you because I wanted to. Now here, you should eat something."

He forced her to eat half a bowl of thin rice-and-lentil soup before he let her go to sleep.

"I will sleep on the floor," he said. "I have a sleeping mat."

But his presence—and his unmistakable sense of contained power—comforted her. And she had been alone for so long. "No," she said. "Sleep here, with me. I want you to."

He hesitated, but in the end he did so, cradling her hand carefully within his.

She awoke the next morning with a fever that made her skin feel like burning rice paper and her throat painfully thick with mucus. She spent a few panicked moments wondering what on earth was wrong with her back before her memories returned to her. She sighed and curled into a fetal position, wondering where she could go now. How long could she rely on Kai's kindness, after all?

With a monumental exertion of will, she forced herself to sit up, and then nearly collapsed again with dizziness. When the world stabilized, she looked around and saw a basket filled with bloody bandages on the floor. He must have changed them while she was sleeping, but looking around she saw no signs of the man himself. She thought about getting up, but decided against it—she didn't feel quite capable of walking from the bed to the sliding door, let alone searching for him outside. Besides, she couldn't seem to find the blanket that she had been using as a cloak. Kai had probably taken it along with her filthy clothes, although perhaps he had done so to make sure she didn't leave his rooms. They both knew that if she were to go outside with the wings in full view she would probably get stoned to death, with him powerless to stop it.

Lana sighed and cast around for some water, which she found in a delicate glass cup beside the bed. She took a few tentative, painful sips before putting it down. Beside the water she noticed a pair of exquisitely woven dark blue pants, with intricate yellow embroidery all along the bottom and up the sides. She wondered how Kai had managed to find something so fine out in this remote part of the island, but then reminded herself that he was, after all, the water guardian.

Very carefully—because her back felt taut, as though the slightest overexertion might rip it open again—she pulled on the pants and tied the drawstring. She didn't see a shirt, but of course how could she expect to wear a normal shirt with the wings? The pounding of her head and the blood rushing past her ears made Lana want to vomit. She lowered her head between her knees and thought about how relaxed she had felt last night, sleeping in the bed of a man who was essentially a stranger. For now, at least, she was entirely at his mercy—and yet she didn't feel afraid. The only other person she had ever met with such power and effortless control was Akua. Here, with Kai, she felt a little less like she was on the verge of drowning every moment. Though she had never sought out someone to take care of her, she didn't think she'd mind it if he did. Perhaps it was because of the way his eyes turned into a rippling, iris-less ocean at the sight of her, so gentle and so inexpressibly sad.

Her stomach heaved violently and she fell halfway out of the bed, barely reaching the bucket before she vomited what looked like the entire meager contents of her stomach. She panted for a few moments, desperately sucking air into her lungs before her stomach began heaving again. This time there was nothing to come up, only a series of incrementally more painful dry heaves. Tears started streaming from her eyes and she realized that she couldn't stop them, no matter how hard she tried. She didn't know what she had expected from the wind spirit, but certainly not what it had given her. She felt as though the remaining fragile core of her sanity had been shattered, and she had no idea of how to put anything together again. How much longer could she survive like this? All that awaited her was a slow and painful death.

She heard the sound of the sliding door opening and Kai's soft footsteps entering the room. Lana's tears redoubled and she became painfully aware of the mucus running from her nose. Kai knelt next to her and put his arm over her shaking shoulders. He handed her a handkerchief, which she took gratefully, and blew her nose. Another dry heave shook her and she gagged over the bucket.

"I didn't know you had woken up. I'm sorry I didn't come earlier," he said.

"It's okay," Lana said, leaning against him gratefully.

He seemed worried but helpless, like a man left alone with a baby he has no idea how to care for. "It's a day's ride by horse, but maybe I should send someone for a doctor in the city. You look so sick ..."

Lana shook her head. She distrusted doctors' methods—some were sound, but all too often they practiced quackery that made their patients sicker than before. "I just need some herbs ... see if they have ginger, boneset, and blue vervain in the kitchen here. Tell them to boil them together in fresh water for about half an hour and then strain it. It should help."

He looked surprised. "Are you a doctor?" he asked.

Lana smiled. "I was apprenticed to a witch. Well ... I suppose I *am* a witch now, aren't I?"

"Of course ... the geas, the wings. You just look so young." His eyes had turned gentle and ocean-like again.

"I'm eighteen," she said, and then paused. "Wait, what's the date?"

He stared at her. "The fifth day of the fourth month, I think. Why?"

Lana started laughing. She couldn't seem to stop herself, even when she had to fight back another dry heave. She wasn't sure if the tears in her eyes were from mirth or grief.

Something about her reaction seemed to worry him. "What is it?"

"My birthday," she said, after the wild, bubbling mirth had left her, "was yesterday. I'm nineteen."

The draught, mercifully, reduced her nausea. She slept for nearly a day straight after she took it, waking up only when Kai forced her to drink water. Three days after he first began caring for her, the fever finally broke. She was still weak, but a numb, stubborn happiness had settled around her. She refused to think about what would happen when she had fully recovered and she and Kai would leave each other. Instead, she waited patiently for him to return from his strange excursions each day, looking forward to their conversations. He must have led a very sheltered life, she realized—a particularly solitary one, growing up virtually alone on the water shrine with no other children his age. In fact, Lana began to suspect that this was the first time he had left the water shrine since he was small. She wondered how people reacted to him, since he obviously wasn't entirely human. People probably preferred honoring their guardians at great distances rather than in person. No one felt comfortable in the face of such alien, overwhelming power. Lana wasn't quite comfortable with such power, either, but it thrilled her.

He never said any of this to her, of course. Kai was always unfailingly polite, but he guarded himself very closely, never saying more about himself than was necessary. The fourth day, he returned when she was sitting on the bed, reading one of his books.

"How are you feeling?" he asked. She wondered if the smile on his flushed face was forced.

Lana thought about feigning more weakness than she felt, but she didn't think it would be fair. "Much better," she said.

He sat on the bed next to her and put down a few packages he had been carrying. "You could probably use a few extra days, though. You don't have to push yourself."

"What are those?" she asked, pointing to the packages.

"Presents. I'm sorry I didn't get this for you sooner …" He pulled out a beautiful blue long shirt, the match to the pants that he had given her a few days ago. In back it had two long slits to fit her wings, and buttons continuing beneath them.

"How did you …" Her hands were trembling. It was such a simple thing—a shirt to fit her wings—but she had never been given such a wonderful present in her life. Perhaps because Kai was a kind of non-human aberration himself, he understood her need to regain some sense of normalcy.

"I had it altered by a seamstress in the nearest village. She's making another now—it should be ready in a few days."

Lana wanted to hug him, do something to show the depth of her gratitude, but she found herself awkwardly unable to move. It had been years since she had shown that kind of affection to any-one outside her family. But she couldn't just *sit* there. She inched forward and, without really thinking, rested her head on his chest. He seemed surprised at first and then, tentatively, he put his arms around her back. She could feel him gently stroking her wings, as though they were sacred objects and not the mark of a black angel.

After a very long time, he pulled away slightly and looked at her. His ocean-eyes rippled with occasional flashes of light. She heard the air moving in and out of her lungs, her heart beating in her chest, but that didn't feel like it had anything to do with her anymore. Her body functioned, but she was lost in those deep, unfathomable, alien eyes. He leaned forward.

This was the third time Lana had ever been kissed. This time, it shocked her how much she wanted it.

She fell asleep soon after, lulled by the comfort of his embrace and his rich, damp smell. When she woke up again several hours later, he was kneeling in front of the writing desk that faced the small private garden. He looked completely absorbed in whatever he was writing, pausing for long moments before each sentence. The sight of his now greenish hair bound at the base of his neck with a leather string, his broad back, and his brown shirt casually hanging over his pantaloons, made her bite her lip against the sudden longing that flooded her. She knew so little about him, but at this moment that didn't seem to matter.

"What are you writing?" she asked.

His hand jerked in surprise, making ink splatter all over the paper.

"Oh, I'm sorry—"

"Don't worry," he said, turning around and smiling at her. "I'll just do it over. I didn't realize you were awake. I can finish this later." He stood up and sat next to her.

"So, what were you writing?" Lana asked again, wondering if she sensed a little evasiveness in his tone.

"Just some letters." He reached over to the foot of the bed and picked up a small wooden box—one of the objects that he had dropped there earlier in the day. "I never got to give you the rest of your presents, you know."

"What is that?" she said. Kai took the top off the box. Inside, she saw several small objects, delicately wrapped in bamboo leaves and tied with a bit of green twine. They smelled sweet.

"The town where the seamstress lives is famous for making these sweets, so I brought some back. Do you want to try one?"

He seemed so hopeful that Lana had to laugh. "Of course," she said.

Kai picked up one of the sweets and undid the twine. Inside the bamboo leaf was a sticky purple oblong ball.

"They make the outside from pounded rice. The filling is made from some kind of red bean, I think—it's hard to understand the accents around here, sometimes." He held it up to her mouth, and after a moment's hesitation she bit into it. The sweet, tangy paste filling had a smooth texture that contrasted beautifully with the chewy stickiness of the outside.

"It's … wonderful," Lana said, surprised.

Kai put the other half in his mouth and his intent expression soon turned to one of delight. "You know, I wasn't sure when I bought them, but they are delicious, aren't they?"

Lana nodded. They stared at each other for an awkward moment, but before it could turn into anything more, the bell outside their door began ringing peremptorily. Kai's eyes abruptly regained their irises—a chilly pale blue.

"Just leave whatever it is outside the door. I believe I left instructions not to be disturbed?" His voice took on that commanding tone that she remembered from the day he took her in.

She heard furious whispering from the people on the other side of the door.

"I apologize, sir," a woman said firmly. "But this matter cannot wait another night." Lana thought the voice belonged to the innkeeper who had refused to invite her over the threshold. "If you won't open the door, then we will be forced to come in ourselves. Do you understand?"

Lana suddenly felt very afraid. She saw the light of several lanterns through the dark screen. Why would so many people decide to come to their room this late in the evening? She had a sudden, horrible premonition of violence.

Kai looked from the door and squeezed her hands. "Don't worry," he said quietly. "I'll deal with this. Go into the garden and close the screen door. Make sure that they can't see you."

Lana swallowed forcibly and walked into the garden. She left the door open a crack, so that she would be able to see what was happening. Kai gave her a tight, reassuring smile before opening the door.

There were more people than she had expected—what looked like every staff member of the inn and possibly all of the guests. What could they want, with their swaying lanterns and angry expressions? They reminded her of the villagers by the lake, and the resemblance didn't reassure her.

The line of Kai's back was tense, but his tone was icy cold. "What reason could possibly warrant this kind of visitation so late?"

"Where's the girl?" The angry voice belonged to a man whose rough clothes and accent made Lana suspect he was a villager. But what business could the villagers have with them? The man tried to push his way into the room and Kai roughly shoved him back.

"That's no business of yours. You still haven't told me your reasons for coming here—I have to say, Miss Oeha, I had heard better things of your hospitality."

The innkeeper had the grace to look slightly embarrassed, but she did not move. "Be that as it may. I've never had such a reason to violate it before. Against my better judgment, I allowed you to take that ... wretched hunchback in, but I can't allow it any longer. You must give that girl to us. She's done enough damage."

Kai's hands tightened on the edge of the door. "Have you lost your mind, Oeha? Haven't I paid you well for the extra days? Why would you let yourself get sucked in with this ... mob?"

The woman looked away from him, but the man next to her shoved his way forward until he was barely an inch from Kai's nose. "Because she has a responsibility, that's why. You had my wife make ... abominations! Shirts with holes in back for your hunchback. But she's a witch! Just as soon as my wife finished the second shirt, our daughter starts coughing ... mostly blood, now. She's about to die, and it's that damn witch's fault. Give her to us, or we'll take her!"

Lana cursed and stared, paralyzed by her bubbling fear. She wondered if she saw the death's smiling mask lurking somewhere in the back of the mob.

"I'm sorry about your daughter, but what possible reason do you have to think that this girl has anything to do with it?"

Still avoiding his eyes, the woman pulled a young girl from deeper in the crowd toward the front. "Tell him what you told me."

The girl stared studiously at the ground. "Few days ago, you came in and told us to boil all these plants I'd never heard of to make a potion for that hunchback. It smelled awful—my grandmother used to work spells. They looked just like that."

Lana closed her eyes and struggled to regain control of her breathing. How could this be happening? That idiot girl had probably never seen a geas worked in her life.

"I'm telling you, my girl is dying! I don't care if you are the water guardian, I won't spare you if you keep protecting her." The man's angry voice sounded rough with tears.

"You won't spare me? *You won't spare me?*" Kai's voice was terrifyingly soft. His skin began taking on silver tones, rippling and splashing light. "You will not touch her. She is under my protection. You'll have to kill me first, and I promise—you can't kill me."

A sheer wall of water burst from the ground before him, separating him from the mob. It sailed yards in the air before falling back down on their heads and extinguishing their lanterns. His skin wasn't just splashing light anymore, it was glowing. She had never seen anything quite like it, and such a palpable demonstration of power awed her in a way that had nothing to do with their desperate situation.

"I won't let that damn witch kill my daughter!" The man's scream of defiance turned into one of surprised pain when he tried to force his way through the wall of water. He stumbled backwards, holding a hand to the left side of his face. The mob fell back, looking at each other in obvious fear.

Something the man had said about his daughter kept coming back to Lana in the part of her mind that wasn't overcome with horror. It reminded her of a detail Akua had once told her about lung diseases. She had said that the rice paddies often carried diseases that would flood the lungs and drown its victims if they weren't treated immediately. That man was convinced that his daughter was about to die, and he was probably right, even if for the wrong reasons.

Barely aware that she had made a decision, Lana slowly finished fastening the buttons on her shirt and pulled back the screen door. Kai whirled around and his wall of water faltered for a second.

"Get back inside, Lana!" He sounded like he was finally panicking, which scared her more than anything else. Behind him, she could hear the horrified whispers of the people as they saw her wings through the water.

She shook her head. "I can help that man's daughter. If he'll let me see her, I can probably save her life."

"They'll kill you if you go out there, keika." His soft, almost helpless use of the endearment nearly made her lose her resolve.

But she knew he had enough power. "Then you'll have to protect me," she said.

He held her gaze for a long time. "Collect our things," he said finally. "Then stand beside me."

Lana ignored the muffled sounds of the mob as she picked up his bag and carefully stuffed his few belongings inside. She paused a moment over his letters—one was addressed to the fire guardian and the other to the Mo'i. When she had finished, she walked beside him and quietly handed him his bag. What little she had was already packed.

"If it were up to me, I would leave now, but she wants to save your daughter. You have come to kill an innocent woman who still feels enough pity for you to help you despite yourself. I hope, one day, you may understand what that means."

"She ... she's a damned black angel ... she'll kill my daughter just by touching her—" A well-placed jet of water suddenly hit the man in his mouth and he began coughing violently.

"What do you need?" he asked her.

"Nightshade mushrooms, bitterwort, pleurisy root, blue cohosh—those are the most important, but they probably won't have them in the kitchen here."

"Any of you who still have a bit of sense left and who would like to see this man's daughter live, find those herbs and take them to the seamstress's house," Kai commanded the crowd. He lowered his voice and turned to her. "Hold my hand tightly and don't let go, no matter what. You understand?"

Lana nodded mutely. He gave her a sudden, gentle smile and caressed her cheek. Then his skin began to glow more brightly and the towering wall of water slowly melded itself into a hollow sphere surrounding them both. Everything looked hazy and blurred to Lana, but Kai seemed sure of his view. He took a step forward and the people around them fell back, cursing and shrieking. The innkeeper, however, actually chased after them, yelling in a shrill voice.

"I demand you compensate me for the damage done to the room. It will cost at least a thousand kala to repair—"

A jet of water suddenly surged from their bubble and knocked her to the ground. Before she could do more than gasp and splutter, another—much stronger—spray of water launched into the beautifully painted wooden pagoda, arching above a small pond. Two of its supports snapped immediately, and the ensuing deluge of water sent it crashing down, a mess of shattered tile and broken wood.

"And that," he said, very deliberately, "is at least fifteen thousand kala, I should think."

And even though she could hardly think of a more inappropriate time to do so, Lana burst out laughing.

Their walk to the village, followed at a respectful distance by a growing crowd of people, took about an hour. When they first set out, some people had sprinted past them—presumably to alert the villagers—but now things were relatively quiet. Kai's skin was slightly damp, but to her surprise the bubble of water around them did not drip at all. He smiled at her occasionally, but he mainly focused his gaze forward. The furrowed line between his pale eyebrows grew deeper as they went along. She finally realized what a strain he was under when he tripped over a small rock and nearly collapsed. She had to hold him up until he said he could go on. She worried about him and then berated herself—he wouldn't have had to expend so much energy if she hadn't demanded to see that sick child. *Why is he doing this for me?* She was as much a stranger to him as he was to her, after all. An answer occurred to her, and she wondered if it could be so simple. Beads of sweat were rolling down his forehead and his irises had turned so pale she could hardly see them.

"Kai, are you all right?" she asked finally, even though she knew it was a useless question. What would he do if he wasn't? Abandon her to the mob?

"Don't worry, we're almost there." When he turned his head to look at her, she saw his expression change to one of dismay. Surprised, she turned around and felt the bottom drop out of her stomach. The death was walking beside them, on the other side of the barrier of water. It must have sensed how weak Kai was getting—almost too weak to enforce his geas.

"Stay away," she said angrily. "He bound you and you haven't broken it."

The death's mask refracted through the water looked like a hideous parody of itself. "I can stay right here. I may not be able to touch you now, but not many geas are kept by dead men."

Lana refused to show fear at his threat. Instead, she reached into her bag and pulled out the flute. She didn't quite know why she did it—she was completely out of her depth and she could think of no geas that would be helpful—but the music comforted her, and she knew it set the death on edge. She found herself playing one of her father's favorite tunes—the very same one, in fact, that he had performed for her on the day of her initiation. She played it slowly and sweetly, not entirely unaware of the irony. She was playing "Yaela's Lament" for the man who had inherited the powers for which Yaela had sacrificed herself.

Kai seemed surprised when she started playing, but he didn't speak. They reached the seamstress's house just as she was finishing the song. A woman waited for them on the porch, surveying the approaching crowd with a wary expression. Kai's breathing began rasping in his throat, but Lana didn't dare show her worry.

The woman looked down at her and held out a loosely wrapped bundle of herbs. "They told me that a black angel was coming. They said that she needed these herbs to cure my daughter. You must be the one I made those shirts for. I wondered, but I never imagined …" She shook her head. "So tell me, why have you come?"

"I know much about illness and healing. Your husband blames me, but I had nothing to do with your daughter's illness. I may be able to save her life, if you let me inside. I can promise nothing, but I swear I will do nothing to harm her."

The woman gave a bitter smile and Lana could see there were tears in her eyes. "Ah, my husband's a fool. Our daughter had the cough a week ago—it only got serious recently. She's in so much pain …" The woman paused and then took a deep breath. "If you think you can, please, will you help her?"

Her husband and a few other men came tearing through the back of the crowd—he must have been with the stragglers.

"What are you doing, you fool!" he screamed. "Do you want her to die? She's the one who did this, and now you'll let her kill our daughter with one touch!"

The woman's mouth twisted. "You ignorant ass. Do you really think anybody but death has such power?"

"She's a black angel, Sei!" he said.

"Then let me be the first to invite a black angel into my house." She turned to Lana and held out her hand. "Come," she said.

Lana looked frantically at Kai. "Go on," he said. "I'll hold them off."

"But, you—"

"I'll hold them off!" he shouted. He gripped her hand tightly and his eyes momentarily regained some color. "Save her, keika." He kissed her briefly on the lips and then shoved her out of the bubble. Lana grabbed the woman's hand and ran inside, only vaguely aware of the wall of water that came shooting up behind her.

The girl was sleeping on a mat on the floor. The windows were shut and cloying incense was burning at her feet—Lana nearly gagged on the smell when she entered the room.

"Throw that incense away and open the windows. This isn't good for a girl with lung sickness." Lana was startled, but pleased at the authority in her voice.

Negotiating the small room was a little difficult with her wings, but she managed to kneel next to the sleeping mat. The girl opened her eyes as she did so, and then they grew round with shock.

"Am I dead?" she asked. Her voice was just the barest rasp in her throat.

Lana shook her head. "No, of course not. You're just a little sick."

The girl began coughing and Lana was shocked to see how much blood was mixed with the phlegm. She wondered if she might have come too late.

"I put some water out to boil, just in case. Do you want it?" The woman was hovering nervously over her shoulder.

"That's good. Put the mushrooms in first, then the rest ten minutes later. When the bitterwort turns pale yellow, strain it and bring a glass to me."

Lana kept a silent vigil by the child, wondering at the irony of a black angel trying not to destroy, but rather to save a life. She could hardly blame this woman's husband or the rest of the villagers for their attitude—the only thing anyone knew about black angels (which was what everyone knew, even children like this girl) was that they brought destruction. It had been far too long for anyone to remember how or why. Lana wondered if all of the black angels had essentially been helpless spectators to the destruction that followed them. Had their existence presaged violence without their ever participating in it?

The woman tapped her on her shoulder. "I think it's ready," she said quietly, handing her the glass.

Lana nodded. She helped the mother force the drink down the girl's throat and her mind raced as she thought of what to do next. The geas needed to be powerful, but though she knew she could use the flute, something inside her warned against it. She had never used the flute for any geas other than those she used to bind the death, and she wondered if playing it now might somehow invite the death inside. No, it had to be a self-sacrifice.

Steadying herself, she felt for the watching presence of the spirits around her. There were more than she ever remembered, in fact, as though she were now an object worthy of far more attention. Lana reached behind her back to where the wings joined her still-tender skin. Remorselessly, she ripped out three large feathers. For once, she barely enjoyed the waiting anticipation of the spirits before the binding. She was too worried about Kai—the sounds from outside were violent and not reassuring.

"No human is a waterbird. No fish breathes air. As the wind blows where water does not belong, so I bind them both to right themselves in the body of this girl."

A strange force began making the tips of the three black feathers vibrate. The girl gasped and Sei held her shoulders as she began coughing uncontrollably, nearly vomiting as vast amounts of discolored phlegm suddenly vacated her lungs. Lana held the feathers still over her torso, hoping that the violence of the purging wouldn't further harm her already weakened body. The feathers crumbled to black ashes that dusted the deep blue of her pants—the terms of the geas were fulfilled.

The three of them were silent for a moment and then the girl took a deep, shuddering breath—probably the healthiest-sounding one she had taken in days.

The woman gasped and felt the girl's forehead. "Her fever's broken," she said quietly. "You've saved her life."

"I only—"

She stopped at the sound of something heavy smashing into the wall just above their heads. The shouts outside that she had tuned out for the past twenty minutes suddenly seemed loud and terrifying. Some of the men had taken up a chant that sounded like, "Kill the freak, then the witch."

"I have to go," Lana said, standing up awkwardly. "Give her more of the draught every few hours until she seems better."

The cries of the mob sounded like a solid wall of noise when she ran outside. The water barrier still surrounded the house, but Kai had sunk to his knees and it looked like he was barely holding on to consciousness. Lana stumbled next to him and held his shoulders. He looked at her with an expression of barely suppressed pain, but he smiled.

"Did you ... do it?" he asked.

Lana realized she was crying when she tasted salt, but she didn't know when she started. She nodded. "The girl will be all right. But we have to leave."

"No, you run away. I can't. Just get away. Fly ... I can't hold this up much longer. When it comes down ..."

"What are you saying?" Lana's head felt like it was going to burst with the sudden pressure.

"Stop it!" The new voice was loud and emphatic. The noise of the crowd tapered off in response to its anger and, Lana realized, its authority: the girl's mother, Sei, was standing beside them.

"You will *not* kill these people. Or you will have to kill me to do it. She saved our daughter, Tope. Why do you want to kill her?"

"She's deluded you! No black angel could save anyone—they only destroy."

"Will you all kill me, then?"

They mob hesitated, then seemed to lose some of its anger.

"I will never forget what you did for me today," the woman said to her. "Tell him to drop his shield. I'll be able to give you enough time to get away."

Lana nodded and nudged Kai. He collapsed against her and the wall of water fell to the muddy ground. Before the mob had a chance to regain their bearings, she grabbed both of their bags and then hugged Kai tightly around the waist. He only seemed partly conscious, but she knew that she would need his help if they even had a prayer of getting off the ground.

"Kai, you have to put your arms around my neck, okay? I won't be able to fly if you don't."

"Just leave me," he mumbled.

"Damn it, Kai! Do you think I could do something like that? Put your arms around my neck!"

Lana thought she heard something like a muffled laugh escape his lips before he slowly complied. She thanked him silently.

Looking around her for the final time, she had a strange, hazy glimpse of glowing lanterns, angry faces, and one brave woman daring to stop them. Then she stood up and with a few painful, powerful strokes heaved herself off of the ground and into the night sky.

She didn't dare spend too long in the air—Kai seemed to be holding onto consciousness by sheer force of will. His breathing was shallow and she knew the air and the wind that was battering them at such a high altitude could only make things worse. The effort of carrying both her and his weight was also ripping open her healing back. She managed to make it to the city, landing less than gracefully on a low roof in the northeast. They both lay there panting for a few moments before Lana forced herself to sit up again. They still wouldn't be safe unless she could somehow conceal her identity. She shoved her own exhaustion away and began rifling through Kai's bag for something she could use as a cloak. To her surprise, she found a real one with a blue silk lining, so long that she knew Kai must have bought it for her. She smiled and put it on, carefully arranging the folds so it disguised the shape of her wings. Then she reached over and shook him by the shoulders.

"Kai, you have to wake up. Just a little longer and then you can rest, okay?"

He opened his eyes and smiled. "You're crazy, keika."

Lana almost started crying again. "You too," she said softly. "Now put your arm over my shoulder."

They were in luck—she had apparently landed on top of a theater and the production was letting out right at that moment. Many of the people below her were wearing outfits so outlandish she felt sure that the two of them would simply blend into the crowd. They climbed down a ladder set into the wall and then Lana half-carried Kai as she walked as nonchalantly as she could through the crowd.

She stopped in front of two men lolling on the side of the theater and smoking something whose smell she didn't recognize. They looked at her raised cloak with the barest flicker of curiosity.

"I'm sorry, but my friend here is a little drunk and, um … I was wondering if you could tell me where the nearest inn would be?"

"Up the street, to the left," one of them said. "It has a red door. You can't miss it."

Lana thanked them and walked with Kai as quickly as she could—his legs were barely moving beneath him. The inn was just as easy to find as the men had said and the proprietor seemed as disinclined as anybody else in this neighborhood to think there was something strange about having a hunchback and a near-albino as guests. Lana fished into Kai's pocket and pulled out a hundred-kala coin that seemed to satisfy the proprietor quite nicely, since he led them to a room in back that was much quieter and a bit larger than the others.

"I'll have a maid bring bedding," he said.

Lana took a ten-kala coin from Kai's pocket and handed it to the man. "Make sure she brings the softest sleeping mats … some food and amant weed wouldn't be amiss either."

The man looked at her a little bemusedly and then nodded before shutting the door behind him. Lana set Kai against a wall and then poured some water from the pitcher on the table. He revived enough to drink half of it and then leaned back against the wall. His skin felt dangerously cold and he had begun shivering. She waited impatiently until she heard someone knock at her door.

Two maids entered, one carrying some of the fluffiest bedding she had ever seen and the other bearing a huge tray of food.

"Is that real?" the younger maid asked after she had set down the food, pointing to Lana's back.

Lana nodded. "I've had it since I was born."

"Does it hurt?" she asked, ignoring the other one's efforts to drag her out of the room.

"Not anymore."

"Oh? Well, good night, then. Just let me know if you want anything else." She closed the door behind her and Lana heard the two girls arguing as they walked back down the hall.

Lana allowed herself a small smile and then locked the door after them. She took off his shoes and then half-dragged Kai to the sleeping mat. Part of her wanted to take off his clothes, but she didn't quite have the nerve. Instead she pulled the thick down quilt over him and adjusted his head on the pillow. Just before she turned to the food, he gripped her hand. Her heartbeat skittered—she had assumed he was asleep.

"Will you come home with me?" he asked. His iris-less eyes rippled the way they had the first time he looked at her. "My father is dead—I must go home and be his successor. But will you come with me?"

"To the water shrine?" she asked, stupidly. Was it possible that they had only kissed just this afternoon? That he had nearly killed himself to save her life? "Why?"

"I can protect you. So long as you're there with me, that death will never be able to touch you. You and your mother will be safe. I ... I want to be with you, keika. Please come?"

Lana's thoughts seemed to have collapsed in on themselves. Safe forever? It must be a dream, but here Kai was offering it to her. And yet, to be so deeply in his debt, so beholden to him? They had only known each other for five days. But more than anything, she wanted to stay alive, and Kai was probably the only one who could help. Safety, he said, and ...

"I'll go with you," she said, burying her face in the crook of his shoulder. "Of course I'll go."

Three weeks after they first boarded the ship to the water shrine, Lana once again awoke without Kai's familiar heat beside her. She was nearly drowned in the folds of the hammock, and once again wondered how he had managed to get up without disturbing her. She pulled up the blankets and attempted to fall asleep again, but her mind wandered back to Kai, her almost-lover, who had grown progressively more introspective and withdrawn as they neared his home. Maybe it was just grief over his father, but something there was haunting him. The same thing, perhaps, that made him refuse to take their relationship beyond a certain level of intimacy. She felt frustrated, but too nervous to demand answers—what if he reconsidered his offer? What if he took away her only chance at peace and safety? How could she go on as she had before, when she knew how much better it could be?

She tumbled out of the hammock and climbed up the hatch to the deck. Kai was standing near the prow, leaning over the railing. His hair was wild in the wind—midnight black and streaked with starlight. Her breath caught, as it always did, at his changeable, inhuman beauty. The water was choppy tonight, but she navigated the deck easily on her bare feet. She didn't think she had made any noise that could be heard over the ocean, but Kai spoke when she was a few feet away.

"I need to ask you a question," he said. His voice was tense.

"Okay," she said, worried but trying not to show it. She joined him at the railing, but he didn't turn to face her.

"The death has been chasing you for months. How well do you know it?"

Lana was confused by the question. "Know? I don't ... I mean, it's a spirit."

She caught the edge of his smile. "And you can't know spirits?"

"Oh." She looked out at the sea, grateful that the night hid her blush. "Well, then ..." She thought of its inscrutable silences, sudden violence, bizarre moments that might have approached affection, and shook her head. "Not very well."

"So you wouldn't know if someone had weakened its bonds." It was a statement that almost sounded like an accusation.

"*Weakened* them? How would I know anything about that? I'm just an herb witch."

He turned to look at her now, and she was surprised by how weary he seemed. His eyes were nearly black. "The death that follows you? It's no pale manifestation of the great spirit, and even that would be surprising for an herb-witch. No, it's a full-fledged projection. Do you understand? The actual death spirit, the one bound by rock and bone in the heart of a dead volcano on the inner islands, has projected *itself* to chase you for your mother's death. Do you think that's normal? Do you think, even with such an ancient and powerful geas, most people are taken past the gates by the Great Spirit itself?"

You are chased by more than you know. Others had told her that, over the course of this torturous journey, but she had been too distraught to pay much attention. A *projection*? She had always imagined that it was one of the lesser death spirits, a reflection of a reflection of a ghost of the true manifestation.

"What are you saying?" Her voice was quiet, but it shook.

"Fire or death," he said softly. "You weakened its bonds, didn't you?" He sounded resigned, not angry.

"I—" Something occurred to her. "All this time? When you invited me and you ... all this time?"

"Yes."

How could he be so calm? She laughed, but it was desperate and a little hysterical. "You've thought I did something that could kill millions of innocent people and you wanted me anyway?"

She couldn't read his face. "I thought ... maybe it wasn't deliberate."

"And if it was?"

"Even so."

She slapped him, hard. He must have seen the blow coming, but he didn't stop it. "Even if I wanted to, I don't know how to weaken a great Binding. And I would never, ever want to."

He didn't say anything, but she could hear his question anyway: then why was the great spirit itself floating just beyond the ship?

He took her hand, quickly, before she could pull away, and touched his fingertips to her palm. "I apologize," he said.

"Kai ... it really didn't matter?"

He leaned forward and brushed his lips against hers. "No."

They arrived a week later. The water shrine was a short but sprawling structure dominating an island at least the same size as her childhood home. On the opposite harbor she saw the famous blue marble arch—the spirit gate. Guarding that gate was the guardian's main task: to prevent the lesser spirits from escaping the islands. The shrine itself was largely made out of the same blue marble, although it looked as though many additions had been made with whatever stone had been available at the time. A small boat awaited them in the harborless waters nearby, and they lowered themselves into it with a rope thrown over the edge of the ship. The death hovered over them until it seemed to hit a wall right on the boundary of the shrine. So Kai had told her the exact truth when he offered her total protection. As long as she stayed here in this beautiful place, she and everyone she loved would always be safe from the death. Certainly, Kai was more than a match for it. Kai paddled the boat slowly around the edge of the island until he reached a part of the shrine that was built over the water. A few other boats were moored inside and Kai pulled alongside with a deft maneuver. The splashing water echoed delicately on the stone, but she heard no other sounds coming from the temple. Was there no one to come and meet him in his own home? He stepped lightly out of the boat and then held out his hand. Lana took it, unable to keep a smile from spreading across her face.

After all this time, she was finally safe.

· 13 ·

KAI WAS SILENT as he led her through a long corridor. The blue-veined marble walls stopped abruptly where the ceiling should be. Instead, jets of water sprayed like arches overhead. Water from the jets misted around them, but somehow neither she nor Kai got wet. Beside her she felt a rush of air and then a brief giggle, like that of a young girl, echo off the stones. Footprints of water appeared and then vanished almost immediately, running far ahead of them down the hall. She froze and turned to Kai.

"What was that?" she asked.

"Just a sprite. I suppose they're going to tell my father I've returned." His voice was tense, distant.

"I thought your father was dead."

He started walking again. "He is."

Lana felt like clicking her tongue in annoyance—he was always this closed off—but she refrained. Kai was clearly disturbed, but she didn't know enough about him to understand why. A few uncomfortable minutes later, Lana, still unbalanced by her wings, slipped on the damp floor and went careening into the wall. Instead of smashing against hard stone like she had expected, she was actually cushioned by the strange film of water rushing, impossibly, along the side. It spread from the wall in the shape of two long-fingered hands and pushed her gently upright. Kai's hands replaced the ones that had already receded into the water, and she wondered at how similar they felt. She shivered at his touch on her arms and looked into his eyes.

"I'm sorry," he said. "I wasn't thinking. Here." He waved his hand and suddenly the area around her feet cleared entirely of water, bone dry under her sandals.

Lana smiled tentatively and wished that he would hold her closer, but he just turned away again and they continued their journey through the hall. She heard more giggles and the sound of running footsteps passing them, but Kai ignored it and eventually she did too. At the end of the hall was an archway festooned with small animal sculptures that she was half-convinced turned their heads to stare at her as she passed through. Kai stopped her just before the path abruptly ended. They stood before a large, dimly lit room filled entirely with water that lapped delicately against the walls. She was about to ask Kai how they could get across when the blue feather in his hair glowed briefly and the water receded a few inches, revealing a series of irregularly shaped stones that led to the other end of the chamber.

Without any warning, Kai picked her up by the waist and jumped lightly to the first stone. She squirmed half-heartedly, laughing. She loved being this close to him.

"Hey, what do you think you're doing?" she said, pounding on his back.

"Would you rather I toss you in?" he said, and for the first time in a week she heard genuine laughter in his tone.

When he was about to jump from the middle stone, a wobbly, glowing glob detached itself from the water and floated up to her face. She nearly choked, but Kai's lack of reaction told her that this thing—whatever it was—couldn't be dangerous. It paused a few inches from her eyes, and she stared back helplessly, feeling uncomfortable at something that felt oddly like an appraisal. Inside its filmy skin she could see dozens of strange whirling objects, but nothing even resembling eyes or a mouth. Eventually it broke her gaze and dropped down to Kai. The thing wrapped itself around his head for a few moments and glowed very brightly before meandering back underneath the water.

"What … what was that?" Lana asked, desperately trying to keep her tone even.

"An old friend," he said. "Well, perhaps it isn't so bad to be back at home, after all."

An old friend? The gulf separating their lives suddenly yawned into a chasm.

The dark room with the rocks led to a large pond, its clear, smooth surface reflecting the green plants surrounding it and the bright blue of the sky above. Kai stepped onto a wooden bridge that spanned the lake and gestured for her to follow him. Lana paused at the top of the bridge and looked down at the glassy surface of the water. For a brief moment, she didn't realize she was staring at her own reflection—she hadn't seen herself since she had left Akua. She was much thinner. Her cheekbones were more sharply defined and her eyes held a certain wariness that she didn't recognize. And her wings …

"Great Kai," she whispered.

Kai put a hand on her shoulder, but didn't say anything. She was grateful for his touch—it grounded her, made her remember who she was. She barely recognized that stranger reflected in the water. She took a shaky breath and looked back up at him. His eyes looked turbulent, filled with sadness and pity and other emotions she didn't quite understand. Her breath caught.

"Just wait here for a bit," he said.

Before she could ask him what he was planning, he smiled and tumbled backwards in an impossibly graceful dive into the water. She leaned over the bridge and called his name a little frantically before she realized how ludicrous her fear was. Kai was as much a part of the water as he was human. His skin looked subtly different when he surfaced moments later, slick and oily—almost like a seal. He splashed water playfully at her but she noticed that no drops ever landed on her wings.

"Hey, stop that!" she shouted, following him around to the other side of the bridge. His mood was infectious, and she laughed even as he lobbed more water in her direction. His attacks took the strangest forms—delicate flowers, stars, fish that swam through the air toward her face with their mouths open. His rapid, easy movements in the water filled her with envy. How long had it been since she dove? Unthinking, she unstrapped her sandals and flexed her legs for her familiar dive into the water.

She looked down at Kai and smiled, wondering why he suddenly looked so worried.

"Lana, what are you—"

He actually launched himself out of the water, landing on top of her with enough force to almost bowl her over the other side of the bridge. She landed on her back, her wings squashed beneath her and the healing skin on her back pulled painfully taut.

"What were you doing?" he shouted, his voice shaking.

"I just wanted to dive ..."

"Lana ... you can't dive anymore. If you do and I'm not around, you'll drown. Promise me you won't ever try that again."

"But, Kai—"

"Promise me!"

His eyes resembled a fast-moving current, and in their depths she imagined she saw that first mandagah fish, opening its dying mouth over and over again as though it would devour her as well as its tainted jewel. She closed her eyes and wished that his words weren't true, that she would be able to dive again. She had known the depth of her sacrifice the second the wind spirit uttered the words "dark angel." Yet to hear it put so plainly ... there could be no more denial.

"I promise," she said.

He touched her wet cheek softly, collecting her tears on his fingers. When her face was dry, he put his hand to his mouth. One by one, he let the gathered tears dissolve on his tongue as his own eyes danced like the sea in a hurricane.

I'm a part of him now, she thought, overwhelmed—like a tiny piece of driftwood tossed on the top of a vast, stormy ocean.

Eventually they reached a drier part of the vast complex. The water in this area confined itself to a few small ponds with bridges and a stream that ran through all of the rooms. He led her up a small flight of stairs and then entered a room whose only door seemed to be an archway of roots covered by thick, hanging vines. He pushed his way through and she saw that it was some kind of sleeping chamber. There was no roof to speak of, but tall green plants shaded the sun's harsh glare. Nestled between the massive roots of one tree was a bed covered with fresh white sheets. Spaces had been carved in the walls where she could place her belongings.

"This is where you can stay. I think it's the nicest room, but if you don't like it, I can find something else."

"Oh no, it's fine. Where's your room, though?"

"Room? I don't have one. Well, I had one before the change, but not anymore."

Lana had never heard him use the term before. "What's a change?"

He seemed surprised. "When I stopped being ... human, I suppose."

"So, where do you sleep,?" she asked.

"The water, mostly. It's usually easiest that way."

Lana couldn't hide her disappointment. She supposed that she had hoped that they would be able to share the same bed, but he seemed so nervous and distant.

"We won't ... you don't want to sleep together? Like before?" She wanted to kick herself for sounding so desperate and tentative.

He looked away from her as though he was too ashamed to meet her eyes. "I'm sorry, Lana. I can't, not now. One day I'll explain, I promise, but ..."

Lana blushed so fiercely, she felt like her face had caught fire.

"Don't worry," she said, forcing her tone to be light. "I'm sure I'll manage without you. It's kindness enough that you allowed me to stay here."

He winced at her sarcasm, but didn't return it, which made Lana feel very petty.

"For now, I think it's better if you don't go wandering too much," he said. "It's very easy to get lost ... not everything here stays exactly where you left it. I'll have some food brought here later. Normally we can eat together, but tonight ..."

"What is it?" Lana asked.

"Tonight ... I release my father. I'll have his Weeping."

Lana kissed him goodbye on the bridge over a deep lake near her room. He returned it tenderly, but with an edge that made her ache for him. Whatever awaited him down there, he was clearly afraid of it.

"Kai ... what's a Weeping? They always said the water guardians couldn't cry."

He sighed. "We can, but just one tear is a massive sacrifice. A Weeping is what the water guardian does to pass his powers to his successor when he's ready to die. My father ... he's wanted to do this for a very long time. I have no right to deny him any longer."

He leaned over and kissed her left ear, where ugly, ridged scar tissue grew over the place where her earlobe had once been. She shivered.

"I'll be back soon," he said. "You don't have to wait for me."

He closed his eyes and dove over the side of the bridge. This time, he didn't resurface.

Lana sat down with her legs dangling over the edge and began her vigil.

Kai allowed his body to change as he pushed himself deeper underwater. Membranous tissue grew between his fingers and toes, his ears adjusted themselves to the increasing pressure and parts of his skin began to open up, allowing him to breathe underwater.

He ignored the growing gaggle of sprites that followed his deep passage—they could only follow him so far, after all. Only the guardians themselves could enter the ancestors' cave. He used their light to guide him through the underwater maze, but he went through the final passage alone, and in the dark. After squeezing through a tiny fissure in the rock face, he emerged in a huge dark cavern. The walls by the fissure were covered in fading murals, painted by the lost civilization that had first built these underground mazes. He had often wondered about that as a child: how had a whole race with powers like the water guardians been so utterly destroyed that only a handful of people even knew that they existed? He sighed and stepped through the rim of the air seal that surrounded most of the cavern.

Weeks ago, when he felt his father enter this sacred chamber for the final time, he had been furious. Ali'ikai hadn't wanted him to leave; he had dismissed his son's concerns as childish delusions. And then, just when Kai was learning how horribly right he had been, his father chose to die. He hadn't wanted to return, though he had known he didn't have much choice. But then he met Lana, and his whole world rearranged itself. The cranes warned him, he remembered. He didn't know where it came from, this crazed love that had lodged itself in him the moment he first looked at her. It had happened to his father—Aunt Pua loved to tell him that story—but he had always considered himself to be more rational, more controlled. He would never sink into a decades-deep pit of grief over the love of one woman. And yet ... now Lana was with him, and he didn't know what he would do if she ever left.

Even here, on the cusp of doing the one thing he had dreaded all his life, he didn't regret returning. He would do whatever was needed to protect her, even if it meant accepting the power he had never wanted. He thought of how she had last looked at him, with a kind of dogged, sad hope that made him want to beg her forgiveness. Of course, how could he possibly give into the constant temptation before she understood what she would be sacrificing?

Selfishly or not, he wanted a little more time with her before he forced her to make such an impossible decision.

His father sat hunched in a tiny crevice above the graves of his ancestors, a desultory white light floating somewhere above his head.

"So, the wayward son has finally returned." His father's voice was cold and oddly distant, as though he was already half-gone. "I had begun to lose hope." He stared at Kai. "You know how long I've wanted this. You know that you were the only reason I remained. Why did you delay? Didn't you think you owed me this much?"

Kai clenched his webbed fingers. "You know why I had to, father. Even if you're too far gone to care, it matters to me what happens in the world of the living."

"Oh, you presume to know me so well?" The listless voice now held a touch of anger.

"I only know who I saw. A man half-mad with grief over a woman I barely even remember. You never were interested in the world, in life … in me …" Seeing his father in this state had stirred something inside of him—he wanted to dam the anger and the old pain, but they suffused him.

"I see. So that's what this is really about. You think I loved my dead wife more than my living son. You're probably right." His face crumpled and he looked away. "I was never worthy of you, was I, Makani?" he whispered, his voice scratchy with agony even twenty-five years after the loss.

"Do you know what it was like, Kai? You think you know so much, but you know nothing of grief. Imagine spending days with it tearing at your insides like a maniac with a dull spoon, knowing that nothing short of death will assuage it and that *you cannot die.* Imagine the mad, terrifying temptation to weep until your very soul drains away and knowing even that recourse isn't open to you. Can you not imagine why I would have felt some resentment toward the one who would keep me in that hellish prison? Can you not even sympathize?"

"Even if that person's crime was merely existing? Merely reminding you of your obligations? Even if you instead chose to give all of your love to someone who could no longer feel it?"

"Don't say that!" And then, a few seconds later, "Why didn't you come sooner?" His father's voice sounded plaintive, almost like a child's.

"Maybe I hoped that if I could find out what had been causing the disturbances, you would change your mind. I hoped I could get to know my own father before everyone I loved died. I hoped ..." Kai paused and shook his head. "What I hoped was naïve. Selfish. I'm sorry, Father, I should have come sooner. Your torment is over—have your release."

Kai closed the gap between them and lowered his head beneath his father's, so their eyes met.

"It wasn't all torment," his father said quietly. "You have a lot of your mother about you ... your pig-headedness, your smile ... not your eyes, though." He chuckled. "No, those are mine."

He gripped Kai's hand one last time. "May fate protect you from loving a woman like I did your mother."

Kai's voice stuck in his throat, but his mind flitted to visions of Lana sleeping on the rocking ship during their journey to the shrine, her tangled hair falling over her face.

And then, with a cough so delicate as to belie the fact that he was overcoming a lifetime of rigid self-control, his father began to weep.

Kai emerged from the lake many hours later, his face haunted and his body sagging with exhaustion. She called out his name, but he didn't seem to hear her at first.

"What are you doing here?" he asked, after he finally snapped out of his reverie.

"Waiting for you," she said. He floated on the top of the water, staring like he didn't quite understand what she was saying. She sighed. "Are you coming up? I can't very well go down and get you."

A thick cord of water lifted him from the lake and deposited him on the bridge. He sprawled onto his back, his ice-blue eyes staring blankly up at the starry night sky. His chest barely moved— anyone not looking closely might have thought him dead.

She moved closer to him and tentatively held his hand. He looked different, she realized. A second feather—this one a deep, oily black—was now entwined with his hair on the right side.

"Kai?" she said softly. He didn't move. "What happened?" Lana didn't dare speak again, even as the seconds ticked away and he showed no sign of having heard her.

"He's gone," he said finally, in a voice so small she could barely hear it. "Do you know, I remember crying when I was just a baby. It's my first memory—me bawling while my mother rocked me and held her hand over my eyes to try and stop the tears. If my father caught me crying he would roar and hold me underwater until I almost drowned ... I haven't cried since I was four years old. Not even when my mother died ... can you imagine that?" He laughed bleakly. "A five-year-old child not shedding a tear over his dead mother? By the time I had the change, I think I had forgotten how." He turned his head to face her. "Is that what you want, keika? A man who wouldn't even be able to shed tears on your grave?"

What did she want? Him; but was it so simple? She smiled a little and helped him sit up. "Sleep with me again? Just for tonight?"

He avoided her eyes. "Lana, I don't think that's a very—"

"Please?"

He sighed, then smiled ruefully. "Okay."

They walked slowly off of the bridge and away from the lake where, one day, Kai too would gain his ultimate release through tears.

The library was a massive warren of books, scrolls, and clay tablets, accessible only by poled boats and water-taut stairs that Kai would obligingly create so she could fetch something down. The only solid bit of floor was a stone island in the center of the library that held a carpet, a large wooden table, and about five cushioned chairs. Kai was still obsessed with learning more about the death and the strange geas that she had used to save her mother. He had decided to search through his library to see if he could find any other references to it. Perhaps, he said, he had been mistaken and something in the geas itself called forth a projection of the death spirit. He had seemed a little subdued after she first told him of her mother's illness, but she realized that it must have been very similar to the way his own mother died. Most of his books were dedicated to the geas and the art of sacrifice, but a month after he started looking, he still hadn't found any useful information about that kind of binding.

Lana was reading a decidedly plebeian book about daring pirate adventures in the days before the spirit bindings while sitting on the edge of the stone island with her feet dangling in the water. Kai had made it warm for her, which she enjoyed.

Kai slammed his book shut and then sneezed in the resulting little explosion dust. "Can I see that flute of yours again, Lana?" he asked.

Lana swiveled around, a little miffed at being distracted from her reading. "Why? Do you want to play it?"

"No, of course not. I just thought looking at it again might help me see if I missed any other reason why it can work geas so powerfully."

Lana shrugged and fished it out of her pocket. "I told you, it's because it's a self-sacrifice."

"You're probably right," he said, fingering the worn holes carefully. "But I'm not getting anywhere with this other stuff."

He held it up to the light. "How old did you say this was?"

"Oh … somewhere between thirty and forty years, I guess."

"Really?" he said, still squinting up at it. "I'm not sure, but the bone seems much older. It's so discolored and brittle." He lowered it to his lips and tentatively blew out a long, high-pitched note.

He frowned. "Nothing." He handed it to Lana. "Why don't you try? Blow the same note I just did."

Despite its offhanded, breathy edge, when Lana played the note, she still felt the familiar instantaneous reaction of spirits waiting, anticipating the geas about to be recited. Of course, she didn't recite a geas and the sensation quickly faded away.

Her palms were slick when she put the flute back in her pocket—she knew this meant something was wrong. He sat down next to her. "So it works for you, but not for me ..." He lapsed into silence and she leaned on his shoulder. "You know ... maybe it's the witch. Even if you're using it, it's still her sacrifice, isn't it? Whenever you use that flute, it's like you have the witch's willing sacrifice, but one far more subtle and nuanced than anything I've ever seen before. She must still have control over who can access the sacrifice."

Kai didn't say it, but Lana knew what he must be thinking. If Akua had given her that power, she could just as easily take it away.

The next day Kai handed her a well-worn tome, his expression so intent she suspected she would not be seeing very much of her pirate book over the next few days.

"What is this?" she asked. It looked old and a little mysterious, like the books in Akua's death temple.

"It's a dictionary of fundamental geas principles. Probably more comprehensive than any you worked with. I don't think your teacher was very thorough ... which is strange, because anyone familiar with a geas like the one you recited for your mother must have known them."

Lana frowned. "Fundamental geas ... I thought you just had to memorize them."

He stared at her. "Lana, you must have created some geas if you made it this far. You actually don't know anything about this?"

"I was desperate! It was either make up a geas and hope it doesn't kill me, or don't make up a geas and know it will." She felt vaguely uncomfortable under his disbelieving gaze.

"I wouldn't trust that flute, Lana," he said slowly. His eyes had gone stormy again. "You shouldn't rely on a gift from a witch who never even told you that you could make up your own geas."

She felt strangely panicked. "But ... it was never meant to

happen this way. I was just supposed to learn enough to make my living—herbs for sickness, for getting rid of babies or helping them along and the geas that could help. I was never supposed to learn them just to survive, not like this. How could she have known?" But maybe *this* was part of the game they had played, and Lana had very nearly lost.

He looked like he wanted to say something more, but finally he just nodded. "Just be careful, okay?" He opened up the book and began speaking, his tone positively academic. "So, the basic principles. You should think of it like, say, geometry. Do you know geometry?"

Lana nodded. Well, she had several years ago, and she wasn't about to make another admission of ignorance.

"So, geometry uses a series of statements, one directly relating to another known statement to prove something. Like ..." He raised his finger and a small stream of water spurt from it, forming a straight line in the air in front of them. "A line is the shortest distance between two points. We make another line on the same plane," he drew a line above the first, "we have two lines that seemingly have no relationship to each other, right?"

Lana nodded tentatively. She was quickly realizing that she must have spent most of her time in class with Kohaku daydreaming about him and not actually paying attention to the lessons.

"But," Kai said, "what if we draw a line going through them both?" He squirted a vaguely diagonal line. "Now, take your book and go check to see which angles are less than the corner." Reluctantly, Lana stood up and measured the angles, trying not to get the book wet. Both of the angles on the left side were slightly smaller than the paper.

"If the angles on one side are both less than ninety degrees, that means that eventually, these two lines that you thought had nothing to do with each other will intersect on that side."

Kai waved his hand and the lines evaporated. He turned back to her, a smug little smile on his face.

"Okay, that was ... interesting, but I don't understand what it has to do with geas."

He sighed. "What I mean is that from one simple premise—a line is the shortest route between two points—we proved how two lines can intersect each other. And if I wanted, I could use that to prove more things. It's the same with a geas, only the fundamental principles are less obvious, and the logic behind many of them has been lost. Once you learn them, though, the process of constructing a geas is virtually the same."

Lana cracked open the tome and flipped to the relatively small section in back about death. "It carries a key of lead," read the first short postulate. She looked up at Kai.

"Everyone learns these?"

"Everyone who wants to master geas."

The book was very thick, and the type was very small. Even if she did commit each of these to memory, would it be enough? If she and Akua were still playing their game, would it at least give her a chance?

After a solid week of studying, she had only managed to memorize the first ten pages of postulates. She had decided to start with wind (alternatively known as air, storm, and—most disconcertingly—light), in some sort of defiant homage to its "gift." Often, she wanted to stop and relax, or at least complain loudly, but Kai had buried himself so deeply in his research that she sometimes felt he forgot her presence entirely. His discovery about Akua's flute had disturbed him. She knew it must have revived his earlier concerns about Lana having something to do with weakening the death spirit's bindings, but she didn't understand how the two could be related. He had told her that the flooding on her island had only been one of dozens of similarly inexplicable disasters throughout the islands. And though the threat was remote—the bindings had held for more than a thousand years, after all—the possibility of one of the three spirits breaking free had consumed him. She wanted to help, but given her ignorance on the subject, there wasn't much she could do. So, she bit her lip and trudged through the postulates, muttering them aloud to herself until she could be reasonably sure she'd remember them. "Even the wind can freeze," she repeated, feeling like a temple officiate at solstice. *Why* hadn't Akua taught her any of this? She didn't doubt that the witch knew every postulate in this book by heart. Quickly, Lana went to the next line. She couldn't stand to think of that for very long.

"Lana," Kai said suddenly, surprising her. "That witch, Akua ... did she frequently invoke death? Was it her affinity?"

"She's a healer!" Lana snapped. "She only ever bound the most minor death sprites, and even then a handful of times." She was distantly surprised at how defensive she felt.

Kai nodded, but he didn't stop looking at her, and she shifted uncomfortably. What had those ancient books told him?

She cleared her throat. "You don't believe me again?"

His eyes were the very clear crystal blue of his most analytical mood. "I think you must be forgetting something."

Almost involuntarily, she recalled the first night Akua took her to death temple at the center of the lake. What were Ino's words? *She belongs to the water, not to that.* Not to death.

"There was a death temple. She took me there ... twice."

She wanted to run away—from both the memory and the implications—but she knew that Kai would never let it go. He was a guardian. He would protect the islands, even from her.

"What did it look like?"

Lana took a shaky breath, acutely aware of the flute in her pocket. "Old. There was a hole in the center ... like a column of air."

He stood up so abruptly that some of his books splashed into the water. They didn't get wet, of course. He walked over to her and gripped her shoulders.

"Lana," he said, "I know you were young, and you didn't understand and she deliberately misled you, but you cannot continue to defend her. I don't know what she intended with you, I don't know how precisely she did it—but she *must* be responsible for the death."

She shook his hands off angrily. "I recited the geas, Kai. I accepted the sacrifice. What could Akua have to do with that? Without the flute I would have died months ago. Why would she set me up and then help save my life?"

"I don't know."

"Then stop accusing her!"

He seemed very lost, suddenly. "I'm not accusing you, keika."

She laughed. "Well, it's a short step, isn't it?"

He found her a few hours later, napping in her room.

"I won't apologize for trying to learn the truth," he said, without preamble when she opened her eyes. "But I promise I won't accuse Akua of anything until I'm sure."

"Okay," she said, rubbing her eyes. "I'm sorry I got so upset. It's just ... I can't believe ..."

She couldn't believe that those four years of her life were some elaborate lie. That her mother might have even suspected and let Akua take her anyway. It was easier to ignore everything.

"I know," Kai said.

A month later the rains began. Even though her room had no roof, the rain ran off an invisible barrier before it reached her. At first it was fun to watch the rain without getting soaked to the skin, but the relentless pounding reminded her of those final months on her island when the mandagah fish were nearly wiped out and Kali fell victim to the flood. When Kai left for several days to check on remote parts of the shrine and make repairs on areas that might be damaged by the flooding, she felt practically oppressed by loneliness. She had grown so used to his presence; now not even the death, her grim companion for so long, could reach her. So, she started wandering around the seemingly endless, bizarre maze of rooms, streams, and passages that always led to places she had never been before. Even though she had lived here for over two months, she could still hardly fathom the kind of sprawling, massive place she had ventured into. She wondered what the fire shrine was like—she had heard that the wives were locked in a tall tower and never allowed to leave because of the constant volcanic eruptions. Before, she had thought the story ridiculous. Now, she was just grateful that she had never run into the fire guardian.

The second day of Kai's absence, she discovered a vine-ladder near her rooms that led to an entirely different section of the shrine. On one side of a forked bridge in this newfound area she saw a series of stairs. She took them, since she so rarely saw anything that led upwards. After five minutes of circular climbing, she arrived, to her surprise, on the roof, in an area that was not protected from the rain. She was about to sprint back downstairs when she realized that from right here she had a perfect view of the spirit gate. The dark blue stone monolith looked particularly magnificent in the rain, and she nearly forgot about the water soaking through her wings as she stared. The wind spirit had given her the wings of a dry-climate bird—when she was flying, she dislodged enough water to stay airborne, but it wasn't a good idea for her to stand still in this kind of a deluge. Inside the arch of the gate, a shape began to form. She watched curiously before she realized what it must be: the death staring at her, its empty hole of a mouth curved into a smile. She stumbled backwards onto the first step, but its voice caught her before she got away.

"You can't stay there forever," it said. "I know you, Lana. I know what you love, what you hate. I know what you don't know, and I know that you will leave. Will you be able to bind me then? Or have you grown soft with your lover?"

"He's not my lover," Lana said, absurdly. Before she could hear anything else, she rushed back down the steps.

Her mood turned much blacker after that, haunted by the death's words and her renewed awareness of its waiting presence. Her wings were heavy and waterlogged, which made walking a far more arduous task than usual. She wandered into a corridor much like the one where she slept—minimal water, as though it was designed for humans and not water guardians. At the end of the corridor she saw a wide gap in the wall, but no door to speak of. The opening led to a large room, decorated with old-fashioned furniture that was caked in dust. There were two doors inside, one that led to a water closet and the other that led to an inner chamber, complete with a small, deep pond and what looked like still-rumpled bedding. That, too, was caked with dust. Who had lived here? She walked to the far wall, where she thought she saw some odd discoloration in the stone. But it wasn't discoloration, she realized, but writing. Someone had taken a rusty object and actually scratched characters into the wall—quite a long time ago, judging by how much it had faded.

> I, Hiapo bei'Polunu, wife of the water guardian, have been imprisoned here for ten years. Should anyone ever find this, please pray for myself and my son, for I do not think I shall be imprisoned for very much longer. I have seen him emerge from that pool too many times. Today my body shall meet him, but my soul will escape forever. *Se maloka selama ua ola, ipa nui.*

What lies beyond the gate, I do not know. The catechism still recited in the ancient dialect at the end of funeral services.

Someone giggled softly behind her. She whirled around, heart pounding, to see that a female water sprite had emerged from the pond. She was made entirely out of water, but each of her features was delicately defined. She sat in its center, smiling and touching the water invitingly.

"What do you want?" Lana asked warily. She rarely saw the water sprites, and with Kai gone she wasn't inclined to trust them.

The sprite just giggled and gestured toward the water again.

"Did you know her?" Lana asked. "The woman who lived in these rooms? Did she actually … in the pool …"

"Did she drown herself, you mean?" The sprite's voice was

hideously bright. "Oh yes. Just after she wrote that, in fact. She jumped, but she might have changed her mind, at the end ... I'm not sure. I helped her stay down, after all."

Lana felt nauseous. "What about her son?" she asked.

"Ah, he's dead too. His son is the guardian now. It's been so long since I last had any visitors!" Her voice grated at Lana's ears like a screeching cat. That poor woman had been Kai's grandmother? But why would the guardian's wife ever be imprisoned?

"Come, won't you look in the water? I'm sure you'll see something you like."

Against all of her better judgment, Lana snuck a peek inside the pond.

She forgot to breathe. The pool was filled with mandagah fish. It had been so long since she had last seen one that she had almost forgotten their peculiar sedate pace, their squashed, sand-colored faces that looked disturbingly human. One of them looked up at her and opened its mouth. Inside were two exquisite blue mandagah jewels, bigger than almost any she had ever seen. She lost track of time as she stared at them, overcome with an unexpected joy. She had to dive and play with them. They wanted to give her their jewels—look, they were practically tossing them at her now. If only she could go in, if only she hadn't promised Kai not to ...

"Go dive with them. Can't you see how they want it? Haven't you missed it?" The sprite's voice now sounded melodious and inviting, yet some small part of Lana still told her to resist it.

"But ... the wings," Lana said, barely able to articulate the words. "Kai says ... I'll drown."

"Don't worry about what Kai says. I see how much you want this, and I can give it to you. I promise, I'll help you so you won't drown. Don't you see? They've all missed you so much."

The mandagah fish had all moved to the edge of the pond and were staring up like they desperately wanted to see her. Some far distant part of her was aware that this wasn't normal mandagah behavior, but she couldn't control herself any longer. Without a conscious decision, she took off her shoes and soaked socks.

"Yes, that's it. Come inside. Come inside."

Lana jumped.

At first the feeling of the water against her skin was like ecstasy. She spread her arms looked for the mandagah fish that were sure to come running to greet her. Then, as horror gripped her stomach like a vise, she realized two things.

First, there were no mandagah fish. Second, she was about to drown.

The weight of her wings began dragging her closer to the bottom of the impossibly deep pond, and it was all she could do to pressurize her ears and struggle to stay above a certain depth. The sprite had told her how she had drowned Kai's grandmother, and still Lana had looked in the lake? Was she so desperate to dive again? Above her she saw the sprite's graceful shape and she reached out in the vain hope that the creature would help her.

It smiled sadistically and flitted away, leaving Lana deep in a lightless night.

What would Kai do, she wondered, when he found her body lying at the bottom of a pond in a deserted part of the shrine? Would he be angry? Would he rage or grieve and then slowly let her image fade to a pleasant memory, sometimes dusted off for reuse? She knew one thing he wouldn't do, though: cry.

As the air in her lungs dwindled to a pittance and she felt black encroaching on the edges of her world, she decided to make one last, desperate bid to save herself. Before she ran out of all of her air, she would try to call for him. Afterwards, she wouldn't be able to stop herself from sucking in water, but there was the vaguest possibility that he would have heard her.

"Kai!" she screamed into the water. "Sweet Kai …"

The water burned as it flooded her lungs, but she thought of him as she slipped into darkness.

Kai heard the sound, impossibly faint, as he was hauling stones to support a crumbling outer wall. It could have been a thousand other things, but his brain shivered when he heard it and he knew it was Lana. He dove back under the water, straining his senses until he could feel practically every part of the shrine. After several long, nerve-wracking moments, he found her. She was barely there—a fast-dimming spark in an abandoned part of the shrine. She was about to die. Barely aware of what he was doing, he allowed his entire physical form to dissolve into the water and then he rushed along, in every tiny rivulet and stream that permeated the water shrine, gradually coming closer to where she was. He had no heart to pound, but fear sped his noncorporeal parts until he felt as though he were falling through air instead of gliding through water. This was an ability he had never had before he became guardian, and one he had never used even since. It was dangerous—even within the water shrine itself—because dissolved like this, his disparate parts could get separated with disastrous results.

He found her a minute later, floating unconscious at the bottom of a pool that he had thought was sealed off forever. He re-formed and picked her up, speeding out of the water like a geyser. She didn't gasp or breathe when he broke the surface, and he wondered, desperately, how long ago she had drowned. Why had she waited so long to call him? When he hauled her onto the cold, dusty stones, he wasn't even sure if her heart was still beating. There was still one thing he could do. He gripped the black waterbird feather and recited a geas, softly, as though he was reciting a prayer.

A jolt of light seemed to pass through her body and water erupted from her mouth as he forced it from her lungs. Kai held her hand, but it still hung limply in his. Even that hadn't revived her.

He called her name frantically, but she didn't respond.

Is this my father's hell?

No, he couldn't give up now, not yet. He touched the black feather and recited the geas again, this time giving it more power even though he knew it could hurt her. The light passed through her body and her legs jerked. One long second later her whole body shook and she began coughing violently in his lap.

He thought that he had never heard a more beautiful sound.

She actually saw the death at the gate.

"So, you came even without my help," it said.

Lana shook her head. Where was Kai? Could he have abandoned her, or did he just come too late?

"He can't save you now. You're in my domain."

"Will you take my mother, too?" she asked.

It nodded. "You didn't have a natural death."

"Mama, I'm so sorry," she whispered. She looked back up at the death. "Tell me, what's beyond the gate?"

It paused and its mask returned to neutral. "You'll see soon enough," it said.

"But you're about to take me there. What's the harm?"

It shook its head and beckoned her to come forward. Against her will, she did so. Did she have wings here, as well? She looked. Yes, even in death, she was still a black angel. The death picked the key up off the chain around his waist and inserted it into the lock.

"Your key," she said suddenly.

It paused and turned to face her. "What?"

"It's made of lead."

The death looked startled. She felt a strange charge flow through her body, like a bolt of lightning, and she suddenly stood several feet further away from the gate.

"You have a clever lover, Lana," it said. "But not clever enough." It started to drag her forward again.

"Lana ... Lana please ..."

It was Kai. She latched onto his image in her mind and resisted the death's relentless pull.

"The death's key is made of lead," she said, frantically searching for a corollary. Of course, a geas without a sacrifice was generally useless, but she refused to just give up. "Made of lead ... the earth!

The death is tied to the earth by that lodestone. It can never fully escape it. For all its power, it is still a creature bound to the grief that it creates. Like all creatures of the earth, it can feel grief, love, anger … even pity. So long as it wields the key, death is bound to petty human emotion."

The death paused. "Pity, you say?" Its voice was filled with disbelieving laughter. "Ah, you are brave. Ignorant, but brave. I never expected this to be such a challenge. So let the guardian call you back—it will be a far greater pleasure to take you myself."

Another, greater, bolt of light rocked her.

The death bowed. "Till next time, brave one."

And then she was coughing on Kai's lap—wet, cold, and alive.

He held her until the coughing subsided, brushing back her hair and murmuring things she couldn't quite understand but which felt very comforting nonetheless. Her body ached all over in a formless kind of way, and she wondered if it had anything to do with the strange light she had felt before. Still trembling, she pulled him down until his face was level with hers. For now, at least, she knew exactly what she wanted.

"Kiss me," she said, teeth chattering.

Blindly, unquestioning, he did so. It was the most gentle, tender thing that she had ever experienced. His fingers glided in delicate, feather-like strokes, even though his arms were shaking with tension. He moved from her mouth and began kissing her nose, eyes, forehead, temple, the hollow of her neck. She felt like her whole existence was being held in those gentle hands. How was it possible to love someone this much? Part of her wanted to tell him so, but she was so afraid of destroying the moment that she held her silence, saying as much as she could without words. He lay with his back on the floor and pulled her on top of him, kissing her gently as he undid her shirt. But when she tried to pull off his, he suddenly stopped and held her wrists, pulling away from her with a tormented expression.

"What … what's wrong?" They had never gone this far before, but she had thought he was enjoying it.

"Lana, I can't. I want to … you don't know how much I want to, but I would never forgive myself. You don't know what you would be sacrificing."

Lana froze. That word choice had to be deliberate, and Kai was half sprite. "What kind of sacrifice?" Her voice was steady.

He looked away. "Do you know where we are? These may look like rooms, but they're just a well-furnished prison. My grandmother lived here a hundred years ago. For the last ten years of her life she never saw any family or friends. She never saw a wall that wasn't contained in her cell. The only two people she was ever allowed to see were her husband and her son—and after he reached a certain age, not even her son. Do you know why she was forced to live like a slave—this woman who was the wife of one of the most powerful men in the islands?"

"Why?" she asked, a little alarmed now at his intensity.

He leaned over her and gripped her shoulder so hard that it hurt. "Because the water guardians are not like normal men. We demand far too much for our love and then, even when love is given freely in return, we never trust it. Understand me, Lana: a water guardian can only give himself to one woman, and when he does, it must be for life. If that woman gives herself to *any-one* afterwards, the guardian will die in slow and painful agony, unable to pass his abilities on to his son. There is no stronger bond in nature. Do you understand? My grandmother, and dozens of women before her, spent their lives imprisoned because their husbands lived in dread of the day their wives would betray them—and in doing so, destroy them."

"Are you saying … are you saying that you would have to imprison me here if I gave myself to you?"

"What if I was?"

Her wings shivered at the thought. "I would leave you and wait until you returned to your senses."

He traced her cheekbones with his cool, smooth fingertips. For a moment, they stared at each other, and then she buried her head in his chest and breathed his scent until she thought her heart would burst. "Oh, keika," he whispered, "of course I would never do that to you. I would die and leave the shrine unguarded before I made you live like that. But … but you would still have to bear my son. Do you really want to do this? I can give you more time to decide—"

"Shh," she said gently, putting her finger to his mouth.

He smiled—joyously, like a child—and closed his eyes. This time, he made no objection when she began to remove his clothes. She leaned into him and breathed his musk of seawater and sweat.

"Great Kai," she said, and then laughed. "How many women can invoke the spirit and their lover at the same time?"

Kai opened his eyes and moved, ever so delicately, directly beneath her. She gasped and bit her lip.

He froze. "Are you okay?" he asked, horrified.

"I've wanted this for so long …"

"So have I."

"Then whatever you do," she said, hugging him so she could hear the reassuring beat of his heart, "don't stop."

Afterwards, looking back at those months, Lana would marvel at how she had managed to reach such an oasis of happiness when everything she had previously loved about her life had been destroyed. She had lost her home, her family, her faith in Akua, her ability to dive, and any pretension to normalcy. She was chased by the manifestation of death itself and the wild wind had turned her into a black angel. And yet, she was happy. She supposed, later, that some of the heady joy of those days with Kai was derived from her never-articulated conviction that it must all end. That the game she had been playing—and losing—with Akua would not end here. The death had said as much to her that day on the roof. She and Kai spent nearly every minute of each day with each other, and Lana made her dogged way through the geas tome. It pleased Kai to see her study it, and that was more than enough motivation. After two months she had memorized all of wind and half of fire (naturally a much longer section). She was aware of a certain perversity in the fact that she hadn't even glanced at the death postulates, but that always brought her thoughts back to Akua. And Kai needed no help from her on that score. If there was any worm in the orange of her happiness, it was their repeated arguments about her former mentor. They began two months after she nearly drowned. Kai came to her room in the early morning, visibly exhausted from spending all night in the library.

"I think she somehow used you to destabilize the death spirit's bonds."

Lana didn't need to ask who "she" was. "I thought you promised not to mention it again."

"Unless I was sure, I said."

Lana scowled at him. "So, you're sure now? What happened, did you pay her a visit?"

He sat on the bed next to her and turned her head to face him. "I did a scrying."

Her stomach clenched. "What did you see?"

He shook his head, and Lana realized why he looked so tired. The geas must have demanded a large sacrifice. "She's very well guarded. I don't know how anyone, let alone a normal human, can keep so many geas active. I've tried before, and I couldn't get through."

"And now?"

"I tried harder. I used … other methods. I only caught a glimpse, Lana, but … I scryed for Akua, and all I could see was death. She's wrapped inside it like a cocoon. It's more than an affinity. I've never seen anything like it."

Lana swallowed. "What do you want me to do, Kai?"

"Help me find out what she did to you."

"Does it matter? Fine, she manipulated me, but she couldn't have weakened a first Binding. No one can do that."

He kissed her. "Except a black angel."

If Kai was right, Lana realized, then she had no future. She could learn as many geas postulates as she wanted, but she had seen Akua's power and she knew she'd never be a match for it. If Akua was her enemy, she might as well slit her own throat now. If wanting to hide from the possibility made her a coward, then so be it. She was too happy with him to care.

It lasted four months. The day that was to end their idyll, Kai said that he had some cleaning he ought to do for the spirit solstice. She tagged along as he maneuvered the still-confusing pathways to a part of the shrine that she had never seen. It amazed her that it had been nearly a year since she had last seen her mother. Was she planning another feast? Did she hope that Lana might come home? Kai grew silent as they went along, but she was so wrapped up in her own thoughts that she hardly noticed. He pushed back the vine-curtain of a small, pleasant-smelling room that looked very homey. A set of colored-glass wind chimes hung from the tree above the tidily made bed. The cubbies held little keepsakes in stout wooden boxes and a few extra sets of clothes. Only a desiccated leaf in the water pitcher gave any indication that whoever owned this room had not been back recently. It certainly didn't have the long-abandoned feel of his grandmother's quarters.

"Whose room is this?" she asked. "I didn't know there was another human living here."

Kai had frozen inside the door and the expression on his face made her pause. His eyes looked like they had when his father died. "There isn't," he said quietly. "At least, not anymore. This was my aunt's bedroom. After my mother died ... she raised me. My whole life she did everything she could for me, and then one day last year she got terribly sick and died a week later. There was nothing I could do."

It sounded so much like her mother's near-death. She hugged Kai until his breathing steadied.

"Why didn't you ever say anything about her before?" she asked.

He shrugged. "I didn't even know how to begin. She was so close to me, and then she died, just like that ... I left here to run away from it. When I brought you back, and my father died, I thought I just shouldn't burden you. But now it's been a year, and I really should put some of her things on the shrine with my mother and mourn her properly."

He broke away from her and walked over to one of the keepsake boxes. "Do you know that she had a mandagah jewel just like yours before she died? I don't know where she got it, but she held onto it the entire time. She said it was for luck, but I think ... I think it reminded her of my mother. They were so close, but my father had so much grief I think she sometimes felt like she didn't even have a right to any of her own."

He opened the box and pulled out a large blue mandagah jewel, strung on a line of shimmering riverweed.

"It reminds me of yours, but I don't know why ... yours is much more striking, with all that red ..." He smiled, but it wavered at his eyes. "They're like a set, aren't they?"

Lana fell back against the wall, smashing her wings and barely feeling it.

"Are you all right?" he said, cutting her with his gentle concern.

She just had to be sure. "Kai, tell me, what was ... your aunt's name?"

He rubbed her arm. "You look really sick. Do you want—"

"Please, please tell me her name."

"Pua," he said, looking confused. "But why—Lana! Okay, we should go back."

She couldn't seem to control her limbs or the blood rushing past her ears. She let Kai pick her up by the waist, feeling like a criminal even as she reveled in his touch.

"When did she die?" she asked, knowing she was grasping at straws. What more evidence did she need?

"She collapsed a week after the solstice. Lana, why are you so interested in this?"

A week after the solstice. The day that Lana had reached Essel to recite the geas that would save her mother. The day she used the linked mandagah jewel that Akua had sworn to her would be harmless—using it despite the taint Lana had somehow sensed.

Kai had fallen in love with the woman responsible for his aunt's death.

He left her in the bedroom with hot tea and a sweet parting glance that made her insides feel like ribboned meat. She had to tell him. He had been right all along, and far more profoundly than even he had realized. For the first time, Lana thought it likely that Akua had somehow weakened the death spirit's Binding. She had betrayed Lana, willingly and knowingly. She had insisted that the linked necklaces would be harmless, and using them had killed Pua. Lana remembered the other hundreds upon hundreds of matched necklaces that the witch had somehow linked with her red jewel. Did each of those pairs represent a dead human, drained of life for one of Akua's esoteric needs? Had she really been the unwitting party to so much death?

The hot cup of tea spilled over her trembling hands and crashed to the floor. She had to tell him. Sweet Kai, it would destroy them both, but she had to tell him.

She thought about what she would say as she walked unsteadily through the shrine. *Kai, you were right, but please don't hate me?* or, *It wasn't my fault.* But now that she was dealing in honesty, that wasn't precisely true, was it? Much as she yearned to lay all the blame on Akua, she knew that it wouldn't be fair. She had known from the start—even if Akua had said otherwise—that using the link would somehow hurt Pua. Wasn't that what wielding geas required, at bottom—sacrifice? She hadn't been ignorant of the possible consequences. And the fact still remained that no matter what her intentions had been, Kai's aunt was dead and Lana was responsible.

He was in the library, of course. Probably still researching any hints about what sort of witch Akua might be. Her news would probably save him a lot of time.

He looked up when she walked in, and then jumped down from his desk to meet her. "Are you feeling better?" he asked, keeping a hand low on her back to steady her.

She shook her head. "We need to talk." Her voice was breathy, but it was the best she could manage.

Kai looked like he might protest, but something stopped his words. He sat down with her on the edge of the platform, their legs dangling in the water. How many times had they sat together like this? Lana wanted to cry at the thought that this would probably be their last time.

"What is it?" he said, quietly.

Lana looked at the distortion of her feet through the water and clenched the edge of the platform. "I'll just say this quickly. I can't ..." She took a deep breath. "I killed your aunt. I didn't know I had until now. I didn't even know she was your aunt. I didn't do it deliberately, but I had reason enough to think something like that might happen, and I ignored it. That blue mandagah jewel is mine. I harvested it with this red one when I was thirteen, just before the floods came. I met her in Ialo. She ... she asked about you, you know. I'm sure it was you. She wanted to know if she would see you again. And then I gave her the jewel and told her not to take it off. I told her it was for good luck, but it was a sacrifice. A willing sacrifice. Akua told me to do it, of course. She said it wouldn't hurt her, but ... I knew. Part of me knew, Kai. I wasn't going to use it, but my then my mama got so sick and I couldn't—" She stopped and turned to face him, her teeth clenched furiously. She felt tears sliding down her neck. "I couldn't let her die. Not after what she had done for me. So I used the necklace. It was ... strange. There was something wrong with it, I felt that. Not just Pua. Something else. The week before, Akua made me accept some kind of sacrifice. Something bound to these thousands of other paired trinkets and I didn't know what it meant! I agreed, but it was so confusing in the column ..."

"What kind of sacrifice?" Kai asked, surprising her. His voice was flat. His eyes had turned black, without a hint of movement. The effect terrified her. "What did she call it?"

"Make'lai," Lana said. That memory, at least, was quite clear.

He shut his eyes. "Make'lai means death, keika. In an ancient language she was sure you wouldn't know. But languages don't matter to spirits. When you used that sacrifice, you invoked something far greater than just your mother's death."

"What?"

"I'm not sure. Her workings are deep and subtle. She's a master's master ... and she has played you like a flute."

She heard the unspoken coda: like he had told her. "Yes," she said.

For nearly a minute, the only sounds in the library were those of the water lapping against the side of the platform and Lana hastily sniffling back her tears. She tried to look at Kai, but his eyes were so black, his face so expressionless, she had to turn away.

"You should have known," he said into that silence. "She deceived you, but you should have known."

"She said nothing would—"

"And you believed her!" the volume of his suddenly raised voice made her jump. She nearly cringed at his fury. "Even you, from the very beginning, even you knew about sacrifice. She couldn't hide that! You wanted to save your mother's life. So you took my Aunt's. You must have known. You can't bring someone back from the shadow of death's gate without an equal sacrifice. What did you think Akua gave you? Magic?"

"Kai, don't. Please don't." In her panic, she tried to hold him, but he shook her off and she nearly tumbled into the water.

"Admit it, Lana. Some part of you must have understood the sacrifice."

"Kai—"

His eyes flashed like lightning over the sea. "Admit it!"

"*It was my mother!* What else could I do?"

He leaned forward until their noses were nearly touching. "Let. Her. Die."

She shook her head—a child's vehement denial—but didn't say anything. She couldn't.

"If you knew everything you knew now—about me and Akua and my aunt—would you still do it? Would you still call the sacrifice?"

Lana closed her eyes. Honesty, right? Could she have saved her mother any other way?

She stood up, distantly pleased that her body still functioned properly, and walked towards the exit.

"I'll be gone in an hour," she said quietly. "Akua is my burden. I can't hide behind you any longer. I have to find her … I have to find out why."

He had stood also, but made no move to stop her. She didn't know if she wished he would. "Don't tell me you still think there's some innocent explanation?"

"I just want to understand."

"And what makes you think she won't just kill you?"

She shrugged. "She's kept me alive this long."

"You didn't answer my question," he said as she reached the door.

Even knowing what she did now, would she still call the sacrifice?

"Yes."

She left by the same staircase that she had discovered so many months ago during the rainy season. The death was there, waiting for her.

"So, you finally came. I knew you would. You're too foolishly strong-willed to hide for very long."

Lana shrugged. "Or perhaps I'm just too foolish." She fingered the flute, but did not play it. She didn't want to warn Akua of her approach.

Kai arrived, even paler than normal, just as she was about to launch herself in the air.

"Don't," he said.

She settled her wings against her back. "Why not? You can't forgive me. I can't stay, knowing what she's done."

"I love you."

Unthinking, she twisted the red jewel between her fingers. "After your mother died … could your father have found someone else? Could someone else have had his children?"

Kai seemed a little confused. "Of course."

"Then don't worry. If I die, you won't have to deal with me again. And if I don't, I'll have your son." She felt lightheaded, suffused with a pain that had nothing to do with her body.

"Do you really think I want you to die?"

Her hand was still on the necklace, and she remembered what it meant. "Do you forgive me?" she asked

A long pause. She almost hoped, but then he met her eyes. "No."

It was all she needed. A few powerful strokes and she was flying, for the first time in months. Had she actually missed it?

"But, keika," he called out, as she soared above him. "I will."

· 14 ·

FOR THE PAST FOUR YEARS, the spirit solstice had always been the happiest time of their lives, but as this one approached, both Leilani and Kapa grew more irritable and depressed. They both knew that this year they would be spending it with only each other. After Leilani's mysterious illness (and even more mysterious recovery) last year, they had heard nothing at all from Lana. It was as though she had disappeared. Leilani knew that Lana was still alive, but she suspected that whatever Lana had done to save her life had come at a horribly high cost. And so Kapa sold his instruments and Leilani taught her swimming lessons and they both held each other very closely at night. Leilani understood that Lana had known she wasn't going to see them again. She had said goodbye for good just before she had been blown out the window like a zephyr.

Leilani sighed and pulled her groceries tighter on her back. It was funny; she had felt so healthy this past year that she sometimes forgot that she had almost died. Of course, she had also taken off the bone necklace for the first time in four years and given it to Kapa for safeguarding. As soon as she had known that Lana was no longer beholden to the witch, she had decided it would be safe.

The streets were crowded at this time of evening, with many people wheeling carts of old good-luck charms and various other offerings through the streets to get to the fire temple. The evening sun was pleasantly warm and she took her time walking home, politely looking at the wares of a few street vendors and tossing a full kala in front of every street musician she saw. She always thought of Kapa when she saw them, and she imagined how grateful he would have been to encounter someone so generous.

When she finally made it back to the shopkeepers' district, she was beginning to hope that this spirit solstice wouldn't be as miserable as she had thought. Perhaps Lana would find some way to come, and even if she couldn't, there were many ways to remember her daughter. Leilani felt sure that she would see her again someday.

Her skin prickled oddly when she turned onto their street and she paused, unaware of a drawn carriage racing perilously close to her. Someone gripped her arm and pulled her out of the way just in time for Leilani to see the emblem of the fire temple on the carriage door. She turned around to thank the person when her words dried in her throat. It was the witch. Her eyes were harder, perhaps, but her skin had not aged at all. Leilani's first thought was to ask what had happened to Lana, but she found herself incapable of speech and her legs incapable of movement.

"Walk," said the woman under her breath. Leilani's legs suddenly sprang into motion, walking industriously back in the direction that she had come. In her mind she was screaming for Kapa, but her mouth didn't move. She didn't know what the witch had planned for her, but she was thoroughly terrified. She knew it must have something to do with Lana, and she immediately suspected that her daughter must be in far more danger now than she had ever been, even this time last year. They rounded the corner and stopped, to her surprise, in front of the same wooden carriage that had nearly run her over two minutes ago. Was this woman in league with the fire temple?

"Get inside," the witch said. Leilani opened the door and climbed inside, amazed at how well her limbs could work without her conscious direction. The witch climbed in after her and slammed the door shut. She slid all of the wooden covers over the windows and then told the driver to leave.

Leilani stared straight ahead because she had to. Utterly helpless, she wondered where this woman was taking her, and prayed that her daughter would be safe.

It took Lana nearly four days of straight flying—only resting when she was in danger of falling out of the sky—to reach Akua's house. She was amazed at how quickly she could travel now. A fast ship could cover the same distance in a little more than a week. The death seemed inexplicably cheery during her journey and hardly made any effort at all to take her, even when she landed to sleep— so exhausted she could hardly blow a single note on the flute. It even refrained from mocking her about Kai, which she felt was almost magnanimous. If it had been a human, she would have said it was anticipating something.

Lana flew over Ialo around midday, and the sight of gathered crowds and brightly painted houses made her realize that today must be solstice eve. She tried to imagine the feast that her mother would be cooking right now—jellied oranges, roast grouper, yucca stuffed with spices and fish meat. She was probably cooking in the faint hope that Lana would find some way to visit. Suddenly she missed her mother so much that she wanted to cry. Would they ever see each other again?

The death, floating below her, cocked its head curiously and she bit her tongue. She would not let it know how afraid she was. Just before sunset she found the lake and Akua's familiar stone house, nestled in a bend in the shoreline. She circled warily, trying to gather her courage to land. She knew how powerful the witch was—Lana would stand no chance in an open confrontation. She supposed Kai was right—some part of her still hoped that Akua could somehow offer her a reasonable explanation. And if she couldn't ... Lana didn't want to think that far. She landed on the earth right in front of the door. It was open, she saw in surprise.

"Threshold," she said to the death, even though it hadn't moved. It nodded, as though a geas without a sacrifice or a person to actually invite her in was perfectly reasonable. She took a deep breath and walked inside.

It became immediately obvious to her that Akua was gone, but she called the witch's name several times before she admitted it. The kitchen looked like a shell of its old self—no more herbs dried on the ceiling, no cauldron hung above the hearth. The cupboards were bare except for a few empty jars. She turned and ran up the stairs, her wings pressing up against the walls.

Her room had been ransacked. Akua had apparently rifled through every item of clothing and every cubbyhole—until she had found her mother's letters. She looked through the scattered pile frantically, wondering why Akua would have been looking for something so trivial. Most of them were still there, she realized. Only two had been taken—ones that her mother had written during Lana's first few months with Akua. What could possibly be important about those? Even as she wondered, she became aware of an overpowering anger, bubbling up under her skin until she thought she would explode with it. Akua had been manipulating her like a puppet for all of these years and Lana had never known. Like a child, she had blindly trusted her mentor—trusted her even into murder.

Lana stormed down the stairs and walked to the edge of the lake, somehow confident that the death would not touch her now.

"Ino," she shouted. "It's me. I need your help." She waited. Moments later, the water before her rippled and she saw his familiar face rise above the surface.

He stared at her for a long time, his opaque eyes taking in her huge black wings and expressing a heavy sadness.

"Oh, little diver," he said. "What have you done?"

"Only what I had to," she said, her heart constricting. Could anyone else but Ino truly understand what she had given up by accepting the wind's sacrifice?

"You said you needed my help. Anything I can, I'll give to you."

"Where has the witch gone, Ino?" she asked.

He shook his head. "I can't say, little diver. But you shouldn't try to find her. You should stay as far away as you can—she has used you too long. If you stay away, maybe she won't be able to use you any longer."

The beginnings of a geas began shimmering around his skin, but he did not move.

"Ino ... it's too late. I can't run away. I have to find out why she's done this. I have to understand what else she's done. You're the only one I know who can help me, and if you don't, I'm as good as dead. Please."

He held his silence for at least a minute. Finally, he nodded. "You've grown strong." The shimmering of the geas suddenly intensified and she saw him wince. "Wait here," he said softly. He ducked back under the surface of the lake.

She stood silently, waiting for Ino to return.

"Now would be a good time to take you," the death whispered in her ear.

She shuddered. "But you don't want to," she said, fingering the flute and wondering if she should use it.

"Perhaps you're right," it said. "Even though it would be convenient, perhaps I am, as you say, bound to passions that render me ... slightly irrational."

"Passions like anticipation?" she asked.

It laughed. "Indeed. You have come to know me well."

Ino reemerged from the lake, gasping and shuddering. She ran forward, amazed that he could still be moving with the force of the geas that she felt. It looked like he was in agony.

"Take this, little diver," he said, handing her a small black book similar to the one she remembered reading in the death temple a year ago. As soon as she took it he let out a high-pitched shriek of agony and collapsed into the water.

"Ino!" She fell to her knees in the shallow mud. "What did you do?"

"Go," he said. "The binding ... won't kill me. Go, before she makes me take it back."

Lana stood up and backed away, stuffing the book in her bag.

"I swear to you that one day I'll find a way to break that geas, Ino," she said.

"Go!"

With one last worried glance, Lana launched herself off the ground. She wasn't going far—she still had one last person she needed to see.

She landed on the outskirts of the village, where one small boy playing by himself in a puddle stared at her with open-mouthed surprise. She smiled at him and began walking. She didn't bother putting on her cloak—it hardly mattered, now. The streets were mostly deserted this solstice eve. The smells of plentiful suppers wafted onto the road and she struggled not to think of her mother. Night had fallen, but the nearly full moon gave off plenty of light. To her surprise, the door to the general store was still open. She would have thought that Apano's daughter would refuse to entertain customers on solstice eve. She walked inside.

Apano was the only person in the front room. He sat in his chair humming to himself as he whittled a piece of driftwood with a small knife. As soon as he heard her footsteps, however, he stopped and stared at the door with his ruined eyes.

"Who is that?" he asked. She walked closer to him. "Lana?" he said. "What happened to you?"

He could always tell. She never knew how, but he could always tell. "Too much," she said quietly. She gripped his hand and led it to the wings on her back.

He stroked them gently, an expression of wonder on his face. "Child ... so you're now ... a black angel?"

"Yes," she said.

"I always thought that woman would drive you to grief ... she used you, you most of all."

"Apa," she said. "The witch is gone. Did you hear anything? Do you have any idea what might have happened?"

"She left about seven months ago, Lana. They told me she hurried through the streets and hired a boat like she was being chased by death. The boat was headed for Ialo, but she could have gone anywhere after that."

Seven months ago? What had happened to scare Akua so much?

Behind her, someone began to scream. Lana whirled around and saw Apano's daughter standing in the inner doorway, her hands plastered to her mouth.

"Help!" she screamed. "It's a black angel! That bitch witch's apprentice has turned herself into a black angel!"

Her husband ran to the door. "Get out!" he shouted. "Leave my family alone."

Apano stood up, his eyebrows furrowed in anger. "How dare you speak that way to a guest of mine!"

"You are a blind old fool," the man said. He pushed Apano, who went sprawling back in his chair. "I will not allow you to keep this … this abomination in our house."

Lana stood up. "I'm sorry, Apa," she said. "I shouldn't have come."

She turned around and walked to the door. As she stood on the threshold, she noticed the death staring eagerly toward the west.

The image in its robes was familiar, but not one she had ever seen there. Why was it showing her Essel?

She watched in horror as Nui'ahi, the sleeping sentinel of the greatest city in the world, erupted in a mass of angry, violent flame. And then the rumbling began, quietly at first, then swelling into a noise too great and too violent to be illusion.

But, keika, I will.

And it hadn't taken very long—just a few hours of sitting miserably in her abandoned room, wondering if she would find the witch and if the witch would kill her. He imagined how he would feel if she died and he hadn't even tried to protect her … it was simple, really. He had wanted to be with her even when he thought she had weakened death's bonds. And that budding desire was a thimble of water compared to the ocean of his current longing.

It had taken Kai all of his self-control not to go chasing after Lana then. The disturbances that he had sensed for years suddenly felt more acute, as though whatever strange, subtle thing had been interfering with the islands had reached critical mass. Confined as he was in this remote place, he did the only thing he could: reinforce the geas that prevented the spirits from leaving the gate. He spent four days in a thick haze of frantic grief, unable to bear the thought of Lana on her own again, only now realizing how deeply embroiled she was in a plot that she hadn't even known existed.

Four days after Lana fled, Kai slept on the small fishing boat that he would use to get to the nearest town. The night of solstice eve, as he anchored in the gently rocking water, he awoke abruptly to the sound of a distant rumbling. Waves lapped harder against the edge of his boat. In some faraway part of the ocean, thousands of creatures screamed out their deaths as the water boiled around them. The echoes of their distress rippled and grew until it reached a single crescendo that Kai had no ability to close his mind against. He put his hand in the water, hoping for a clearer expression of what had happened. He received it, slowly, from those sprites and water creatures that could form the words:

Nui'ahi.

Fire or death. He had guessed, and he had been wrong.

On solstice eve, Manuku snuck up to the 'Ana's rooms without quite knowing why. His daughter had just gone to bed, but he couldn't bring himself to do the same. There was an inexplicable mood of nervous anticipation in the death temple—he could see it on the faces of the priests and officiates as they hurried by, pretending not to notice he was there. He could also tell that they understood the reason no more than he did. So, even though he had done his weekly cleaning three days before, he climbed the hundreds of stairs within the 'Ana's tower.

Everything remained exactly where he had left it. The mirror that he had broken months before lay facedown on the dresser— he knew that no one but he would ever dare pick it up, so his secret was safe. He walked around the room slowly, gently running his fingers over every surface to make sure that it remained dust-free. In his peripheral vision, he saw images floating in and out of definition within the column of air. The death spirit was certainly agitated—the flow of images seemed far more frantic and gleeful than normal. He thought he saw the now-familiar image of the girl with the horrible black wings, but thankfully she didn't remain visible for long.

He paused near the doorway, wondering why he had felt so compelled to visit a place he usually hated.

A slight tremor passed under his feet. He barely noticed—tremors were relatively common, here at the center. He glanced at the column and felt a frisson of disbelief run through his stomach.

It was blank. For a bare moment, the column of air was free of any roiling hints of imagery.

The next image was a volcano, spewing glowing chunks of molten lava in the air and raining ash. And then the frantic pace resumed—this time of people dying one after another, consumed by fire and ash.

Erlun had blessed Yechtak when he left the tribe. The old shaman's voice had been so full of pride that after he returned, Yechtak had been too cowardly to tell him of his failures near the ruins. But he swore to the old man that he would do everything in his power to do the bidding of the wild spirit. To himself, he swore that he would find Iolana again and make true amends for his behavior. And perhaps, when he had proven himself worthy, she would not find his kiss so repugnant.

At his mother's request, he had delayed leaving on his next journey for a month so she would have time to arrange a marriage for him. He had told his bride that she could only be his second wife, but she had seemed content with that and they had married just before he left. His mother had suffered too much, he decided, for him to deny her the grandchildren for which she longed. She was a sweet girl, Yechtak thought, but he knew that he would never be able to feel true passion for her. No, that emotion was reserved for the one who had spent three days on the wind altar in mute agony to emerge, metamorphosed, as a beautiful, pitiable creature of destruction and power. For a brief moment, he had felt himself underneath her as he called the wind for her first flight. He had shared her exhilaration and her fear. Yes, he thought, it fell to him to tell the world of the coming of the black angel.

His love for her kept him warm during yet another cold night on the vast island they called Okua. Here, this far inland, early fall meant layers of frost and sometimes even dusty coatings of snow on the verdant bamboo leaves. He longed to sleep away from the cold, but he had long since run out of his small stash of Binder money, and few of these cold people took barter. Of course, even if he had money, people often turned inhospitable as soon as he mentioned the words "black angel." No one, he discovered, wanted to hear his news. But he still felt just as honor-bound to say it. Sometimes he heard the wind around him, but it never felt as strong or as comforting here as it had on his island.

Hiking through the night to keep warm, he paused in startled surprise when three nearby cranes keened in unison and then flew off. The wind that suddenly gusted past his ears sounded like soft crying, and for the barest of moments he thought it carried the scent of ash and scorched flesh.

In a tower at the northeast corner of the fire temple, two novice nuns practically carried Nahoa up the stairs as she gripped her swollen belly and tried to ignore the way birthing fluid dripped from her pants onto the stairs as she walked.

"Come, my lady, we're almost there," said one. Nahoa groaned and forced one foot to follow another. The baby was coming a few weeks early and had caught everyone by surprise. Apparently this tower was the safest area in the temple—they had been planning to move her there just after the spirit solstice. She knew that Kohaku's spies would be rushing to the Mo'i's house with the news. She wondered how he would take it. Would he try to contact her again? Sometimes she missed him so much that she actually considered going back. Then she would remember how Nahe had looked as he died and how even now the disappearances continued. Kohaku refused to promise her the one thing she needed from him: that he would never harm anyone again. And so she found herself giving birth at the top of a tower in the fire temple, surrounded by nuns and guards so she would be safe from her husband.

Makaho, the head nun, was already in the room when she staggered inside.

"Get her in the bed," she said.

The two novices helped Nahoa lie down on the sheets. She was grateful it was a sleeping mat instead of the raised beds that she had been using for the past year—it reminded her of home. Someone pulled off her wet pants and someone else rubbed a balm on her swollen belly that made it tingle and cleared her nose.

In the moments in between the wracking pain, she felt oddly distant from the situation. Her child would have good luck, she thought, being born on solstice eve. She stared out the single window and admired the powerful figure of Nui'ahi framing the dying sunset. She wondered if Kohaku was seeing the same thing right now. Was he keeping vigil in his aerie for the fires that so terrified him? Even tonight, the day most appropriate for joy and celebration, was he still afraid of whatever ghost his scorched left hand represented? Did he still speak to it?

A pain twisted at her stomach so violently that she screamed. The head nun was by her side, her eyes bright with concern and eagerness.

"Here, take this for the pain, my lady," she said, holding a drink to Nahoa's lips that smelled like urine and rotten fruit. Another contraction and she opened her mouth, swallowing as much of the vile concoction as she could without tasting it.

An hour later, when night had fallen and the moon bathed

Nui'ahi in her light, the baby still seemed no closer to being born. Sweat from her body had soaked the sheets beneath her, and she shivered as it cooled.

"It's a girl, I think," Makaho said as she massaged her belly. "They are always more stubborn."

Nahoa smiled, thinking about how her mother had given birth to seven girls.

She was still smiling when Nui'ahi exploded, spewing molten lava high into the air. How pretty, Nahoa thought, absurdly, before the lava began running into the streets and the roaring wind flattened whole neighborhoods in seconds.

The contraction that ripped through her then nearly made her lose consciousness. She wept as she screamed, for the thousands of people dying below her, and for her baby girl, who would be born in this river of fire and blood.

Makaho stayed by her side, but the two novices rushed to the window, keening with shocked disbelief. The ground rocked beneath them and the tower swayed alarmingly, but remained upright. One of the girls shrieked and sank to the floor, weeping into her hands.

"My family," she said, "they live southside. Right underneath …" she began sobbing again.

Nahoa wanted to say something, but the contractions were coming faster and far more painfully now. She gasped under another onslaught, but the growing chorus of screams and wails coming from far below drowned her voice.

Two hours later, when ash had blotted the moon and the stars so that the only light came from the red-orange lava that flowed through the streets, Nahoa gave birth to a baby girl.

Lei'ahi, she called her: child of fire.

In the moments before the world exploded, it spoke to him.

He did not see her reflection in the glass of the aerie, but he knew she was there nonetheless. How could anyone not recognize the presence of a great spirit?

"I owe you thanks," said her hateful voice.

Kohaku did not turn to face it. He could not bear to look at its eyes. "Why?" he asked. Nahoa was giving birth, he had heard, locked away in a tall, hidden tower of the fire temple. He had only revenge to live for, and this simulacrum of his sister. It was mostly the fire spirit, of that he was sure, but his infrequent glimpses of the true Emea sickened him. When it begged him for revenge, he could never be sure who was begging.

"Tonight's festivities wouldn't have been possible without your contribution."

Kohaku glanced behind him. She was smiling. "Festivities?" he said.

"Turn around."

He did.

"Three, two, one ..."

Nui'ahi exploded.

"Merry solstice eve, dear brother."

When he looked back, she was gone.

"Why do you wish to become Mo'i?" it had asked, those many months ago.

"I ... I mean ... for love. And especially for revenge."

The flames suddenly billowed out and Kohaku danced backwards in fear. The tongues of fire seemed to form in shapes of a dozen crudely grinning mouths, but they vanished as quickly as he had seen them.

"Better," it said, "much better. Many have come here for revenge and many have come here for love, but very few for both. Those few almost agreed, but in the end, they were too weak. Will you be different?"

"Different how?" Kohaku felt terrified but somehow exhilarated, talking with this inhuman spirit that could kill him at any moment.

"Will you," said the spirit, "take a handful of ashes from Konani's urn?" The flames thinned briefly so that he got a clearer view of that dark center of the flames—an urn containing the remains of Konani, the one who had given the ultimate self-sacrifice to bind the fire spirit. On the outside of the urn he had written the words of the geas that still bound the spirit and allowed civilization on the islands to survive.

He suddenly understood what that morose voice was asking him to do. It wanted Kohaku to remove a support that could destroy all the advances made by humans in the last thousand years. If the hundreds of volcanoes throughout the islands began to erupt again, millions would die and the survivors would be forced to scrabble a living in the ashes.

And in return, Kohaku would get revenge.

"You're trying to break free," he whispered, wishing that he were strong enough to refuse.

"I'm always trying to break free. But even if you take a handful of the ashes, I'll still be bound. I'll just have a little more leeway, a few small ways to show myself in the world aside from candles and hearth fires. I long to *burn,* penitent. As much as I'm able."

The spirit's obvious desire sent a wave of terror through him. Still, beneath that terror was a sudden sense of possibility. He had come here expecting to die and instead he had been offered a chance to have everything he ever wanted—and to commit the greatest crime humanity had ever known.

"Kohaku."

His head snapped up at the sound of her voice and his breath strangled in his throat. It was impossible. He hadn't heard that voice since he was ten years old. Reluctantly, he looked up and saw her in the flames, smiling sadly at him.

"It's me," Emea said.

"Stop it!" he yelled suddenly. Angry tears were forming in a hot ball in the back of his throat. "Don't mock me like this!"

"It's not mocking you," she said. "I can come here because I was burned in Nui'ahi. My spirit melded with the fire."

Kohaku met her eyes—where her green irises should have been, he only saw licking flames. Could it be real?

"Please, Kohaku ... do what it says. Take revenge for me. Promise me you won't let Nahe get away with my death."

He couldn't hold back the tears. He stared helplessly at the wavering figure of his sister. "But ... what about everyone else? How many people will I kill if I do what he says?"

"It is just a little fire, Kohaku ... no one in the world would be harmed by just a little more fire."

Her image flickered and vanished, replaced by featureless blue flames.

"Have you made your decision?" the spirit asked. "Do you take revenge for your sister and become Mo'i, or do you join the ashes?"

He couldn't even be sure if what he had seen had been his sister, but he wanted to believe it. He wanted to believe the fire spirit's assurances of how harmless his actions would be. He wanted revenge and he wanted Nahoa.

"I agree," he said finally. "I'll take the ashes."

"The fire will burn you," the spirit said, a crackling excitement in its voice, "and the ashes will sear your skin, but you must not let go. If you do, you will be consumed—just another sacrifice. If you succeed, you will be Mo'i."

Kohaku nodded, his heart thudding.

"Do you make this sacrifice willingly, supplicant?"

"Yes," Kohaku said.

Before he could think about it, he put his arm in the fire.

It burned so badly he was afraid he would faint, but he bit down on his tongue until he tasted blood, just to clear his head. His fingertips could barely reach over the edge of the urn, but as quickly as he could he reached inside and scooped out a tiny handful of ashes.

The pain that he felt then did make him scream—the ashes were eating into his muscle and bone but leaving his nerves to shriek in misery. He almost dropped them, despite the warning of the fire spirit, but he held on, keeping Emea's image in his mind as he pulled his arm carefully out of the fire. He held it close to his chest as he collapsed on the floor, uncaring of the ashes that mingled with his sweat and tears into a grimy paste on his cheeks.

"You were the first one," Kohaku heard the spirit say softly, barely audible over his own low moans. "No one else held on. You must have truly loved your sister."

When the officiates opened the door, they had been shocked to discover Kohaku still on the floor beside the great fire, covered in ashes and holding his mangled left arm to his chest.

I long to burn ...

Below him, distantly, he heard his guards pounding on his door, desperate to tell him what had happened. Soon, he would have to wipe the guilt off of his face and go back down to meet with his advisors and those district chiefs who had survived the carnage. He would have to conduct the relief effort for what was left of this once-great city, as though his missing left hand wasn't an indictment for hundreds of thousands dead and wounded.

Kohaku walked down the stairs and opened the doors, his eyes dry as ash.

Akua hadn't expected Nui'ahi to erupt. She hadn't expected events to go that far. She stared at the burning city and the flowing lava with as much horror as anyone else on the small ship that had just cast off from the docks. Leilani was facing the other direction, only her rigid neck muscles giving away the fact that she was desperate to turn around. Feeling an unexpected moment of pity, Akua loosened the geas holding her. Leilani turned around slowly, a gasp escaping her lips when she saw what had happened. She mouthed her husband's name.

Akua tried to imagine how many people would die before the night was out and, despite everything, felt staggered by the number. She, who knew death perhaps better than anyone, could hardly believe it.

"What have you done to my daughter?" Leilani asked quietly, staring at Nui'ahi as though she was still bound by the geas.

Akua thought about the black angel that soon the whole world would know about. "Nothing," she said, just as quietly. "What she did, she did entirely to herself."

The Essel that Lana saw when she arrived two days later was a smoking, ashen husk of its old self. Southside, most of the buildings had been smothered by nearly four feet of ash that still fell from the gray sky, barely lightened by the sun. The east side, where her parents lived, had been ravaged by fires, some still burning, but most now contained by the simple fact that there was nothing left to burn. Survivors hurried through the streets with their remaining possessions clutched to their chests with one hand, and a cloth clamped over their mouths and noses with the other. Some people noticed her as she glided overhead, but they all stared at her with glazed eyes, and then looked away like they had been hallucinating.

The death had vanished after the eruption. She knew it would return, but something about the abundance of death in Essel had lured it away.

She thought she would scream when she finally found her parents' street. All but three of the houses had been burned to their foundations, and the three still standing were merely gutted frames. She landed and walked slowly up the street, telling herself that her parents weren't necessarily dead, that maybe they hadn't been at home. She had to laugh at herself, then. The eruption had taken place solstice eve—everyone in Essel had been at home.

People stared at her as she walked down the street, and some even pointed, but none seemed inclined to do more than that. Perhaps part of the reason she refused to hide her wings was because she felt a responsibility now to show people that they were living in the time of a black angel. That all the destruction they saw here was probably only a taste of what was to come. The bottom of her wings collected a gum of ash and water, but she didn't try to shake it off.

Her father's shop was one of the places that had burned to the foundations. Looking at the heap of charred wood and ash, she knew that anyone caught in the blaze would have had no chance of survival. Tears swelled in her throat, but she couldn't seem to force them out. They just made her whole body ache without the luxury of any release. Was this how Kai felt? He must be the strongest man she knew. She looked up and saw a man rifling through the ruins in the back of the house.

"Stop that!" she said sharply, even though she knew it was absurd to deny another victim the possessions for which her parents would no longer have any use.

The man stood up and she realized it was her father.

They stared at each other for a long time.

"You ... you're not ... you can't be," he stammered. His hands were covered in soot and his left cheek was puckered with an angry red burn. He looked exhausted enough to fall asleep where he stood.

"It's me, Papa," she said.

He stepped closer. "Lana?" he said, disbelieving. "But you have ..." He ran the next few steps and enveloped her in a desperate, shuddering embrace.

"We never thought we'd see you again," he said.

The tears that had been building burst like a dam and she sobbed on his shoulder, the way she had as a child.

"Where's Mama?" she asked.

He froze and pulled slightly away from her. "She's gone," he said quietly.

Lana felt more sobs rising in her throat. "She ... died?" she asked. Was that why the death left her?

He shook his head. "No ... I don't think so. Just before the eruption, she disappeared. She went out for a quick trip to the market, and she never came back. I went out to look for her ... so I wasn't here when the house caught on fire."

As if to prove her father's words, she felt the death suddenly reappear behind her.

"Lana," her father said, gripping her elbow. "Your mother made me promise to give this to you if I ever saw you again. I don't know why ... maybe she knew something might happen to her." He reached into his pocket and pulled out a necklace. Strung on the leather cord was a key carved out of bone—the exact match of a necklace Lana had seen countless times before, and never suspected a thing.

"She wore this every day for four years, and then just after you saved her last year she gave it to me. She said you might know what it meant. Do you, Lana?"

She nodded mutely, unable to speak past the grief and anger. Instead, she took the necklace and put it in her pocket. Slowly, the pieces of this puzzle were falling into place. Behind her, she heard the whispers of a growing crowd.

She looked up at her father. "Did the fire destroy all of your instruments?" she asked.

"Everything except this." He held out one of his old tortoise-shell lutes. It had been his favorite back on their island, but she hadn't heard him play it for years. "I kept it in a different place than the others," he said. "I think I always liked this old thing the best, I was just too embarrassed to play it."

"Would you ... would you be embarrassed to play with me?" she asked, pulling the arm bone flute out of her pocket.

He looked surprised—she had never been particularly interested in music before—but he nodded. She turned around and faced the growing crowd of survivors, their faces haggard and disbelieving.

"Have you come here to kill the rest of us?" one asked, sounding as though he wouldn't mind if the answer were yes.

Suddenly unable to speak, she simply shook her head. She squatted down in the ashes next to her father and put the flute to her lips. The flute always had the right to go first. She waited in the dead silence, wondering what could possibly be equal to this disaster.

The song she picked was simple—one woman's lament over how she would soon be leaving everything she loved forever. The sound of her flute had never carried so far, and her father had never played his lute so delicately. Hundreds of people listened in dead silence as her father sang, and the black angel mourned the destruction she had foretold.

> *Come dawn's red gaze I must leave here*
> *And the leaving some may think is fate*
> *But within my heart, love battles fear*
> *For I do not know what lies beyond the gate*

High and sweet, she played, until even the death seemed to weep for what it could not help but do.

Note on Pronunciation

The language of the islands in *Racing the Dark* is based mainly on Hawaiian, with some Japanese and a dash of invention. The use of an apostrophe (') in a proper noun (for anything besides a possessive) denotes a glottal stop—the sound one makes between the first and second syllables of "uh-oh," for example.

Otherwise, names generally sound the way they look, with each syllable pronounced and no "silent e," as in English. For example, "kale" would *not* rhyme with "quail" but with "ballet." The letter combination of "ei" rhymes with "hay." The combination of "ai" rhymes with "sky." Below is a list of the pronunciations a few representative names and places.

Iolana – "EE-oh-LAH-nah"
Leilani – "lay-LAH-knee"
Mandagah – "mahn-DAH-gah"
Nui'ahi – "new-ee ' AH-hee"
Emea – "eh-MAY-ah"
Ino – "EE-no"
Pua – "POO-ah"
Malie – "MAH-lee-eh"
Kalakoa – "KAH-lah-coe-ah"
Ali'ikai – "AH-lee ' EE-kah-ee"
Kaleakai – "kah-LEH-ah-kah-ee"

Acknowledgments

This is my first novel and any thanks must begin with my family. My father, Ford Johnson, remains a constant inspiration to me. My mother, Mary Fogg Johnson, taught me to read and has supported everything I've tried since. Phillip, Lauren, Alexis, Aunt Vanessa, Aunt Betty and Uncle Darrell. Joan and Gary Pellegrino, who have so lovingly made me a part of their family.

High school left an indelible stamp on my writer's soul. At the National Cathedral School, I had the luck to encounter teachers whose effect on my life and my writing continue to the present. I must mention three in particular: Mr. John Wood, Ms. Jessica Neely, and Ms. Mari Schindele. And of course Frank Njuki-Katende, my favorite friend from Zamunda.

I began this novel in Japan, listening obsessively to Beatles music, and though I don't imagine that a country and a band really need to be acknowledged, I'll do it anyway. Also, my friends and fellow writers who have read and critiqued my work over the years: Amanda Hollander, Bianca Redhead, Bill Steinmetz, Fleur Beckwith, Rachel Lenz, Robert Sietsema, Dan Bush, Tamar Bihari, Aimee Kratz, and others.

My agent, Ken Atchity, bowled me over with his enthusiasm for this book from the first. And I couldn't have asked for a more insightful publisher and editor than Doug Seibold.

The earth-shattering importance of my first novel dwindles in a global context: Iraq, Afghanistan, Darfur, global warming, and rampant social inequality here in the states. Individual actions make a difference. I'd suggest FAIR (www.fair.org) as a place for concerned readers to start.

About the Author

Alaya Dawn Johnson was born in 1982 in Washington, DC and graduated from Columbia University, where she studied East Asian languages and cultures. She has published short fiction in several magazines, and two of her stories were republished in the anthologies *Year's Best SF 11* and *Year's Best Fantasy 6*. She lives in New York. *Racing the Dark,* the first book in the trilogy *The Spirit Binders,* is her first novel.